D0241641

THE OTHER HALF
OF AUGUSTA HOPE

Joanna Glen read Spanish at the University of London, with a stint at the Faculty of Arts at Córdoba University in the south of Spain. She went on to teach Spanish and English to all ages, and, latterly, was a school principal in London. She has edited a variety of non-fiction books and her short fiction has appeared in the Bath Flash Fiction Anthology. She lives with her husband and children on the River Thames in Battersea, returning to Andalusia whenever it gets too grey.

The
Other
Half
of
Augusta
Hope

JOANNA GLEN

THE BOROUGH PRESS

The Borough Press
An imprint of HarperCollins*Publishers* Ltd
1 London Bridge Street
London SE1 9GF

www.harpercollins.co.uk

First published by HarperCollins*Publishers* 2019
1

A catalogue record for this book is available from the British Library

HB ISBN: 978-0-00-831415-6
TPB ISBN: 978-0-00-831416-3

This novel is entirely a work of fiction.
The names, characters and incidents portrayed in it are
the work of the author's imagination. Any resemblance to
actual persons, living or dead, events or localities is
entirely coincidental.

Excerpt from *The Collected Poems and Drawings of Stevie Smith*, ed. by Will May
reprinted by permission of Faber and Faber Ltd.

Excerpt from *The Complete Poems of Philip Larkin*, ed. by Archie Burnett
reprinted by permission of Faber and Faber Ltd.

Excerpt from *Los Puentes Colgados*, 1921, Fundación Federico García Lorca. Translation
and transcription to music, 2007, reprinted by permission of Keith James.

Every effort has been made to trace and contact copyright holders.
If there are any inadvertent omissions we apologise to those concerned and will undertake
to include suitable acknowledgements in all future editions.

Set in Bell MT by Palimpsest Book Production Limited, Falkirk, Stirlingshire

Printed and bound in the UK by CPI Group (UK) Ltd, Croydon CR0 4YY

MIX
Paper from
responsible sources

FSC
www.fsc.org
FSC™ C007454

For Mark, Charlie and Nina.

A time to weep and a time to laugh,
A time to mourn and a time to dance,
A time to scatter stones and a time to gather them . . .

Ecclesiastes 3:4–5

Augusta

My parents didn't seem the sort of people who would end up killing someone. Everyone would say that – except the boy who died, who isn't saying anything. He carried his story with him off the edges of the earth, like the others who died along the way.

This story, my story, belongs to them too.

My story starts, like all stories do, with a mother and a father, and here they are – Stanley and Jilly Hope.

Stanley, tall, and stooping to apologise for this, liked to wear a dark wool suit, which, when he sat down, would rise to reveal two white and entirely hairless shins. Jilly was well below his eyeline, squashy as marshmallow and keen on aprons. She had pale curly hair, cut to just above the shoulder, which she patted, to little effect.

My parents put down a deposit on the house in Willow Crescent, in Hedley Green, before there was a house there at all. The riskiest thing they ever did. Empty out their bank account for a pile of mud.

From then on, no more risks to be taken. Life best lived within the crescent, which was circular, and round and round they went with their lives, contented, with no desire for exit.

I, as soon as I was *out* of my mother's womb, looked to be *out* of anywhere I was put *in*, striving, with some success, to exit the cot, the playpen or the pram.

My first exit (out of my mother) was fraught. I'd turned the wrong way up and wrapped the umbilical cord around my neck, whilst Julia slid serenely into the world shortly before midnight on 31 July. I didn't appear until some minutes later, by which time it was August, and we were twins with different birthdays.

My sister, born in July, was named Julia; I, born in August, would be Augusta. A thematic and paired approach, as advised by the library of books on naming babies which my mother had stacked on her bedside table throughout the long months of our gestation. Our double exit was complete. Exit was a word I liked, *ex* meaning out in Latin, and *x* meaning anything at all in maths, and exit signs in green and white everywhere at school, but with limited opportunities to do so.

Stanley and Jilly Hope were much more inclined towards the in than the out, the staying than the going. They were the first to move into the crescent, and they wore this like a badge amongst the neighbours. We live at *number 1*. As if this made them winners.

But the thought crept into my mind quite early on that they were losers.

'Go away!' I said to the thought, but it didn't.

I never told anyone about it, even Julia, though I know it showed in the expression on my face, and this made her sad – and I am truly sorry about that now, sorrier than you know.

She and I were Snow White and Rose Red: Julia, fair, quiet and contained, happy inside herself, inside the house, humming; and me, quite the opposite, straining to leave, dark, outspoken, walking in the wind, *railing*. Railing, from the Latin, to bray like a donkey (*ragulare*) and railing meaning barrier or fence from straight stick (*regula*), which is how I looked, skinny as a ruler.

Our fifth birthday, one year of school done, and my legs and arms narrowing as I rose an inch above Julia's head. We were given tricycles, mine, yellow, and Julia's, pink. Julia drew chalk lines on the drive and spent the day reversing into parking spaces. I rode out of the drive, turned left, curved around to number 13, at the top of the crescent, twelve o'clock, crossed the road precariously to the roundabout and drove my trike into the fishpond singing 'We All Live in a Yellow Submarine'.

At school, in Year 4, 1998, when I was seven years old, and we were doing an underwater project (remaining, ourselves, disappointingly, on land), Miss April told us that *marinus* meant *of the sea* in Latin, and *sub* meant *under*, hence submarine. But when I put up my hand and told her, excuse me, Miss April, but your pen has rolled *sub* your desk, she told me not to be a show-off, Augusta.

I've always loved words like other people love sweets or ice cream or puddings, words made of letters so that sounds turn into things, actual things. And miraculously we remember which sounds match which things, hundreds and thousands of sound-combinations – because that's language. It mesmerised me as a child, and I would hang about, spellbound, whenever I heard people speaking Spanish or French or Gujarati.

I realised with some pride that I must sound as clever to foreigners when I spoke English, rattling off the words like a total pro, as we all do – well most of us, not Graham Cook, who lived next door, whose mouth didn't manage to make any words at all.

'You pity the Cooks,' said my father, lightly, with no sign of pity on his face. 'It could happen to anyone.'

I liked to pop next door and talk to Jim Cook when he was out washing his car in the drive, because he always had new dreams up his sleeve. But the truth was that none of them ever seemed to slip out of his sleeve into real life.

Barbara Cook used to take Julia and me swimming when she had respite care days for Graham because, my mother told me, the poor woman liked the chance to do normal things and do them normally, without a palaver. I tried to make swimming the best possible time for Barbara Cook, although she wasn't a person who said much about how she was feeling.

One day, after swimming, I couldn't find my skirt or my pants, and I had to walk into Barbara's changing cubicle wearing a red T-shirt and nothing else – but all she said was, 'Augusta, you look the living image of Winnie the Pooh!'

She laughed until her eyes were streaming tears, she wrapped my wet towel around my waist, and I had to waddle into the car park like that, my face on fire with the shame of it.

I wanted to like Barbara Cook, and I did like Barbara Cook, I might even have loved her, so I tried not to mind that she laughed at me when I already felt ashamed. I also learnt a valuable lesson: that the people we like, and might even love, will still disappoint us – in the same way, I suppose, as we disappoint them.

'Why do you think Barbara laughed at me?' I said to Julia later.

Julia shrugged and went on making some kind of woollen knitted rope which came out of the head of a painted wooden doll. I hated that thing. I had one too. Of course. Still sealed. Suffocating in her box. Like the rest of us.

My mother, inexplicably, tied Julia's woollen rope onto the pull-on pull-off light string in the bathroom, to join the gallery of miscellany hung around the house. There were crêpe butterflies, paper mobiles on coat-hangers, doilies taped to windows and paintings magnetised to the fridge – a kind of shrine to us, the twins, their girls.

No more children followed.

'When you have two perfect children,' said my father, 'why ask for trouble?'

'Perfect, are we?' said Julia, smiling, and stretching on the sofa like a cat, with that lovely aura of contentment she had, a kind of giant body-shaped halo.

'No complications, I mean,' said my father, nodding towards number 2, and reaching out his small pale hand to Julia's shoulder. 'All there. Not – you know.'

My father drew spirals out of his right temple.

My mother patted the front of her apron as if she'd baked us, and we'd risen just right.

'Graham Cook *is all there*,' I said, and I was off. 'Why do you think it's OK to make mental spiral signs with your fingers? And how do you think that would that make the Cooks feel? And what on earth does perfect mean anyway, because sometimes the people *you* think are so perfect in fact end up doing the worst—'

'Can you slow down, Augusta? I can't think straight,' said my father.

'—things in the world?'

I kept going because I loved the sound of my own voice even though I was scarcely seven years old, and I could only imagine how clever I would sound if someone foreign was listening. Someone from one of the many countries in the world that was not our boring country, afloat on a grey ocean, when other countries got turquoise and aquamarine and azure blue as the colour of *their* sea.

As you see, I never had that gold halo of contentment around me. I don't know why that was. I guess it's the way we were made, Julia and I.

The way I was made was wanting to write a book. From as far back as I can remember.

But first I wanted to memorise as many words as I could, so that I could write it with precision and a bit of pzazz – which is the only word in the dictionary starting with *pz*, acronyms excepted.

I liked to open the dictionary at the first and tiniest word, *a* (which has thirty-seven entries), and to work my way through all the letters of the alphabet, exclaiming and memorising, until I ended up at zyzzogeton (a genus of large South American leafhopper), and then I'd try out the words I'd found in new and unlikely combinations. Then I'd go back to the beginning and start at *a* again.

People typically use 5,000 words in their speech, and twice as many in their writing, but an educated person might use 80,000, and the twenty-volume Oxford English Dictionary has full entries for 171,476 words in current use, 47,156 obsolete words, with 9,500 derivatives as sub-entries.

When I was at Hedley Green library for the morning, I decided to try to find my favourite name for a country, going on sounds, without knowing anything about the place.

I was supposed to be doing a puppet workshop, but I crept away and let Julia make two stripy sock snakes with plastic eyes and felt tongues, which weren't completely my cup of tea.

I crept past Jean, the librarian, who had a habit of ripping her own hair out, and I sat quietly in the shadows of the bookshelves. I went through all the countries, starting at A and ending at Z, in the index of the atlas, and I came to the conclusion that the best country name in the world was Burundi.

Burundi Burundi Burundi. I said it so many times it stopped meaning anything. It was like the sea lapping against my mind.

I went to the left-hand corner of the library where they had a huge globe on wheels, and I found Burundi, land-locked in Africa between Tanzania and Rwanda and the Democratic Republic of Congo. I turned the globe slowly, staring at all the countries and trying to memorise every name and every location and where they joined, and the shapes they made up against the sea, up against each other, and then I spun the globe round and round really fast, letting it turn into a greeny-blue blur, and I imagined myself at Hedley Green library, a tiny pin-prick in the South of England, rotating, and I tried to work out why we didn't all fall off the earth – me, Julia, the puppet lady and all the stripy socks.

When I looked up Burundi in the encyclopaedias and information books at Hedley Green library, I found out that the Tutsis looked down their noses at the Hutus, who arrived there first – even though they all spoke the same Bantu language called Kirundi, and had the same colour skin and the same Christian religion. European men called by in ships, and they said that the Hutus should look after the Tutsis' cows. To cut a very long story short, this in the end made them want to kill each other. I was struck by how sad and unnecessary this was – and then by how many other sad and unnecessary things human beings make happen on this earth. I decided to turn my attention to the sky.

When I started my research into the sky, a cloud seemed a simple thing to me – a puff of floating water-vapour, and that was that. But the more I researched, the more cloud meant. The five letters were elastic, and they stretched through the years, as I realised that someone somewhere was probably doing their PhD on clouds, or on one tiny aspect of clouds, and maybe that would take up half their brain for their whole life.

It made me feel dizzy when I realised everything the simple word *cloud* carried around inside it. It made me feel dizzy when I realised that this was true of every word there is. It made me feel both dizzy and small – and, in my dizziness and smallness, I watched the clouds go by, and they looked like speech bubbles. As I grew older and started to spend more time inside the row of dictionaries lined up on the reference shelves of the library, I put words inside them, words I loved, in alphabetical order A–Z. Acanthus, admiral, aeronaut, bean-stalk, bergamot, chrysanthemum, calabash, cicada. I thought about the size of different words – or should I say the depth, or the space they take up? I wasn't referring to the number of letters they had but to what manner of thing or things were held within those letters.

I thought of hundreds and thousands of words all meaning hundreds and thousands of things, and it made me realise that, in the course of my own life, I would end up knowing almost nothing. But the almost nothing I ended up knowing would, I supposed, be different from the almost nothing other people would end up knowing, and between us all, I thought we would know a bit more than almost nothing. And, of course, death would come along, and everything we'd found out would be buried with us. Which seemed a terrible waste. Shouldn't we first be tipped upside down to let all our knowledge out – like when you empty a piggy bank of its coins?

For days, I went around chewing Burundi like you might chew gum. Burundi, I discovered, was a big, capacious word, and it stretched, stretched, stretched. Because Burundi meant a million things.

It was made up of 27,816 square kilometres, much of it hilly and mountainous, and 10 per cent of it water, mainly the huge Lake Tanganyika which contained 250 species of cichlid fish, rainbow-striped and dazzling.

There were about ten and a half million people living in Burundi – Hutu (85 per cent), Tutsi (14 per cent) and Twa (1 per cent) – and most of them were sad. Their land was running out of soil, their forests were running out of trees and the ones who hadn't been killed by each other were dying of AIDs.

Only the other day, when they did one of those world happiness surveys, Burundi turned out to be the world's least happy nation in 2016.

Burundi was my first unlikely choice before I realised how much I like unlikely choices – and, once I'd picked it, I couldn't let it go. I tried to imagine how different my life would have been if I'd been born there and not here. And I did my best to keep up with what was going on there through the years, including writing letters to each one of its American ambassadors.

The American ambassadors never so much as replied to me, so I turned my attention back to words, which seemed more readily available.

The word Asda was created in 1965, when the *As*quith brothers approached Associated *Da*iries to run the butchery departments in their chain of shops.

If you made a similar combination out of *Ju*lia and Augu*sta*, I worked out that you could call us *Justa* – and we would be one. Like we were, we really were – back in 1999 when we were both nine years old and wearing matching pleated skirts, modelled on Jane in the interminable *Peter and Jane* series, from my mother's second-hand Ladybird book collection.

Justa, I would later discover, is the feminine of *justus*, a Latin adjective meaning just and fair and proper and reasonable and a load of other things besides.

Asda is a word which sums up the life I was born into, a life in which Asda was news. And the news was that there was going to be a *massive* new Asda as part of the *massive* new shopping centre in Hedley Green, out on the main road. This was *massive* news in our house, in Willow Crescent, in the school playground, in Hedley Green high street – in 1999.

This new Asda would be the biggest Asda in Hertfordshire, or the South of England, or the whole world, depending who you were listening to. It was going to be huge and white and made of curved glass – like a great big UFO. Everyone was excited. Except me. They saw Asda as a big word, but I saw it as small. Size had nothing to do with it.

'I can't think of anything *less exciting* than the new Asda,' I said to my mother and Julia. Because I liked to be dramatic and difficult, my mother would say. And *oppositional*, I would say, because I like finding new words.

'Don't be such an old grump, Augusta,' said my mother, icing cupcakes in pastel colours, at breakfast, to eat at tea, like fashion houses show their autumn collections in the spring. She liked to be at least one meal ahead, sometimes more, which makes you feel breathless, if you think about it too hard. She rarely sat down.

Despite what I said, I quickly thought of about twenty-five things that *were* less exciting than the new Asda. Lard and washing up liquid and fingernail clippings and trowels and the hymn that begins 'Forty Days and Forty Nights' which we had to sing at school.

Although everyone called the new development Asda, there was going to be (eventually if all went to plan) a Homebase, a Next, a Mothercare and, rumour had it – because rumour *has* a lot of things – a cinema complex, possibly, and even a bowling alley. The cinema and bowling alley never came, as I might have predicted. (Think what a huge word rumour is, positively bulging with stuff, like a massive delusional warehouse.)

When I was a child and I told people my name, they said back at me, 'Augusta?' They said it with as big a question mark in their voice as you can imagine. Like they thought I'd got my own name wrong.

I replied, 'Yes, Augusta.'

They said, 'Oh, I see.'

Some people said, 'And what are you actually called?'

I said, again, 'Augusta.'

They said, 'I haven't heard that name before.'

But I soon grew to like my name.

It fits with my unusual choices.

Augusta, feminine version of Augustus – majestic, grand, venerable – a name originally given to the female relatives of Roman emperors.

Just saying.

Antsy Augusta, my mother used to call me.

'Ants in your pants, can you please sit still and stop talking all the time?'

My mother kept saying over and over again how much she wished the Mothercare had come when we were little. I couldn't see the point of saying this even once.

Julia reminded me that having twins was my mother's idea of heaven: pastel-coloured Babygros, pin-tucked girls' dresses and gingham bloomers.

I wondered what *my* heaven would be full of. But then I thought that I probably wouldn't get a choice, bearing in mind the communal aspect of the project.

I prefer the word paradise to heaven, a word which joins us all the way from the Greek *paradeisos*, giving us one of my favourite ever adjectives – *paradisiacal* – a word which nobody actually uses.

My grandmother Nellie (who gave me her middle name, and her straight dark hair and skinny limbs) said that in heaven we'd be in white, wearing crowns and waiting around, like in the carol. I knew I didn't want to wear a crown and I *hated* waiting around. So I hoped she was wrong. I still have no idea how it works, and I'd like to find out. Like we all would, I guess.

Julia said that heaven would be full of roses and waterfalls and flocks of white doves, which were three of her favourite things.

'Oh, that I had wings like a dove! I would fly away and be at rest,' said my grandmother, who liked to talk in bible verses, set off by a word or a thought or a curse on somebody she didn't like. She particularly liked to divide people into sheep and goats, popping my goat grandfather into the jaws of hell at every possible opportunity because he had gone off with his secretary soon after my mother was born.

My grandmother would sit in the corner of the lounge on Friday evenings and Saturday afternoons, commenting on our lives like a one-woman Greek chorus, whilst also playing with the silver crucifix which she wore around her neck. It had a little Jesus Christ on it, permanently dying. It bothered me.

To make room for the magical *Asda Development,* the terraced houses on the main road were being taken down, with the residents compensated, *very generously,* everybody said. The way they did it looked like slicing a rectangular block of Wall's ice cream, one oblong at a time, and I thought that this was one of my best similes (bearing in mind the name of the brand of ice cream), though nobody else in the family appreciated my brilliance.

Mrs Venditti, who was married to the ice cream-van man, cried as number 3 was sliced, and my mother explained that this was because her baby had died inside that house of cot death. I'd heard this was to do with lying babies on their front, and I asked my mother if Mrs Venditti had done this, by mistake, but my mother said, 'Can we change the subject?'

'Why?' I said.

'Because I don't like thinking about dead babies,' she said.

My father added, 'Mrs Venditti is also Italian.'

I said, 'What do you mean?'

He said, 'Stop asking questions all the time.'

A driver in an old Renault 5 crashed into a minibus of school children because he was watching number 8 fall down, but nobody was badly hurt. A sign went up saying, 'Keep your eyes on the road,' except you had to take your eyes off the road to look at the sign. Sometimes, I thought, adults just don't think things through.

My mother let me wait on the main road in the evenings to meet our father on his way home from work. It made her feel that everything about our life was utterly perfect. Like the families in her second-hand Ladybird books, which continued to proliferate along the shelves of the somewhat over-varnished pine dresser.

The Greens' house was the last to come down, and all six Greens stood on the opposite pavement watching, as I waited for my father, who soon came walking past, whistling, on his way back from Stanley Hope Uniforms.

'This must be a very sad day for you,' he said to Mr Green cheerfully, as if the thought of Mr Green's sadness made him feel safer inside his own happiness.

'It's only bricks and mortar,' said Mr Green, with his hands in his pockets.

'It's a *home*,' said my father.

'That's sentimental, Stanley,' said Mr Green.

My father didn't seem to be able to find an answer for that.

'Aren't you worried?' said Mr Green to my father as his old house crashed to the ground.

'Why would *I* be *worried?*' said my father.

'Too much *worry*, Jilly,' my father would say when my mother suggested owning a dog, or going on an aeroplane, or having another baby, which was her favourite suggestion through the years.

'School uniform!' shouted Mr Green over the noise of the crashing bricks, jerking his head at the place behind the hoarding where the biggest Asda in the whole universe would be.

'School uniform?' shouted my father back.

Then the crashing stopped for a moment.

'Asda sells school uniform,' said Mr Green very slowly and very loudly as if my father had special needs. 'Lots of it. And cheap. The whole shaboodle.'

I watched my father's face, and I saw, for a tiny fragment of a second, a crack run across it, a hairline fracture, like on a china pot. I looked down at the pavement. I didn't like to see my father's face break like that. When I looked up, the hairline crack was gone. But my father's face was covered in a layer of sweat like see-through Uhu glue, which I hoped might mend the crack, although I knew the truth, that cracks grow and split rather than shrink or mend. I had a premonition of my father's face splitting in two.

'Better be on our way then,' said my father to Mr Green, and he shot his arm up in a wave to Mrs Green and the four bored children.

'What's a *shaboodle*?' I said, thinking I had a new word to add to my S page.

My father didn't answer Mr Green, and he didn't answer me. He practically ran home, whereas normally we walked along together, talking about how my day had been at school. His fingers were trembling, and I could tell he wanted to see my mother really badly.

'Peas in a pod,' says my mother – still, despite, or maybe because of, everything. 'That's what marriage is. For better. For worse. In sickness. And in health.'

'I need to talk to you, Jilly,' said my father, with his key still in the door, and I noticed he was panting with worry. I took up my position underneath the serving hatch (an arched hole in the wall) on the lounge side, which enabled me to listen to all their kitchen conversations.

'Oh, darling,' said my mother, laughing. 'Asda can't compete with Stanley Hope Uniforms!'

'Really?' said my father. 'Really?'

'It's the personal service,' said my mother. 'Who's going to measure

13

the kids up at Asda? Who's going to sew initials onto their shoe bags at Asda?'

'Really?' said my father again. 'So nothing to worry about?'

And he walked into the hall saying under his breath, 'Nothing to worry about. Nothing to worry about.'

'Were the Greens sad to see their home come crashing down?' said my mother when we were eating supper.

'Mr Green said it was only bricks and mortar,' I said.

'How heartless,' said my mother. 'It's where they brought up their children.'

'Mr Green told Dad he was being sentimental,' I said.

My father blushed.

'I like you sentimental,' said my mother.

Julia and I looked at each other, waiting for my mother to kiss my father on his head, on his sweaty hair – which she did. I always found that my father's hair smelled a bit funny.

'We have something to tell you, Daddy,' said my mother.

'Oh yes,' said my father, spearing his fifth sausage with his fork.

'Julia has come home with the Poet of the Week certificate,' said my mother. 'It's a very special *award* from school.'

'Well done,' said my father, before adding, 'I'm sure Augusta's poem was good too.'

'Julia is going to read it to you,' said my mother to my father.

'The title,' said Julia, glancing at me, slightly flushed, as, strictly speaking, poetry was my thing, 'is "My Mother's Name".'

'Everyone's title was the same,' I said, by way of information, though my mother took it as a slight against Julia, and left her eyes on me that fraction too long.

'Fire away,' said my father.

Julia stood up, and she started to read, though she wasn't excellent at reading out and tended to stumble a bit, which made me clench my jaw.

'My mother's name is Jilly
And she likes things that are frilly
In summer she can be silly
And in winter she's rather chilly.'

'Bravo,' said my father, laughing, ignoring the stumbles.

'She's just got me, hasn't she?' said my mother. 'Down to a tee. I do like things that are frilly, don't I, Stan?'

I was so happy that Julia got the Poet of the Week certificate, and I loved the way her little nose wrinkled like a rabbit when she read it, but I knew that this was not a good poem. Either the teacher had no idea about poetry or she had some other motive like balancing out the awards.

My mother and father laughed for some time together after Julia read the poem, which made me think they must be losing their minds. Even if you liked the rhymes, the poem was really not that funny.

'I do get chilly in winter,' laughed my mother, wiping her eyes, 'and I am a bit silly in summer.'

Summer was coming, and my father would close the shop on 30 or 31 July (Julia's birthday) for two weeks because so many people went away, and because my mother required that we too took a fortnight's holiday.

My mother spent fifty weeks of the year planning our two-week holiday, which would be the only one my father was prepared to take because he never liked anyone else to run the shop, the way some mothers won't pass their babies around. He had a sign in the window showing the whole calendar year. OPEN, it said in luminous ruled capital letters, with a single spindly pencil line through his holiday fortnight.

'Six months until we go away,' my mother would say.

'Five'

'Four'

'Three'

'Two'

'One'

When we left for our holiday, my father would leave lights on timer switches around the house, mimicking our family routines, and he would go around checking them about five times before we left, and then one for luck. I told him that I'd never seen any burglars lurking about in Willow Crescent, and he said that they didn't carry swag bags and wear striped T-shirts – burglars could be anyone, even people we knew and liked, even neighbours in Willow Crescent.

'Even Barbara Cook?' I said.

'Obviously not Barbara Cook,' he said.

'You're the Neighbourhood Watch man,' I said. 'Shouldn't you have found out if any of our neighbours are burglars?'

'Don't worry your father when he's so busy,' said my mother, with her holiday glow, hoping my insolence wouldn't make my father's fingers start shaking, as it sometimes did, particularly on the day we left for our holiday, when he was taut with tension.

My mother started her trips to the travel agent in the autumn. She kept an eye on the newsagent board. She scoured the Sunday papers. She also used the school magazine where people advertised holiday homes and caravans.

Julia's poem ended up being published in the school magazine. My mother cut it out and framed it, and my father nailed it to the hall wall. Julia put a chewy Werther's toffee under my pillow with a note saying, 'You are the real poet in the family.'

I chewed it with great humility as Julia said (not incorrectly), 'My poem is actually quite bad.'

I wanted my mouth to make the words, 'No it isn't.' But my mouth didn't seem able to make those words, and, if it had, Julia would have known it was a total fib.

That's the thing with being a twin, and maybe it's the same with all brothers and sisters. You know the outside of each other, the body you bath with every night of your life, until you become too big to fit in together. Then one of you sits on the toilet lid and chats to the other in the bath until you run some more hot water and swap around.

You know the little splodge of birthmark on Julia's right upper arm and the dark freckle on her left ring finger that helps her tell her right from her left, and you know her inside too just the same. You feel her tears before they fall – and you want to stop them, you so want to stop them, though you can't, that's the truth of it. You hear her laugh before it comes, and hearing her laugh makes you laugh too. Her lovely bright laugh.

In this way, your twin is your home.

Or mine was, anyway.

Far more than my home was ever my home.

What a word it is – home – a million meanings packed up in a giant handkerchief and hanging from a pole which we carry across our shoulder.

'Didn't you write a poem, Augusta?' said my mother.

I nodded.

'You must show me it,' she said.

'Don't worry,' I said.

'I will worry,' said my mother, which meant I had to go and get my English exercise book although I really didn't want to.

'Here it is,' I said. 'Miss Rae didn't especially like it.'

'I'm sure she did,' said my mother, who obviously couldn't be sure she did, especially as I could be absolutely sure she didn't.

I opened the exercise book at the right page.

This is what my mother read:

<u>'My Mother's Name' by Augusta Hope</u>
'My mother's name is Jilly
Which (apparently) is an affectionate
Shortened version of Jill
Although it is longer by y

Which makes me ask y
You don't call a pill you love
Such as aspirin
(which removes head-aches)
A pilly
Or a hill you love
Such as Old John Brown's
A hilly
Or a window sill you love
A window silly
But that would just be silly.'

Underneath, the teacher had written:

'This is quite a strange poem, Augusta, and your rhyme pattern is not regular. Well done!'

My mother stared at the teacher's comment.

Then she stared at the ruled grey line underneath. She was trying to read the indentations, and she was also trying to think what on earth she could say to me about my weird poem.

Underneath the teacher's comment I had written:

'I didn't actually want a regular rhyme pattern FYI (which I'd discovered meant *for your information*). Then I'd rubbed it out because I knew that, though it was true, it was also a bit rude – and precocious.

My mother went on straining her eyes to read underneath the rubbing out.

'What did it say here?' she said.

'I can't remember,' I said.

'It's . . .' said my mother, and she couldn't think what to say.

'It's OK,' I said. 'You don't have to like it. I know it's a bit strange.'

'Sometimes I wonder what is going on in that little head of yours,' said my mother.

She did not frame my poem.

Parfait

My mother was called Aurore, which means dawn.

And my motherland, still waiting for its dawn, is called Burundi.

Burundi carries its poetry in the hummingbirds drinking from the purple throats of flowers, the leaves glistening green after a night of rain; in the cichlid fish which flash like jewels deep beneath the surface of Lake Tanganyika, where crocodiles slumber like logs, still and deceptive, and hippos paddle downriver, in a line.

It carries its spirit in the dignified faces of all who are willing to forgive in the belief that Burundi will one day be beautiful again.

Dignified faces like my father's.

I was his first son, and he prayed that by the time I was grown, we'd be living in peace.

'You were born smiling,' he told me. 'And you were so perfect. Everything we'd ever dreamt of.'

'So we called you Parfait,' said my mother.

'Parfait Nduwimana,' said my father (which means *I'm in God's hands*).

'You were the most beautiful baby,' said my mother 'with those little dimples in your cheeks.'

'Why would dimples be beautiful?' I said.

'Just because!' she answered, hopping over to me on her wiry legs, and stroking my left-hand dimple with her right hand.

She reminded me of a bird, my mother.

I loved to spot birds when I was out and about: the hoopoe, or the Malachite kingfisher, or my favourite, the Fischer's lovebird – a little rainbow-feathered parrot which used to bathe in the stream up above our homestead.

'That bird is so . . .' I said.

And my father said, 'Unnecessary.'

Which I suppose is what beauty is.

Yet later I found I couldn't live without it.

Then my father said, 'Unnecessarily extravagant.'

I said, 'What's extravagant?'

He said, 'This is,' turning in a circle and pointing all around him, at the sky and the trees and the water running, clear, over the pebbles.

My family went on washing in the stream, like the birds.

There were nine of us in the beginning.

The girl twins: Gloria and Douce, who liked to dress up in the shiny bridesmaid dresses brought down the hill by the Baptists in plastic sacks.

The boy twins: Wilfred, named after an English missionary who lived (and died) on our *colline*, and Claude, named after a French one.

Pierre was strong and stubborn, and you couldn't tell what he was thinking.

Zion was the baby, and you could. Even from when he was tiny, he wore his heart on his sleeve, as they say in English.

My father's face always had a glow about it as if he had a candle inside him, shining light through his eyes. I see his smile, so wide it seemed to reach from one earlobe to the other, and I hear his laughter, bubbling up from some mysterious source inside him. I see his fingers sculpting a whistle from a stick, or fashioning a football for us out of coconut and twine.

I feel my mother's arms around me, the slight damp of her armpits on my shoulders, the warmth of my cheek against her soft chest and the deep shiver of belonging running down my spine to the soles of my feet.

All of us would sit around the fire, the twin girls singing; the twin boys tied together at the ankle and refusing to separate; Pierre quiet and brooding; the baby in my mother's arms, with something still of heaven about him.

'We'll call him Zion,' said my father, as my mother pushed him out between her legs to the sound of gunfire in the homestead on the left.

The women tied the umbilical cord into his navel.

'Yes, Zion!' said my father. 'And we'll all keep dreaming of the city that is to come!'

Augusta

On the last day of 1999, the last day of the twentieth century, the last day of the old millennium, a day full of potential drama, there was a New Year's Eve party at the Pattons' house, number 13, the only detached house on the crescent, which was empty except for several towers of identical beige cardboard boxes in every room, each labelled in black marker pen with strange vowel-less codes on them like R1/shf or R3/cpd, which made you think that Mr Patton was a member of MI5.

The point of the party, whilst allegedly to celebrate the new millennium, was in fact to have lots of musical performances by the Patton children, practically every five minutes. Cello, violin, clarinet and a recorder ensemble, and then the whole lot all over again, until the rest of us nearly died of boredom.

Then it was 1 January 2000 – Julia and I were nine and a half years old, and the sci-fi millennium was here.

It made me hopeful. As if something monumental was about to happen. As if a battalion of silver robots was about to walk around the crescent. But actually, the next day, 2 January, in the rain, a grand piano rolled down the pavement. Because the Pattons (who were, as you've seen, *very musical*) were moving out of Willow Crescent. We saw Tabitha Patton through the window in an entirely empty house practising her violin amongst the boxes. She was ten years old and doing Grade 8. She went to private school, where apparently everyone is a genius.

Grade 8!

'It's cruel,' said my mother.

'Or brilliant,' I said (to be oppositional because, to be honest, I couldn't stand Tabitha Patton).

'Do you always have to disagree with me?' said my mother.

Next thing we knew, a huge removal lorry arrived, with foreign words down its side, and the removal men started bringing out carved benches and jewelled cushions, antique bird cages and hat stands, and cardboard boxes in bright canary colours.

But better than any of these things was the appearance of a dark-haired boy, who could carry four boxes at once, easy as anything.

Julia and I went and hung around in our raincoats, pretending to have lost something on the roundabout, and we spied on him from behind the ragged branches of the willow tree, which were actually pathetic for spying because they were too thin and straggly, and only covered us down to our waists.

We walked over and started looking for our *lost thing* on the wet pavement outside number 13, and we found out that the boy's name was Diego, and then we completely forgot about our lost thing, and when Diego asked us the next day if we'd found it, we had no idea what he was talking about.

Looking back, Diego was a chubby twelve-year-old, but he was three years older than us, and we thought he was the bee's knees with his dark Spanish skin and his black eyes. His sister was called Paloma which means Dove, though she wasn't at all bird-like, and this possibly wasn't the right name for her.

'Which animal *does* she remind you of?' I said to Julia.

'I'm not saying,' she replied.

But we burst out laughing anyway.

Then we felt bad, and Julia said, 'She has a lovely face,' which is what people say about fat girls.

My mother made a large dish of lasagne for the new arrivals, as was her custom. My father was the Neighbourhood Watch man, and she considered this *the least she could do.* She handed it over at the front door, looking up the hall, hoping for an invitation.

'It was quite bare inside,' she said on her return, 'from what I could see.'

'They have only been there an hour,' said my father. 'Anyhow, they'll have different customs.'

'Yes, but I imagine they'll have furniture,' I said.

A few days later, Diego's foreign mother committed the error of not returning my mother's lasagne dish, one she'd bought on holiday in Brittany in 1998, which said along the bottom, *Quimper, Bretagne.*

'You don't expect that of a new neighbour,' said my mother, who didn't have the necessary imagination to understand people.

Julia went to number 13 for the missing lasagne dish, with her smile. On the way back, she put a little sprig of yellow wintersweet flowers from our garden in the dish for my mother, so that when she came through the door, the kitchen smelled of petals. She just had that way with her. I could have thought for a hundred years and I would never have thought of putting yellow flowers in my mother's lasagne dish.

As I write my story here in La Higuera in the south of Spain, though Hedley Green is over two thousand kilometres away, I can smell the wintersweet flowers in the front garden of number 1, to the left of the front door, and I can smell Julia's soft fair hair, washed with Timotei shampoo, still wet, over her pale pink dressing gown, waiting to be dried. We'd sit, legs apart, us two, and sometimes Angela Dunnett from the crescent, and Julia's slightly dizzy school-friend, Amy Atkins, drying and plaiting and crimping, and taking turns to be the person at the back of the line who had nobody to play with her hair.

'If Angela Dunnett wanted to frizz her hair, she would need quimpers,' I said, looking at the lasagne dish from Quimper.

'She can't help having a speech impediment,' said my mother. 'So don't be a clever clogs.'

I felt ashamed – but I also found it a bit funny that Angela Dunnett, who was so full of herself, couldn't say her rs. She was only two years older than us, but she acted like she knew everything there was to know about the world.

Julia said that Diego's mother was called *Lola Alvárez*, trying to make the Spanish sounds come out just right. The name made the most gorgeous sounds I'd ever heard. Also, Julia added, she thought Lola Alvárez would end up being a very good neighbour; she had a lovely smile.

But three months later, Julia's prediction had not come true on account of the fact that there were weeds growing all over the front garden of number 13, which quite ruined the appearance of the crescent, and my mother felt that, if the Neighbourhood Watch man couldn't say this to Lola Alvárez, who could?

My father was dispatched, but when he came back, he said it hadn't quite come out how he meant it to.

'Did you say anything at all?' said my mother.

'I said that an English man's home is his castle,' he said.

'Well, I suppose that's a start,' my mother said.

'I wondered if perhaps they don't know the difference between weeds and flowers,' said my father. 'It's probably different over there.'

He pointed towards the level crossing, as if Spain was behind the railway line.

'Then I shall tell them the difference, Stanley,' said my mother.

I was there, cringing, at her side, when she did so, patting her curly hair and going pink on her cheeks even though she had paley-cream make-up on.

'*Your* weeds are *my* flowers,' Diego's mother said to my mother, winking, with her hands in the pockets of her baggy dungarees, smiling in the way she had that made her eyes wrinkle up at the edges.

My mother never learnt to wink. Nor did she wish to. Neither did she have any understanding of dungarees for adults.

The weeds went on growing – white, blue, yellow and red – in the garden of number 13, and I loved the look of them.

Your weeds are my flowers – I am still thinking it years after.

I knew I was going to love Diego's mother from the word go. Diego's father, Fermín, was large and dark, a top scientist, who had come over to run the huge science laboratory out in the Tattershall Industrial Park. His mother had found a job teaching Spanish in the Sixth Form College in Hinton, and she wore her hair in plaits, with a rose fixed to each elastic. Fermín would pull her face towards him by holding her two plaits, and give her mouth-to-mouth kisses in the kitchen. I found this completely transfixing.

Parfait

My mother used to lean back against the big wall of my father's dark chest, and he'd put his arms around her, clasped together like a belt at the front. I knew that nothing bad could ever happen to us because he was here, and he would save us, whatever happened.

'We all need a Saviour,' he used to say, smiling at us.

'No we don't,' Pierre would answer, and this pained my father, the way he loved to say no to everything.

But now a saviour was coming.

Not down to earth from heaven.

But over the border from Rwanda.

With the name, Melchior, like my father, like one of the three wise kings.

He was a Hutu, like us.

And this Hutu was going to be *president of Burundi*.

Although Hutu people weren't presidents, not ordinarily, not ever so far.

I'll never forget the day that Melchior Ndadaye took power. The hope we felt in our new *Hutu president*, a hope that blew in the smoke of a thousand fires cooking a thousand celebration chickens, rising above the conical roofs of our huts on the *collines* above Bujumbura.

'We have a choice to love the Tutsi even if they've killed half the people we loved,' my father told us. 'We have a choice to love our neighbour.'

We nodded because we hated to disappoint our father.

27

'And who is your neighbour?' said our father.

'Anyone God made,' we said, all together, as we'd been taught. 'Hutu, Tutsi or Twa.'

'Hurray for the new president!' said my father.

'Hurray for the new president!' we all echoed.

Little did we know that one hundred and two days later, men from the army – the president's army – would come to kill their president. Little did we know that his thirty-eight palace guards would make no attempt to defend him.

In revenge, the Hutu massacred the Tutsi. Which, my father said, the president would not have wanted. The conflict cost three hundred thousand lives in the end, and one of those three hundred thousand was my father, who chose to turn the other cheek because, as he'd often told us, someone has to *break the chain*.

I was eight years old at the time.

I watched the fruit bats flying north in a big black cloud, and I knew I couldn't bear to be here on the *colline* without him. Perhaps the bats would fly all the way up the continent of Africa to Europe – and perhaps I could go there too one day.

The countries of Europe were joining together to make one big happy continent. That's what the Baptists said – and they should have known, being from England and France, themselves. Through the years that followed, in addition to clothes, they brought us second-hand paperback books and atlases and foreign-language dictionaries and old magazines, and I stayed up at night reading about this other world, extending my French vocabulary, learning English and the capitals of European countries.

I read about a pop band called the Spice Girls and a nun called Mother Teresa and a beautiful princess who died in a tunnel in Paris and a woman who spent eighty-one days rowing alone across the Atlantic Ocean.

So it obviously was possible, getting away to somewhere else, if you were brave enough.

I could take my whole family somewhere better. We could leave the *colline*, catch a boat up the lake, walk through Rwanda to the Democratic Republic of Congo, up through the Central African Republic into Chad, through Niger to Algeria, and then we'd reach Morocco, and I'd seen on the map that there was a tiny strip of sea, thin as a river. We could cross it by boat and go and live in the south of Spain.

Perhaps we would find a new life.

But the years passed, and we didn't find a new life. Everything went on just the same.

Except something was about to change.

The *one thousands* were coming to an end.

We sat, all of us, on 31 December 1999, crouched on our haunches, our bare brown feet caked in red mud, looking expectantly over Lake Tanganyika, whose waters flowed over our borders and out beyond, imagining that something extraordinary might happen as we crossed over at midnight to the new millennium.

'It's the longest lake in the world,' I said to my brothers and sisters, trying to copy my father's jolly tone of voice, though the exact timbre of it was fading away from me, six years from his death. I found it hard to conjure it at night inside my head but I could still see his big wide smile and his twinkling eyes.

'It's the second deepest and the second largest, after Lake Baikal in Siberia,' I said. 'It holds 18 per cent of the world's fresh water – and the fish in the lake are so special and so colourful that they are sold all around the world to rich men who like to keep them in glass boxes in their dining rooms.'

'Do soldiers break in and smash the glass boxes?' said Zion.

'They don't need soldiers in those countries,' I said, authoritatively – I was fourteen years old now, my voice had broken and I was growing body hair. 'No, these rich men live in peace.'

'Peace?' said Zion, creasing his brow.

And he and I walked across the hillside, looking up at the sky.

'Let's imagine that the clouds are boats,' I said, crouching down and putting my arm around Zion's shoulder, just as my father did with me when I was a little boy. 'And let's imagine that they'll dip down to earth, Little Bro, and we'll climb in, you and I. And, you know what? We'll float right across the border of Burundi and way over the whole continent of Africa to the sea.'

'Will we really?' said Zion.

'Really really,' I said, and I wished it was true. I wished I could make things not as they were. I wished I could save Zion from the place where he'd been born.

Augusta

My mother had always been fond of knitting, sewing and tapestry, and she tried to interest us in terrible craft projects where you made stuffed owls or knitted blankets for dolls.

She offered a special service for Stanley Hope Uniforms, which involved embroidering names onto PE bags, pencil cases, aertex shirts, anything really.

The minute we were born, our names were sewn and embroidered and painted and framed, with creeping flowers twisting and turning on the ascenders and descenders.

Barbara Cook at number 2 was inspired by my mother's craft work, and it was this that sent her off to art classes, and this that caused her to start wearing wrap-around Indian skirts, which didn't go well with her leather slip-on court shoes, flesh-coloured tights and anoraks.

Helen Dunnett at number 3 (who had a very thin grey whippet) liked to crochet things such as little boys' ties, babies' bonnets and holders for toilet rolls – and even a coat for the whippet, in pale green.

The craft craze must have been contagious because before you knew it, over half of Willow Crescent's women were crafting away in their spare time, creating rag dolls, candles in the shape of triangular prisms, baby clothes, three-dimensional special-occasion cards – you name it, they made it.

*   *   *

My mother said her dream was to have a craft room, like my father had a study, but, although he was out of the house six days a week, he never once offered to share.

His study (the third bedroom) was the only part of the interior of the house of which he was in charge. His desk was immaculate, his dark green files hung in alphabetical order and his cork boards were papered in taut rectangles. He was also in charge of the double garage and the extra single garage and the garden, in which not one thing was out of place.

It was Barbara Cook who had the idea of the Willow Crescent Craft Fair. Everybody agreed that Number 1 would be the best location for it, not only because of our larger-than-average garden, but, in the event of rain, our immaculate double garage, with the additional single garage for the side shows, which the children would organise.

'We've been thinking of a way to raise funds for the farm school where Graham Cook goes,' said my mother to my father. 'We all thought a Craft Fair would be a good idea.'

'Lovely,' said my father. 'That would give the Cooks a bit of a boost.'

'Yes, exactly,' said my mother, allowing this burst of good-heartedness to flourish before slipping in the suggested venue.

'I wouldn't want everyone tramping over the carpets to use our toilet,' said my father.

It was some hours later, when my mother and father had undergone several circular arguments and become rather tetchy with each other, and by which time Julia and I had gone to bed, listening out anxiously, in case our parents were about to get divorced, that we heard my father exclaim, 'I shall damn well build an outside toilet.'

My father laboured on this outside toilet through the spring and summer, and when it was finished, he painted it, and bought a special red/green lock to show if the toilet was vacant or occupied. My mother made an arrangement of dried flowers for the shelf, and bought one of Helen Dunnett's crocheted toilet-roll holders – in what Helen called burnt russet.

After that, my father looked a little lost on Sundays, as if some great purpose had been removed from his life.

My mother and her friends held committee meetings every five minutes around our kitchen table, and the children started planning side shows like Count the Number of Sweets in the Jar or Guess the Weight of the Cake.

I offered to sort through the second-hand toys and put prices on them, which, I discovered, my mother would over-write in permanent marker. Amongst them, I found the ugliest rag doll with yellow plaits, a brand-new Peter Rabbit and a drawn-on doll with one arm and one leg, and, in my fury about the wasted time I'd spent pricing the toys, I pulled off her remaining limbs, feeling strange. I put her torso and her separated arm and leg in my bedside drawer, and then I wrote a story where a dead baby was wrapped in cellophane like the un-used Peter Rabbit.

I asked Julia to read it so somebody would know how terrible I was inside my mind where you don't always have control of things. She hesitated, breathed deeply and said, 'Everyone has strange thoughts. And maybe you've read too many horrible things about Burundi. But we'll burn it anyway, shall we, Aug? Because that would also be quite fun, don't you think?'

I did think, but now I wish I hadn't made her read that story.

I hear her childish voice so clearly, all these years later, that it makes me jump.

I hear her trying to draw me towards the fun, towards the joy, away from the darkness.

There's a pale moth fluttering towards the light of the candle, here, at the front of the caravan, in the dusk, where I'm writing. I bat her away. She has dark squiggles on her wings, like letters written on sepia paper.

Julia went inside for matches, and we crept to a lovely hidden place behind the shed – I can feel the rough texture of the wooden slats which pulled threads out of our jumpers when we brushed against them and I can see the wire fire basket hung with spider webs. There, in a lovely empty pocket of time, the sort of pocket reserved for brothers and sisters, she and I made a little bonfire in the wire cage, and we stood together, in the warm evening, watching the pages of the story turn into flames.

My father went hysterical when he found us.

I said it was all my fault.

Julia joined in the blame, using a very soft, calm voice at his rage, like a warm shower.

'We're sorry, Dad, we're sorry,' she said, with her little heart-shaped face crinkled with sorry-ness.

It came to me then, and it comes to me now, that I didn't feel sorry at all.

One thing the committee could not talk about, as Barbara Cook was running the Craft Fair, was what Graham Cook would do on the day, as, although nobody said it, they all thought the strange drowning noises he made might put people off buying.

But one Saturday, Barbara Cook went to visit her sister, so the committee arranged an ad hoc meeting. My father walked in and out of the kitchen, hoping the meeting would soon be over, practically before it had begun.

'Perhaps Barbara's brother might come over and look after Graham at the Craft Fair,' said my mother. 'He's very good with him.'

My father shook his head.

'He's unpredictable,' he said, as he passed through. 'We wouldn't want him running amok in the garden.'

'I would be very happy to look after Graham Cook,' I said. I knew that Graham was five years older than me, but, in the circumstances, I thought this might still work.

'Oh no, darling, you couldn't possibly look after Graham Cook,' said my mother and father, practically in unison, as my father passed through again. 'You're only ten.'

'I'm nearly eleven,' I said.

'If Graham Cook's angry,' said Hilary Hawkins, 'he loses his rag – it's quite frightening, to be honest.'

In the end, Barbara Cook told the Craft Committee how much Graham was looking forward to the Craft Fair, and on the day, he sat down at the end of the garden in a shady corner next to the candle stall with his red bus, making drowning noises and putting people off coming near.

I went to the second-hand toy stall and bought a red plastic bus, and I sat with my red plastic bus right next to Graham with his red plastic bus, so that holding a red plastic bus would seem more of a normal thing to do. I considered whether I should also make some drowning noises and shoot my limbs out, but came to the conclusion that this might cause a bit too much of a commotion.

Graham Cook and I sat with our red plastic buses in the unexpected sunshine, and he seemed comforted and hardly made any strange noises at all. Julia couldn't move from her position at the Lucky Dip over by the outside toilet, but she smiled at me in that way she had.

My father came over to me and, once Barbara Cook was out of earshot, he said under his breath, 'For God's sake get up, Augusta. You're making a fool of yourself – and people will think *you're* a bit . . .'

'A bit what?' I said.

'A bit . . .' said my father. 'A bit, you know, not all there. *Spasticated.*'

'I'm staying right here,' I said, 'in solidarity with Graham Cook.'

Then my father took hold of my upper arm and dragged me upwards with a big tug, which made me feel as if my arm and my shoulder were going to come apart from each other, and in a strange tight voice, quite menacing, he whispered in my ear, 'Get over to the Lucky Dip and help your sister.'

Graham Cook moaned and wailed and tried to run away, so Jim Cook had to hold him in an arm lock.

I shut myself in the outside toilet and cried and cried at the shock of it all, and when I came out, with my red bus, there was a long queue, and Angela Dunnett said, 'We were about to call the Fire Bwigade. We thought you were locked in.'

I felt really bad that Angela Dunnett was being so nice to me, and had gone and bought me a cupcake with butter icing from the cake stall to help cheer me up, and I determined that I would never ever again make jokes about the way she said *r*.

My friend, Ian, turned up and he bought the ugly ragdoll with the yellow plaits as a joke, and we went behind the outside toilet and had a tug-of-war with her – and all her stuffing fell out of her middle.

Then I went and stood next to Julia at the Lucky Dip holding the red bus. Julia didn't ask me why I'd been crying. She just reached for my hand, but when my father came by, his face all tense and contorted, she let it go. He did another loud whisper in my ear which said, 'Put that damned bus down.'

Julia bit her lip and she puffed up the sawdust in the Lucky Dip to bring the remaining prizes to the surface.

All the happiness had seeped out of her face.

Parfait

I remember the day I met Víctor, the Spanish priest, out on the road on his bike. We started talking, and I found that things came pouring out of my mouth, things I'd been storing up inside, not knowing what I could do with them.

I told Víctor that, the week after Melchior Ndadaye was assassinated, my father, Melchior, died too.

'The soldiers came to our *colline*,' I said. 'And my father turned his cheek because he wanted to break the chain.'

I told him that the next time they came, Wilfred the English missionary stepped in front of our pregnant neighbour, Honorine, so that the soldiers would shoot him instead of her.

'I'll never forget the way he was smiling, though he was dead,' I said. 'He was lying there amongst the daffodils his mother had sent over from England. I felt so bad about what our country had done to her son.'

Víctor nodded.

'My mother went with the women to the rubbish dump,' I said, 'and they made daffodils out of old tin cans to put around his grave.'

I took a deep breath because I didn't want to speak about Claude.

I'd told Claude to run when the soldiers came with flaming torches, but as I counted everyone in, behind the bush by the stream, he wasn't there. We found his burnt body too late, cowering in the corner of our hut.

'Wilfred's still got the rope around his ankle,' I said to Víctor. 'The one that used to join onto Claude's ankle. He won't take it off, and I can't ask him why because he won't speak any more. Not a word since Claude died.'

I told him that my mother wasn't feeling too good, but she wouldn't go and see the doctor because all doctors were Tutsi and she didn't trust them.

Things went on pouring out of my mouth, and Victor went on nodding.

He told me some things about his life. How he was setting up a school for deaf and blind children, up the hill, bringing them out of the shadows so that they wouldn't feel ashamed of themselves any more. He invited me to come and see them, and I shook their hands, and Víctor gave me mango fruit chopped up in porridge in the little kitchen of his house.

'Is Spain really over there?' I asked him. 'At the top of Africa and over the sea?'

I felt light coming into my body at the thought of this country that was real and full of peace and sunshine, and not so very far away.

'It really is over there,' said Víctor.

'What's it like?' I asked him.

'There's sea pretty much all the way round, and people take picnics to the beach in the summer, and go swimming. We have festivals in the street at Christmas and Easter, when the men wear felt hats, and the women wear spotty dresses and roses in their hair – and we have this dance called *flamenco*.'

'Did you ever dance *flamenco*?' I asked him.

Víctor nodded.

'I wasn't always a priest,' he said, laughing.

'Is it like our dancing?' I asked.

'It goes something like this,' said Víctor.

He got up off the little wooden chair and threw his hands in the air, and he started to dance about, with his hips swaying and his feet stamping.

'The woman dances like this . . .' he said, and now he was really laughing, and so was I, and he looked very funny with his big grey beard and his pinky skin, and his baggy trousers, swaying his hips and turning in circles and swishing out his imaginary dress.

A man called Nelson Mandela came on the radio.

Víctor stopped dancing and turned the volume up.

This Nelson Mandela had a voice you didn't forget – kind of soft but hard underneath – like wool with steel inside it.

Nelson Mandela had made a suggestion to President Buyoya that the Tutsi and the Hutu could take it in turns to lead the country because this might stop Burundians fighting each other and dying all the time.

Víctor clapped his hands and said, 'Yes! Yes!'

I said, 'It's so obvious. Why didn't anyone think of it before?'

'Because nobody likes to share power,' said Víctor.

Augusta

Power-sharing was proving a trial in Willow Crescent as, a year after the first Craft Fair, the committee prepared, with renewed vigour, for the second.

Janice Brown brought up the subject of whether the Craft Fair really was the best place for Graham Cook, and Barbara Cook got straight up from the table, and, as she did so, her wrap-around Indian skirt started to unwrap itself, revealing her large white pants and her spongey right buttock.

A terrible silence fell on the committee meeting, as the front door slammed shut.

My mother said, 'Oh dear.'

Then the others all started saying that when you are on a committee you have to have difficult conversations, and you couldn't hide from the truth, which was plain to see, that Graham Cook put off buyers from buying.

Julia and I were sitting there, good and quiet. She was pressing flowers in a wood-framed flower press, and I was leafing through my book of Latin phrases, when out of my mouth came the words, 'If this Craft Fair is to help Graham Cook, then he might rather you didn't bother so much about how much money his school got, and you just let him come.'

Julia raised her hand, the way my mother used to do when my father didn't brake early enough in the car.

My mother sat completely still as if someone had pressed pause on her, before Hilary Hawkins said, 'Nobody ever told me that this was about raising money for Graham Cook's school.'

'Who got the money last year?' I said to my mother. 'Didn't it go to Graham Cook's school?'

Now Julia took my hand in hers, which meant shut up.

'I'm not sure,' said my mother. 'I'm not the treasurer. The treasurer is Janice Brown.'

Julia looked at my mother and then at me and then at my mother, and I knew that my mother had lied to my father to get him to agree to hold the Craft Fair in our garden.

'Perhaps we could give a percentage this year,' said Janice Brown, blushing, and also glowering at me when she thought my mother wasn't looking – and thus not loving her neighbour at all, like it said on the white plastic sacks in which she collected our old clothes to send on to African children.

After that burst of noise, there was an even bigger silence, and into that silence came the noise of the train. We let the train blast into our silence. We were quite used to it. We didn't know that Barbara Cook had gone for a walk to compose herself. We didn't know that she'd got stuck the other side of what everyone in Hedley Green called, with a sigh, *the crossing*.

Hedley Green Level Crossing was always in the news – it caused people to give birth to babies in their cars and miss their A level exams, and it was a temptation to school boys, people said, and there were always bunches of dead roses tied to the fence where a boy called Fatty Jenkins had died playing with his friends at the crossing. Except, once he was dead, you were supposed to call him Frank Jenkins, or even Francis, which was the name he was christened.

His mother had a plaque nailed to the gate, and she would often be seen there, polishing it and watching the trains go by and staring about the place as if there was some small chance that Fatty Jenkins might come walking out of the long grass, after a very long game of hide-and-seek.

Francis Jenkins, 1980–1992, who died at the crossing and is now with the angels.

Parfait

To me, sitting on the *colline*, trying to think of a way to change our future, the crossing meant the little stretch of water between Africa and Europe.

It meant peace and hope and the chance of a new life.

Augusta

The train passed and the crossing gates came up – and Barbara Cook marched back through the door, her face set, her skirt done up, and she said that she was resigning. My mother said that of course she wasn't, and they'd all agreed that Graham Cook was most welcome at the Craft Fair, and they went on having their committee meeting as if nothing at all had happened.

This time, I'd asked to be in charge of second-hand books. Amongst the tatty Enid Blyton paperbacks, I found an old leather book of Victorian children's poems and rhymes, published in 1900, illustrated with beautiful watercolour plates, and I took this without asking my mother, and I put it under my mattress without telling anyone, even Julia.

I knew deep down that this was stealing.

But I wanted this book so badly.

Inside it were all the normal nursery rhymes that Julia and I knew off by heart and used to say so fast that the words blurred into each other when we were younger. 'Humpty Dumpty', 'Little Bo Peep', and 'Mary, Mary, Quite Contrary', which was another of my mother's nicknames for me and drove me absolutely mad.

My favourite poem was called 'The Pedlar's Caravan' by William Brighty Rands. The illustration showed trees and birds and caterpillars – and a Victorian caravan, made of wooden slats, yellow and red, with flowers painted in vertical plaited lines to the right and left at the front, and butterflies fluttering above them. It had tiny windows with geraniums in boxes, and ladder steps, and wooden wheels with cream-coloured spokes, and a smoking tin chimney, and it was passing under a huge tree, with a dark-looking woman and child at the window, and the pedlar man leading a dapple-grey horse to a dusky not quite see-able horizon.

When I was alone, I read it and I read it, and it made my heart beat and my soul soar, and I heard the noise of singing coming from deep down inside me, *where he comes from nobody knows*, and I was in the caravan, *or where he goes to, but on he goes*, and I was leading the dapple-grey horse, and my horizon was unknowable, and every time I climbed the ladder, I gave my own life story a different ending. And I never once ended up in Hedley Green.

Perhaps the reason I didn't show Julia the book was that I couldn't bear to admit to her that I wanted to leave.

Go anywhere but where I was.

The minute I could.

Of course, I knew that she would want to stay.

And, if I left and she stayed, we wouldn't be *Justa* any more.

We'd be ripped apart like the ragdoll, with our stuffing falling out.

Parfait

The stuffing was falling out of my mother.

When Douce came running out of the hut, shrieking, I knew.

I wasn't brave enough to face what I knew.

Not again.

So I ran up to Víctor's house, and we zoomed back down the hillside, with me on the back of his bike, my long legs sticking out either side. As I looked at Víctor's strong back in front of me, his prominent shoulder blades, his thick white-skinned neck and his mop of grey hair, I felt that perhaps this time, this time, it was all going to be OK.

But by the time we got into the hut, the feeling started to dissolve. Because Gloria and Douce and Wilfred and Zion were all sitting in a semi-circle, and in front of them was my mother. It was, in some ways, my mother, but she looked like an empty sack.

Breathe, I thought, breathe in, breathe out, breathe in, breathe out.

I remembered the feel of her skin on my cheek.

The softness of her.

Zion got up.

'She'll be with Pa,' he said, clenching his fingers, then stretching them out. 'Isn't that a good thing, that she'll be with Pa? That they'll be together.'

'That's right,' I said, and I wiped away my own tears as fast as they fell because I was the oldest and I had to be brave.

'Yes, Little Bro,' I said, trying to find a smile from somewhere, 'she'll be right there where there's a huge river, and trees with fruit every month – do you remember? – and leaves for the healing of the nations.'

'Leaves don't heal nations,' said Pierre, coming in through the open door. 'Leaves don't do anything.'

'Except photosynthesis,' said Zion.

Zion remembered everything I taught him. He listened to me like I'd listened to my father, and this steadied me. He loved me much more than the others did, and this gave me purpose. If he was beside me, it was worth going on.

'Yes, Zion,' said Víctor. 'Your mother's crossed over to the eternal city.'

'Like my name!' said Zion.

'Like your name!' said Víctor. 'And she'll be dancing down its golden streets with your father.'

'What do you think it was?' Pierre said to Víctor, crossly, sounding as if he couldn't stand hearing another thing about the golden streets. 'The thing that killed her?'

'It could have been cholera,' said Víctor.

'Could the doctor have saved her?' I asked Víctor.

Víctor put his arm around my shoulder.

Pierre said, 'Well, could he?' in that voice he had that made me feel as if everything that happened in our lives was my fault.

'Oh, cholera's a tricky one,' said Víctor.

Then, he dug a hole, and each one of us in turn thanked God for our little bird mother, Aurore, whose name meant dawn. We gathered around the hole where she lay, and as Víctor filled it up with red earth, he led us in singing, *Freedom is coming, freedom is coming, freedom is coming, oh yes I know!*

Except Pierre walked off in the middle.

I understood.

Freedom didn't seem to be coming at all.

The more the years passed, the less free we felt.

Augusta

I noticed that the older you got, the more careful you had to be about things you said. In Reception, you could let anything blurt out of your mouth. But by secondary school, you weighed things up before you spoke.

For example, we couldn't say *gardening* aloud in Year 8, and for a few years after that. Robin Fox had introduced the class to *double-entendre*, and frankly one hardly dared open one's mouth at school. Girls in our class were starting to grow hair in awkward places, and Robin Fox would take a look at our fuzzy legs and the hairs appearing in our armpits and say, 'A bit of *gardening* at the weekend, maybe, for you?'

What could we do but use our pocket money on Bic razors or depilating cream or wax strips that didn't work? And looking back, what power he wielded.

Robin Fox had four older brothers, and he knew how to turn ordinary sentences sexual by raising one eyebrow. For the whole of our lives, we'd been able to say, 'Are you coming?' without even thinking about it. But not now. Now we would have Robin Fox's one raised eyebrow, and, if there was enough of an audience, we would have the full fake orgasm scene from *When Harry Met Sally*, with Robin Fox thrashing about moaning and gasping at the dining table.

*　　*　　*

I remember a spring day when we were heading for thirteen. My father was mowing the lawn with not a hint of *double entendre* in his clean and ordered mind; my mother was cutting the edges into perfect curves (ditto); and Julia was weeding (relieved from the burden of Robin Fox's raised eyebrow).

I wasn't thinking of Robin Fox either. Part of the joy of the school holidays was getting away from him.

No, I was thinking of Lola Alvárez saying, 'Your weeds are my flowers.'

The weeds, which looked exactly like flowers to me, were lying with their pretty blue petals, ready to be piled into thick green sacks where they would suffocate in polythene on their way to the dump to die in a yellow metal skip.

I was suffocating too, on purpose, hiding in my bedroom to avoid the tedium of the gardening. I was also watching Pally's dove, which lived in a cream dovecote Fermín had made in their garden. It liked to fly down and flit among the luscious creamy petals of the magnolia tree, which my father had planted dead in the centre of our front lawn. Sometimes he would do the measurements all over again for the pleasure of knowing that he'd got it just right.

Today the dove had flown over the top of our house to the three lacy cherry blossom trees which stood at the back. It flitted from tree to tree, before flying off to the Cooks' garden and landing on Graham Cook's swing-set, which had been there for years, but to which I'd paid little attention.

I'd watched Barbara Cook pushing Graham in his enormous cage of a swing in the rain, and I'd watched Jim Cook with his shirt off and his big balloon tummy, shouting, 'Hey ho and up she rises.'

That day, it struck me, as I stared out of my bedroom window, that nobody had ever sat next to Graham Cook on the spare normal swing. Nobody ever in his entire life.

So I crept downstairs out of the front door, up our little grey paved drive, and I went next door and asked Barbara Cook if Graham would like me to come and swing with him on the swing-set.

Graham was in his baby pen, rocking back and forward, and he sounded almost like a vacuum cleaner going up and down the carpet.

Barbara Cook talked to him, and she guided him into the garden, holding his arm. It was quite an effort getting him into the swing, but once he was in with his red bus, and swinging, he stopped making the hoover noises.

Barbara Cook pushed Graham, and I started to swing, back and forth in time with him. I went higher higher higher, and I could see my mother digging, my father digging, Julia digging.

Back down.

Up again – they were still digging.

Back down.

Up again – so odd to watch my family being my family without me.

Digging.

Very intently.

My father turned around.

Back down.

I loved it that they didn't know I was watching them.

It made me feel powerful.

It also made me feel odd watching them.

I sang, 'Hey ho and up she rises,' like Jim Cook, and Graham and I made laughing noises together.

Up I went – my family remained oblivious.

I breathed in the smell of mown grass.

Barbara Cook went inside for a moment, and I heard her shouting at Jim, 'You're drunk again!'

When she came out, she was carrying a camera. She shouted, 'Cheese!' and she stood in front of the swing-set, laughing and laughing, as if she couldn't stop, as if she'd been storing this laughter somewhere deep down for a long time, and, while she went on laughing, she kept taking photos of the same thing – Graham Cook and me swinging on the swing-set.

She gave Graham a push and went inside again. She came out with a flowered cushion, and she sat on her white plastic garden chair and she put her cup of tea on her white plastic garden table, and she sighed very loudly and she dipped in a digestive biscuit so that its edges went soft. When she lifted her head, I saw that she was crying, in the same way that she'd been laughing, as if she'd never stop.

Graham's swing had come to rest, and he was moaning and twisting, and Barbara Cook was crying tears from deep inside of her, and I pictured all of our stomachs full of bubbles, which would turn acid-red for crying, or alkaline-blue for laughing, like litmus paper. I supposed that we all had an endless supply of these bubbles, and I didn't know whether my life would be a laughing kind of life, mainly blue, or a crying kind of life, mainly red. None of us knows.

No, none of us knows.

Barbara Cook went on crying, and Graham and I went on swinging, and after a while, I thanked Barbara for having me and I crept through the double garage and sped through the back door and up to my room, where I bumped into my mother, on the landing.

'We've been calling,' she said. 'Where on earth were you?'

'In the toilet,' I said.

'We're all going to the dump,' she said.

'Thrilling,' I said, which was not the right answer.

Julia and I sat strapped into the back of the car.

'What on earth have you been doing all this time?' said my mother.

'Nothing,' I said.

When I went round to the Cooks a week later, there was a large photo of Graham and me swinging on the swing-set framed on the wall of the hall, above the shelf.

As I came in, Barbara Cook called out to Graham, 'Your girlfriend's here.'

That made me feel really strange inside, and I hoped that I could be a nice person without having to be Graham Cook's girlfriend. Then I realised that Graham Cook would never ever in his entire life have a girlfriend.

The real problem came when my father went to visit the Cooks and saw the photo on the hall wall, and when Barbara Cook called out to Graham, 'It's your girlfriend's dad.'

My father told Barbara Cook not to say that. Then he came home and told me I was not to visit Graham Cook's house, and nor was Julia, that Graham Cook was not a suitable friend for me. What was I thinking, going and swinging with him as if, as if . . . he spluttered to a stop.

My mother looked shocked and wrung her apron in her hands, and mentioned all Barbara Cook's good qualities.

'I like swinging with Graham Cook,' I said to my father. 'I like being his friend.'

My father's neck went red and his fingers started shaking.

'There is to be no more swinging,' he said.

Then I said something very rude. I said some *double-entendre* I'd learnt at school, which my father did not appreciate.

I said, 'I heard at school that there has been plenty of *swinging* in Willow Crescent. That is, amongst the adults.'

My mother and father went very quiet, and then my father told Julia and me to please go to our bedroom.

Straight away.

Now.

NOW.

'NOW,' screamed my father.

Julia asked me why he was so cross about me swinging with Graham Cook.

'Because he's stupid enough to think . . .' I began.

'Please don't say that,' said Julia.

' . . . that I would want to be Graham's girlfriend, when it's perfectly obvious that I want to be Diego's!'

'Me too,' said Julia.

'We can't both have Diego,' I said. 'We can't exactly share him. We might be twins but that would be taking things too far.'

'But how will he choose?' said Julia. 'Surely it's got to be one of us. We've fancied him for years.'

'It will be quite easy for him to choose,' I said. 'We're really not very alike. Especially for twins.'

As I said it, I knew exactly who he would choose.

'People say our faces are quite similar,' said Julia. 'It's only the colour of our hair and the shape of our bodies which have turned out a bit different.'

I looked down at my skinny legs with dark hairs on them.

'Well, he'll just have to choose the hair and body he likes best, I suppose,' said Julia.

'That's a terrible thing to say,' I said. 'You're supposed to fall in love with someone's *personality*. Not the shape of their body. It's very sexist to think of women as bodies, Jules.'

'I still don't get why Dad has stopped you visiting Graham Cook.'

'He doesn't want me with a spastic,' I said.

'Stop it,' said Julia.

'That's what he said to me at the first Craft Fair,' I said. 'That if I sat with Graham, I'd look spasticated too. And he nearly pulled my arm out of my socket to force me to get up.'

'I still don't get why he's sent us to bed,' said Julia, who never liked to criticise our parents.

'Because I did the *double-entendre*.'

'The what?'

'Robin Fox told me that swinging is what adults do when they swap husbands and wives, and he said there was a lot of it going on in places like Willow Crescent.'

'But Dad's Neighbourhood Watch,' said Julia. 'Wouldn't he stop it?'

'It happens inside people's houses,' I said. 'Apparently, they all throw their keys on the floor and then see where they end up.'

'What? Do they deliberately go to the wrong house?' said Julia.

'Yes,' I said. 'To have sex.'

'What? People like Helen Dunnett and Janice Brown?' said Julia, with a massive frown wrinkling up her forehead.

'Robin Fox said it's typical of the suburbs, but I didn't know what he was on about.'

'Do you really mean that Mum and Dad would do this too?' said Julia again. 'Like, would Dad have had sex with Helen Dunnett or Janice Brown?'

I nodded very seriously, and then I said, 'Come to think of it, nobody else would put up with Dad's pants!'

That set Julia off, thinking of his grey Y-fronts with little slits at the front to put his thingie through. (We knew masses of words for his thingie these days, but neither of us could quite bring ourselves to use any of them – the whole idea of it appalled us. Not to mention the necessity of his thingie in our very own creation. With our very own mother!)

My father came raging up the stairs because, instead of being contrite and ashamed of the rudeness of my *double-entendre*, he'd heard me laughing again. When he came in, shaking and bursting a blood vessel in his neck, we put our hands over our mouths because seeing him there screaming at us and knowing he was wearing those slitty grey Y-fronts underneath his grey trousers made us squirt laughter between our fingers in big gasps and splurts. This sent him totally round the bend.

Then our mother came in, smelling of talcum powder, from her bath, and we could see her big stretchy pants because she'd got her nightie on which was a bit see-through, and we could also see the tyre of fat around her middle, like a ring doughnut.

'If you go on laughing like this,' said my mother, 'you will give your father a heart attack.'

At the mention of the word heart attack, and I don't know why this was, a big squelch of laughter burst out of my mouth through my fingers – and that set Julia off.

My mother turned bright red in the face.

She looked at Julia and said, 'I expected more of you.'

And I realised that she didn't expect more of me.

I couldn't decide whether to try and be good like Julia or whether to pay her back by being extremely bad.

Parfait

When my mind clogged up with stuff, I used to go down to the lake, and I'd let the water wash it clean as I swam deep, like a dolphin, remembering that I was Parfait Nduwimana, and I was *in God's hands.*

'Come on then,' I said to the rest of them. 'Who wants to learn to swim? It's a beautiful day.'

'There are crocodiles in the lake!' said Gloria. 'You must be mad!'

'Not in the part where I go,' I said.

'We'll all get bilharzia,' said Douce.

'Or leeches on our legs,' said Pierre.

'How about if we come and watch you?' said Gloria. 'Come on, Wilfred, you can come too.'

Wilfred stared back at her, with no words.

'Pierre?'

'Maybe,' he said, his brow creased up as if he had a war going on inside him, as usual.

'Zion?'

'If Parfait's going, I'm going.'

It was quite a walk down the hill, but the lake was shimmering, and there were butterflies about, and we almost felt like a family again, walking along together in a line in the sunshine.

Gloria and Douce linked arms, but they didn't sing together like they used to; Wilfred ambled along with the rope still round his ankle;

Zion was wearing the red-and-white nylon football top that he liked to believe had once belonged to David Beckham; and Pierre walked some distance behind.

'This is what it would be like if we walked to Spain,' I said to them. 'Except when we arrived, we'd be swimming in the turquoise sea. In the actual Atlantic Ocean. And we'd be getting out onto the yellow sandy beach and having a picnic together. Possibly with a bottle of Spanish wine.'

'I'm not sure we'd make it all that way up Africa,' said Douce. 'Or I'm not sure *I* would.'

'We could go a little at a time,' I said. 'I'd make sure you all had time to rest, I promise you. And if you were tired, we'd wait a day before moving on.'

'We don't need to decide now,' said Gloria.

'We have to go,' said Zion with that determined look on his face. 'I can't believe you don't want to. We can go to Europe and build a new life, with our own house on the beach, all of us together. And we can drink Spanish wine and go to festivals together. What on earth is stopping you? I just don't understand.'

'We don't know what Europe's like,' said Douce quietly. 'It could be worse than here.'

'Nothing could be worse than here,' said Zion. 'And I'm going with Parfait for sure. If you don't want to, don't bother.'

'It's such a long journey,' said Gloria.

'God gave us legs,' said Zion. 'What do you suppose they're for? Except walking.'

I put my arm around Zion and squeezed him.

'Give them time, Little Bro,' I said.

'I'm serious,' he said. 'If I could choose, we'd set out for Spain tomorrow. I want us to be happy again.'

Augusta

I first heard the word *España* when Diego moved into Willow Crescent. If somebody had told me there was a word for a country which sounded as light and airy and beautiful as this, I might never have chosen Burundi.

I thought (obviously) that the country which joined on to France had the name of Spain, which rhymes with pain and plain and rain.

We'd ventured as far as France on our August holidays, which we documented in sticky photo albums, covered by cellophane, annotated by my mother and arranged in date order.

People loved to comment on the differences between Julia and me, never looking through the albums without saying which one of us was taller, smaller, thinner, fatter, paler, darker.

This is what happens with twins.

I quickly became the clever one – and Julia was obliged to oppose me. Julia quickly became the pretty one – and you see where I am going with this. And, in seasons, being objective, I was not an attractive child.

There I was, knobbly-kneed and squinting on the beach in Benodet, twenty kilometres from Quimper, where we were staying, and where my mother bought the lasagne dish.

There I was in Wales, skinny and tall, with slightly lank hair.

It rained a lot on that holiday, but we swam in the pool anyway.

My father stood under an umbrella with our towels over his arm, and my mother stood next to him, holding my glasses and intercepting me as I climbed out, so that I didn't bump into anything. My grandmother sat in the pool café, storing up criticisms of our fellow guests to share with us later.

'Far too much squinting at books,' said my mother, hooking the spectacle arms around my damp ears, then trying to pat me on my upper arm. I wriggled from her touch. I didn't like my parents to touch me, and because I wriggled, they gave up trying and lavished their touch on Julia.

In our tiny pinewood bedroom, I read Julia poems, which she tolerated, and excerpts from a book called *An Instant in the Wind* which I'd found on my grandmother's shelves. I'd marked the sex scenes between the white woman and her black slave with shop receipts so I could read them aloud to her in bed.

My mother followed us around the damp log cabin camp, 'keeping an eye' because Amanda Dowler went missing on her way home from school and her body was found in the River Thames. Then, would you believe it? On the fourth day of the holiday, two girls called Holly and Jessica went missing in a place called Soham. Julia and I prayed so hard that they would be found safe and well. But they weren't. Their plight sent my mother nearly over the edge, and she started saying that she didn't want us to walk to school any more. We would be kidnapped and sold to traffickers and turned into prostitutes.

'Ha ha ha,' said my grandmother.

Parfait

The soldiers, when they felt like it, broke into our hut and broke my sisters' bodies as if they were clay jars with nothing inside them.

Although we were broken, I thought, we would fly away to Spain, and I pictured us all up above the clouds like grey-crowned cranes, or angels, with white-feathered wings. Oh yes, please send angels to swoop down and rescue Douce and Gloria, right now this minute, I prayed.

But failing that, and in the absence of angels, I would take them to Spain where no man could touch them, and I'd build them all a little white stone house down by the water, and I'd tie each one of them a hammock between two palm trees, and they could lie there, swinging, and I'd go fishing in the blue sea, and when I came home, we'd all sit around the fire barbecuing fish and reading Spanish poetry.

Augusta

My mother and father wanted Julia and me to go on with French. But for the first year ever in our new school, Hedley Heights, we could choose Spanish in Year 9, or, if you were in the top set, you could do French and Spanish together.

Julia was not in the top set, and she chose to carry on with French. She didn't really want to because she was in love with Diego at number 13, as I was too, but she did French (which she was awful at) because she always liked to do what my parents wanted.

'It hurts me when they look disappointed,' she said.

'They're manipulating you,' I said.

If you wanted, as an extra, at Hedley Heights, you could also do Latin at lunchtimes. I put my name down in the first week of Year 7, which meant I would miss Cookery Club, one of its most significant attractions. In the beginning. Before I loved everything else about it.

My mother had signed us both up for Cookery Club, cooking being her thing. I'd spotted that some people assumed cooking would be my thing, by dint of me being a girl, and the best way, it seemed, to destroy that assumption would be never to learn to cook. Either in Cookery Club or in the many invitations made to me by my mother in the kitchen at number 1.

'Oh, Augusta,' said my mother. 'What good will Latin be to you later on?'

'Perhaps I will be a professor at Cambridge University,' I said.

'Professors at Cambridge University still need to cook,' said my mother.

Which was a perfect example of the knack she had of entirely missing the point.

'I don't know what you're planning to do with all these words you're so keen on,' said my mother.

'You wait and see,' I said.

Here I was, alone in Spanish, in Year 9, with *España* dancing on the air around my head, light as a fairy-sprite, like a butterfly, like the feeling of spring.

Before I could stop myself, I put up my hand and asked the teacher what the word was for sprite in Spanish. Because I couldn't stop myself. And I didn't want to know how to say *I am called Augusta*, which was clearly where we were heading.

'Fairy or sprite – *hada*,' said the teacher, but his mouth was all soft like a bean bag when he said it. I wondered if I could do that with my own mouth, soften the d to the point of collapse.

'Or *duende*, I suppose,' said the teacher, 'which actually means spirit, except it's untranslatable.'

Untranslatable, my ears pricked up – what a lovely, complicated thought. I saved it away for later, hoping that I was untranslatable, myself.

'A book has just come out called *Duende*,' said the teacher. 'A book by Jason Webster – you may want to read it.'

Duende – I tried the word out on my tongue, imitating the teacher.

'*Duende*,' said the teacher, 'is that . . .'

He hesitated.

'That . . .'

We stared at him.

'That moment of ecstasy.'

He stopped.

I thought of how much I wanted to find *it*, that thing I couldn't find, whatever *it* was.

Parfait

I knew where to find it, the thing I couldn't find. It was up there, to
the north − I just knew it was.

I headed up the hill to see Víctor, who was out in the vegetable
garden, digging. Because I'd decided.

'We have a Hutu president again, Parfait,' he said. 'They really are
sharing power − and maybe peace is in sight!'

I watched him pull the big flappy leaves off a broccoli stalk, putting
them in one basket, the little tree-like head in the other, and I thought,
I'm not interested in the new president.

The chickens went on clucking about in the mud, beside the pen,
and Víctor's band of blind children were in the yard, swinging their
white sticks, chanting: 'Left foot out, stick to the right, right foot out,
stick to the left.'

'I've made up my mind, Víctor,' I said. 'I'm going to travel to your
country and set up home there.'

'Are you now?' said Víctor, kneeling back with his buttocks resting
on his heels, winking at me.

'What's the point of staying here?' I said.

'Well, it sounds a great plan, Parfait,' said Víctor. 'But it might be
a bit ambitious for your first trip. After all, Spain is eight thousand
kilometres away.'

'We can go one step at a time,' I said, furious at Víctor's patronising tone, at not being taken seriously, 'and it doesn't matter how long it takes. There's nothing to keep us here.'

'You do know that there's a sea between Africa and Spain?' said Víctor, as if I was an idiot.

'But it's a very small sea,' I said, not smiling. 'I've looked on the map in my atlas, and it's more like a river. We can cross by boat from Tangier. Have you ever been to Tangier?'

'As a matter of fact, I have,' said Víctor.

'When did you go?'

'Before I came here, at the start of my little road trip through Africa.'

'What did you do there?'

'I stayed with my friend – he's a priest and he lives in the port . . .'

Víctor stopped talking, and he closed his eyes for a second.

'But it can be quite dangerous at night, Parfait, thugs about, you wouldn't want to be out late, or there at all on your own, to be frank—'

'So your friend's still there?' I said.

'I believe so,' he said.

'You *believe* or you *know*?' I said, because I could see what he was up to, trying to put me off.

Víctor fiddled with the broccoli leaves.

'Don't say you're not sure because you want to stop me going,' I said. 'I feel like your friend would be willing to help us, wouldn't he? If I say I know you.'

Víctor creased up his eyes.

'Maybe I just don't want to lose you,' said Víctor. 'After all, I've only just got you helping up here, driving the van for me . . .'

His voice petered out.

'You will give me his name and number, Víctor, won't you?' I said. 'It feels like the whole plan is coming together.'

'Well,' said Víctor, 'maybe our first job is to teach you Spanish. You've got English under your belt already . . .'

'That was my father,' I said. 'And the Baptists . . .'

'And Spanish is pretty similar to French . . .' said Víctor.

'So can we start now?' I said.

'We'll start with the verbs,' said Víctor.

'Pa said I learnt quickly,' I said. 'He said I was like a sponge.'

This was true – if I set my mind to it, I could keep going for hours, and if I kept on repeating things, they seemed to stick.

The chickens went on clucking, and Víctor went on gardening, and the blind children went on swinging their sticks in the yard, and I sat under a eucalyptus tree, with hope in my heart, saying, '*Hablo, hablas, habla, hablamos, habláis, hablan.*'

Augusta

Mr Sánchez gathered himself together.

'In a performance of flamenco, *duende* happens when all the conditions are right – the guitar, the voice and the dance somehow melt into the clapping of the audience and the heat of the night and, sometimes for a moment, like a firework almost, except better, there is an intoxicating energy, and the atmosphere changes. And somebody near you might very quietly, under cover of dark, from inside the spell, murmur *Olé.*'

I thought *duende* had possibly come through the grey walls of the classroom, or under the door. The atmosphere had changed, and everyone was dead silent. We sat staring at Mr Sánchez as if we were in a trance.

The silence drained away, and the tiniest whisper of noise came back, like butterflies' wings.

I put up my hand.

'And the word for butterfly?'

But my voice had gone funny.

All I could think about was *duende.*

'Butterfly – *mariposa,*' said Mr Sánchez.

'Oh,' I said. 'Thank you.'

Because if you say *mariposa* – try it – you will find that a butterfly has flown out of your mouth.

'Let's all say it,' said Mr Sánchez.

Mariposa mariposa mariposa.

Butterflies flew around the classroom like thrown confetti.

'What's the Spanish for spring?' I said.

'Spring?' said Mr Sánchez. '*Primavera.*'

Primavera primavera primavera.

I liked making up Latin sentences, and in fact I was trying to write some of my diary in Latin. I didn't tell anyone in the family as they all thought I was mad enough already.

Primavera.

I could hear Latin underneath the word.

Primum – first.

Verum – truth.

I put up my hand.

'Mr Sánchez,' I said. 'The word for spring sounds like first truth.'

Around me people got that expression they always got around me.

But Mr Sánchez nodded.

His face looked so thoughtful and sad and I wondered why.

'Spring,' he said, with his eyes as doleful as that sad cow the Hendersons kept in their field for no reason. 'Spring – the first truth. Yes, yes, probably.'

Again, the classroom went silent.

As if *duende* had come back.

Mr Sánchez was the only teacher I'd ever had who could make silence out of his own silence. Most teachers had to wave their arms around and shout and make threats.

'Spring,' he said again. 'The first truth.'

It seemed impossible but the bell went.

Mr Sánchez jolted.

I later found out that he'd lost his wife, who was called Leonor like the wife of the Spanish poet, Antonio Machado. She'd died in the spring. As she lay bald and fading to nothing in the English hospice, the apple blossom fell past her window and rotted in the grass.

'We must have spent a long time handing all the books out at the beginning,' said Mr Sánchez. 'I can't think where the time went.'

'Where it always goes, Mr Sánchez,' I said.

He laughed.

Then he stopped and looked as if he was about to cry.

'So where is all that time, Augusta?' he said.

'Perhaps we'll find it in heaven,' I said, which was a surprising thing to say, and came out of my mouth without me thinking about it.

'Or would it be hell?' said Mr Sánchez. 'If you found the past, all piled up by the side of the road. All the things you'd ever said. All the things you'd ever thought. All the things you'd ever done.'

That was one of those questions that Mr Sánchez asked that made you stop dead, as if the question had shot you through the heart.

As we all stood up to leave our first ever Spanish lesson, Mr Sánchez said, 'Of course, Spanish is the language of Miguel de Cervantes, Federico García Lorca, Gabriel García Márquez, Isabel Allende, not to mention Picasso, Dalí and Velázquez.'

The sounds of their names!

That's my heaven.

All of them sitting together under an eternal palm tree discussing important things forever, in gorgeous Spanish, like gunfire and joy mixed up together.

We all filed out of the room, but I stopped and said, 'Thank you so much, Mr Sánchez. That was the best lesson I've ever had – and please may I borrow your book on *Duende*?'

He nodded and stroked his beard as if he had just had a great shock, and all I could think of was how desperately I had to get to Spain.

To *España*.

Parfait

I told Víctor I was planning to be a teacher or a doctor, an artist or a poet once I made it to Spain.

'Well let's start with the art,' he said. 'I can help you with the art.'

He went and got an old easel and a case of mucky paints and sketching pencils from a store cupboard out at the back of his little house.

I started off copying great Spanish artists from his *History of Art* book in pencil. We moved on to pastel. Then we tried some paint.

Looking through Víctor's book about living European artists, I found an artist called Sami Terre who had skin the same colour as mine and wore his black hair in lots of long plaits. He'd been born in what he called a *shithole* on the outskirts of Brussels and started out making graffiti.

'Can you make my hair like this?' I asked Gloria and Douce, pointing to his photograph.

'Who are *you* getting yourself so handsome for?' said Gloria.

I shook my head.

They got to work on my hair, with Amie Santiana who lived on the homestead next to us and knew all about hairdressing.

As I walked out of the hut the next day, I found I was standing a little taller. Because, if Sami Terre was raised in a *shithole* but went on to be famous and written about in books, it could happen to anyone. It could even happen to me.

The African mourning doves were calling in the acacia tree opposite the hut – krrrrrr, oo-OO-oo – as I took the photograph of my parents' wedding out of the Memory Box. In it I found the little card my father had given my mother on their wedding night.

'*God grant me the serenity to accept the things I cannot change,*' it said. '*The courage to change the things I can. And the wisdom to know the difference.*'

It made my mind up.

This was something I could change.

The place we lived.

I did have the courage, I knew I did.

I began to paint a portrait of my parents, falling into each other on their wedding day, my father in a dark suit and my mother in the shiny wedding dress lent to her by the Baptists.

'Tell me I'm right to go,' I said to my father's photograph, but it didn't answer.

I worked at the painting hour after hour, covering it with an old mat, telling everyone they mustn't look at it, not yet.

Even when my arms ached from banana-picking, I still painted.

Then it was finished.

Víctor came down on his bike, and the rest of them gathered around, and, feeling suddenly shy, I took off the mat to reveal the painting.

'You're a genius,' said Víctor. 'A total natural! Stay here and you'll become a famous Burundian artist.'

The rest of them stared at our mother and father, perhaps hoping that they might walk off the page and come and live with us in the hut again.

'This is how we'll earn money as we go,' I said to them all. 'By painting portraits.'

'I'm not coming,' said Pierre. 'I'm going to stay here and fight.'

'Fight?' I said. 'Fight as in struggle?'

'Fight as in anything it takes,' said Pierre.

My father's twinkly eyes and his cheek, his turning-the-other-cheek, stared out at us from the easel and stopped twinkling for a second.

'What would Pa say?' I said.

'And what good did it do him? Refusing to retaliate? Breaking the chain?' said Pierre.

Wilfred sat staring.

The girls looked sad.

Víctor said nothing.

'When are we leaving?' said Zion.

Then, one by one, we all walked quietly away from the easel where my mother and father stayed laughing love into each other's eyes.

'Patience, Little Bro,' I said, and I tried to cheer myself up by dancing about with him, the way I imagined flamenco dancers might dance, though, looking back, it was some other way altogether.

'Come and join in!' I said to the girls. 'You sway your hips like this, and you lift your arms and twist around – and the girls wear bright-coloured dresses like butterflies.'

'You can shout out *Olé* whenever you feel like it!' said Zion.

But Gloria said, 'You dance, boys. I like watching.'

Douce nodded.

Whenever Zion and I found ourselves alone together, we'd say *Olé* and do our special up-down high-five as a way of believing in the journey we would make.

'*Olé Olé Olé Olé.*'

Augusta

My mother was starting to circle possible destinations for the summer of 2004 in red biro, and I asked Mr Sánchez whether Spain would be a good place for a holiday.

'I'd avoid the Costa del Sol, Augusta,' said Mr Sánchez. 'It's full of English people!'

Then we both laughed like conspirators, as if we knew how boring English people were, and I started to wonder if I were actually Spanish and the stork (ha ha) had dropped me in the wrong place. I obviously knew quite a bit about sex by now — and not only from the scenes in *An Instant in the Wind*. No, the internet had arrived — at other people's houses. My parents continued to favour paper. My mother had bought us a book on sex, and she threw it into our hands, keeping the focus on how *special* it was to have babies, a great privilege for every woman, she kept saying.

'Not for every woman,' I said. 'Some women can't have children.'

She gave me the you're-being-difficult look so I didn't bother to bring up the way the privilege could also be suffering, or the way Barbara Cook loved and suffered every day of being a mother so that the two things became one. I didn't bother to talk about the fact that love might be the hugest word there is in the world and that we would never, across a whole lifetime, work out what it meant. I didn't say that if we put love on one side of the weighing scales and suffering

73

on the other, we might change our minds and decide suffering was bigger. Then I found myself wondering if actually love and suffering were on the same side of the scales. And you couldn't have the one without the other. Then I couldn't decide what was on the other side of the weighing scales. But I didn't say any of this aloud, and my mother went on running through her list of warnings against the use of tampons, in particular the risk of toxic shock syndrome.

'But, quite apart from that,' she said, 'they can be extremely painful when you *put them in your. Put them in your. Put them in your.*'

She never found the word.

'Vagina,' I said.

My mother squeezed the new packet of extra-thin sanitary towels she was holding in her hand at the shock of the word said aloud, and she started to talk about holidays instead, putting down the sanitary towels and picking up her holiday spiral notepad.

'Spain is supposed to be very safe,' I said. 'And I would also be able to practise my Spanish like we practised French in Brittany.'

Spain, my mother wrote, underlining it twice.

The Alvárez family's Spanish house wasn't on the Costa del Sol, but on the Costa de la Luz, I told my mother. In a village by the beach, called La Higuera. Which means fig tree. *Higos* are figs and you don't pronounce the h.

The next year, in August, Diego's family would be going to Argentina for a family wedding so we could (possibly) rent their holiday house with fig trees in the garden for a much-reduced price. They'd be going at Christmas for the special festivals.

My father said, 'It's all very different out there. Apparently, Lola sunbathes without a swimsuit on in the garden. They probably all do that sort of thing over there. And it's jolly hot, you know, in summer. Sweltering. It may not suit us.'

He was right.

It didn't suit him.

Yet we plotted and persuaded to get him there.

I look around me as I write, here in La Higuera, thirteen years after we first came. How I love its fig trees and its palms, its warm air and wild winds.

There we were, innocent and dreamy.

So excited.

'Two months to go,' I said to Julia, crossing off another day on the chart we'd stuck to the back of the wardrobe door.

'Will we be different when we come back?' said Julia.

'Course we will,' I said, smiling.

I remember us packing for Spain, suitcases open on the bed and the sun coming through the bedroom window and landing in that little pool, over in the corner, where there was, where there is, one of those triangular-shaped stands, made to fit in corners. On it are our awards – all my academic cups, made of fake silver, and my one riding rosette clipped to the top, and Julia's dancing trophies in the shape of gold ballet shoes. I remember specks of dust falling through the sheet of light, bits of our own skin.

I'm looking down at my hand, brown from the sun because I live here now.

The skin of my hand.

Mano in Spanish.

Mano mano mano – man-o – man-oeuvre – man-overboard – man-o-tee, but I think it's manatee actually.

They are sometimes called sea cows – dolphin things with rounded noses. Like the pilot whales we saw from the boat out in the Straits of Gibraltar, heading off from the port at Tarifa.

That day.

Parfait

'Will you come?' I said to Wilfred. 'This is the last time I'm going to ask you.'

Wilfred shook his head.

'We'll make a new home with hammocks in the garden.'

He shook his head again.

'A hundred per cent?' I said. 'Because once we've gone, you won't be able to change your mind. This is the day to decide.'

Wilfred pointed to the rope around his ankle.

'You want to stay with Claude?' I said.

Wilfred took me by the arm, leading me to the patch of earth where we'd buried Claude, and there, at the foot of a cypress tree, was a pile of stones, with a fresh red rose in a little clay pot. He'd scratched the name CLAUDE into the bark, and he'd drawn tally marks, four upright lines and one diagonal, in fives, for every day since he died – they went stretching up and around the trunk.

When I saw those tally marks, I put my arms around him. I was taller than him, and his face fell into my chest.

It made me cry to feel him crying.

To feel his feelings and not be able to change them.

Three years since Claude died – and what it must be to lose a twin.

I couldn't bear to remember the sight of Claude in the corner of the burnt hut.

Three months since the girls disappeared, and no one had seen a sign of them since.

The pain was too much for me.

And the guilt.

Wilfred pulled away, still holding my hand, and he drew two question marks in the earth.

'What are you wondering?' I asked. 'Why you didn't hold Claude's hand? Where the girls have gone?'

He nodded, then nodded again.

'Me too,' I said. 'Me too.'

He pointed to the rope around his ankle, and our tears made trails down our legs and ran along our dry feet into the earth.

'Will you forgive me if I go?' I said.

Wilfred nodded and pointed to the tree.

'Do you find a flower every day for Claude?'

He nodded again.

'I can't bear the pain here,' I said, and I knew that this was really why I was going.

I wasn't really going for Zion.

I was going for myself.

'I'm going because I can't bear the pain here,' I told Víctor. 'So don't say I shouldn't go. Because I can't hear it any more. And I can't bear it any more. And I can't live here any more. Without them all.'

Víctor looked away.

'I'll miss you, Parfait,' he said.

'I'll miss you too,' I said, clenching my jaw.

'Perhaps Wilfred would like to come and live here at my school,' said Víctor. 'He can help me with the garden, do some odd jobs, teach the children football, learn sign language.'

Víctor paused.

'That's a thought,' he said to himself, his face brightening. 'Sign language might bring him out of himself.'

'He's not deaf, you know,' I said. 'It's just that he has nothing left to say.'

'He might find some new things to say by living somewhere new, doing new things,' said Víctor. 'What do you think?'

'Are you serious?' I said. 'That you'd have him here?'

'Of course. And I'd have Pierre too. The girls, if . . .'

'You'll keep on looking for them?' I said.

Víctor nodded.

'You're my blessing number one,' I said. 'My father told us to count our blessings, and I count you a thousand times, Víctor. You're a thousand – a million – blessings. Maybe more. *Bendiciones infinitas.*'

'Well, look at you, Mr Fluent!' said Víctor, and he hugged me.

'It feels like thank you doesn't quite cover it,' I said, smiling at him.

'Don't give up hope in this place,' he said. 'Even if you go, you could always come back. I think peace is coming, I can smell it. They say that the civil war could be over by the end of November. Things change, you know, Parfait.'

Augusta

Things change.

Sometimes quite unexpectedly.

With one tiny action.

Like booking tickets to Seville.

My mother kissed my father's sweaty hair and bided her time. There were aeroplanes and foreigners and a language he didn't know and renting a car and driving on the right and he was full of *worries*.

But my mother had taken to the idea with some passion, and Julia and I fanned that passion like a pair of bellows. We blew and we blew so that we all three burned to go to Diego's family house, which sat at the back of a huge slab of beach, where the Atlantic waves came crashing in.

My father had no hope of denying us Spain, the Coast of Light, the little village called The Fig Tree. We heard the rise and fall of the crashing tide in our dreams from our beds in number 1 Willow Crescent for months before we got there.

We *anticipated*.

Do you know how big and powerful that word is – *anticipating*? It fills you up so that you're tingling inside, and we tingled with Spain, with heat, with the Coast of Light, with fig trees, and castanets and guitars, so that by the time we were on the aeroplane, we were like champagne, with the cork coming off.

Just coming off.

Just coming off.

Cabin crew ten minutes to landing.

My mother and father clutched each other's hands, amazed that we'd made it thus far, praying under their breath. The aeroplane wheels came down, making noisy jolts underneath us.

Bump bump.

Welcome to Seville.

Where the temperature is.

Where the temperature is thirty-five degrees.

My father drew a handkerchief across his worried forehead. He'd survived the flight but would he survive the thirty-five degrees? We bundled into our hire car, my mother with the map spread out on her knees, shaking.

'Concentrate!' said my father. 'Concentrate!'

'Just keep driving on the right!' said my mother. 'The right! The right!'

'We mustn't get this wrong!' yelled my father. 'Don't let us end up in the city centre!'

It felt like the city centre was some kind of black hole from which we'd never return.

'Don't let us end up in the city centre!' said my father again.

'That's it!' said my mother. 'That's the road!'

'Don't tell me so late!' said my father.

'Drive on the right! The right!' said my mother.

'I *am* driving on the right!' said my father.

Somehow, corks starting to rise, to rise, we found ourselves driving along the road at the back of the beach, turning in, and Julia and I leapt out to open the gate in the way that Diego had explained to us, and the cork came off and we were there!

We ran down the track to the beach in our bikinis, in bare feet, and the waves were as big and as crashing as Diego had told us, and there was a man at the back of the beach with a little trolley selling polystyrene kites, and my father bought one.

My father bought one.

Of his own volition.

When he didn't like buying things.

He didn't like spending money on things he considered to be *junk*.

Julia tied the kite to her plait, and the white polystyrene bird followed us as we walked, the four of us together, as we paddled, as we saw tiny slithers of silver fish jumping on the rolling waves, iridescent and catching sun rays.

We laughed.

We pointed.

We felt the spray on our faces.

And we were.

Happy.

I stop writing for a moment, and I climb up the tiny ladder to the roof of the caravan. I look out at the beach, and I think, the four of us were there. We were right there with the sand dissolving in vertical tunnels under the heels and soles of our feet. The sand where we stood is long gone, but the house remains.

The house belonging to the Alvárez family is made of rough stone, inside and out, and it has wall-hangings in Indian fabrics on black iron poles. The beds have metal bedheads and white sheets, with linen bedspreads in washed-out colours: aquamarine, sand, palest pink and coral. On every window sill, there are shells that Diego and Pally collected on the beach and bits of misshapen driftwood. The windows have wooden shutters, and the floor is made of terracotta stone. The front of the house opens onto a sandy garden with swirls of palm and olive trees, with hammocks hanging between them. The back of the house has a veranda with a thatched roof, and dotted around the lawn are fig trees, and there's a tiny stone dip pool, and if you're lucky, you can find baby frogs swimming up and down doing breast stroke.

There's also a four-poster carved wooden bed made in Morocco, which you can pile up with jewelled cushions. Like the bed of a

North-African ancient king. It's a throne of a bed. It demands attention – and it stands right at the centre of my life.

It is, in every sense, forgive me, seminal.

(That wasn't really supposed to be a joke – I just have no control
over the way words strike me, how extraordinary they are, layered
with meaning.)

I look at the Moroccan bed, and it looks at me.

I loved that house from the moment I first saw it in August 2004.
I loved it again when I went back in 2011, though I wished Julia had
come with me. And I loved it again – and much more deeply, and
much more painfully – when Diego and I escaped here before Christmas
in 2015. And I love it still, despite everything.

But now I wonder if I'll ever go inside it again.

Now that I have no key.

I walk past it and stare over the gates.

The Alvárez family rent it out to strangers these days.

I watch different couples in shorts and bikinis lying together on
the Moroccan bed in the back garden – you can see it from the left-
hand side, if you stand at the right angle, looking over the prickly
pear bushes.

I watch these strangers cook fish on the stone barbecue late at
night.

When we went there as a family in 2004, Julia wanted to have a
barbecue, but my father said he didn't know where to get the charcoal.

My mother said they didn't eat sausages here, she'd looked in the
butcher's window, and there weren't any – there were only fish, alive-
looking with eyes and mouths and tails.

'I think that was the fishmonger,' I said.

'And, anyway, how would you clean the barbecue?' she said.

So, instead, we used the gas hob and the microwave and got take-
away chickens that turned on spits.

As a treat one lunchtime, we ate at the restaurant on the beach –
Restaurante Raúl, whose owner (unsurprisingly) was called Raúl. He

had thick dark hair and a fat hairy belly and he wore a straw hat. He took Julia and me to see the donkey he kept in his field, with its thickset furry neck and cross face, and he let us stroke his thorough-bred mares. He said he rode his horses in the early morning when no one was about, and he suggested that this was a lovely time to have a picnic on the beach and see the sun rise over the mountains. I trans-lated for my family. He mimed to my mother and father that Julia and I could have a little ride around the field, but they mimed back pointing at their heads and the ground.

'*Sombrero!*' said my father. '*Sombrero!*'

Not only did my father look like a total English idiot, but we also missed our chance to go riding.

Raúl's wife, Teodora, had the smoothest caramel skin, and the kindest black eyes, and, when she heard how disappointed we were, she gave Julia and me free *crema catalana* ice creams.

She made us *paella* with mussels in and fried *chanquete* fish which you ate whole with your fingers (even their eyes) and the local speci-ality of seared tuna, cooked with grapes. My father refused everything except Spanish omelette.

Raúl didn't seem to do much work. He walked about chatting to everybody, eating sunflower seeds.

'Do you think they can understand each other, talking that fast?' said my mother.

'Sounds like a bloody aviary,' said my father, pulling up the sports socks my mother had bought him. He did not look himself in shorts, and I preferred it in the evenings when he put trousers on over his burnt pink legs.

We visited the dark church in the square on the Sunday evening. It was full of gold with alabaster statues and gloomy paintings of the Virgin Mary, and Jesus writhing on the cross, like my grandmother's necklace.

Each day, we went to the tiny village shop by the roundabout, and we pointed to baked *barras* of bread, to fat tomatoes and nectarines, which the woman in the pale blue housecoat put in brown paper bags, and my mother put in Lola Alvárez's Moroccan basket for our lunch.

My father let me buy the daily newspaper in Spanish so that I could spend all day translating it with my dictionary on the beach, happy as anything.

We paddled and swam and surfed on body boards and got knocked over by the waves, and we went for walks way down the beach to have our picnic in *our special spot*, where nobody else went.

Our special spot, my mother named it.

Our special spot was right at the end of the beach, marked by a crop of holey rocks, and a glade of pine trees and little pools left behind at low tide. There was a blue wooden boat buried in the sand, and we often sat amongst its contoured edges to eat our lunch.

Looking back, I see that my father was trying to get away from the Spanish men with dark skin and hairy chests, who stood, legs apart, at the busier part of the beach, swigging from beer cans and addressing comments to him he couldn't understand.

This spot was special for him because he could hide his burnt knees and his inadequacies, and he didn't have to ask for ice creams at the kiosk, pointing furiously, panicking, handing over the wrong money.

'We could get a family pack of ice creams from the shop,' said my mother.

'Much better,' said my father. 'Whichever one I point to, they never have it. But the Spanish people get whichever ice cream they want.'

'I'm sure that's not true,' I said.

'When I ask for things, they all start laughing,' said my father. 'I feel as though they're mocking me.'

There were no ice cream stalls or laughing foreigners in *our special spot*.

There was only us.

I make myself go down there some days, and I wonder if I should put something up to remember us – the four of us – a sign saying: 'The Hope family was happy here. For a bit.'

The place now hangs heavy with sadness, not just my own.

Perhaps I should commission a sculpture – maybe a tree, I was thinking, with four outstretched branches, like human arms.

Parfait

There are places – aren't there?

Places which are so full of feeling you hardly dare return to them. I wonder which place it is for you.

For me, one of those places is Tangier.

Before we got there, the *port of Tangier,* where Víctor had once stayed with a Spanish priest, was a fairy-tale town from *One Thousand and One Nights,* with narrow streets full of lamp-lit cubic houses tumbling down to the harbour.

When we arrived, it was even more magical than that, I guess, because of what had come before. And in my mind, it's made of jewels: emerald, sapphire and aquamarine.

I'm sure there was a hexagonal courtyard with a tiled fountain. I'm sure there was a shady garden at the back of the priest's rust-coloured house, and I'm sure he served us food on pottery plates with geometric designs in green and sapphire-blue like a peacock's tail. I'm imagining peacocks strutting about on the lawn, but they weren't there.

'José *María?*' Zion said to the priest, in his best Spanish accent, screwing up his face, with that slightly cocky way he had.

The priest smiled.

'*María?*' said Zion, turning his voice high, like a girl.

'I'm so sorry,' I said, thinking, Zion, please don't offend him, he's our only hope.

But the priest laughed, a throaty laugh, like Víctor's, and I missed him. I missed his voice. I missed his big hands gesticulating. His bad flamenco dancing. The way he loved me.

'It means Joseph Mary,' the priest said to me, gesturing towards Zion. 'And girls can be called María José – the other way round.'

I explained this to Zion, as well as glaring at him.

'It's a bit like heaven here,' I said, 'after the places we've been,' and I looked out over the bright green lawn, and the little jets of water spurting in turning arcs around the edges so that the palms trembled and glistened.

'You honestly walked?' said José María. 'You're not having me on.'

'Well, we did whatever worked,' I said. 'Walked. Hitched lifts. Hid in trains.'

There were things I didn't want to remember about the journey, things that we'd chosen not to talk about. How long the nights were. And how dark. The man in Algeria who tried to sell us to old men; the roadside fights; the dumps where gangs sniffed glue; where the storks strode over the rubbish pecking out human eyes – that's what people said.

When I look back, what I remember most is never daring to sleep at night. And how tired I felt.

'Was it worth it?' said José María.

'I hope so,' I said, looking at Zion, feeling that it had to be worth it.

'What makes you want to live there?' said José María.

'It's a peaceful country,' I said, and my voice came out hard and determined, in case he was going to try to contradict me, or dissuade me – it was far too late to be wrong. 'We've known so much violence, you see, in our lives, and a lot of death. So we're going to build a new life where we can be happy and safe. That's the plan, anyway.'

'Ask him if it's true,' Zion said to me. 'Ask him if Spain is as wonderful as we think it is.'

'Is Spain the most wonderful country?' I said to the priest.

He smiled.

'It all depends,' he began.

'He says it is,' I said. 'And we're nearly there. OK?'

'OK,' said Zion.

'*Olé?*' I said.

'*Olé,*' said Zion.

Augusta

On the twelfth day of the holiday, when we were two thirds of the way to *our special spot*, we came across four or five groups of people sunbathing with no clothes on at all. The men had willies like big dripping sea slugs, and the women didn't hold their legs together to hide their private parts and their triangle of hair. And the children bounced about not seeming to find it alarming that their parents had no swimsuits on.

My father said, 'Keep going!' and he accelerated through them as if he was walking through a battlefield and we were all about to get shot.

'Come on come on come on,' he shouted at us, as we practically ran to *our special spot*.

But it was as if something had spooked my father. He couldn't quite settle with his book. He kept saying, 'I hope the paedos won't be there on the way back.'

'They aren't necessarily paedophiles,' I said, with my mother shaking her head at me behind my father's back, her eyes wide and glaring. 'They may just like to take their clothes off.'

My father kept getting up from his towel to see if they were coming any closer.

My mother kept saying, 'Are you all right, darling?'

'It's disgusting,' said my father. 'There are children about.'

My mother pushed her fingers into the nape of my neck under my hair, which is what she always did to stop me saying things, as if I had an on-off switch like a doll.

'Why don't you read us some poems out of your book?' said my mother.

So I read to them.

'Nobody heard him, the dead man.
But still he lay moaning:
I was much further out than you thought
And not waving but drowning.'

'Haven't you got something a bit more cheerful?' said my mother.

'But don't you see?' I said. 'It's about how we can misinterpret each other. They thought he was waving but actually he was drowning. Dad thinks they're paedophiles but actually . . .'

'How about another one?' said my mother. 'Something funny.'

'They fuck you up, your mum and dad.'

Julia gave me a funny look.

My mother pursed her lips.

My father stared at me as if the f-word had paralysed him like a stun gun.

'They may not mean to, but they do.
They fill you with the faults they had
And add some extra, just for you.'

'I think that's enough of that one,' said my mother. 'I didn't know poets were allowed to swear. What about that one about ducks I used to read you? Julia, you know that one.'

'I won't have that language,' said my father.

'Oh I'm not sure I remember all the words of the duck one,' said Julia.

And I thought how strange language was – one letter turned duck into fuck. Just like that.

'Go on,' said my mother.

Julia had the pained look on her face she used to get when she couldn't find a way to love us all at the same time. When she felt our happiness dissolving. But she started, looking awkward, because this was really a children's poem and we were fourteen, and about to start our GCSE courses:

'All along the backwater,
Through the rushes tall,
Ducks are a-dabbling,
Up tails all!'

'You go on, Aug,' said Julia.

So I chose this verse:

'Everyone for what he likes!
We like to be
Heads down, tails up,
Dabbling free!'

Then I said, quick as anything: 'You could read that verse as pro-naturism, if you think about it. Look over there!'

They all tried not to look over there, at the diving buttocks in the sea, at the dabbling free, and we all sat in silence, with my mother shooting bullets at me from her eyeballs.

The wind came up, and palm fronds and sea holly and people's sunhats started flying down the beach.

We looked out over the sea as the waves grew, as they started to pound the beach, curling at the top, making the letter C.

Cccccccc – joined together – like children drawing waves across a page in cursive writing.

The waves rushed up the beach and soaked our towels, and the gusts sent sand whipping into our mouths and our eyes, and this was the perfect excuse for us to leave – because everyone was leaving.

That evening, we were going to eat spaghetti at the house, but my mother couldn't get the gas to light so we ended up having the leftovers of the picnic. My father rang and left a very loud slow message on the gas people's answerphone in English with a slight Spanish accent, although I'd offered to make the phone call in Spanish.

The wind only blew harder, and you could hear the palms creaking and the shutters shaking.

Parfait

We sat sipping special tea with mint and sugar in it, which José María poured from a silver teapot into little glasses, so hot you couldn't hold them. We'd had a bath, and the housekeeper had given us funny leather slipper-things that kept coming off our feet. We weren't used to shoes. Ours had worn out.

I was trying to pluck up the courage to say what I had to say, but sometimes words, though they are only words – are almost impossible to say.

God grant me the courage, I thought, and I felt inside the pocket of my jacket where I kept both the prayer card and my mother's metal daffodil, which I'd stolen from the Memory Box. It was probably selfish of me, but I'd persuaded myself they meant more to me than to the others.

Go on, I said to myself, go on, spit it out.

Finally.

'Víctor said you would lend us your boat to go on the final leg of our journey,' I said.

'Lend?' said the priest, laughing, in a way I didn't like. 'How will you return it to me?'

I hadn't thought of that, and it made me feel stupid.

I didn't have another plan, and I was tired now, and desperate.

Desperate to arrive, as well as fearful, terrified in fact, that I would fail this last test.

I stood up straight and I shook my head so that I could see the plaits out of the corner of each eye, and I felt them on my cheeks, and I remembered the European artist, Sami Terre, who pulled himself out of a *shithole*, and I looked directly into the priest's eyes.

'I have some money,' I said.

'Money?' said the priest.

'From painting portraits,' I said, thinking that the priest might be impressed.

'I'm an artist,' I said, which I'd never said before, and it made me feel not much better, as I'd hoped, but much more stupid.

'I see,' said José María, with a wry smile.

I thought how strange it was that you could walk eight thousand kilometres across a continent, and adults would still laugh at you.

'So I have the money to buy your boat,' I said, feeling like an idiot.

'Oh, it's only a flimsy thing, for excursions down the coast, or fishing,' said José María, taking a keyring from a hook by the back door. 'Come and have a look at it. And you'll see.'

We walked down to the harbour, and José María let us through the gate, and I remember my heart beating hard because the thing I'd imagined was now too real.

'There it is,' said José María.

The boat was made of rubber, thick rubber, with a big old engine.

A man with a moustache climbed off his yacht to come and talk to José María in a language I didn't understand.

'It looks good and strong,' I said to Zion, trying to make my voice sound confident and assertive. Because I'd seen the shape of Spain over the water, right there, right there.

The man with the moustache went back to his yacht, and José María let us get into the boat to see what it was like.

'You see,' he said. 'It's only a rubber dinghy really. For messing about. When the wind's died down, we'll go out on a fishing trip.'

We sat down on the bench seats.

'You can stay at my house as long as you like!' said José María. 'We'll have some fun together.'

We climbed out of the boat, went out through the harbour gate and walked up the hill to his house.

'Anyhow,' José María said to us as we went through the gates to his garden, 'they're saying the civil war is nearly over in Burundi. It may be better to have a nice holiday here and head home. And I might be able to help you with that. Getting you back there.'

He winked at us.

'Listen to that wind!' he said.

'What's he saying?' said Zion.

'The war might be over,' I said, keeping off the subject of the wind.

'We've come all this way and the war's over?' said Zion, as the housekeeper came in to ask us what we'd like for supper – chicken or fish in the *tagine*.

'They're always saying the war's over,' I said. 'Let's wait and see! Chicken or fish?'

'Chicken, please,' said Zion.

The tagine smelled of spices and was warm and delicious, and we ate it with rice, and then the lady came with watermelon and bowls of ice cream. Soon we were sleepy and over-fed, and it was time for bed.

I went back to the kitchen for two glasses of water, and I thought how easy it would be not to go. I thought if we stay even one night here, we'll get too comfortable. If we stay even one night, we'll find a reason not to go. We'll get to know him better, and we won't be able to make ourselves sneak away. Grant me the courage, grant me the courage. I slipped the boat keyring into my pocket.

'You wait until we get to Spain,' I said to Zion in our bedroom.

'You do still want to go, don't you?' I said, though I think I might have been asking myself. I thought of mentioning the wind, but the truth is that I didn't. I know I didn't.

'I think the priest wants us to stay,' said Zion.

'Why do you think that is?' I said.

'I think he wants to put us on a plane back to Burundi,' said Zion. 'I think he's in cahoots with Víctor. He's trying to tempt us with fishing trips.'

'I think you may have a point,' I said. 'And what do you think we should do?'

'I think go to Spain, and quickly,' said Zion. 'Otherwise it will all be for nothing.'

'I agree,' I said as fast as I could, in case I didn't, I had to be sure I did.

Zion put his thumbs up.

'Thank you for coming with me, Zion,' I said, holding up the keyring with the gate key and the boat key, and a tiny plastic dolphin. 'And for being so brave, Little Bro. And putting up with so much.'

'Thank you for being braver,' said Zion. 'You're the bravest. You've always been the bravest.'

That made me feel good.

Because I didn't feel brave at all.

'So shall we do it?' I said, and I took out my mother's metal daffodil and stroked it like Aladdin and the lamp, but no genie appeared to magic us to Spain.

'Let's do it,' said Zion. 'Let's go and build our new life.'

'Nothing will ever be the same for us again,' I said, staring at the daffodil. 'We're actually leaving Africa, Zion! We're off to Europe! Like we said, when we used to look up at the clouds.'

We did our special high-five with the up-down moves, looking into each other's eyes for signs of cracking or weakness or lack of faith.

'Will we stay there forever?' said Zion. 'Because I never want to go back. We'll have houses next door to each other on the beach, and we'll marry and have children and good jobs. When we have the money, we'll invite the others over and we'll pay for their plane tickets and we'll have a huge party on the beach with Spanish wine and flamenco dancing. I can see it all in my mind.'

'The new life is coming,' I said, and I put my mother's metal daffodil back in my pocket, and I tried to believe it.

'*Olé*,' said Zion.

'*Olé*,' I said back.

I left all my money in the priest's soft leather shoe, and we set off through the dark streets, like children playing a game of hide and seek, creeping past the cubed houses which spilled down the hill, and into the port.

Augusta

My father couldn't sleep.

He watched the digital clock going round, so he said in the morning, 10.30, 10.33, 10.56 – he always slept well – 11.17, 11.37, 11.51, 00.00, he didn't like the look of that time, and he was never awake at midnight, so he woke my mother up, to keep him company.

Which, come to think of it, is rather sweet.

Though at the time, I thought it utterly pathetic.

While they were walking about not sleeping and worrying about the gas, and the wind, my father started to get his own gas and wind, as he used to call it, because he hadn't had a *hot meal*, and his stomach liked a hot meal in the evening, ideally with potatoes.

Anyway, I assume my father was walking about with his *terrible indigestion* and I assume my mother might even have been off getting the Gaviscon out of his wash bag when a huge lizard ran out from under the sofa, and my father shrieked into the silent house and woke us all up.

Parfait

As I untied the rope in the port of Tangier, I expected to hear a shout, a searchlight, the roar of an engine.

I expected to be caught.

Wanted to be caught?

I don't think so.

This was the fulfilment of a dream.

But I was terrified.

Getting through the gate and into the port was easy.

Starting the engine was easy.

I felt myself calm down.

It was going to be OK.

Spain was literally over there.

I was making a fuss about nothing.

We'd be there in no time.

The water in the port was calm, clinking against the side of the boats. But the sea, once we passed the harbour walls and were out in the open, was big – such a big unwieldy thing – bigger than you could imagine if you hadn't seen it before, even if on a map it looked like a river.

The waves swelled and the boat pitched.

Our stomachs started to groan with the motion.

I tried to stop myself.

Tried.

Tried.

But it was impossible.

The chicken tagine was rolling around my stomach, and I was dizzy, couldn't stop myself, I threw up over the side of the boat.

Then Zion did.

There was no relief from it.

We felt worse.

We didn't speak.

It was so dark.

And the rolling sea seemed to be inside our bellies.

I was pretty sure I was still heading in the right direction. I had the compass, and I assumed it was working, but the needle danced in front of me – and I threw up again. The compass slipped out of my hands.

'Not much longer,' I shouted through the roar of the sea and the wind, through the acid in my throat, my head swimming.

But the waves were getting bigger all the time, and it was so dark, the sky like tar. I thought maybe we should go back, definitely we should go back, yes definitely, but I didn't know any more where back was.

'Tie yourself in,' I said to Zion because I was terrified. 'Tie yourself to this rope so you don't get thrown over.'

I tried to sound strong and calm, but my breathing was laboured now, and the boat wasn't handling right, it was being knocked about, side to side, up and down, and I was throwing up again, and the waves were getting bigger and coming into the boat, and our feet were soaking wet to our ankles, lurching lurching in the dark, water bursting over the sides as we rocked and rolled, side to side, back, forward, back forward – and I was more frightened by far, by far, than I had ever been in the whole of my frightening life.

'Tie yourself in,' I shouted again, slipping on the wet rubber and falling, and getting up, and falling again.

Zion tried to steady himself, but he slipped too, was thrown into the rising water gathering at the bottom of the boat, soaked through now and flailing about.

'I'm frightened,' he yelped, lying on his back, struggling to tie the rope to his belt. 'I want to go back.'

'It's OK,' I said, swallowing my own vomit, eyes and throat stinging with salt. 'It's OK.'

We were diving down, then flying up to the peak of the swell, and down again, and we were being jolted from one side, and then another, the boat spinning, and from below came what seemed like a giant fist punching the bottom of the boat, and I saw Zion flung down, flipped on his side, smashed into the bow, flattened against the floor, up again, like a ragdoll.

I reached for him.

Augusta

'As we're awake,' my mother said, coming into our room at seven o'clock in the morning, with her fake cheerful voice on, the one she uses when my father is in a sweat, 'we thought we might go down to the beach and see the sunrise, like Raúl said. We thought we'd go down to our special spot for breakfast. Wouldn't that be *lovely?*'

Julia leapt out of bed and opened the shutters.

'It's still pretty dark,' she said.

'We've been up for hours,' said my mother. 'Wouldn't it be *special* to have breakfast on the beach. In *our special spot?*'

'I think I'll stay,' I said.

'What about the lizard?' said my mother.

'I like lizards,' I said.

'Do you think it's safe?' said my mother. 'Leaving you here. It's not so much the lizard as, you know, strangers.'

'Of course it's safe,' I said. 'I'm going to turn over and go back to sleep.'

'I'd prefer you to come with us,' said my mother.

'You know she's not good in the morning,' said Julia. 'Let's leave her. We won't be long.'

The three of them left, and I was – gloriously – alone.

Which was what I'd been hoping for.

Longing for.

Selfishly.

Yes, so selfishly.

I got up and put on Lola Alvárez's Moroccan robe, and I wandered from room to room, imagining that the house was mine, that I was a famous writer, who lived here on my own. I thought how much I'd like to spend my whole life writing stories. And perhaps I'd start by telling stories about people in Burundi who never seemed to get their story told anywhere.

I picked up my leather notebook, which I'd bought with my birthday money at the market, and I grabbed my ink pen, and carelessly wrote down anything that came into my head.

Then I went around to the side of the house to climb the steps to the roof terrace, from where I planned to watch the sun rise behind the mountains.

The wind had died, very suddenly, and the clouds were shaped like puffer fish, fat-bodied with little fins and tails. As the sun rose, flaming behind me, the puffer fish clouds swam, in a shoal, down the beach, where I assumed that my mother and father and Julia would see them as they ate their dawn breakfast. The clouds left behind a perfect morning, the sky glowing magenta to indigo to turquoise blue which merged, dazzling, with the sea.

I lay down with the sun on my face, inviting the right words into my brain in A–Z formation as was my way. And here came the words: argan, Berber, carnelian – I started to write. A list in English – A to Z. A list in Spanish, which took me longer.

I still have the lists – they're here with me in the caravan.

I turn the pages.

Salvación, tragedia, ultramarino.

Ultramarine, the pigment made from lapis lazuli, a brilliant deep blue.

I stared at the sky and I was flying.

Free.

Volante.
Peces volantes.

Flying fish.

We went out on a boat trip that day, where we had a chance of seeing flying fish – though, in the end, we didn't.

The minute the three of them came back, they started emptying out the beach bags and repacking them with things we might need for the trip. Cagoules in case we got wet on the boat. Camera. A pair of binoculars. A change of clothes. My father put money in the strange plastic container he liked to wear around his neck on the beach.

As they made these preparations, at lightning speed, they didn't speak to each other.

I stared at them all.

Julia had a red cheek, like one side of her had been burnt by the sun.

'In the end, we stopped and had breakfast on the beach *in front of the shop*,' said my father. 'We didn't bother to go down to the end. As I said, *we didn't go down to the end. We had our breakfast in front of the shop.*'

'Did you see how the clouds looked like puffer fish?' I said, to try and take my mind off my mother and father's tendency to repeat things.

'Clouds?' said my father.

'Puffer fish?' said my mother.

'You must have seen them,' I said.

'Oh yes,' said my mother.

'Julia, did you see the clouds?' I said.

'I don't know,' she said.

'You don't know what puffer fish look like?'

'I don't know anything,' said Julia.

'I think Julia's just excited about the boat trip,' said my mother.

But it wasn't excitement I saw in her face.

'Your cheek looks burnt,' I said to Julia. 'Is it sore? Right there . . .'

I moved my hand towards her cheek.

'I'll get the aftersun,' said my mother a bit too loudly.

'It's nothing,' said Julia, and she didn't look at me – she looked at the floor.

My mother rushed out of the room and rushed back in again, and then she started slathering the aftersun onto Julia's cheek, staring into Julia's eyes, the way she did when she was trying to stop you saying something.

We left in the hire car, accelerating out of the gate with the air conditioning blasting.

I leaned over to Julia.

'What's wrong with Mum?' I whispered.

Julia shrugged and looked out of the window.

'Have they had an argument?' I whispered.

She shook her head.

'Well what happened then? You all seem so stressed out.'

'Let's talk when we get there,' said Julia, and she looked out of the window at the beach, straining her neck.

Parfait

I looked around me at the huge beach.

'We're here,' I said, as the beach spun.

'We're here,' I said again, looking around, closing my salty eyes, rubbing my temples.

'Zion, we made it,' I said. 'We made it!'

I touched my arms to check I was real.

God grant me the serenity.

I tried to find myself, to remember how we got here, to see a picture in my mind of us reaching the beach. But my head spun only with memories of the thwack of waves and the spinning boat and the dark and my feet slipping on wet rubber and the living thing, the ocean, like a broiling liquid beast – and the beach was turning around me, and I was in the centre, and it spun faster.

'Zion!' I said, quieter at first, then louder.

'Zion!'

To accept the things I cannot change.

The courage.

Yes, I must have the courage.

Zion was tying himself into the boat, that's what I'd told him to do.

'Zion!'

I felt a jolt inside me.

The giant fist of the wave.

To change the things I can.

And the wisdom.

I couldn't see the priest's boat anywhere, but perhaps if I went down to the rocks.

The wisdom, the wisdom.

I got up, with difficulty, legs gelatinous, wondering if I could get myself together to walk. I was rocking, but I pulled myself up and concentrating hard, focusing on a rock, I headed down the beach.

Perhaps if you tie yourself in.

To know the difference.

'Zion!' I said.

But there was no answer.

I remembered.

He was flipped like a ragdoll.

But I reached out for him.

Screaming for him.

I leapt into the sea, I was grabbing at the rubber, I was reaching for him, I struggled, I fought, I slipped between the waves, water shot up my nose and in my eyes and burned my throat, and then nothing but turning, turning, nothing but salt and water, and gasping, and praying, and gasping, and fighting, and the sudden shock of sand.

'Zion!' I said, dizzy again, watery, spinning.

We shall stay in the country we love, that's what my father said, didn't he?

And we'll go on dreaming of the city that is to come.

Everything went round and round, round and round.

Stop, I said, stop.

I'm falling, I thought.

I'm going to be sick.

The boat isn't here.

He isn't here.

I started walking up the beach.

Everything was falling, falling with me, the trees, the three houses along the back of the beach, all sliding down into the sea.

Augusta

At the marine centre in Tarifa, there was a short talk, where the lecturer told us we might see pilot whales, different species of dolphins, flying fish. She told us the seas were filling up with plastic, not only the big Pacific blob we all knew about, but tiny beads of plastic, which fish were eating, which were floating through the baleen of whales, making their stomachs feel so full that they thought they didn't need to eat, and swam about, plastically dying.

'Don't buy plastic bags,' said the woman, who had a strong German accent.

'I definitely won't,' I said.

My mother gave me the strange look, as if the rules about plastic didn't apply to us, they were just something for lectures.

My father was tapping his fingers on the table.

When they held up the photos of the different species of dolphins and whales, I kept saying, 'I hope we see that one,' but nobody else spoke. Not even Julia, who normally got excited about things like this.

The dolphins were beautiful. Full of such joy.

I want to be a dolphin, I thought.

I want to be joyful.

As I ran about the deck, right to left, left to right, gasping at every dolphin-leap, Julia stood in one place, staring.

'You'll miss them if you stay there,' I said. 'You won't see anything.'
But still she didn't move.

'Why are you being so weird?' I said, and I knew I sounded frustrated, and I didn't care. 'Come and see the dolphins with me.'

'It's fine,' she said in an angry voice.

'It quite obviously isn't fine,' I said and I'd raised my voice now, almost to a shout, and my mother turned around to glare at us because this was a public place and she didn't approve of raising your voice in a public place, she didn't approve of *airing your dirty linen.*

And Julia went red in the face and exploded.

'I'm FINE!' she said. 'Can you stop bloody asking me all the time?'

It felt as if every single person on the boat had stopped talking.

And my mother was paralysed at the bow because Julia had sworn *in public.*

Then a dolphin leapt over to the right.

The volume of voices rose again.

Julia stood at the bow of the boat.

I ignored her.

After the trip, we went to a hot bar in Tarifa which had English television, and my mother wasn't talking to us.

'Did something happen on the beach?' I said to them.

They all three shook their heads.

My father said, 'It's so good to watch the English news,' and he sat, oddly upright and urgent, asking our opinions on things that wouldn't normally interest him.

On the way home, we saw that behind the tiny village of La Higuera, there was a huge building project going on, stretching for miles. The boards on the outside were in English: NEW TOURIST COMPLEX – LUXURY ACCOMMODATION, LUXURY POOLS, LUXURY SPA, LUXURY GOLF COURSE, LUXURY WATER PARK, LUXURY EXCURSIONS. There were black men pushing wheelbarrows, digging, putting up scaffolding in the burning heat.

'Terrible smell of sewage,' said my father.

I felt sorry for the black men working so hard in the searing heat.

The next morning, when we went to the table with the daily news-paper on it in the village shop, there was a photo of the fish-clouds shoaling down the beach. But underneath, beyond the buried boat, under the trees, there was a black man, lying face down on the sand – maybe, I thought, one of those workers from out on the main road, sleeping on the beach.

'That's our special spot!' I said. 'I'm sure of it.'

My father hurried us out of the shop, and said that there was no money for the newspaper today.

'Come on, Julia!' he said. 'Why are you dawdling about in there? Here, let me carry the basket. Let's go! We're going to have our last day in the garden.'

'Not the beach?' I said.

'It's such a lovely garden and we've hardly spent any time in it,' said my mother.

'I'd like to go to the beach,' I said.

'We're staying in the *garden*,' said my mother.

My father walked about wiping his face with a handkerchief and looking at his watch, and we were allowed to dip into the natural pool. Julia sat in the shade reading.

'Are you sad we're leaving?' I said.

She shook her head.

'I can't wait to go home now,' she said.

'You can't wait? But we were marking off the days for months before we came.'

'It'll be nice to be back where everything's normal and familiar and there's nothing to worry about,' said Julia.

'Nothing to *worry* about?' I said. 'What is there to worry about here?'

'We've got the Half-Term Fair to look forward to,' she said. 'And then it's Angela Dunnett's Hallowe'en party.'

'That's over two months away.'

'But she's having fairy lights and a DJ,' said Julia sadly.

'I couldn't care less about Angela Dunnett's Hallowe'en party,' I said. 'I want to stay here forever.'

'I'm ready to be home,' said Julia, and she smiled, half-closing her eyes as if she was looking right through my eyeballs to somewhere beyond.

'Julia, what is wrong with you?' I said.

'Probably homesickness,' she said.

'But I'm home, aren't I? You can't miss a house with no one in it.'

'I just don't want to be here any more, that's all I'm saying.'

'You don't want to be *here*? You'd rather be *there*?'

She nodded, and it seemed as if her eyes filled with tears.

'Will you tell me, Julia? What's wrong?'

'Everything will be the same again once we're home,' she said.

'Promise?' I said.

'Promise,' she said.

But there are some things you can't promise.

You can never promise that everything will be the same again. Nothing is ever the same again.

On our last evening, my stomach aching with the pain of seeing it all and smelling it all for the last time, we went to the square, to the Tienda de la Playa, which sold towels and jewellery and sunhats and sunglasses.

I expected that Julia and I would spend ages deciding how to spend our five euros, but we walked in, I pointed to some leather wristbands on a rotating stand, and Julia said, 'Yes fine.'

'But there might be other things,' I said.

'These are fine,' she said.

We walked out into the square in the warm evening air, which tickled my shoulders and smelled of honeysuckle and sea. The cobbles were lumpy beneath my espadrilles, and, as we walked along the beach road, the crickets were summer-crazy in the long dry grass, and the egrets were flying to the big old tree where they loved to perch, hundreds of them, lighting up the dark under the moon.

I tried to slip my arm through Julia's, but the minute I did that, my arm felt like it wasn't mine, or like it was dead. So I took it out again.

'So what's been your best moment?' I said.

'Oh I can't think. The dolphins?' said Julia.

'You didn't even look at the dolphins,' I said.

'Why are you interrogating me?' said Julia, and my stomach knotted because I couldn't reach her.

'What's been your worst moment?' I said.

She looked away.

'What kind of question is that?' said Julia. 'There are no worst moments on holiday.'

'This is my worst moment,' I said.

Julia said nothing.

'This is the worst moment in my life,' I said. 'You won't talk to me.'

'I'm probably just tired,' said Julia.

What else could I say?

I remember a heaviness in my stomach as I lay in bed in the thick dark of the shuttered room. I remember hearing her turn over one way and then another, and I remember the air, as it is here on summer nights, dense, nearly solid, suffocating me.

I too turned over. Over. Over.

We were both awake.

We both knew that we were both awake.

But we didn't speak.

I tried lying still.

Dead still.

That's what I would do – I would die to make her love me.

But I still didn't dare talk to her.

I didn't dare say to her, 'What's wrong?'

Hours seemed to pass.

Then I heard her rhythmic breathing.

And I felt as if I could breathe again too.

But I couldn't sleep.

When it was still dark, the sun about to rise, without saying a word to anyone, without asking permission from my parents, I got up and walked down to the beach, to *our special spot*, and I sat on the sand, with the pine trees behind me where you could see through to the three white houses at the back of the beach road.

I wanted to see if anything had changed.

It hadn't.

There were only the shadows of the trees and the noise of the waves, crashing in, back and forth.

I sat right at the edge, picking up shells and putting them in my pocket, and letting the waves spray my face.

I could feel little specks of anxiety inside me, moving, like bacteria under a microscope.

It was time for me to say goodbye.

It made me feel sick inside.

To be leaving.

Especially to be leaving behind something much bigger than Spain.

Something that I would never have back.

I didn't know this, but I knew something.

I felt a strange pain in my stomach.

As if something inside me was breaking.

'Where on earth were you?' said my father.

'We were worried sick,' said my mother.

'Are we still *Justa*?' I whispered to Julia in the car on the way to the airport.

She smiled at me.

'Are you thinking we're too old for *Justa*?' I said.

'We can be *Justa* if you want us to,' said Julia.

I hated that reply, the way it wasn't a reply at all.

I knew what *I* wanted.

I was asking her what *she* wanted.

I looked down and she was drawing on her hand with a biro.

She was drawing waves in the sea, completely even, rows of joined cs like they'd been that day on the beach.

She had such a steady hand, such beautiful writing, even in the car, driving.

Cccccccccccccccccccc

There was our house, orange-bricked, triple-garaged, static, ugly and entirely unchanged by what had happened to us.

My mother seemed energised by arranging the washing into piles of whites and coloureds. My father retreated to his shop. Julia went to show Angela Dunnett and Amy Atkins her tanned skin and leather wristband. She'd bought them each a rubber with the Spanish flag on.

I hadn't bought anything for Ian or Ali or Moira. Ian was only interested in computers, and Ali, who I knew from riding, would have wanted something horsey even though she already had everything horsey you could buy anywhere in the world. Moira had the kind of family who only believed in home-made presents, and I certainly wasn't going to be making her something out of shells. None of them, in short, would have wanted a rubber with the Spanish flag on. Anyway, Ian and Moira were still on holiday, and Ali had gone to see her aunt who had a horse.

I felt lonely.

So I carried on with my research into Burundi.

When Julia came back, my mother said, 'Did they like the rubbers?'

'In America, rubber means condom,' I said. 'So it's advisable to say eraser. In case any Americans are around.'

'There aren't any in this house,' said Julia.

I started to laugh.

But she wasn't laughing.

My mother made a special album of the holiday, and the photos she'd taken on the beach made Julia's boobs look enormous. My body – lying on the sand – looked as long and flat as an ironing board.

The photos made me blush.

I couldn't believe my mother was showing these half-naked photos of us quite casually to the neighbours, to Jim and Barbara Cook, to John and Janice Brown, to David and Hilary Hawkins, to the Dunnetts, to Diego Alvárez.

To Diego Alvárez.

What was the woman thinking?

'I think we need a little trip to Debenhams,' said my mother the next day.

'What for?'

'Seeing as you two are becoming young ladies.'

'What are you insinuating?' I said.

We did go to Debenhams.

A lady with enormous bosoms came at us with a tape measure.

'*You* don't need a bra,' she said to me. 'There's nothing there yet!'

Perhaps you could auction off some of yours, I thought, in batches.

She brought a selection of bras for Julia, white with tiny coloured bows in the middle.

I sat on a small plastic chair.

'Do you want anything else, Augusta?' said my mother.

'No thank you,' I said.

I went back to my research on Burundi.

Lake Tanganyika was forged from the earth's crust as the tectonic plates moved and tore apart, forming a huge split and a kind of freshwater reef.

'In Lake Tanganyika, there are two hundred and fifty endemic cichlid species,' I said to Julia.

'Can't you say fish?' said Julia.

'Do you find me annoying?' I said, smiling, trying to smile – except that my lips were turning down at the ends.

'Course I don't,' she said.

I tried to get control of my mouth, thinking, Pull yourself together, what's wrong with you?

'Sorry,' she said. 'I didn't mean to snap. I love your words. You know I do.'

She reached out her hand and touched my shoulder, and I couldn't think what to do so I just sat there, thinking, Why does everything feel like this? Like we don't know each other – or something.

I got up.

'I'm going to see Jim Cook,' I said, thinking that perhaps he might have another dream up his sleeve, and, even if he didn't, I couldn't bear to stay here any longer.

Although my father had banned us from visiting the Cooks, we both used to sneak to number 2 through a gap in the hedge in the back garden, so that the other neighbours wouldn't see us and tell our father.

My mother had asked me more than once if I'd ever seen Jim drinking alcohol in the daytime, and I said no, although actually I had. I didn't want to get him into trouble.

When I went through the hedge to talk to Jim Cook about my research into cichlid fish, he said, 'Why don't we make an aquarium which looks like a miniature version of Lake Tanganyika?'

I assumed he wouldn't do anything about it, but he did.

He bought a special filter and bluish lights and an antique-looking Roman pot and he set the water at 78 degrees Fahrenheit, which is 25.5 degrees Celsius, and we waited for the nitrogen cycle to establish.

Then came the best bit: choosing the fish.

The fish man, also known as an aquarist, by the way, helped us to choose *callochromis melanostigma* – which had long gold fins like hair combs – and *callochromis* raspberry heads (what a name!) with a pale pink blush about their faces, and *cyprichromis leptosoma katete*, my total favourite, as these little fish glowed gold and sapphire and aquamarine.

Parfait

I walked up and down the beach by the sea, looking for signs – real physical signs. The boat. As well as other kinds of signs. From above. I hoped God would speak to me, but God didn't. Not aloud anyway.

But perhaps God was speaking to me in the fish surfing in on the waves. Perhaps the fish were God's way of saying that Zion had come in on the waves. Or perhaps the fish were God's way of saying that he hadn't. That's the problem with reading signs from God.

'What are you saying?' I said aloud.

'What was that?' said a voice in Spanish. 'Can I help you?'

It was a guy about my age.

He was smoking weed.

'No,' I said.

He tried to do a high five.

But our hands just missed each other.

He laughed.

'Who the hell were you talking to?' he said, still laughing, kind of hysterically.

'*Nadie*,' I said. 'No one.'

He laughed even more.

I wasn't laughing.

He walked on.

I could swim out.

And keep swimming.

And swimming.

But I didn't let myself get in the water.

As a punishment.

'Have you lost something?' a girl said to me when I was down on the beach. 'I once lost my engagement ring in the sea.'

'I'm so sorry,' I said to her.

'I found it,' she said, putting out her tanned hand. 'It was kind of a miracle. So maybe you'll find whatever you've lost.'

Was it a sign?

'What have you lost?' said an old lady as she put on her swimming hat in the early morning, before people arrived.

I stared at her.

She was covered in freckles, and the skin on her arms and legs hung in folds.

No words came out of my mouth.

There were no words to describe what I'd lost anyway.

She shook her head at me and plunged her body into the sea.

Augusta

One day, something went wrong with Jim Cook's tank, and he found all the cichlid fish floating on the surface, dead. Graham moaned and bashed his head against the tank, smash, smash, smash.

Jim Cook, who'd been so keen to create Lake Tanganyika in his sitting room for Graham, lost heart when the fish died, and he said he was done with fish and he put the aquarium up for sale in the *Hedley Green Gazette* that same day, without telling Barbara.

Barbara moved into the spare bedroom.

When I was listening the other side of the serving hatch, I heard her say to my mother, 'There's nothing that would fit neatly into the gap where the aquarium went.'

The gap sat there staring at you in the sitting room, reminding you of how beautiful it once was. In fact, Barbara Cook said to my mother, the hole was like the hole in their marriage.

My mother and Barbara Cook spent hours leafing through the Ikea catalogue thinking what might fit snugly into the space where the Tanganyikan tank had been. In the end, they settled on a special teak drinks cabinet, with an up-and-over door. But Jim Cook could never keep his hand out of that cabinet.

Now that the aquarium had gone, Barbara had to take Graham out and about much more, which was totally exhausting her, she said, though she might have been exaggerating to make Jim feel bad. I did my best to bump into Graham whenever he was out in his adapted buggy because I always had this feeling that I had a special responsibility towards him.

As I analyse my own behaviour, sitting some distance now from being a child, I wonder if I just liked to be different from everybody by being friends with Graham Cook. Was it one more of my unusual choices? I certainly liked to think I had special linguistic powers that made me understand his noises. Or maybe there was actually something nice about me.

Who knows?

But soon after the selling of the aquarium, I bumped into Graham up by the roundabout, and I swear he said to me, hidden under all the moaning noises, 'Fish fish fish.'

That made my mind up.

Parfait

The waves came in and out, in and out.
    But the waves brought nothing with them.
    Except plastic bottles, with rubbed-off labels.
    Bits of broken-off polystyrene.
    Weed.
    Cuttlefish bones like little white surfboards.
    A flip-flop.
    I stared at the flip-flop.
    Zion didn't wear flip-flops.

Augusta

It wasn't long until the Fair – it came every year for one day in the October half-term and closed down the whole of Hedley Green high street.

Poor Graham Cook could never go to the fair because he found it over-stimulating.

And my father didn't go because all the fair people were *crooks*.

I had started practising my hoop-la skills with a kind of manic zeal in the garage some weeks before. In order to win Graham Cook some new fish (a good thing), I stole £20 from my mother's purse (a bad thing). You got 3 goes for £1. And 3 x 20 = 60 goes.

Now, if I had been truly a good person, I would not have stolen the £20 but rather used the £15 which my parents had already given me for my own enjoyment at the Fair. But the £15 I kept for my own pleasure, prioritising the gorgeous old merry-go-round with its painted horses, palomino and dapple grey, with real hair manes and red leather stirrups. We always went on the merry-go-round first, and had done since we were tiny children. There were still grown women finding their favourite horse. There was also the big wheel, which gave me a special kind of thrill, the way we soared over Stanley Hope Uniforms, the way we could see the top of Old John Brown's Hill and the back gardens of Willow Crescent.

Next stop, the hoop-la stall, and it turned out that, should hoop-la ever become an Olympic sport, I would win gold, no problem at all.

I got to Graham Cook at the pond in Willow Crescent, with seven plastic bags of goldfish making grooves in the skin of my arms, and I tried to act like we were both pouring the fish into the pond, but actually Graham's hands were twisted and didn't manage to do things like that.

Julia had meanwhile been instructed to distract my mother with plausible stories about me meeting Ali and going on the dodgems.

When Graham saw the goldfish with the longest silkiest tail come swimming up to the surface, he started making cooing noises like a dove.

Next thing we knew, my mother and Julia were up on the round-about panting and my mother was saying, in her furious voice, 'I've never been more worried in my life.'

The Hedley Green Fair doesn't happen any more. Nowadays, one big fair comes for all of half-term to Tattershall Common.

They moved the fireworks there too, around the same time.

It's hard to remember that I used to love Fireworks Night.

Before my life exploded in my face.

Parfait

I walked.

That's all I did.

In the evenings, the bakeries threw out their stale bread. In the markets, you could pick up unsold fish from the barrows, bits of octopus tentacle, squid rings on the turn.

I walked practically to Algeciras. I walked all the way back. The sky was the deepest blue and the beach was golden.

Unnecessarily extravagant.

Beauty.

It kept me going.

Pa, I said, Pa.

Help me.

I was back at the holey rocks and the trees.

Don't give up.

Don't give up.

That's what Pa said, or I said to myself, or God said, or someone said, the pine trees or the sea, or all of us together.

I sat right by the water.

I watched the little waves roll in.

There were no fish jumping today.

Augusta

Julia and I used to sit dangling willow fronds into the pond, trying to get the fish to swim up to the surface before we fed them.

But one day, no fish swam up.

The same thing happened the next day, and the next.

So we got our wellies on and dug about, but could see no sign of them.

'Do you think they're lying dead at the bottom of the pond?' I said. 'Like Jim Cook's cichlids? Or do you think a heron got them?'

Julia looked very strange.

And much sadder than anyone would look about goldfish.

'Why would all the fish be dying round here?' she said, peering into the pond water.

And now she didn't so much look sad as frightened.

'Are you OK, Julia?' I said.

'Oh yes I'm fine,' she said in a very flat voice. 'Mum thinks it's my hormones.'

'Do you think you got all my hormones too?' I said, trying to make a joke about the way my boobs weren't growing.

But Julia didn't seem to hear.

The first time that Mr Sánchez showed us a film of flamenco dancing, the women were all wearing bright orange dresses which they flashed around in layers of fiery golden frills, and I thought that perhaps the seven goldfish had come to life like in a fairy tale.

Raúl and Teo sometimes have flamenco dancing shows in their restaurant, but we never saw them on our family holiday in 2004 because the dancing started at midnight, and my parents liked to be in bed by ten thirty – or eleven o'clock at weekends.

I had no idea then that Raúl and Teo would become so dear to me, so very central in my life, or that I'd be living here in the field at the back of their white stone house, with the flat roof terrace looking out to Africa. I had no idea that the three of us would gallop their mares down the beach at sunrise and sunset, and sometimes in the dark under the stars.

I had no idea then what it would be like in La Higuera at Christmas for the celebrations of the live Nativity, or at *fiesta* time, when the sound of flamenco is carried on the *Levante* wind, when we celebrate the procession of the Virgin, wearing frilled dresses. I had no idea that I would learn to dance flamenco. That I would buy myself a tangerine-orange dress, with white embroidery and layers of frills which are called *volantes*.

Volante, from the Latin verb – *volare* – to fly.

The same word used for flying fish.

And when you dance flamenco, you can sometimes fly right out of your own body.

On Sunday 31 October 2004, Angela Dunnett had her much-anticipated Hallowe'en party under a striped gazebo.

Nobody really has a clue where the word, gazebo, comes from. It popped up (get it?) in 1752 in a book about oriental design, which was quite the fad in eighteenth-century England.

People think the author took the 'ebo' of the Latin future tense and added it to 'gaze'.

I will look, kind of thing, out of the gazebo.

It doesn't sound that likely an explanation to me, but then I'm not an etymologist.

I did indeed spend much of the long evening of Angela Dunnett's Hallowe'en party looking out of the gazebo and seeing nothing.

Julia had refused to go as a ghost or a witch or a skeleton or a corpse. So, in the end, we both went as fruit bats, and I rammed a quarter of an orange into my mouth, which I refused to take out to speak to anyone. Though, after a while, it was quite wearing, and people got a bit bored of finding it funny. So I took the orange out and put it in my pocket. Then everyone took off their spooky costumes, and the juice from the orange dripped down my leg, making me feel as if I was peeing myself.

Underneath their costumes, people had put on the coolest clothes they owned, and some girls had brought make-up bags with them and they all crowded into the Dunnetts' toilet to put on lipstick.

Angela Dunnett's cousin, Ricky, said, 'Are you Julia's younger sister? You're very tall.'

First, there was some karaoke – and Angela Dunnett pranced around in black leggings and her mother's wooden Scholls, shaking her boobs and yelling, 'You're the one that I want!'

Then we all danced in the garden underneath the fairy lights in a big group, and I saw out of the corner of my eye that Diego and Julia were deliberately dancing away from the main group, further, further, further, until they entirely disappeared behind Mr Dunnett's shed.

I tried dancing to the right and to the left to see if I could get a good look at what might be going on behind that shed, but my view was entirely blocked, by two apple trees on one side, and by a high trellis fence on the other.

I kept dancing around under the fairy lights, trying to look normal, but feeling really abnormal – dance, dance, dance.

When things got a bit boring, I put the orange-quarter back in my mouth, but nobody noticed, so I took it out again.

Then I spent some time stroking the whippet.

The evening went on and on and on, forever.

I wasn't used to doing this kind of thing without Julia.

I kept going into the Dunnetts' toilet and checking my watch and thinking surely surely this party will end soon. Surely surely it will be over by midnight.

Then – joy! – Mr Dunnett pulled the plug out of the wall, turned off the fairy lights and shouted in the karaoke microphone, 'That's it, folks!'

Julia and I walked home in dead silence.

When we got to the porch, I noticed that her lipstick was all smudged and her mascara was running.

'Have you been crying?' I said.

'Oh, Aug,' said Julia.

I took my orange-quarter out of my pocket and shoved it in my mouth.

She said, 'It's finally happened.'

'Did you have a nice time?' said my mother, coming down in her dressing gown.

'Great,' said Julia.

'What did you do?'

Julia blushed.

I started making strange groaning noises with the orange still blocking up my mouth.

'Take that out, Augusta,' said my mother.

But I kept going, saying, 'We just danced really and slaughtered a few of the neighbours,' except you couldn't hear me because of the orange.

'Off to bed,' said my mother.

We lay in bed, still in silence.

'So?' I said. 'Tell me.'

'Oh, it's nothing,' said Julia.

'Nothing!' I said. 'We've been after that boy for four years.'

'But I feel a bit bad,' said Julia. 'We always said he'd have to choose between us.'

'Please don't worry, Jules,' I said. 'I think I might have gone off him anyway – and also I don't have any tits.'

Then it all came out.

Diego apparently put his right arm around her shoulder and then he swung around until he was holding her with both arms. He put his hands to her jaw, cupping her chin like an egg in an egg-cup, and he moved his face forward and put his tongue right inside her mouth, and, although she'd never done this kind of thing before, she knew exactly what to do.

'It made me forget everything,' she said. 'I wanted to go on and on kissing forever.'

'Could you breathe?' I said.

'It made you breathe more,' she said. 'My own breath got louder and louder and drowned everything else out. All my thoughts. All my worries.'

'What kind of thoughts? What kind of worries?' I said. 'I wish you'd tell me. You never tell me. Not since Spain.'

'Let me keep telling you this,' she said. 'This is much more interesting.'

She told me that feeling the palms of his hands on the skin of her face and his tongue wrapping up in hers made her whole body start quivering and shaking and she felt as if she might well collapse.

'Really?' I said. 'And did you? Did you collapse?'

'Yes,' she said. 'Yes.'

'What? You actually fainted?'

'Well, it was more accidentally on purpose,' she said. 'And we were lying on the grass by now, and I could feel his willy all hard inside his trousers.'

'Really?' I said. 'Was that a bit gross?'

'No,' she said.

She honestly liked that.

That's what she said.

The fact that she had caused it. Ta-dah! Like a magician!

131

She and Diego lay right on top of each other – her underneath and him on top.

'Didn't you get squashed?' I said. 'Wasn't he really heavy?'

'No.'

'That is weird,' I said. 'Come and lie on top of me. I'm sure I'd feel squashed. And you're not nearly as heavy as Diego.'

'What?' said Julia.

'Go on, let's do an experiment,' I said. 'Remember I have had a really shit evening. At least let's have a laugh.'

'Really?' said Julia.

'Let's be like we used to be,' I said. 'Silly.'

'Silly?' said Julia.

'Oh go on, don't get all serious and up yourself just because you've learnt how to kiss. Just because you're the willy-magician.'

Julia laughed.

She leapt out of her bed and she lay down right on top of me, face down, and she raised her arms and legs the way seals do when they sunbathe on the beach, being as dead a weight as she could manage.

We started laughing and laughing so hard, and Julia started wriggling about doing all the strange humpy actions he'd done on top of her.

'Did he really do that?' I squealed.

She kept putting her hands on my cheeks and touching my hair.

We were properly hysterical by now.

Then my father came in.

'Stop this right now!' he yelled. 'Get into your own beds!'

We were laughing so hard that we couldn't stop.

'Get into your own beds!' shouted my father again.

'I *am* in my own bed,' I said.

'Don't you dare cheek me,' he said, and he rushed out.

In the morning, our mother appeared to tell us how rude and disrespectful we'd been to our father.

'I want you to tell me what on earth you were doing,' she said.

I realised at once that explaining was problematic, without revealing what had happened to Julia behind the shed – and this was not something that I was going to be describing to my mother. Though one assumes that some time long ago she might have collapsed on the grass with my father – it's just that I really really couldn't imagine it.

'We were messing about,' I said.

'Were you drunk?' she said. 'Or hiding a boy in here?'

I knew I could do better.

'We were being *fruit bats*,' I said, and I knew I was a genius, and I went and got the sucked-dry orange-quarter and I shoved it in my mouth, and I started flailing about, humping and twisting, on my bed.

'Oh,' said my mother, frowning a little. 'Is that what fruit bats do?'

'Yes,' I said. 'Always. In the wild.'

'Oh, I see,' said my mother. 'I'll tell your father.'

She went out.

'Call me a genius,' I said to Julia. 'I've revealed nothing.'

'I feel a bit odd this morning,' said Julia. 'When Diego was kissing me, I felt like it would solve everything. But I don't think it did.'

Julia had started spending hours and hours with Diego.

And not with me.

I felt – what did I feel? – lost.

'Are you feeling a bit jealous?' said my mother.

'What of?' I said, casual as anything.

'Don't be like that,' said my mother.

'Like what?' I said.

The truth was that yes, I *was* feeling jealous.

But the person I wanted was Julia.

Not Diego.

I hadn't known that would be true.

But seeing him mooning around after her made him undesirable to me.

'He's so handsome,' said my mother.

He's so desperate, I thought.

I kept on with my research – several files for Burundi, a file for Andalusia, majoring on horses, and a file for each of my favourite Spanish novelists, poets, dramatists and artists.

'Who's that photo of?' said my mother, from some way away over by the cooker.

'Federico García Lorca,' I said.

'Someone you're interested in?' she said, coming closer. 'A boy?'

'Very much so,' I said.

'He sounds Spanish too,' said my mother.

'Yes,' I said.

'Tell me more.'

'He was shot on the nineteenth of August 1936,' I said. 'He was a homosexual poet.'

'Augusta,' she said. 'I don't know what's the matter with you. I think you need to get out a bit more.'

So I went round to Ian's house.

Ian was growing his hair long and he had a layer of dark down above his lip which he refused to shave. It made me feel a bit ill.

'Do you fancy me?' he said, out of the blue, while we were sitting on his bed.

I shook my head.

'I didn't think so,' he said.

I smiled.

'I don't fancy you either,' he said.

'Great,' I said, and then we played computer games.

'Don't you get bored with all that kissing?' I said to Julia. 'Kissing and kissing all day long? Does your tongue get a bit sore?'

She looked away.

'It's nice,' she said.

'What do you talk about for all those hours on end?'

'Stuff.'

'Do you still love me?' I said.

'Course I still love you,' said Julia.

Diego bought Julia a gold heart pendant.

'Love is in the air,' sang my father, which was quite out of character.

Love was not in my air.

Love had sprouted a new season of letters and gifts in Julia and Diego's air.

Julia bought an italic pen set with little cream cards and matching envelopes, and she wrote Diego inky love letters, sometimes choosing to copy awful rhymes from greetings cards you could buy in the newsagent by Hedley Green station, next to our secret glade with the trees to climb and bluebells in spring.

Julia never wanted to stop off there any more.

She was always rushing to meet Diego on Hedley Green high street.

'Ian's given me some cigarettes,' I said. 'Shall we go and smoke them in the bluebell wood?'

She grimaced.

'You don't want to try smoking?'

'Diego doesn't like it,' she said. 'Especially not on a girl.'

'Not on a *girl?*' I said. 'What the hell's being a girl got to do with it?'

'Well, anyway,' she said. 'Apparently, it's like kissing an ashtray.'

'Has he tried kissing an ashtray?'

'Don't be silly, Aug.'

'When did he kiss a girl who smoked?'

'I don't know.'

'Aren't you jealous?'

'Anyway, it gives you lung cancer,' said Julia.

'Not one cigarette,' I said.

'You smoke one and then you're addicted,' said Julia.

'You are addicted to Diego,' I said. 'I challenge you to give up French kissing for Lent.'

'I don't really do Lent,' said Julia.

'Or you could give up Diego for Lent,' I said, trying to sound as if I was being funny, trying not to sound hurt.

'I need to go,' she said.

That did hurt me.

That she couldn't stay for three seconds to have a conversation with me.

'You always need to go, don't you?' I said, and it came out quite mean. 'You're always rushing off.'

'I like being busy,' she said quietly. 'That's no crime, is it?'

'You never used to,' I said in quite a hard voice because I wasn't going to be needy if she wasn't going to be nice.

'Things change,' she said.

'*You've* changed,' I said. 'You didn't use to be cold.'

'I've just got a boyfriend,' she said, and her measured and rather *adult* tone of voice annoyed me.

'You changed before you had a boyfriend. You changed in Spain.'

Now her cheeks coloured, and I could see something altering in her face, and I watched her pull at her sleeve, and her lips looked as if they were trembling.

'Maybe I grew up,' she said, but on the *up*, her voice broke.

'It isn't that, Jules,' I said. 'It's something else.'

I tried to smile at her because I hated us arguing.

'I'll be late,' she said. 'Diego hates it when I'm late.'

She turned to go, but, as she turned, I could see her face crumpling up the way it always did before she cried.

When she came home, she'd bought me a bunch of daffodils – they were still buds, closed up, green-ish yellow.

'I feel terrible,' she said. 'I feel like you think I abandoned you. Diego and I wanted to say that you're always welcome to be with us. Literally, any time.'

'Thank you,' I said.

'I'm so sorry about earlier,' she said. 'I don't know what got into me.'

Something happened inside me.

In my heart.

It was hurting my chest.

'You're crying,' said Julia. 'You never cry. Please don't cry.'

She took me in her arms and she smelled of Timotei shampoo and Diego's aftershave and the tears were coming in big bursts, like when Barbara Cook was watching Graham and me on the swing-set.

'I love you, Aug,' she said, again and again.

Then my mother came in.

'What on earth is the matter?' she said.

'It's OK,' said Julia.

'Is it to do with Diego?' she said, her face colouring and her neck rash coming on underneath her garnet birthstone.

I look back and think she must have seen that it was me who was crying, not Julia.

Surely.

Julia wrote me a card in italic writing.

I still have it.

It says: 'I can't imagine life without you.'

I brought it with me to La Higuera but I don't look at it.

Life without you.

The card has a baby chick on the outside.

The daffodil buds burst out, yellow and full of sunshine.

They made me hopeful.

Spring was coming.

Parfait

It was Good Friday.

Not that good.

I was sitting on a wall, with hundreds of other people sitting on a wall, above the square in Tarifa.

I'd got myself a job as a security guard in a car park – six in the evening until six in the morning. It was terrible pay, but it was pay, and I now had somewhere to go at night.

I sat on my broken armchair in the hut next to the up-down barrier, with the radio playing bad Spanish pop music and the street light shining in my eyes, and my alarm going off every ten minutes to keep me awake.

Every time I woke, I jumped, and every time I slept, even for ten minutes, I was in the sea. And so was Zion. But we'd become separated, and the sea was cloudy. He was turning, spiralling downwards through the water, right into the depths, facing away from me. I was trying to catch his attention, trying to say something to him from far away. But every time I opened my mouth, it filled with sea.

The sound of the alarm.

The strange shocked jump, as if I was falling off a cliff, and I came to on the chair, and I set my alarm again.

I felt exhausted, inside my veins, inside my bones, as I watched the

Holy Week procession come by: big platforms called *pasos*, swaying on the shoulders of the *costaleros*, who were hidden underneath.

The first *paso* carried three wooden crosses.

I thought of my father telling us that the thief on the cross was forgiven, on the spot, despite everything he'd done.

Everything I'd done.

I couldn't bear to think of it.

I thought of my mother, and I fingered my tin daffodil as the next *paso* came by, a huge single wooden cross, with the choir following – boys and girls, their jeans and trainers sticking out of the bottom of their white robes; men with beards; women in red lipstick. All singing *forgiven, forgiven, forgiven.*

A woman in black, with a Spanish comb in her hair, came onto the square, bent double and started to lament loudly using what seemed to be words from the bible. And when she'd finished, she got straight up off her knees and went to the side to smoke a cigarette and chat to her friends.

Round came the choir again into the square.

Forgiven forgiven forgiven.

Perdonados.

The words disappeared down the hill, a faint echo now on the air. Going going going. Like watching a bird fly away. Smaller smaller smaller until it was nothing. But the bird sang inside of me.

Loud inside of me.

Forgiven, forgiven, forgiven.

'Your choice, boy, but I'd take it!' my father used to say with that big wide smile across his face. 'Otherwise, it was a waste of all his pain!'

Augusta

Diego bought Julia an incubator of chicken eggs for Easter because she liked baby anythings. She put the incubator on the side table, and on the first night, the biggest egg started to wobble when we were eating supper, and a tiny cheep came from inside it and it made us all feel a bit tense.

My father kept staring at it, saying, 'I'm not sure I want to get wrapped up in this.'

We ate our raspberry jelly without speaking, and somehow when it went down my throat, I felt like I was eating egg yolk and albumin and vitelline membrane.

The other eggs lay still in the incubator.

Diego called around, and we all said what a great idea the eggs were.

The next day, the wobbling and the cheeping started again in the biggest egg, and the tip of a small beak pushed through the shell. It struggled about, pecking, tapping, smashing, and we all held our breath.

Then the miracle!

The chick shoved itself through, exhausted and wet, and collapsed on its side in a nest of eggshell.

It lay panting as my father took loud gulps of water.

The chick still didn't move.

Diego came, and by the time Julia had let him in, the chick had resurrected and dried and puffed out and was strutting about, yellow and fluffy as anything, and it was the sweetest thing we'd ever seen.

So it went on, night after night, until the final chick came out of the final egg, collapsed, panting, got up and walked round and round in circles, leaning left, with a twisted wing, smashed into the side of the incubator and died. We waited and waited, we prayed and prayed, but it didn't come back to life.

After Easter, we had revision sessions at lunchtime.

I remember it was Latin revision, and I was looking out of the window, when I saw Julia walking alone on the path.

She stopped by the sundial and stared at it, the way the shadow fell on the hour-lines, to tell the time.

The earliest sundials are shadow clocks from Egypt, dated at 1500 BC. I guess human beings have always wanted to tell the time.

To know how long is left.

Julia was reading the quote that is engraved on the bronze plaque. *'The butterfly counts not months but moments, and has time enough.'*

'Adjectives,' said the teacher, 'come after nouns in Latin. Like in French. And Spanish. But not English.'

I put up my hand.

'There are exceptions,' I said, looking out at Julia still reading the sundial.

'For example?' said the teacher.

'For example, *time enough,*' I said.

'Yes yes yes,' said the teacher. 'Time enough.'

When I looked out of the window, Julia was still staring at the sundial.

Her face had turned quite still.

Parfait

Now I had a little bit of money in my pocket, I liked to sit at a café in the Paseo de la Alameda – an open kind of square (though more of a rectangle) framed by palm trees, near the port. I would drink black tea in the sun and watch people – their bodies, their faces, the way they walked, or held hands – especially the couples. I wondered what it would be like to be a couple.

'I often see you here,' said a voice, and the owner of the voice came over.

He was a small stocky man – I'd seen him here before.

His skin was like leather and he had a scar on his left cheek, thick dark hair and stubby fingers.

He drew up his chair.

'You always look troubled,' he said, and the smoke from his black tobacco floated up my nose.

I plucked the lemon out of my tea and bit at its green skin, and I tried to smile at him.

I liked his face.

He'd seen things.

He knew things.

A bit of pain.

Pleasure too, I thought.

'Biting the lemon – you know the song?' he said.

I shook my head.

'*Cante Jondo,*' said the man, and he looked around him, as if he was about to tell me some great secret, and then he whispered, 'You know about it? People call it *flamenco* but it should be called *Cante Jondo*. Deep song.'

'*Flamenco!*' I said, remembering Víctor dancing round the kitchen. 'Yes! Spanish dancing – I know about that.'

'Well, it doesn't start with the dancing,' said the man, shaking his head. 'It starts with the song.'

'I've never heard about *flamenco songs,*' I said. 'I thought it was a dance.'

'Then you've never lived,' he said, and he sat back, as if he was weighing up whether to go on, and he inhaled with a big sucking noise, held the smoke inside, sitting quite still, before exhaling.

'Spanish dancing!' he said to himself, once, twice, three times, and shaking his head, and we sat there for a while, on our wicker chairs, the man smoking and me biting the green skin of the lemon.

'It doesn't actually start with the song,' said the man, laughing.

'You said it did start with the song!' I said, and I smiled at him – it was so good to talk. It was so good – something about this encounter was so good.

The man went on laughing. Then he leant forward, so that his face was up close to mine, and he winked at me, and he took my hand, and he held it in his, and he squeezed it. Then he put his other stubby hand on top, so my one hand was sandwiched between his two hands.

Touch.

The touch of a person.

'So does it start with the song or doesn't it start with the song?' I said.

'Oh, if I'm going to teach you about *Cante Jondo,*' said the man. 'You will have to enjoy a little mystery, a little paradox, a little *razón incorpórea.*'

Disembodied reasoning, I translated in my head, probably frowning; it didn't seem to make much sense to me.

'What's that?'

'Who knows?' said the man. 'It's untranslatable. And anyway, only gypsies have it. Only gypsies have *flamencura*. *Duende*.'

I hadn't heard either of those words, and I was still chewing on how I was supposed to have disembodied reasoning.

'Are you a gypsy?'

The man knocked back his head and started laughing again.

'*Claro!*' he said. '*Claro!* Look at me!'

The man picked up a napkin and took a pen from his pocket and, on it, he wrote some Spanish words, shaped like a verse of poetry.

'This is one of the *soleares*,' he said, giving me the napkin.

I took it.

'It's a present,' he said. '*Un regalito.*'

'Thank you,' I said, folding it.

'There are all different types of song in *Cante Jondo*. The *seguiriya* and the *soleá* help us when we feel we're beyond consolation. So we'll start there, shall we, with a *soleá*? There'll be time to get to the *alegrías* later – the cheery ones. That's the right order for you, don't you think?'

The man smiled into my eyes, getting up from the chair.

'You'll read the words, won't you?' he said. 'They bear re-reading.'

'I will,' I said. 'Thank you. Will I see you again?'

'I'm going back to Seville for a while,' he said. 'Things are a bit complicated. But I'll be back.'

Augusta

Diego had started buying me a present whenever he bought one for Julia. She'd clearly told him to.

The best of Diego's double presents were two stunt kites. He'd ordered them from Spain, where they held competitions near La Higuera. They were great big things – a giant pink butterfly for Julia, and a kind of ferocious-looking turquoise dragonfly for me. If you were good at it, you could make them leap and dive and circle round each other.

We were not good at it. As it turned out. We took them up to Old John Brown's and the kites dive-bombed repeatedly to the ground on top of us, leaving us all crying with laughter.

It was good to hear Julia laugh, but she laughed less, and when she wasn't thinking about *anything*, you could tell she was thinking about *something*.

'No no no!' she shrieked in her sleep. 'He is!'

'Who is?' I said.

'He is,' she whispered back at me.

'Diego?'

'No no no!' she said, with a strange rasping voice. 'His hand.'

'You're shouting things out in your dreams,' I said. 'Are you OK?'

'Nobody can help dreaming,' she said.

And that is true.

I spent hours inside my own head, dreaming too. There was not a lot happening outside – my body seemed to have come to a standstill, and even my periods only turned up when they felt like it.

I was the caterpillar who went into the chrysalis and came out a longer and thinner caterpillar, while Julia grew wings and flew, dazzling, into the sky.

Julia's boobs grew round, and every three months, she went up a bra size, it seemed to me. My nipples turned from flat to pointed, two pencil leads under the thin fabric of my school shirt, which, mortifyingly, *showed through*. And I still – *still* – didn't need a bra.

But that November, when I was fifteen and three months, and giving up hope, a slight swelling took place underneath my pointed nipples, as if someone had injected my chest with yeast. I stood in front of the bathroom mirror, and joy surged through my body.

Transmogrification!

Metamorphosis!

Finally!

Julia went through her underwear and I slipped on one of her old bras – and it fitted!

The future was coming.

I took the cream book out from under my mattress and I stood in our bedroom, and I said the words of the pedlar-man poem over and over again, staring out of the window.

Then I felt a bit of an idiot.

After I stopped feeling an idiot, I let myself dream of the life I would have when I grew older, when I would flee from Hedley Green in a gypsy caravan and travel across the globe at the reins of a dapple-grey horse, with pans clanking from hooks in the roof and geraniums growing in the tiny window-boxes and my wooden gypsy bed draped in Indian saris like our neighbours, the Hassans, wore.

I'd read stories in the Sunday magazines of real people who didn't care about going to school or washing their car or mowing the lawn – they crossed the Sahara Desert on camels or cycled over mountain ranges or sailed around the globe, living in far-away ports underneath starry skies.

Parfait

In the port, there was a huge cruise ship moored up with rows and rows of thousand-euro windows and two hydrofoils which took tourists to the markets at Tangier – oh, Tangier!

On the tarmac at the back, in front of a row of tiny modern shops, there were folding boards set out on the concrete, advertising trips to see dolphins and whales, or diving courses.

I sat and translated what the gypsy man had written on the napkin.

I wished he hadn't gone back to Seville.

It was nice to talk to someone.

Me muero yo – I'm dying.

De pena voy a morirme – of sorrow I'm going to die, or I'm going to die of sorrow, more like.

Como me muero mordiendo la corteza del verde limón – as I die biting the skin of a green lemon.

The taste of grief.

That's what it was about.

Grief like green lemons.

I'd paint it.

As soon as I had enough money, I'd buy paints.

I learnt it off by heart, wondering why the adjective green wasn't after the noun lemon, like it was supposed to be in Spanish.

Augusta

Year 11 rushed by.

Twelve subjects.

The Second World War, the parables of Jesus, algebraic equations, butterflies in mixed media, conductors and insulators, defining and non-defining clauses, cell vacuoles, chemical formulae, *To Kill a Mocking Bird*, verb declensions in three languages, active and passive mood, indicative, subjunctive.

In June, Julia laboured, sweating and sighing in exam halls, whilst I cruised through to A levels with hardly a backward glance.

My mother tried to cheer her up in the evenings by planning our sixteenth-birthday barbecue which would be held in the garden for our friends in the crescent, Julia's friends from the dance school, mine from riding and the library club – and our favourite school friends, who, except the slightly odd ones – Ian and Moira – preferred Julia to me.

'Who are parties for in general?' I said to my mother.

'What do you mean?' said my mother.

'Is this party for us or for the people coming?'

'Well, obviously for both,' she said.

'Do you think my library friends *want* to meet Julia's dance friends then?' I said. 'Because I don't think they'll get on at all.'

'But that's what happens at parties,' said my mother.

'My riding friends are a bit *too* into horses. Like, it's a bit weird,' I said. 'They have horse stickers on their cars and horse earrings and horse wash bags. And my library friends only like poems. Like, in the whole world.'

'I'm sure there are some poems about horses somewhere,' said my mother.

I just stared at her, because what on earth could you say to that? Did she honestly think people would be sitting about reading horse poems when they were sixteen, when actually they'd be smuggling in alcohol and snogging each other behind the blossom trees. At the very very least.

'It makes me feel stressed thinking about it,' I said.

She looked at me strangely.

'Isn't it fun to invite all your friends?' she said.

I shook my head.

'The most fun,' I said, 'is not inviting Robin Fox.'

We'd decided to ask for doves for our presents, inspired by Pally Alvárez, but my father was not at all keen.

'We can't be traipsing around the crescent trying to catch birds every night,' he said.

'I've got a surprise for you both. At the party,' said my mother.

Which took my dread to new and dizzying levels.

'Her surprise is going to be awful, I know it is,' I said to Julia.

'Stop it, Aug,' she said. 'Let's try these new wax strips on our legs. I'll do yours. You do mine.'

'You haven't got any hairs.'

'I have, but they're blonde.'

'Your children will be apes like me,' I said. 'Look at Diego – he's turning into a werewolf.'

'Stop it!' said Julia, giggling.

'His chest's going really hairy,' I said, screwing up my nose. 'It's creeping out of his shirt collar. Do you like it?'

'I like him so I like it,' she said, sounding a bit defensive, I thought.

'Do you really?' I said. 'Go on, be honest.'

Julia looked flustered.

'Would you like him if he got fat? Totally obese? Twenty-three stone?' I said, and I was enjoying myself, marching about the bedroom as I talked.

'Aug, stop it,' she said, and it was as if she couldn't decide whether to laugh, or stay sensible, and I felt determined to win her over.

'Would you like him if all the hair on his head fell out and he was totally bald?'

A little giggle bubbled up inside her.

'You're laughing like you used to!' I said. 'Don't stop!'

'Let's get on with the waxing,' she said.

'Let's get on with the laughing,' I said. 'What do you think Mum's surprise is?'

'I don't know,' said Julia.

'Dad as a Strip-o-gram?' I said. 'He'll come in dancing in a mankini with a rose between his teeth.'

'Stop it,' she said, but the giggle was down there, bubbling, like it used to, and it bubbled right out – she laughed, out loud, couldn't stop.

'You're laughing!' I said. 'It's like old times.'

I grabbed her and hugged her.

'Oh stop it!' she said.

I knew that Julia's *Stop it* meant I like it.

I also knew that there was quite a lot of *Stop it I like it* going on with Diego because we caught them at it on the sofa when they thought we were all out at the A level Choices Evening and we came home early because we didn't have any supplementary questions.

I'd already chosen.

English, French, Spanish and Latin.

And that for me was perfect, *parfait, perfecto* and *perfectus.* I wouldn't have said no to some heavy petting on the side, but as yet there were no offers. I put it down to my lack of meaningful bosoms.

When it came to the moment of the cake-cutting at our sixteenth birthday barbecue, my mother had Diego lined up to bring in a wicker basket, which opened, releasing a volley of white doves, which flew over the blossom trees in our back garden as everyone sang *Happy Birthday to you* and showered us with presents and kisses.

Then my father gave quite a bad and awkward speech, with some jokes he'd got from a book called *After-Dinner Speeches.*

But everyone listened and laughed and clapped at the right time.

Was that a bit self-indulgent, I wondered, asking a load of people to come round to your house to find out from your parents how great you were?

And bring presents.

But actually, it was quite nice, being liked.

En masse.

Parfait

Time seemed to pass very slowly in the hut in the car park, but – with little to demarcate the days – the weeks and months merged with my grief, and before I knew it, I'd been there over a year.

I went to the café every day to give myself some kind of rhythm, but the gypsy man was never there.

Augusta

Diego had bought Julia her own dove for her birthday, which had a ruffle on its head like the letter Z. My father looked anxious, but the dove would be kept at number 13, with Pally's dove, in the creamy dovecote.

So it was only me who was doveless, which rhymes with loveless. And I was that, too.

Julia spent hours training the dove to land on her hand.

She liked to say that it would come to her call.

But that was actually bullshit.

Julia and Diego's love went on growing and his chest-hair went on growing, and the dove learnt to carry messages between their houses, written on rolled paper and placed into a small tube attached to the bird's leg.

'Does that thing have fleas?' my father asked.

'I'm sure it's fine,' said my mother.

'The neighbours must think it's a bit strange,' said my father.

'It's nothing strange at all,' I told my parents. 'This was the usual thing in Persia in the fifth century. And in the twelfth century, all the main cities of Syria and Egypt were linked by pigeon messages. And, in fact, for years, there was a proper pigeon airmail service between Great Barrier Island and Auckland. And India's Police Pigeon service was only stopped in 2002. And also Paul Reuter, who you may have heard of . . .'

'Where do you get all this stuff from?' said my father.

Maybe this was why I didn't get any heavy petting – too much weird information spilling out of my mouth.

Parfait

One day the gypsy man was back.

He was sitting smoking, holding a small lemon tree in an earthen-ware pot, which partly hid his face. He peeped out to one side when he saw me, like you do with babies, and a kind of warmth came over me – I hadn't felt that for a while.

'You never told me your name,' I said.

'Antonio.'

'Parfait.'

We shook hands, and I had the feeling I'd arrived, or I'd fully left, or I wouldn't be this sad forever.

'I thought of you,' he said.

'I thought of you too,' I said.

'Did you keep on reading the verse?'

I nodded.

'And here's a lemon tree!' said Antonio.

'Is it for me?' I asked. 'How did you know I'd be here?'

'They told me you came every day.'

He handed me the tree.

'First you taste the lemon skin,' he said. 'Then you plant one of the pips and let the lemons grow.'

He smiled broadly, then gestured that I should come closer.

'Then you make lemonade! Get it?'

He looked very pleased with, well, everything – himself, me, the lemon tree.

I put the little lemon tree on the table, and I found I couldn't stop smiling.

'So, have you ever actually listened to this *Cante Jondo*?' said Antonio.

'The concerts here for the tourists?' I said.

'No no no,' he said. '*Cante Jondo* should never be organised. Or booked. Or paid for. It must be spontaneous. Just rise up wherever. Wherever there are people and emotions and something in the air, and gypsies – *gitanos* – plenty of wine, plenty of life. *La juerga!*'

I nodded, trying to imagine what that would feel like.

Duende. Flamencura. Razón incorpórea. Juerga.

The untranslatable words were multiplying.

'Where all of us live who came down from Seville,' he said, 'in the streets behind the port, it sometimes happens. I'll take you with me. First, grow your lemons.'

As I walked to work in the security hut, I felt that something was changing in me.

I put the lemon tree on the little stool outside the hut, and I watered it. Then I sat out there on my chair, trying to imagine what Antonio had told me: the tone of the guitar; and the *compás* – the rhythm of the clapping; and the twists and turns of the performer; and the way that when all three came together, spontaneously, wrapping around each other in the dark, *duende* came.

The lemon tree grew new lemons, with skin that was yellow as sunshine.

Augusta

Julia became even more radiantly beautiful.

But her eyes still didn't sparkle.

If you looked carefully.

Which most people didn't seem to.

Her beauty blinded them.

This can happen, I guess.

Marilyn Monroe?

Princess Diana?

My mother had a scrapbook about Princess Diana, and when she died, she made my father plant a white rose called Tranquillity, and for a while there was a little framed photograph – that one of her sitting alone in front of the Taj Mahal – in our flower bed.

'You don't think Julia looks a bit sad?' I said to Diego.

'Sad?' he said.

He took photos of her, with her long blonde hair falling over her shoulders like Rapunzel, and the dove on her hand.

The whole world was in love with her.

The whole world was not in love with me.

But, on the appearance front, things were most definitely looking up. Proper tits, no spots, legs less spindly now, a bit – only a bit – of a bum, skin that kept its tan (my best feature). It wasn't all bad.

Julia spotted that Specsavers were doing cool black framed glasses for £20, so I dispensed with the wire frames and danced down the high street like a *new woman*.

I decided to go to the student hairdressers called Fringe Benefits where Julia's friend, Amy Atkins, who wasn't so dizzy any more, cut my black hair into a blunt fringe and chopped half of its length off. My mother nearly collapsed.

I have a photo of myself, holding a Hallowe'en pumpkin, my eyes gleaming underneath my ruler-straight fringe, ringed by the thick black frames of my glasses, with a very determined look on my face.

I *was* determined.

I was determined that now was my moment.

I was sixteen and three months – and no tongue but my own had ever been inside my mouth.

This was pitiful.

Tragic.

I had to get kissed.

We were off to Tattershall Common Fireworks in Diego's car, and Diego, who was now nineteen, had a friend over from Cádiz called Javier, who told me he worked in the sales office of the massive new holiday complex outside La Higuera, where people could pre-order their apartments before they were built and design them to their own specifications.

Javier was sitting in the back seat with me.

'I know exactly where you mean,' I said in Spanish.

'*Exactamente*,' I said again.

Then I couldn't think what else to say.

But what I could think was how nice his after-shave smelled.

Exactamente.

How much he smelled of.

Well.

Man.

And how very close he was.

To.

Me.

Parfait

'Miss work tonight, Parfait,' said Antonio. 'Come with me.'

'I can't,' I said.

'Find a day job.'

'Where?'

'Why don't you try that massive building site just before you get to La Higuera? They're always looking for people.'

'I don't have any papers.'

'You won't need papers there.'

I smiled.

'So how's your pain?' he said.

'How did you know about my pain?'

'I assume it was a death – or the end of a love affair?'

'How did you know?'

'That's all there is, isn't there? Love and death. Is there anything I can do to help?'

'Keep giving me the napkins,' I said. 'I like to memorise the words. It helps.'

'Read this,' he said.

I folded the napkin and put it in my pocket for later.

I had quite a collection now.

Su grito fue terrible – his cries were terrifying.

Los viejos – the old people, the old ones.

Dicen que se erizaban los cabellos – say it made their hairs stand on end.

Y se abría el azoque de los espejos – and the mercury flowed from the mirrors.

I wrote the words on the dusty window of the hut.

I memorised them.

His cries *were* terrifying.

Too loud for my dreams to contain.

But now, as I walked, the huge *Levante* wind blew down across the hills to my right, bending the palms and causing the sea, to my left, to eddy and surge and swell and spray.

As it did that terrible night.

And perhaps I could ask the wind, which now whipped great sheets of sand from the beach and tore branches from trees, to take Zion's cries.

And perhaps I could ask the God of the wind to take him.

And keep him safe for me.

Perhaps, as I walked into what I hoped was a new beginning, I could try to face what was un-faceable in the thick air of my dark hut.

Zion wasn't coming back.

Whether fish were jumping in the sea or not.

Whether the woman found her engagement ring or not.

Whether Zion spoke to me in dreams at night or not.

And what would he want me to do now?

That young boy whose head was full of hopes and dreams and plans, plans of houses on the beach, and well-paid jobs, and the money to buy plane tickets for Wilfred and Pierre and Douce and Gloria so that we could collect them by car from Seville Airport and party on the sand, and drink Spanish wine, and be happy.

Zion wouldn't have wanted me to go back.

He would have wanted me to stay and live and work and love and dance.

Olé olé olé olé.

I was coming to the building site, and the clouds floated past like boats – the boats I'd told Zion would carry us to Spain, when it was all make-believe.

I threw out my shoulders, like I used to when I was still a boy trying to be a man for Zion, yes, for Zion, I drew myself tall and I asked to see the foreman.

After I'd taken the job, I saw a signpost.

1 kilometre.

Palomar de la Breña.

Paloma means dove, so *palomar* must mean dovehouse, dovecote, I supposed.

I walked down the dusty track to what looked like an old country farmhouse in the natural park – and there was a huge dovecote, with slightly crumbling stone arched walls, over ten metres high, arranged in parallel streets, with thousands and thousands of dove nests, and a central canal where they gathered to bathe and drink.

I sat on the wall, and I thought of the Fischer's lovebird bathing in the stream above the *colline* – its face olive green and coral, its wings bright green, with a golden yellow neck and a purple-ish tail, like a rainbow – and I thought of my little bird mother, and how much my father loved her.

I wondered if I could find love that was as true as theirs.

Augusta

What I was waiting to receive, in the backseat of Diego's car, was not, of course, true love.

Not even fake love.

Not love of any sort.

I was waiting for a tongue, and, being honest, pretty much any tongue would have done, up to a point.

The level crossing gates were down and we sat, Javier and I in the back, with Diego driving and Julia beside him, waiting forever in the traffic jam.

There I was, bra full to bursting, frayed denim skirt, black tights and Converse trainers on which I'd written poetry in green felt-tip pen.

There I was, cusping, which isn't a word, but I needed a new word for this strange breathless bubbling-up feeling – a heady mixture of desire and hope and hormones.

Javier turned around. He suckered his mouth onto mine, and he started digging his tongue down my throat like a drill. Diego turned the radio up. The crossing gates opened.

The train shot past.

Drills, trains, opening gates and fireworks in the distance – it was sexual metaphors galore as we kissed and kissed and kissed, before jumping out of the car and rushing along in the rain to Ooh and Aah at the jewelled sky, me feeling as if some important threshold had been crossed, holding my heart to try to stop it jumping out of my chest.

Paradisiacal!

Parfait

On the building site, I was working alongside dozens of Senegalese men, building a huge holiday complex, a kind of fake new city, which would extend across the fields as far as you could see.

The Senegalese men offered me a bed in their *casa patera, patera* being the name of the little wooden boats they'd come over in. It was – though I didn't like to think it – not much better than a squat.

I took my lemon tree, and I put it in the tiny inner patio where we all kept our trainers so they didn't smell the house out. There were ten beds in a biggish room, a kitchen and a bathroom – and we had to put coins in the metre for hot water. They smiled at me, and they faced Mecca and kneeled on the floor to pray, and everyone took it in turns to clean and make dinner.

The thinnest one, who called himself Carlos, offered me his phone.

'I've got a discount to Africa – you're welcome to use it,' he said.

But there was nobody I wanted to phone.

It was too painful.

The thought of what I might say.

The first night, I couldn't sleep with the strangeness of having so many unknown human bodies around me, and with the noises bodies make and the smell of too many men in too small a space.

The second night wasn't much better.

On the third, I said goodnight to the Senegalese men and set off along the main road to Tarifa to see if I could find Antonio.

Or maybe, the thought came to me, to see if I could meet a Spanish girl down where he lived, where there was *duende* and *flamencura* and *juerga* and all those other untranslatable words.

Perhaps there, behind the port, with Antonio's friends, I would find that girl I was always dreaming of, the one who I hoped was dreaming of me.

Augusta

Julia found me taking my old cream book from under my mattress.

So I had to come clean about the pedlar man.

'Start looking from the outside in,' I said, and I let her digest the illustration, from the ridged bark of the trees, the tiny segmented bodies of the caterpillars in graduated shades of green, and then, nervously to the centre, to the majestic gypsy caravan, too beautiful to look at – with the butterflies whose markings and names I knew off by heart: the Adonis Blue, the ragged orange-black Comma, the luminous Green Hairstreak and the purple-eyed Peacock, flashing red. And beyond the caravan, the wide-open horizon.

It made me long for something so much it ached.

Parfait

Antonio was at the café.

'Will it be happening tonight?' I said.

'You never know,' said Antonio. 'But we'll head down there around midnight.'

I wandered around Tarifa. I found an art shop and stared at the paints and brushes and canvases.

When midnight came, I set off, quite nervous, with Antonio, down to the dark streets, where men were sitting on ripped armchairs, passing round wine.

'You know the music is not only music,' a man with a ponytail and a hat said to me, offering me the bottle, not really looking at me.

I nodded.

'*Duende* can be destroyed in a second,' said a tattooed man with a white vest who was sitting alone on a sofa with a guitar beside him taking up the rest of the space as if it were his pet dog.

'*Como la vida*,' I said. 'Like life.'

When I said this, the hat-man with the ponytail moved to a stool over in the corner, and he closed his eyes, and he opened his mouth, and he started to sing, and his voice split up into strands, fraying, as if there was blood on his vocal cords, or in his heart. The man in the vest picked up his guitar, which turned out, indeed, to be a living thing, and a woman appeared from behind the curtain of a doorway, with a black shawl around her shoulders, holding her skirt. She started to dance.

'Ay!' she said, a single stifled cry. 'Ay!'

People came out of doorways saying, 'Ay!'

I felt a lifetime of longing.

Actual physical longing.

Which I didn't know I had inside me.

It just came out.

The man squeezed his arms to his sides as if he were holding in something utterly uncontainable. The dancers' eyes locked. Their feet slammed against the stone.

I couldn't work out what I felt.

Other than terrified.

Of what they chose not to hide.

Things that were inside me too, hidden.

Inside us all, I assume, if we dare let ourselves feel them.

And then the song.

El querer quita sentido – I knew this verse, I had it on one of my napkins – love makes you lose your mind.

Lo digo por experiencia – I say this from experience.

The man with the ponytail went on singing, with his eyes tightly closed.

Porque a mi me ha sucedido – because it has happened to me.

Augusta

I have the old book on a shelf inside the caravan.

It's open at that page, the page where Julia's eyes fell.

I read her the poem aloud.

'Which verse do you like?' I asked her.

'The one where he gets himself a wife and a baby,' she said, smiling.

'I find that a bit too tidy,' I said, 'and I wonder if it's racist to talk about a *baby brown*. Though, if I'm honest, I think black babies are cuter than white ones, don't you?'

'They're all cute,' she said. 'Even the ugly ones.'

His caravan has windows, too,
And a chimney of tin, that the smoke comes through;
He has a wife, with a baby brown,
And they go riding from town to town!

'I'd like to go riding from town to town,' I said. 'I love the thought of never settling anywhere, always being on the move, and I guess I wouldn't mind a brown baby.'

'I like the thought of getting married, building a home and making it beautiful,' said Julia. 'So does that mean we'll never see each other, when we're adults?'

'Not if you stay here in Hedley Green,' I said. 'Because by then I will be travelling through Burundi in a gypsy caravan or taking my holiday on a dhow in Zanzibar or riding across the Sahara Desert on a camel.'

'Could you maybe come and visit me sometimes in Hedley Green?' said Julia.

'Don't you want to be extraordinary?' I said. 'To have an extraordinary life?'

'I'm happy to be ordinary,' said Julia.

'You wouldn't seriously stay here?' I said. 'What do you like about here?'

'It's home,' said Julia.

'Not my home,' I said. 'You're my home.'

'But I won't be forever. We'll both marry different men and live different lives,' said Julia. 'You spend the first part of life binding yourselves together and the second tearing yourselves apart. It's like there's something wrong with the system.'

Parfait

I went back night after night.

I couldn't stop myself.

It consumed me.

Paco jabbed my arm and held his own heart.

'*Cante Jondo* is for when you're beyond consolation. You know that.'

I felt my eyes fill with tears.

'I do know that,' I said, and I felt the ache of my loss – of all my losses – inside me, as if all my organs were bursting.

'It's like the lament of the land that can never be sky,' said Paco.

'Yes,' I said, and I let the words into me without trying to make sense of them because this was what I was learning. That making sense isn't everything. Perhaps this was disembodied reasoning. *Razón incorpórea*.

It was a windy night, and Paco began to sing with the gusts coming in from the sea, and the man in the vest took his guitar, and a woman, a new woman I hadn't seen before, came from a doorway, and a man rose from a chair to dance with her.

As they pursued each other, in the dance, they were somehow more alive than anyone else alive on the planet, that's what it seemed to me. These dancers could burst through walls, I thought, walk over water, through fire. As they danced, they were bound together as if by an invisible thread, holding them as they tried to tear apart.

Then it rose up, *duende*, it was here, and everyone rose up together, as if the whole earth was rising up from its core, as if the dead were rising from graves, the dead and the not yet born.

Paco sang:

'*If anyone doubts the love I have for you.*
Take this knife and open my heart.'

I found that I was starting to move, and with my body I was speaking, and this was new to me, that you could say things with your body – *If anyone doubts the love I have for you* – for you, Zion, wherever you are at sea, at sea, at sea, I am at sea but I am dancing because we said we would – *take this knife and open my heart.*

There seemed to be people emerging from every door, up the street, down the street, and all you had to do was let go and become part of the pattern, as if you were a tiny jewel in a kaleidoscope, being turned by a power on the outside.

I let go.

Augusta

Julia and Diego would go to parties together and dance and kiss in the corner and park Diego's car in the car park at the bottom of Old John Brown's Hill to have sex. Or 'make love' as Julia liked to call it.

'I'm not sure love is something you can make,' I said. 'Like in Craft Club.'

And Julia said, 'Oh, Augusta!'

She said she'd done it quite a lot of times now, but it was still a mystery to her. Sometimes it made her feel happy and sometimes it made her feel sad, but she had nothing to be sad about.

'Is that true?' I said.

'Well, perhaps we all have things to feel sad about,' she said.

'Please tell me the things that are making you sad, Julia,' I said. 'Is it that you grew up too quickly once you started going out with Diego? Is it that your childhood ended too fast?'

'I don't know,' she said.

'Something happened in Spain,' I said.

'We just had breakfast on the beach,' she said, 'and Dad was in quite a weird mood.'

'Dad's always in quite a weird mood,' I said.

'Not when he's at the shop,' she said. 'That's where he's his happiest. I guess we all have different dreams for our lives.'

'P-lease!' I said. 'Please don't tell me that when he was our age, his

174

dream was to own a shop selling school uniform. Because if that's true, it is *sad sad sad.*'

'Or if it's true, he's the luckiest man alive – because his dream came true. Maybe small dreams are better than big ones.'

'I like making up daydreams where I have sex with Javier on the beach at La Higuera, in the dunes, or down at our special spot,' I said. 'Do you think that's normal?'

'Probably,' she said. 'But *the thing is,* Aug . . .'

'I know Javier doesn't like me,' I said. 'You don't have to tell me. It makes no difference to the dreams. I don't like him either.'

She looked sad.

The thing is what?

Why didn't I let her finish?

'Do you like sex?' I said.

'Sex is quite strange,' said Julia.

'Does it feel as though you turn into one person while you're doing it?' I said. 'Like they told us at youth club.'

'I never thought about it,' she said.

'And when you come apart, does it hurt?'

'Not really.'

'Does it make a kind suction noise?' I said. 'Like this?'

I stuck my finger in my cheek.

'Augusta!' said Julia.

'I just wondered,' I said.

'Sex isn't really something you can talk about.'

'Is that because I haven't done it yet?' I said.

'Well, there are some things you have to experience to know how they feel.'

'But don't we all have experiences all the time that are only ours. None of us can ever imagine being someone else. Isn't that why being human is lonely? Because however many words there are in a language, they never express the actual thing, the actual feeling, the actual being ourselves?'

'You're probably right,' said Julia, and the skin on her face changed, gained a strange bumpy texture, and tiny hairs stood up all over her cheeks.

'Are you OK?' I said. 'What other experiences have you had that are making you lonely?'

'I've gone on the pill,' she said. 'But I still make Diego wear a condom. For double protection. And sometimes I feel bad for all those little half-babies slopping about at the bottom of the condom. Little dead tadpoles, which served no purpose at all. They lost a race. And that was it.'

Parfait

'When we fall down,' my father used to say, 'we get up again and keep running. Run with perseverance the race marked out for you.'

That was what I thought when the Senegalese men told me the news.

One day, we were paid.

The next day, we were unemployed.

The building boom was over.

The *crisis* had come.

Across Spain, half-built *urbanizaciones* lay like giant skeletons, flailing over hills and plateaux.

In La Higuera, people left the complex overnight, abandoning cement mixers and stacks of paving slabs and bathtubs, even a coach that hadn't yet been fitted for its luxury tourist excursions.

A perimeter fence was built around the grey bones of the houses, which stood in the wind, with rusting wires sticking out of them, gaping doorways, dark spaces for windows – and the Senegalese men, who'd lost their earnings, filled shopping trolleys with pipes and refrigerators, patio chairs and iron fencing, to sell on.

'*Inshallah,*' said Carlos. 'Whatever God wants.'

I walked around the building site, trying to work out what to do. Absent-mindedly, I tried the door of the coach that had been abandoned, and it opened.

It opened!

The keys were dangling from the ignition.

I set to work. I built partitions, a little kitchen, a bedroom with a view out of the large back picture window.

A home, I thought.

Zion, I said aloud, I've got myself a home.

Get up and keep running, I thought.

Augusta

I used to love autumn, the way it begins mellow and warm, its sleepy wasps drunk on last fruit. I read *The Lotos-Eaters* to Julia on our picnic on the first day of October by the stream on Tattershall Common, when we'd drunk too much cider. I would soon be leaving her for Durham, and we were hanging on to each other.

The Lotos-Eaters, I told Julia, was inspired by a visit that the poet, Alfred Tennyson, made with his friend, Arthur Hallam, to the Spanish mountains in 1829.

'Our Spain, Julia, where we shall go again, the two of us. Let's go to the mountains next time. The Pyrenees maybe. Or the Sierra Nevada.'

I read aloud:

'And deep-asleep he seem'd, yet all awake,
And music in his ears his beating heart did make.'

We drank more cider.

And read more poetry.

'Let us alone. Time driveth onward fast.'

More cider.

Leaves were starting to fall.

Julia waded through the stream, glugging cider from the bottle, drawing her glass through the water where so many times we'd caught minnows and sticklebacks and tiddlers with our nets.

I sat on the bank, watching her.

The dipping sun caught the arched flecks of spray, caught the shapes of leaves, caught the outline of her hair, made it fuzzy, made her golden-haloed.

'I love you too much, Julia,' I said. 'I can't imagine life without you.'

'It will feel so strange when you're not here,' she said, coming to sit beside me.

'I'll be lost without you,' I said, holding her hand.

'Course you won't.'

She picked up a double conker with her other hand, still wrapped and spiky, she gave it to me and I put it in my pocket.

'Are you nervous?' she said.

'Terrified. Exhilarated. Both.'

More cider.

More cider.

'Promise you'll stay in touch?' said Julia.

'Promise.'

'We've made lots of promises to each other, Diego and I,' said Julia, and I looked down at her feet in the stream, so white in the water, with perfect red nails.

'I'm terrified of promises,' I said. 'What if you can't keep them?'

'You just do keep them,' said Julia, and she drew up her knees, and rested her chin on them, and her pretty feet dripped water.

'What if you make a bad promise?' I said. 'It wouldn't be right to keep a bad promise.'

'Like what?'

She turned to look at me, with that expression she used to get, as if she couldn't believe the stuff that came out of my mouth.

'Ian says his mum stays with his dad even though he beats her up. Because she made a promise when she married him,' I said.

'Is that why he wants to become a Druid?' said Julia.

I shrugged my shoulders.

'You're not getting engaged, Julia, are you?' I said. 'We're so young.'

'Not yet,' she said, and she smiled. 'We'll wait a bit.'

'I feel a million miles from doing that,' I said.

'You haven't got a boyfriend,' said Julia. 'Once it's a person, it's different.'

'What if you get bored of him?' I asked.

'You don't if you promised not to,' said Julia.

'But what if you make the promise and then you do get bored?'

'Then you act like you haven't,' said Julia.

'Which is lying.'

'Well then, you don't let yourself.'

'What if he gets boring?'

'He won't because you love him.'

'But what if he does?'

'You don't think about it.'

'That's suppressing the truth.'

'Oh, Aug,' said Julia, groaning at me and poking me in the upper arm. 'You're like a persistent wasp. Let's have some more cider.'

We went back to the rug and opened two new bottles and glugged the cider down.

'I will always love you, Aug,' said Julia.

She really was starting to slur her words, as, I realised, listening to myself, was I.

'I will always love you too,' I said, slurrily.

'Look at you making promises!' said Julia. 'Once you're thinking of a real person, you see, it's all much easier.'

'But I will,' I said.

'I will too,' Julia said. 'Course I'll always love you.'

'Shall we have rings?' I said.

'Oh, any excuse for jewellery!' she said, except her j slightly collapsed into a sh sound.

'And we'll still have no secrets, won't we, from each other?' I said. Shewellery and shecrets.

Julia was twirling off in the wind, with autumn leaves falling around her, and her secret was twirling with her, but however fast she turned, she was never able to dislodge it.

Parfait

I drove the coach to a scrap of scrubland outside Tarifa.

I went down to the art shop, and I bought paints and brushes and an easel, a big sketch pad, different sized canvases.

I set myself up outside the coach, amongst the lorries, my easel in the sand, with a stone stuffed under to keep it even, and I took the small canvas. I painted a man sitting on a rock as the sea came in. The holey rock was sticking out of a sheen of water, with a slight mist across it, and the man was looking out to the horizon, biting the skin of a green lemon.

On the next canvas, I painted a mirror, and inside the mirror was the square where we danced, with the old sofas, and Paco in his hat, and beyond and behind was the port. The mirror was dissolving into streams of mercury.

Then, on the largest canvas, I painted a girl who could have been my sister, Gloria. The skirt of her dress was made of satin ribbons in rainbow colours, and as she danced, turning in circles, faster, faster, the different colours flew out of the ribbons like paint, splashing the white walls around her, making unlikely shapes like countries that don't exist. As I went on painting, her dark plaited hair started releasing brown paint, as she twirled, and then the paint shot out of the skin on her arms, and the gold of her earrings.

Augusta

'I'll tell you a secret,' I called after Julia as she twirled. 'I'd rather have a gypsy caravan than a husband.'

'If I get rich,' she called, 'I'll buy you one like the pedlar man's, and you can go travelling from town to town.'

'Is the pedlar man thrown in?'

'I thought you didn't want the husband.'

'Let's have some more cider.'

On we went into a bleary evening in our bedroom looking at old photo albums, which were losing their stickiness so that photos flew out onto the floor as we turned the pages. We lay on our fronts on the carpet, our legs kicking into each other's legs, with the ease of familiar flesh, and with cider headaches, and a lingering hum of dread about our separation – mixed, for me, with the gorgeous anticipation of finally getting away from Willow Crescent. From my father. From my mother.

My mother opened the door and took photos of us. Double-conkered, legs entwined, and me jumpy with nerves and excitement.

My mother was always crying in the weeks before I left for Durham.

'I can't believe it's all over,' she kept saying.

'What's all over?' I said.

'Us,' she said. 'This.'

She gestured around her at the walls and the floor and the airer which was suspended over the boiler, where our knickers hung in a tidy row, stretched taut, as she liked them.

'Will you miss my knickers?' I said, smiling.

'You'll buy new ones in Durham,' said my mother, 'and I won't be able to recognise them.'

She lurched for the back door and went outside.

'Is she crying?' I said to Julia.

'It will be so strange without you,' she said.

'Do you remember we used to have those pants with the days of the week on?' I said to Julia. 'And Mum used to get in a total stress when I wore Tuesday on Friday.'

'You loved wearing Tuesday on Friday,' said Julia. 'I never understood why.'

I kept finding my mother staring at herself in the mirror in the days before I went to Durham.

'What are you looking at?' I said.

'The future,' she said. 'I'm starting to look like my mother. I can see wrinkles coming in the same places she has them.'

My mother's bathroom mirror fell off the wall, and she brought it to us, as if it meant something.

'Bad luck,' she said. 'Seven years of it. Until 2015.'

'That's all nonsense,' I replied.

'It's all breaking up,' she said.

'We'll make a mosaic,' said Julia.

I never knew how to comfort my mother, but Julia did.

She tried to see the future in the mirror, and the mirror cracked.

I'm really not superstitious – I happily walk under ladders, and I don't touch wood or throw salt over my shoulder – but the future, the seven years that would take us to 2015, was coming at us like a train.

Yes, like a train.

The future was a train.

And the train could not be stopped.

* * *

Autumn strode onwards, browning the leaves, loosening them, as I too was being loosened.

'They'd never cope with us both leaving at once,' said Julia, who was going to train to be what was apparently called an Early Years Practitioner, which my mother called a nursery nurse.

She would go to a local college, living at home, in our half-empty bedroom, with my tightly made bed which would remain tightly made for weeks at a time.

I felt guilty, as usual, but nothing would have made me stay in Willow Crescent. I was pawing at the ground.

I was making my way down the Durham University reading list. I was reading *El Cid* and *Don Quijote*, Unamuno and Calderón, St John of the Cross, Teresa of Ávila, Isabel Allende, Gabriel García Márquez, Federico García Lorca.

Crickets, frogs and the lurking night . . .

Like the garden at the back of the house in La Higuera, where I once lay dreaming on the Moroccan bed.

That Moroccan bed.

I read the line to Julia to see if it made her think of the Spanish garden. She said it didn't.

Lorca hypnotised me – I read him in Spanish, I read him in English, I was back in the South of Spain, I was surrounded by blood and knives and roses, drowning in his symbols – life like running water, death, a river stopped.

Parfait

Antonio visited me at my coach in the scrubby car park, and he brought Paco with him, in his hat, with a book of poetry, and Luis, in his vest with his tattoos on display all down his arms – roses and knives and drops of blood, or were they tears?

'Lorca understood us,' said Paco, opening his book. 'Love, longing and death. He got it. And they killed him for it. Antonio says there's a lot of killing in your country – is that right?'

'Oh there is,' I said. 'Far too much killing. But enough of that. Won't you read me a poem?'

> *'The guitar weeps . . .*
> *like water weeps,*
> *like wind weeps*
> *over snow.*
> *It cannot be silenced.*
> *It weeps for things*
> *far away . . .*
> *Evening without morning,*
> *the first bird dead*
> *on the branch.'*

I started to paint.

I painted the Fischer's lovebird, rainbow-feathered, dead by the stream – and Luis picked up his guitar, and Antonio went on smoking.

Sometimes when they came, Paco sang, but mainly he read, and his voice painted Lorca's poems in my mind.

So vivid, so rich with colour.

I'd never experienced words as alive as these.

I painted twilight trembling in the bulrushes at the river's edge, and a flock of captive birds moving their long tails in the shadows, and fields of olive trees opening and closing between the hills like a fan.

Augusta

'In Lorca's poems, he talks about a pinned butterfly pondering its flight. If you think about it, it makes you feel kind of dizzy,' I said to Julia.

'I hate pinned butterflies in glass cases.'

'Do you think that's what we all are?' I said. 'Pinned butterflies who think we can fly?'

'I don't know what you mean,' said Julia, 'and I'm not sure thinking too much is good for people. It sends them a bit crazy. Stop thinking so much, Aug. Be happy.'

'In Lorca's plays, there's this character who's supposed to be Death. Listen, I'll translate. *I'm coming, freezing my way through walls and through windows! Slice open your roofs and slice open your hearts to warm me up!*'

'I think it's horrible,' said Julia. 'I hate the sound of Lorca.'

'Listen to this one!' I said to Julia. 'This one isn't horrible. Doesn't this make you think of the road to La Higuera? The olive fields opening and closing like a fan?'

'Aug,' she said. 'Can you stop reading bits out? They really don't mean anything to me.'

Parfait

It was Paco who persuaded me to try to sell my paintings to the art gallery in the old town.

'They might not be able to feel the emotions in them like you can,' I said, because I was nervous. 'We all see things differently.'

The paintings were part of our secret life together. The thought of exposing them to other people, the thought of assuming people might pay money for them, that was something altogether different.

'What's the worst that could happen?' said Paco. 'The gallery doesn't take them. Life goes on.'

'But I'd feel such a fool,' I said.

'We've told you they're beautiful,' said Paco. 'Why won't you trust us?'

So, in the end, we walked together — or perhaps more accurately they walked me — through the medieval stone arch, down the cobbled streets of the old town, and I forced myself, sweating with nerves, after several false starts, to open the door of the gallery.

I stood tall, I threw out my shoulders and I shook my head so that I could feel my plaits on my cheeks like Sami Terre.

I introduced myself, smiling, tripping over my Spanish words.

The thin man who owned the gallery, who was wearing a buttoned-up white shirt with a kind of black shoe-lace tie, shook my hand.

He asked to see the paintings.

Antonio, Paco and Luis were waiting outside the door with the canvases.

I nodded at them, and they burst in.

The gallery owner eyed them with some suspicion.

Antonio talked too much.

I sweated.

Luis looked a bit violent in his vest.

Paco kept saying, 'The paintings were inspired by the poetry of Lorca, and by *Cante Jondo*. Did he say?'

'I'll take them all,' said the gallery owner, without asking to see my documents, without asking me anything at all.

He called me over.

'This one,' he said, pointing to the man chewing lemon skin, looking out over the sea. 'What does it mean?'

'What do you think it means?' I said.

'Loss,' said the man. 'The pain of it.'

I nodded.

'Yours?' said the man.

'Everyone's,' I said.

'This one, the girl with the ribbons?'

'It's everything we feel underneath,' I said, 'coming out.'

The man nodded.

As I turned, I caught sight of the girl's long neck and her dignified face, and she was singing Hosanna, I could hear her.

And I went back.

'On second thoughts, I'm going to keep the dancer with the ribbon skirt,' I said. 'She's my sister. And.'

I stopped.

'It doesn't matter,' I said.

The man handed me back the canvas.

As we walked back to the coach, Antonio said, 'Parfait, it's time to call Víctor. The poor man must think you're dead. You need to tell him about your paintings, how they're going to sell them in the gallery.

Then you need to tell him what happened to Zion, and find out how the rest of them are.'

'Is it really you?' Víctor asked me.

His voice trembled.

The wind blew up in my heart.

'You're alive,' he said, and his voice sounded strangled. 'You're alive.'

'Víctor,' I said, my heart beating. 'Zion didn't make it. I didn't know how to tell you.'

Víctor said nothing, and it made me hold my breath and clench my fingers.

'It was my fault,' I said. 'Your friend told us it was too windy to cross.'

'He never told me,' said Víctor. 'He didn't return my calls.'

Antonio was hooking smoke rings on a stick, trying to catch them before they disappeared, and Paco and Luis were looking at the ground, and I felt the first tear running down my cheek.

'Wilfred!' called Víctor. 'Come over here! Parfait's alive!'

Then something quite unexpected happened.

Wilfred opened his mouth.

He said, loudly, 'My brother!'

I heard it down the phone, and I yelled out, 'Wilfred!'

I hadn't heard his voice in so long I'd forgotten the texture of it.

The second tear came, the third, the fourth, I was wiping my cheek with the back of my hand.

'Put him on,' I said.

Wilfred said down the phone, 'My brother!'

The best words.

My brother.

And the worst.

My brother.

Then nothing else.

Only his breathing.

Víctor came back on.

'Also, Víctor,' I said, now a bit bashful. 'I sold some paintings to an art gallery in Tarifa.'

Now it was Víctor's turn to yell at me.

'Parfait,' he said, when he'd stopped yelling. 'Peace is on its way. This time, it's going to happen. The ceasefire's holding. The government soldiers and the rebels are working together. Our dreams are coming true.'

Augusta

It was time for me to leave home. Julia and I went to Claire's Accessories on the high street and bought each other cheap silver rings, in double, and A and J initials, and hung them on chains around our necks, and I felt warm inside, and then cold at the thought of being without her.

We all drove up the A1, with my mother handing out sandwiches which tasted of Tupperware, and my father saying, 'Put your lid underneath. Or the crumbs'll go everywhere.'

We queued for keys and student cards and gowns, with my mother and father anxious to be getting onto the A1 and back to Willow Crescent.

Julia kept holding my arm, and saying, 'It feels so far away.'

The three of them drove away from Hild and Bede College, leaving me on the black tarmac, wearing my A and J necklace, waving with one hand, feeling the shape of two conkers in my pocket with my other. Julia was looking the other way. They drove down the A1 in silence, Julia told me later, and this made me wonder if perhaps my mother and father would miss me, as I'd always suspected they wouldn't. That perhaps they would be sad to be without me.

When their car had disappeared out of sight, I sat at my desk, switching the silver desk light on and off and turning the pages of my dictionary – A-B-C-D.

'Come on Augusta,' I said aloud, and I didn't recognise my own voice, here in my little room at the end of the corridor, at the top of the stairs.

I got up from the desk chair and looked out of the window at a small patch of grass with nothing and nobody on it.

A room with *one bed* in it.

Would I ever get used to that?

I opened my door.

Then I closed it again.

I went back to my dictionary.

Dingle – a deep wooded valley.

Dingoes; dining cars; dinner jackets, with which I would become accustomed at Durham; dioestrus, a period of sexual inactivity, that is, my whole life; and on to Diogenes, the Greek philosopher who highlighted the need for natural, uninhibited behaviour regardless of social conventions; and diogenite, which was a stony meteorite.

Which would I go for? Who would I be? Would I follow Diogenes into wild self-expression at Durham University or continue my journey as a stony meteorite?

Someone put some music on in the next-door room, and I couldn't hear anything except the beat. I wondered what my neighbour looked like and what he or she was doing the other side of the thin wall.

I opened the cupboard door and swapped my T-shirts with my jumpers because you wore T-shirts more, so, logically, they should be on the middle shelf – and more accessible.

I sat back down and picked up one of my Converse trainers and wrote *Shit-scared* in green pen. Because I could. Because my mother couldn't tell me not to swear.

Then I wondered if I really wanted to walk around with Shit on my shoe. So I coloured Shit inside a green rectangle.

And it looked. Well. Shit. Then I felt really cold.

And I remembered everyone had said how freezing it would be in Durham, and I swapped the T-shirts and jumpers back, because, actually, in a place like Durham, which is practically in Scotland, you want to have your jumpers on the middle shelf, where you can get your hands on them.

I looked at the big grey jumper I'd bought when we went to a shop in Wales called Shelley's Sheep. My mother tried to buy me one of those awful ones with rows of white sheep on, and one black sheep, third row down.

No, I chose something that was made in the Andean mountains. I pulled it out of my newly folded Durham cupboard, which smelled of bleach. Pachamama it said on the label. The fertility goddess who causes earthquakes in the Andes.

I'd like to cause an earthquake, I thought, just one, just once, inside a gorgeous man, of which there might be a few, behind all these brown doors, waiting to explode at the sight of me.

I pulled on the huge grey jumper with knitted Aztec symbols on the back in cream.

I looked at my watch.

One hour until the drinks.

I read the pink sheet again.

6.30 pm. Drinks with the academic staff.

I circled *6.30 pm* with the green felt-tip pen and drew flowers around the academic staff, still feeling cold.

I needed to pee but I wasn't sure I wanted to go out into the corridor, or into the communal bathrooms, where I would meet somebody.

At six o'clock, I pulled off my Andean jumper and pulled on a black dress I'd bought in Hedley Green Oxfam (where I loved, to my mother's horror, to shop).

I looked at my watch.

Five past.

I put on some bright red lipstick.

I wouldn't have worn it in Hedley Green because everyone would have said, 'Look at you in your bright red lipstick,' as if I was still five years old and I'd have felt embarrassed. But presumably here they would see me as a person who wore bright red lipstick.

Ten past.

I added another coat of mascara.

Quarter past.

Time can be very slow.

Eventually it was twenty-five past – and I grabbed my coat and key and lurched onto the landing and down the stairs.

Whilst going down the stairs, a girl came up behind me and said, 'I'm Laura,' and then burst out laughing, grabbing my arm and walking with me.

She had her auburn hair in a high ponytail, rucking up at each side, where she'd arranged a row of metal grips, and she was wearing a velvet dress in pine green. She had perfume on that smelled slightly of toilet freshener.

It was a relief to walk into the rather sombre room with Laura. There were lots of people in it, but it was extremely quiet. The new students walked about stiffly talking to the academic staff and sipping wine, and we left little trails of crumbling cheese straws behind us.

After an hour or so, all the lecturers walked out and a very tall boy came in, wearing a red T-shirt saying WELCOME across his chest, holding his left arm across his front and putting his hand under his right bicep so that it bulged outwards. He was surrounded by others in the same red T-shirts saying WELCOME, and he said, 'Let's all go to the bar!'

The red T-shirt people gathered, talking loudly to each other, addressing the barman (also loudly) as Dave or Mate. The non-red-T-shirt people sat in our awkward circle, in our awkward clothes, saying, over and over, 'What did you do for A level?' Occasionally, one of the red-T-shirt people came over and said, 'How's it going?' and then went back to their friends and proceeded to get completely off their faces on cheap pints of beer and vodka shots.

Then a boy arrived wearing a Barbour jacket and a dotty cravat, with blond hair, which flopped over his face at one side.

'Olly Macintosh,' he said. 'I missed the drinks thing. How was it?'

He had a hint of a lisp, which he seemed to know made him cute.

People murmured, 'OK.'

'Great to meet you all,' he said. 'Who wants a drink?'

He went up to the bar and returned with exactly what we'd ordered. Then he said, 'If you were a character in *Winnie the Pooh*, which would you be?'

I wasn't expecting him to say that.

Everyone looked a bit surprised, and went on sipping their drinks in silence. I was sitting next to him, so close that the wax smell of his jacket was getting up my nose, and I was praying in my head that he would start the questioning to his right, so that I, on his left, could answer last.

And, please God, not first.

Because my mind had gone blank and the only character I could remember in *Winnie the Pooh* was Winnie the Pooh himself – wearing a red T-shirt and nothing else. I remembered the day I went swimming with Barbara Cook and lost my pants. Then I thought about all the fantasy sex I'd had with Javier from Cádiz, and how I was probably the only one here who had never managed to lose their pants in real life. And how from now on I was going to be a total Pachamama.

A girl with a big beak-ish nose to the right of Olly Macintosh said, 'I'm Owl. I want to stay on and do a PhD.'

This seemed quite an odd thing to say when she hadn't even tried out her first lecture.

A sporty boy with over-curly hair, who turned out to be called Tom Jones (no relation to the singer) said, 'Tigger', and then he felt obliged to be a bit more energetic after that. He started leaping up shaking hands with everyone and offering to buy them drinks.

Laura, swaying her auburn ponytail and continuing to neigh with laughter, said, 'I'll be Tigger too.'

The question was getting nearer to me, and I realised that I still didn't have an answer, and anyway I didn't want to label myself when I'd just got away from ugly, clever and odd in Hedley Green, and had started wearing red lipstick. I suddenly had a rush of characters – Piglet, Kanga, Roo, Rabbit – but couldn't think of one who would wear red lipstick or cause earthquakes in young men.

'What about you?' said Olly Macintosh.

'I'm none of them,' I said.

Everybody stared at me and a serious pale boy who crossed his legs like a girl, which might be offensive to both sexes, said, 'Every possible human character is said to be represented in those books.'

'That's ridiculous,' I said. 'The world has 6.7 billion people in it.'

'But not 6.7 billion character types,' said the pale boy, who never smiled, and who had the straightest parting I'd ever seen.

'I shall be a Heffalump,' I said.

'And why is that?' said Olly Macintosh.

'Because I like blurry edges,' I said. 'I don't want to be typecast, and perhaps I don't know exactly who I am yet. I can't yet conceive of myself.'

Tom and Laura laughed – in time with each other.

The pale boy sighed.

I knew I was weird, but it was a weird I was starting to like now I had black-framed glasses and a blunt fringe and red lipstick and written-on Converse trainers with a mysterious blotchy green rectangle on the left-hand shoe.

Olly Macintosh took off his Barbour in a big waft of wax, and the questioning was over. Then he took off his dotty cravat and gave it to me, saying, 'Winning answer' rather seriously.

I had somehow arrived. It was going to be OK at Durham University. I felt pretty – now I wasn't the ugly one. I held the dotty cravat limply in my hand and didn't know at all what to do with it. In a burst of confidence, I tied it around my wrist. Then I wondered if that looked absurd, or as if I was in love with Olly Macintosh, which

I wasn't yet, and I took it off again, and I held it in my left hand, a little away from me, and drank a glass of wine with my right.

When I got back to my room, it was quite a relief to be reunited with my dictionary – *dionysiac*, relating to the sensual, spontaneous and emotional aspects of human nature, which were the aspects of myself I needed to develop.

I leafed through *D* and went on to *E*, recovering from the shock of being surrounded by so many new people. The words had stopped lurching though I was possibly lurching a bit from all the drink.

It was very quiet in my single room.

But I felt calm.

Expansive even.

Expectant.

Experimental.

Explosive.

Then I must have fallen asleep.

A few weeks later, I had sex with Olly Macintosh when we went camping for the weekend.

He had a strange kind of tent with a transparent rectangle in the roof, and when it happened, I was looking at the stars. He made love to me and I made love to him and the voice that always narrated inside my head, commenting, criticising, wondering, finding words, asking questions, that voice which never stopped, stopped.

It was like I was properly in the present, for the first time ever – and the minute it was over, I wanted to do it again, and again.

You see, it turned out that I *was* Pachamama. It shocked me to find that I, the child who wouldn't be touched, just couldn't get enough of it. It was like feeling thirsty all the time. I tried not to think about it. It made me feel odd.

Soon after we had sex, Olly and I began to read the dictionary together, and it wasn't long after that that we started keeping our underwear in each other's drawers, mixed up together, for convenience on overnight stays. My mother was right: some of that underwear she would not have recognised, or indeed recommended.

I watched the leaves fall into the River Wear, saw the towered cathedral rise out of burnished trees and I walked, hand in hand with Olly Macintosh over the cobbles, wrapped in scarves and coats – and desire.

Olly started to call me Dragonfly – because my mind flitted about in so many directions, he told me.

Every time he said it, I felt warm.

I did think of Julia in Hedley Green.

But not enough.

I assumed I'd go home for the holidays and everything would be the same.

I texted her.

But not enough.

I phoned her.

But not enough.

Olly Macintosh and I bought sparklers and wrote messages on the air to each other. I was now more obsessed than ever with the poetry of Federico García Lorca, and on Hallowe'en, we sat in a candlelit bath together drinking champagne, and I read *Poeta en Nueva York* to him in a ghostly voice.

> '*I realised that I'd been murdered.*
> *They made their way through cafés and graveyards and churches . . .*
> *Still they didn't find me.*
> *They didn't find me?*
> *No.*
> *They never found me.*'

November froze our breath, and we puffed words at each other, Olly Macintosh and I, always talking, forever talking and touching, we couldn't get enough of each other, we were a bottomless pit.

I watched the fireworks explode over the cathedral towers and hardly thought once of Tattershall Common. The shop windows filled with Christmas. We huddled under rugs drinking mugs of hot chocolate outside; we woke together, legs entwined, in Olly's bed, to see the morning dawn frosted white; we studied together, two at a desk.

I had re-twinned myself – and I felt as if I was tearing in two when Olly and I said goodbye on the tarmac outside our halls with my father's engine still running.

'Any news in Hedley Green?' I asked my father, sitting in the passenger seat, driving down the A1, just he and I.

'A flock of blinking parrots,' said my father. 'Causing total havoc. Foreign birds. Over-running the native species. Like grey squirrels.'

'Any other news?'

'Same old same old,' said my father.

'I hate that expression,' I said.

I noticed that my father was blushing, and I looked at his white hands, with the steering wheel running through them, making clock times, face set forward.

'Sorry,' I said.

He didn't answer.

'I find it hard to drive and talk,' he said. 'I can't concentrate.'

'OK,' I said.

And we drove in silence.

We stopped off at a service station, which had gold Christmas decorations in drooping loops along the corridor, and he got out the two Tupperware boxes we'd always had. My whole life. With the white lids. And our surname.

HOPE.

That's what it said across each lid.

HOPE HOPE.

'Cheese or ham?' said my father.

I don't know why, but I felt like getting up and holding him in my arms, up close, chest to chest.

I didn't.

The truth was that I couldn't, I didn't know how.

I never had.

I never have.

When we walked into the house, there were carols playing on the radio, and my mother came out in her apron, looking shy. She moved forward, and I moved forward. She put her lips – briefly – against my cheek, and they felt soft and velvety, and then she ran off to the kitchen and brought back a tray of iced cupcakes, which spelt out WELCOME HOME in a line.

'Did Dad tell you about the birds?' said my mother. 'They're called rose-ringed parakeets. Green things. Make a terrible racket.'

'Yes,' I said. 'Where's Julia?'

'Her term doesn't end for another week,' she said.

I texted Ali.

No reply.

I texted Ian.

No reply.

I texted Moira.

'I'm in Devon,' she replied.

'Doing what?'

'Selling incense.'

'Cool.'

Julia came home.

'*Justa!*' I said.

She held me in her arms, and I held her in my arms.

'You smell different,' she said.

We all slightly over-laughed.

As I was getting undressed that evening, she stared at me.

'What?' I said.

'You're wearing a thong,' she said. 'You never used to wear a thong. Is it weird to have something up your bum?'

'You tell me,' I said.

And I laughed.

And she said, 'Aug, that's disgusting.'

And I panicked.

Had I become disgusting at university?

Would she still like me?

The next day I woke up and found that the house was empty and so quiet it made a hum of silence.

I walked into every room and stared at it.

Every room looked smaller, and I felt bigger.

It was a doll's house with a tiny orange wooden dresser, and a circular fake-mahogany table, a piano, a fireplace made of crazy paving with a gas fire stuck on the wall with fake glowing wood, with stairs carpeted the colour of olives, taking you upstairs to a cramped landing, lined with photos of us, in date order, so that you could almost watch time chub out our faces, thin them down, grow our teeth too big for our mouths, grow our faces the right size for our teeth, oil our spotty skin, smooth it out, and on, and on, to now.

I walked into my mother and father's bedroom.

I stared at their double bed with the shiny green quilted bedspread with matching cushions, the cream plasticky bedside tables with nothing on them but my father's alarm clock, ticking loudly.

Tick tick tick.

The white washbasin in the corner, with the neatly folded towel on the rail, pale green, with a satin oyster shell.

I picked up the towel.

I smelled it.

It smelled of Bold washing powder, lavender fragrance.

Like we all smelled, my mother, my father, Julia and I.

Our smell.

I bought the same stuff in Durham.

I wondered if I would buy it forever.

Or if I'd make a break.

The towel had not been used.

I wondered if it was ever used.

Or if it was for display.

To nobody.

You could see the creases from the iron.

It had been ironed so that the satin oyster shell fell right in the centre.

I can't be here, I said to the air.

I went to the library. I headed for the ornithology section, where I'd never been, and looked up rose-ringed parakeets – large, long-tailed, lime green, faces ringed in pink and black, *wild parrots*, for goodness sake, in Hedley Green!

'Guess where the rose-ringed parakeets came from!' I said over supper that night, my father sitting, pale and grey, with trembling hands because the bell above the door hadn't rung once, not once, all day.

'The first pair might have escaped from the set of *The African Queen* in 1951,' I said, trying to fill our quiet kitchen with happy stories. 'It was filmed in Burundi. Around Lake Tanganyika.'

Nobody spoke.

'Has anyone seen that film?' I said.

They shook their heads.

'Welcome home,' said my mother, lifting her glass of water.

We all stared at my father's fingers.

'Or perhaps,' I said, making a little drum roll on the table. 'Perhaps you remember the hurricane in 1987?'

'A year before I opened the shop,' said my father, and his voice sounded shaky. 'I was still working at John Lewis.'

'Well, the first two birds might have escaped from an aviary in the hurricane in 1987,' I said. 'Or possibly Jimi Hendrix released a pair in Carnaby Street in the 1960s.'

'When we were children,' said my mother, glancing at my father. 'Happy times, the 1960s.'

'England was England in the 1960s,' said my father. 'You never heard a foreign voice.'

'Apparently, in Angela Dunnett's class, half the children don't understand English,' said my mother.

'Peter Dunnett says he's got half a mind to go and shoot them himself,' said my father.

'The birds or the children?' I said.

'Crumble?' said my mother.

And I thought *my father is crumbling*.

'Would anyone like to come on a bird-watching trip with me?' I said, in an unusually cheerful voice, because somebody had to lift the mood, and also I'd become quite engrossed in the ornithology section of Hedley Green library, and also I couldn't stand the thought of being here all through the Easter Holidays as well. 'I'm thinking of a weekend in Norfolk – maybe in April.'

'Oh, it's very cold on that east coast,' said my mother, 'and anyway we don't go away in the spring, do we, Stan?'

'Just a weekend,' I said.

'Your father has never had a weekend,' said my mother. 'Not since he opened the shop.'

'Julia?' I said.

'I'll talk to Diego,' she said.

'We can only go away in *August*,' said my mother. 'Because of the shop.'

'We may not be able to go away in August this year,' said my father, and his voice broke on *year*, splitting into a strange kind of sob.

A shadow passed over my mother's face.

'I think it's time I told you all,' said my father, in an awful broken cracking voice, and sweat was forming above his lip and on his cheekbones, and he undid the buttons on the cuffs of his white shirt, and he rolled up his sleeves, showing his pale arms, with little clumps of wiry grey hairs on them. Like a wolf.

Lupine, I thought, to distract myself from what was happening to my father's face, from *lupus*, wolf. The only thing lupine would really rhyme with is supine, I thought, meaning lying with your face turned upwards, like you do, I suppose, when you're dead.

My father's face was shiny with sweat, and I could see the hairline crack again, the one that came the night the Greens' house was pulled down. The face crack was waiting for the stroke, which hadn't happened yet, the way the conker shell swells towards its fracture.

He was swelling towards his fracture: he was starting the process of coming undone.

My father started to cry.

We'd never seen my father cry.

Julia and I looked down.

We all let the apple crumble fall off our spoons.

Then we looked up.

And we stared at him.

As he started to crumble.

My mother opened her mouth but no words came out.

'Darling,' she said finally.

My father's shoulders hunched and convulsed in terrible sobs which seemed to shake his whole body.

'Darling,' said my mother. 'Do you want to go somewhere else?'

I opened my mouth.

I closed it.

My father's sobs got louder, and, between them, he started to squeeze out broken words: 'I,' he said.

Then he kept saying *I* again and again, but he couldn't get past it. Until the next burst came out.

'– am – go – ing – to –'

We waited.

He struggled.

'– have – to –'

We knew what was coming.

'– get – rid – of – the – shop.'

We all looked down at our crumble, and we couldn't think of one thing to say.

'I'm sure you'll find another job,' I said.

But that was not the right thing to say.

My father shouted at me, 'You don't understand,' and it sounded as if all the flesh was stripping off his throat.

'You,' he yelled, and the noise was kind of animal-like, like a roar, or a howl, lupine, even, 'you', and again, 'you'.

I'd never heard that sound before, but I've heard it since.

My mother reached for his hand.

His small pale hand.

He waved her away.

'I'm sure she,' Julia began, but her voice started shaking.

'YOU DON'T UNDERSTAND EITHER,' yelled my father at Julia.

I watched Julia pick up her napkin and scrunch it together in the palm of her hand, like one of those strange plastic balls they give my grandmother for her arthritis.

'Darling,' my mother started.

'YOU DON'T UNDERSTAND EITHER,' yelled my father at my mother, and he got up, and he picked up his chair and he smashed it into the sliding glass door, which shattered.

Then he put down the chair and walked out, through the jagged circular frame of broken glass onto the terrace, onto the lawn, and he walked round and round the circumference of the back garden, like a lion at the zoo.

'It was the internet that killed the shop,' said my mother. 'We were never a country that relied on the internet before. We were a great manufacturing nation.'

'Mum, we couldn't rely on the internet when the internet didn't exist,' I said. 'Before.'

This was the beginning of what I decided we would call the obnubilation, which comes from the Latin word *nubilus*, cloudy, and the verb, *nubilare*, to cloud over.

Number 1 Willow Crescent had clouded over, and the sparkling lights of Christmas couldn't penetrate the gloom.

Number 1 stood under a storm cloud, weeping.

I went back to Durham.

My mother ended up working in the pet shop on the parade near Tattershall Common. My father got a job in the Homebase next to the hugest Asda ever in the entire universe.

I went home for my father's birthday.

My mother and father came in the door together around six o'clock, my mother with a slight whiff of rabbit food about her, and my father in his dark wool suit, carrying his leather briefcase with his Homebase uniform folded inside it. We ate supper, and by seven thirty, it felt like midnight.

Back in Durham, conversely, midnight felt like seven thirty in the evening, as if time worked differently there.

Olly and I walked with foxes through the streets.

We went snowballing under a full moon.

We laughed and laughed.

Olly laughed so loudly it disturbed Barry, the boy next door, who liked doing Sudoku puzzles in bed. Barry slipped a complaint under the door, which made us laugh even more.

We laughed until we cried.

We rarely slept before two, three, four in the morning.

February brought snowdrops and candle-lit dinners.

And soon it was spring.

Parfait

It was Good Friday again, my fourth since I'd arrived, and I decided to drive my coach along the coast road, stopping to paint spring flowers, wild and abundant amongst the Roman ruins of Baelo Claudia, which was dotted with metal information plates, dug into the ground on poles. The flowers seemed to sprout straight from the stone of the old tuna *garum* vats (*garum – a fermented sauce made of fish intestines, used as a condiment in the cuisine of Ancient Rome*). I loved to think that the vats had sat here by the beach, according to the sign, for nearly two thousand years, *since the time of Emperor Claudius, eight years after the crucifixion*. There were sketches of Romans carrying pottery amphora, and, in the distance, three crosses on a hill.

Red, white, blue, pink, purple, golden yellow – wild flowers spreading all the way to the beach.

As I painted the spring, I remembered my father saying that crucifixion–resurrection was the pattern of the seasons, and of our lives, throughout nature, throughout the world.

I never knew exactly what he meant.

I couldn't follow the logic of it.

But today, here, painting the spring flowers, I did know.

I felt the pattern inside me, in the new way of unreasoned knowing that Paco had taught me without teaching me.

I phoned Víctor.

'Spring is exploding here,' I said. 'It makes me feel as if something good's going to happen.'

'It has!' said Víctor.

'The girls?' I said, holding my breath, it had to be, here amongst the flowers, it had to be.

I remembered the blood on their dresses and their changed faces, the tears coming up from deep inside. I remembered telling them that the shame didn't belong to them – it belonged to the men. Possibly all men. I remembered saying I was ashamed to be a man. That they shouldn't be ashamed. I'd carry their shame for them because I was stained by what had happened to them.

'Oh, I'm sorry,' said Víctor. 'No, not the girls, I'm afraid. We go on praying, Parfait. Every day. But there's no news there.'

I took a moment to collect myself.

'So is it something to do with Wilfred?' I asked.

'Much warmer now,' said Víctor. 'Positively hot! Wilfred has said his first sentence!'

I practically jumped on the spot.

'We've had a resurrection before we even get to Easter Sunday!' said Víctor.

'Tell me what he said.'

He said, 'I want to start a rose farm.'

'Put him on the phone!' I said.

'Hello,' said Wilfred.

Just hello.

'Well hello hello hello,' I said.

And hello had never sounded so good.

So momentous.

'I hear you want to start a rose farm,' I said.

'Yes,' he said.

'That's such a beautiful idea, Wilfred,' I said.

'Thank you,' he said.

I waited.

I hoped he might say more.

But he didn't.

I moved inland to Seville, catching the end of the Easter Sunday processions, the streets light with hope, and in the Plaza de España, a girl was singing with such raw yearning in her voice that it quietened the crowd, and all that any of us could say, above the rhythm of the clapping was, at unexpected moments, *Olé, Olé.*

Olé, Zion, *olé.*

Olé, Wilfred, *olé.*

The moon came out over the square.

Augusta

It was Easter, and Julia was arranging her pale pink roses from Diego in a glass jug.

'Rose thorns aren't actually thorns. They should be called prickles. They're where the epidermis bulges outwards,' I said.

Julia nodded.

'The Romans used to wear roses on strings around their necks,' I said. 'Anything said *under the rose* had to be kept a secret.'

Julia nodded.

'A rose fossil was found in Colorado which was thirty-five million years old.'

Julia nodded.

'Did you know that more than 80 per cent of the land in Zambia is covered in roses?'

'No more,' said Julia. 'That's enough. No more research, Aug. Let me love roses because I do.'

'Do you honestly prefer *not knowing* all this stuff?' I said.

'We're just different,' said Julia.

I remember a chill in the room, a dark shadow like when a cloud crosses the sun.

Perhaps we were losing each other after two terms apart. Perhaps absence hadn't made the heart grow fonder.

Julia went on cutting the stems, which fell, almost soundlessly onto the carpet. I sat on the floor, made a launcher out of an elastic band and pinged a cut stem into Julia's face.

Julia said, 'Stop it will you, Aug?'

I took each stem she'd cut and put them, one by one, in the bin.

I wanted to tell her that Lorca had written a play about a spinster called Rose. That her botanist uncle had a rose called the *rosa mutabile*, which was red in the morning, brighter red at midday, white in the afternoon, shattered and fallen apart at night. I wanted to tell her that roses budded but they also decayed.

I wanted to talk to her about death, how it frightened me, how I didn't want to die alone, without her, and perhaps we could do it together, like roses on the same bush.

Julia's roses didn't last long.

The water greened in the jug and stank, and the petals fell off on the carpet.

On the Tuesday after Easter, using our Christmas money, Julia and I went and stayed at a cheap bed and breakfast near Brancaster Staithe for our ornithology weekend.

The roadsides were lined with daffodils.

'Do you remember when you bought me those daffodil buds?' I asked her. 'To help me get over you having a boyfriend?'

She nodded, smiling at me.

'Well, I prefer daffodils to roses,' I told her. 'I like the way they're shaped like trumpets. Trumpets are supposed to pass messages between worlds. And announce extraordinary things. And new beginnings. And I like the way daffodils grow through the snow. How strong they are. Like nothing can mess with them.'

'Well, you'll have to get married in the spring then,' said Julia. Which wasn't at all what the daffodils made me think.

'I don't *have* to get married,' I said. 'The only thing any of us *has* to do is die.'

'Aug, don't say things like that,' said Julia.

'Don't you ever think that?' I said.

'I want to concentrate on living,' she said.

'Living and dying are basically the same thing,' I said.

We set off across the marshes, arm in arm, *Justa* again, and, on the sand dunes, we sat and looked out over the little lagoon where the water-birds gathered. I took the wine out of my rucksack, and I said, 'To sisters!'

We clinked our glasses and drank our wine in big gulps, and we stared at the ducks, as they flew over the marshes in great flocks, landing in twos and threes, skittering and skating over the water; and the geese flying in V formation into the pale grey sky.

The birds took our minds off our conversation about dying, the way living things do, the way the present does, until it dies too, which it does, constantly.

Parfait

It was time to go home from Seville.

Home!

The word floated through my mind like smoke from a fire.

I might have expected home to be Tarifa, but I found I was heading to La Higuera. I was driving between the olive fields and turning into the village, fig trees each side of the road. I was going through the square, down to the beach road, and I was parking on the raised scrubland.

Just there.

Just where.

I got out and I walked through the pine trees down to the beach, where it comes to an end, where the holey rocks make shapes in the dusk. I sat and watched the waves darkening the beach, drying, dying, disappearing.

A sea mist blew in.

I looked out over the sea.

Zion's body was out there, under there, somewhere.

It was a horrible thought, so I spoke aloud over it.

'I'm rebuilding my life, Little Bro,' I said. 'But I miss you. I miss you so much.'

My phone shook in my pocket.

As if.

Never mind.

It was Víctor.

He'd gone with Wilfred to see his new farm.

'We were standing on the hillside . . .' he said.

I could smell the hillside, I could hear it, I could feel it on my skin, and I wondered – can home be more than one place?

As Víctor and Wilfred stood there together, about five thousand African pochard had landed in a huge great flock on Lake Tanganyika, and Wilfred thought it meant something.

'Also, I asked him why he stopped speaking,' said Víctor. 'He said there was too much death, and he had nothing to say about death.'

'There's been too much of it in our family,' I said.

'I know how much you loved them,' said Víctor.

But I wasn't sure if he did.

He'd never met my father, who was the most lovable man on earth.

Perhaps love comes in shades like colours, depending on the person you're trying to love. Or maybe on how good you are at loving. I'm not sure which.

'Your mother told Wilfred that flowers have meanings,' said Víctor. 'She said that roses meant love. And he's planning to send these roses from Burundi all around the world. So that Burundi will be known as a place of love and not of hate.'

Augusta

'Does it feel odd that you and Diego will probably stick together forever now?' I said to Julia, watching the ducks on the lagoon. 'That you're never going to love anyone else.'

'Not really, Aug,' she said. 'It was always meant to be.'

'Don't you ever want to be on your own?'

She shook her head.

'Or try someone else?'

'For me there's only ever been Diego. From the day he moved in.'

'You were nine,' I said. 'Is that not a bit weird?'

She shook her head.

'Nine years and you're sure you don't find it a tiny bit boring?'

We looked out to the marshy inlet − the gathering of ordinary mallards and coots, and a handsome pair, rather exotic, a little apart from the others.

We got up and started to walk.

'What about you and Olly?'

'What about us?'

'Is it serious?'

'It feels kind of un-serious,' I said, 'which is how I like it.'

We went into the little wooden hide, and I looked down the telescope.

'Jules, look at this duck.'

It was orange with a striped head in white and blue and rust, with tangerine sails, sticking up each side. The female was brown and speckled, duller but quite stylish, like a posh wedding fascinator, I thought, with a spark of green-blue.

'Mandarin ducks,' Julia read from the poster. 'Introduced from China and escaped from captivity. Occasional sightings.'

'Not more invaders,' I said. 'Don't tell Mum and Dad.'

'Shall we not talk about Mum and Dad?' said Julia. 'I think I need to get away from their sadness.'

'It's making them bitter,' I said.

'It would make anyone bitter,' said Julia. 'Think of the hours Dad put into that shop. It's too sad for words.'

I wasn't sure I could find the words for it either. You can't always, even though there are so many in the dictionary to choose from.

No, we would definitely do our best not to think of Stanley Hope Uniforms, which was being refurbished and turned into a Costa Coffee shop, and which soon wouldn't exist.

I'm sitting here thinking that, although I was so embarrassed by that shop my whole childhood, it was actually quite nice. I kind of miss it. Especially the wooden pull-out drawers with glass fronts where he kept the socks. I kind of miss all the shops like that which don't exist any more.

'Could Olly be the pedlar man?' said Julia. *'Where he comes from nobody knows?'*

'He comes from Cirencester. Everybody knows!' I said, laughing.

'Might he travel across the Sahara with you one day or sail dhows in Zanzibar or ride round the world in a gypsy caravan?'

'Probably not. He'll probably stay in Cirencester and pass on the farm to his children,' I said.

'Would Mum and Dad like Olly?' said Julia.

'Does it matter?' I said.

'It does to me,' said Julia.

Julia and I sat together on the little wooden bench, watching the ducks through the huge glass window as they upturned themselves, diving for algae – and I thought that, however strange it seemed, the only thing on their minds – at all – was probably algae.

'Why do you think people have children?' said Julia.

'I have no idea,' I said.

'Why do you think they had us?' said Julia.

'I've never thought about it.'

'Don't we owe them something?'

'I don't know,' I said.

I didn't want to owe them anything, however mean that sounds.

'Don't people have children so that they can all stick together?' said Julia. 'But nowadays families all split apart across the world and never see each other. So what's the point in being a family?'

'I've never thought about it like that,' I said. 'Not in those actual words.'

'In all that thinking, why have you never thought about it?' said Julia.

But I couldn't answer her.

'What would you like to buy as a souvenir?' said the bed and break-fast woman as we were paying, showing us a selection of hand-made toys and home-made jams.

I bought Olly an awful patchwork owl hot-water bottle cover (iron-ically), though we didn't need any more heat.

Heat is what we had all through our second year.

Then it was summer and we went to festivals and we danced in the mud and slept in a small tent in a happy chaos of wellington boots and vodka.

I didn't think about the past.

Or the future.

I tried to live like a duck.

Symbols of Death in Spanish Literature of the Early Twentieth Century.

The title of my final-year dissertation.

'Why on earth did you choose that?' said my mother. 'It sounds horrible.'

So, I didn't tell her the way the Beggar Woman plotted with the moon and carried the three characters of *Blood Wedding* to their inevitable end, *death in the beauty of the night.*

I didn't tell her it was everyone's inevitable end.

Most of us die in the early hours of the morning.

As I worked alone, I thought too much.

About living and dying.

What it meant to exist.

It's hard to explain, but perhaps you've felt it.

I delved so far down that I slipped out of myself and fell away, away, away.

I clawed myself back inside myself.

'Hold me,' I said to Olly. 'I'm frightened I don't exist.'

'Too much dissertation, Dragonfly,' said Olly. 'Too much death. Come here.'

I wanted to, I wanted to *come here*, wherever here was, to lose my consciousness, to stop the voice, to block the questions.

Sex, the relief of it, the weakening of consciousness, the almost spiritual release, *la petite mort* as it's called – the little death.

That little blast of melancholy or transcendence.

And then reality again.

Bursting in on you.

'Oh, Dragonfly!' said Olly. 'So gorgeous and so flitty.'

In the June of 2011, we gathered respectably with our families, like people who didn't have sex with each other in the afternoons, gowned in black, on a piece of grass called Palace Green, next to Durham Cathedral.

Olly's parents couldn't, or didn't, come. He was their fifth child, and I think they were running out of steam.

There were cream-coloured marquees, bunting and ice creams, gold-lacquered chairs and tables with cloths on. You could hear clinking glass and murmurs and laughter – and barbecued pig floated on the breeze.

Olly was standing on Palace Green, with his blond wavy hair, his lop-sided smile and his magnetic lisp, pouring Pimm's for Laura and Tom.

My mother watched him as if he was some kind of rare bird.

'Will you marry Olly Macintosh?' she'd asked me the night before.

'Promising love forever to one person sounds dangerous to me,' I said. 'And I'm not sure I could promise love forever to a man who passes his leisure time killing birds.'

My mother said, 'I don't know where you got this obsession with birds from. A lot of men like killing. Think of them all fishing at Tattershall Pond.'

A lot of men like killing?

'Does Dad like killing?' I said.

My mother flushed, and her rash grew in whitey-red blotches, spreading all down her chest.

'Take a photo of us, will you, Julia?' she said.

Olly and Diego watched us – my mother, father and me.

'Do you shoot?' said Olly to Diego.

Diego shook his head.

We struggled to find the right position for our arms.

In the photo which my mother would later choose to frame in silver and place on a window sill, my father's right arm looks like a set square, sticking out, in a triangular fashion, to the right.

'Cheese!' said Julia.

'Cheese!' we all said.

We laughed.

Then we stopped laughing and sat down.

Julia tried to smile happiness into me.

My father looked at all the other fathers and mothers pouring jugs of Pimm's, holding forth – and then he looked at the sky.

I looked up.

There was nothing in the sky.

Not even clouds.

Which was unusual for Durham, for England.

But my father went on looking at the sky.

'What's your favourite book, Mrs Hope?' said Olly Macintosh, because posh people get taught how to start conversations at school.

'My favourite book?' said my mother, and she held her white handbag on her knee, like a pet cat.

'Yes,' said Olly to my mother.

I looked at my mother: her cheap white pearl earrings protruding from large lobes, like little ping-pong balls; her curly hair corkscrewing tighter in the heat.

'*Bunnikin's Picnic,*' said my mother to Olly. 'That's my favourite book.'

'Oh, I see,' he said.

My mother sat and stroked her handbag.

I couldn't look up.

I didn't want to see Laura and Tom's faces.

'By whom?' said Olly.

'It's Ladybird,' said my mother. 'I'm not sure they have authors.'

'I think all books would have authors,' said Laura.

But Olly stepped into her sentence, like my mother does with her mother.

'Ladybird?' said Olly on top of Laura.

'I'm fond of ladybirds,' said my mother, looking away, still holding her white bag. 'Pretty little things, ladybirds. I like the dots.'

She paused.

Sweat bubbles spawned above her top lip.

Then she added, 'I've always liked dots. From when I was a little girl. They used to call me Spotty Dotty.'

Laura pursed her lips.

Spotty Dotty.

They are only words.

Julia smiled at my mother, crinkling her eyes as if she was in pain.

I was in pain too.

Agony.

I don't know if I was more ashamed of my mother or more ashamed of being ashamed of her.

'I know what you mean, Mrs Hope,' said Olly. 'I had a dotty cravat once. I was rather fond of it.'

That was kind of Olly.

I thought of his dotty cravat lying amongst my knickers, the knickers my mother wouldn't recognise.

Soon I would have to hand back my black robe and pack up my student house and go home. To Willow Crescent, where there is one ragged willow tree on the roundabout, and where I once emptied goldfish into the communal pond for Graham Cook. They looked beautiful, like orange petals. But they didn't help in the end.

To Willow Crescent, where the roundabout pond had been filled in, and where people's favourite books were not *The Brothers Karamazov*, not *1984*, not *Bleak House*, not *Don Quijote* nor *One Hundred Years of Solitude*. But *Bunnikin's Picnic*. And I knew I was wrong to judge them. And wrong to mind. They could like any books they wanted to like.

My mother invited Olly to the Willow Crescent Collective Supper, which was held in our garage in July, and when he arrived in his convertible Mini in sheeting rain, my mother said, 'So where did you come?'

Olly peered at her, narrowing his blue eyes, and I realised how very tiny our hall was, and I noticed that Julia's poem was still on the wall above the shelf, in a cheap clip frame.

My mother said, 'I gather Augusta was first.'

'*Got* a first,' I said.

My mother nodded.

'I came a poor second,' said Olly, laughing.

'Well done, dear,' she said. 'Well done.'

'In truth, it's tragic,' said Olly. 'A 2:2 is tragic.'

Olly Macintosh was quite the centre of attention at the Collective Supper with his floppy blond hair and his charm.

'Hasn't Augusta changed?' said Hilary Hawkins, rather too loudly.

'She's quite a different girl,' Janice Brown replied.

'You'd hardly recognise her,' said someone I couldn't identify.

'She actually looks quite pretty,' said Helen Dunnett.

Parfait

I'd bought a ladder which enabled me climb onto the roof of the coach, and I could sit on a deckchair, high up, staring out to sea, to Africa, or, if I turned around, looking out to the miles of farmland and the hills beyond.

I watched the egrets on the cows' backs, pecking at the ticks, seeming to whisper in their soft ears. As dusk fell, the birds would rise up, in white clouds, against the darkening sky, heading to roost in the needled branches of a huge old araucaria tree, which stood at the side of the beach road.

I counted the egrets, and got to six hundred, tiny white flames flecking the branches, like an old-fashioned Christmas tree in a European children's book.

Augusta

Diego's family had given me their house in La Higuera rent-free for one week to celebrate adult life, freedom, whatever it was, wherever we'd arrived – our metamorphosis.

I liked that word.

I liked imagining the feeling of it.

A tadpole stretching into new limbs; a caterpillar expanding into flight; a dragonfly arching out of itself, turning turquoise-blue, growing fairy wings – we saw it happening on the wall of Olly's garden.

I dreamt of who I might turn into now that I was graduating and would be free to be anyone I chose to be.

I could hardly sleep, imagining that I would be back on the roof terrace, back on the Moroccan bed piled with jewelled cushions, transmogrifying.

'Five more days.'

Olly smiled.

'Four more days.'

Olly smiled again.

'Three more days.'

Olly went on reading.

'Are you excited?' I said.

'Course I am,' he said.

I didn't say two more days or one more day. I tried to act a bit cool. But it was seven years since I'd been there.

On the plane, Olly fell asleep with his inflatable horseshoe-thing around his neck before the air steward had finished pretending to pull down the oxygen mask.

I wanted to *anticipate* with Olly.

But he was asleep, and asleep he stayed for two and a half hours.

I opened my mouth to say, 'Look! Palm trees!' but he'd put his jumper over his face.

When we arrived in La Higuera, my heart leaping to the palm fronds, my body tingling to the smell of heat, Olly said, 'Why do you keep looking at me like that?'

'What do you think?' I said.

'Lovely beach.'

'No, but do you see?'

'See what?'

'What I mean?'

It was more fun arriving here with Julia.

Olly and I set out to explore, and I kept looking at him. But he just walked along as if we were in a normal kind of place by the sea.

There was an artist with his easel beside the beach road, his skin smooth and conker-coloured, his bunch of plaits tied up so that his cheekbones stuck out – and he was painting the egrets. I stopped and watched, quietly. I hoped Olly would do the same. But he kept on asking me loud questions about restaurants. I said I only knew Restaurante Raúl and the tuna with grapes was delicious, and the *paella*, and the *chanquete* fish which you ate whole. And the *crema catalana* ice cream which tasted of burnt sugar. But still he didn't shut up.

The egrets flew across the canvas in a big burst against the dusk, though when I drew closer to the painting, it seemed as if the egrets weren't there at all. There was only a kind of blast of white light. I wanted to say something to the artist. But he didn't look up. And I felt awkward. I pulled Olly away.

The woman in the shop was wearing the same short-sleeved light blue housecoat that she'd worn in 2004, when I was fourteen and translating Spanish newspapers. Strangely, she remembered me from then.

I felt stiff and odd in the shop, and my Spanish came out constricted on my tongue. I moved my mouth around, stretching my lips, to find my rolling rs and guttural js.

'What are you doing?' said Olly, frowning at me.

'Trying to find my Spanish,' I said.

'Your sister!' said the woman. 'Quite a little pickle! She'd pop something in the basket without anyone looking!'

'My *sister* stealing things?' I said. 'That doesn't sound right.'

'How *is* your sister these days?'

'Very well,' I said. 'Looking after babies. She loves babies.'

'You won't sleep well,' she said. 'The egrets are roosting in the tree up by your house – and they make a terrible noise.'

'I always sleep well,' I said, which wasn't true.

I'm starting to sleep again.

It feels good.

'You must try some of my *dulce de membrillo*,' the woman said. 'Beautiful with salads. Cured meats. *Manchego* cheese.'

I translated, and Olly lit up. He loved new food combinations. I imagine he still does. Over in Cirencester. After a long day out on the farm. They've probably opened a farm shop. Everybody does these days.

'What is this stuff?' Olly asked me.

'A kind of quince paste. Very Spanish.'

'Where are you going to have your picnic?' said the woman.

'Down where the boat's buried,' I said. 'Before the trees. At the end.'

'No one likes to go there,' she said. 'That little wooden boat blew ashore on New Year's Day years back, and the passengers' bodies were never found.'

I translated.

'After that, more of them came in. Thousands of them all down the coast,' said the woman, and her lips turned right down at the end as if her mouth was a croquet hoop.

'Where did they come from?' I asked.

'Africa – they set off from Morocco, but often they'd walked all the way from Senegal, or further,' she said. 'For a few years, they kept being blown ashore in their tiny little *patera* boats.'

'*Patera*,' I said. 'New word.'

'Quite inadequate for the job, those *pateras*,' said the woman. 'Hundreds of them drowned. The ones who made it got jobs building houses. But then we had *la crisis*. And there weren't any jobs. And now with the sea patrols, it's harder to get across. Very good thing, I say. Better we all stay where we are.'

We left the shop.

'That is actually Africa,' I said, gesturing over the sea.

'You don't say,' said Olly.

Stupid expression, you don't say.

'I couldn't believe it when we first came. The thought of Africa. Just over there. And Burundi – way down south.'

'Had you never seen a map of the world, Dragonfly?'

Don't dragonfly me, I thought.

I let go of his hand.

I willed myself to feel ecstatic and happy, which was what I'd planned for the trip.

The nudists were still here – more of them.

I remembered reading my mother and father those poems.

Not waving but drowning.

They fuck you up, your mum and dad.

It made me smile.

It made me sad.

We sat a bit beyond the nudists, who were diving into the sea, *heads down, tails up, dabbling free.*

I thought of telling Olly about the morning of the poems, about the day my family went to the beach without me, about the boat trip in Tarifa, the last day in the garden, Julia, my fears.

But I didn't want to – and not talking about these things made me wonder what I really felt about Olly.

It wasn't yet lunchtime – and certainly not Spanish lunchtime – but Olly wanted to try the quince paste and *Manchego* cheese.

'The Spanish never have lunch before two,' I said, 'and sometimes nearer four.'

'Delicious with the cheese,' said Olly, with his mouth full. 'Let me try it with the *chorizo.*'

'It's not lunchtime,' I said.

'Are there rules about eating on this beach?' said Olly, and then he found a little burst of laughter, as if he was joking.

I wasn't sure if he really liked the quince paste that much. Or if it was something to say.

Olly suggested that we should go naked.

It was a way of blowing away our flat feelings with a little gulp of novelty, which I suppose is how capitalism works, or unusual sex.

I wondered what Julia would say. I wasn't sure that she and Diego would go naked. I wasn't sure if it was something I particularly wanted to do either, but it was too late by then. I'd taken my bikini off.

Olly seemed to find it enormously amusing. I didn't like that. This obsession he had with laughing all the time. The thing I loved when I first met him was becoming the thing I really didn't love. I started to feel my jaw clenching every time he laughed. Did he need to laugh so loudly? So Englishly? On this beach?

Being naked really isn't that funny.

Olly wanted us to take photos of each other, to mark the moment.

I didn't argue.

It felt easier not to.

In the photos, I look bony as anything, with my little high breasts and my nipples darkened by the sun, my skin brown as an acorn, all over, my long hair dragged up in a tie-dye band, and Olly, tall and covered in blond hairs all over, his nose slightly pink, holding his Hawaiian shorts over his private parts for the photo. As if that was, in some way, hilarious.

In the photos, I look sad.

You maybe know how horrible it is to feel sad on a day when you're supposed to feel happy.

'Come here, Dragonfly,' Olly would say, and we'd roll about in the sand dunes, kissing and climbing on top of each other, but all the time I was rolling about, I was analysing whether I wanted to be rolling about. I didn't lose my consciousness like I used to.

The voice kept narrating, and afterwards I felt emptied out.

Like one of the shells on the beach.

Conch shells.

You can make conch shells into bugles, apparently, and play them, but most of them only have one note.

Olly bought me a necklace with a silver conch shell on it. He said he loved me when he put it round my neck.

Then he looked at me, right into my eyes, waiting for me to say it back.

I said, 'I tried to use conch in a rhyming poem once. But I couldn't find one single word it could rhyme with. And then I wondered if no one rhymes with me.'

Olly Macintosh's parents wanted to take the whole family, with girl-friends and boyfriends, to Australia for Christmas because they had no drawing pins on the continent of Oceania on the wall map in their smart downstairs toilet.

I wanted to go to Australia because I wanted not to have Christmas in Hedley Green.

My mother was distraught.

Julia gave me an antique silver writing set with a feather quill, and a tiny tray and an inkpot, and she said, 'This is to say that you are going to be a famous writer.'

I felt really bad that I'd given her Primark pyjamas.

My father drove me to the airport, terse and strange.

'Have a lovely Christmas!' I said, kissing him on his cold perspiring cheek.

He didn't answer. I dragged my case behind me. He chased after me, and said, 'For God's sake, don't forget to ring your mother on Christmas Day!'

'Did you notice that Qantas doesn't have a u?' I said to Olly's mother, who was wearing a denim shirt dress and practical shoes.

'Only you would notice that,' she said.

'Does your mother like me?' I said to Olly on the plane.

'She likes everybody,' said Olly, which was the wrong answer.

When we landed in Sydney, disorientated and upside-down, I sat on the steps of the Opera House staring at its white solid sails, as if it couldn't possibly be real. Or as if I couldn't.

I thought, weirdly, of the framed photo of Princess Diana in front of the Taj Majal, which used to be in our flower bed.

I fiddled with my conch-shell necklace.

Olly clowned around pretending to push his oldest brother in the water. His oldest brother was called Quentin.

Qentin, I thought.

At the first hotel, there were kangaroos on the lawn.

'Do you remember the first night we met?' said Olly, drinking a glass of white wine too quickly, pouring another. 'Nobody ever said Kanga or Roo, did they?'

He took my hand and squeezed it.

'Kanga never had much about her,' I said. 'Except Roo! Obviously!'

We both let out a small odd laugh.

'Will you want to be a mother, Dragonfly?' said Olly.

'If I was a kangaroo, I might consider it,' I said. 'I like the idea of putting the baby in my pocket.'

Olly and I sat staring at the kangaroos together, holding hands, but the longer we sat there, the more his hand started to feel like the plastic doll hand I had inside my bedside table drawer in Hedley Green.

We travelled about in two Winnebago vans, stopping at beaches, and if one of his brothers or sisters fell asleep, they would write on each other's faces with black pen and take photos on their phones and find it hilarious.

I caught Olly watching me as I watched him, as I watched them. I think he knew. We were both starting to know. We screwed up our eyes to try not to see our differences.

We spent Christmas Day on the beach, wearing red-and-white Santa hats. Later, I phoned my mother. They were just back from church.

'Diego's bought us a laptop,' said my mother. 'We're not sure if we'll manage it, though. Have you seen any kangaroos with their babies?'

'Only one,' I said. 'She ran away.'

'I won't keep you,' said my mother.

On New Year's Day of 2012, Olly and I were coming back to land after a day at sea in Port Stephens, sitting in a strange green net attached to the bow of a yacht, and we'd seen dolphins, leaping out of the sea, like in Tarifa, right around us, so close we could almost touch them.

I said, 'We used to feel like that around each other.'

Olly Macintosh said, 'Oh, Dragonfly.'

And I said, 'Thank you for turning me into a person. Making me a bit more normal. Perhaps we need a bit of a break. And then it will be the way it always was.'

We both cried, and then we kept going all the way around the globe until we arrived at Gatwick Airport, where my father and mother and

Julia were waiting in the car park, hiding, because they were nervous about meeting Olly's posh family.

'So, safely home,' said my mother, embracing her handbag on her lap.

The inside of the car felt very cramped.

I said, 'I've split up with Olly. As a trial.'

My father went on driving.

'Julia has some news,' said my mother.

'Not now,' said Julia, trying to put her right hand over her left. 'Let's just—'

'Congratulations,' I said, and I embraced her, as much as you can when you're both wearing seat belts. 'I'm so happy for you.'

'We'll talk about it some other time,' said Julia, and she held my hand with her diamond hand.

'It's OK,' I said. 'I'm fine. Olly and I are going to have a break until Easter. We seem to have run out of steam.'

We drove along quietly for a while, and the seat belt cut into my neck.

'We waited until you were home to have the engagement party,' said my mother.

'Thank you,' I said.

'Will Olly come?' said my father.

'No.'

'We're going to have the party in the garage and fill it with red roses,' said my mother.

The diamond glistened on Julia's finger.

I held her hand and squeezed it.

It was warm, and her skin was smooth with hand-cream because she didn't want to end up with old lady skin.

'Put up your hand and let me look at it,' I said to Julia.

She did, and it seemed as if her face darkened a little.

'You are totally happy, aren't you?' I said, trying to look into her eyes though we weren't at quite the right angle.

'Of course she is,' said my mother.

I raised my eyes at Julia – but she wasn't looking.

'So when will you get married?' I said.

'We think June 2013,' said Julia. 'And I'm not going to properly move in with him until then.'

'A year and a half of still having you,' I said, and a wave of nausea came over me, which I assumed was jet lag.

'Please will you stay at home, Aug?' said Julia. 'Until then. So that we can be together.'

I'd spent the last term sending short stories to competitions and not winning, and now it was time to open all my files and write the great Burundian novel.

I knew I should get a job and earn some money. But I couldn't think what job I would do. Except write.

I'd never met a novelist.

I wasn't sure how one would go about being one – as an actual job.

'How's the book going?' my mother would ask, but when I tried to answer, she tended to change the subject.

'She doesn't know what to say,' Julia said.

'I'm setting it in Burundi,' I said.

'Oh you've always gone on about Burundi,' said my mother. 'Even when you were a little girl. Where is it again?'

'It's in Africa, between Tanzania, Rwanda and the Democratic Republic of Congo – and terrible things have happened there. For years.'

'It's odd that it never comes up on the news,' said my father, with a face that suggested I was exaggerating.

'That's because nobody cares,' I said, in a rather fierce voice, the one I often used when I spoke to my parents, which I regret now, thinking about it. But on I went. 'We gain nothing from Burundi, and nothing it could do would ever threaten us. It has no influence at all. It only matters if we care about people we haven't met.'

'But we've got problems of our own,' said my father.

'We really can't take the burdens of the world on our shoulders, Augusta,' said my mother, sighing. 'You're too much of a dreamer.'

'Anyhow,' said my father. 'It's time you got a job. Sitting tapping at your typewriter isn't going to put bread on the table.'

'What are you going to do with all those notes?' said my mother.

I didn't answer.

'Perhaps Julia could find you something at the nursery. Apparently lots of the parents speak other languages there. Or there's always the Flight Centre.'

I went to the library to write. I put my antique writing set on the back right-hand corner of the desk like a talisman.

On my laptop, I went on looking amongst the hundreds and thousands of stories I'd gathered for the one story. Then I found it. A journalist had gone with her tape recorder to interview a young man who'd started a rose farm outside Bujumbura, the capital of Burundi, but when she arrived, she found he didn't want to speak. He wrote on a piece of cardboard: 'I let my roses speak for me.'

'Did you ever speak?' the journalist asked.

'I stopped when my twin brother died,' he wrote – and she'd photographed the cardboard.

'Have you spoken at all since?' she asked.

'I started but I stopped,' he wrote.

'Why did you stop?'

'The elections came and the only candidate we could vote for was Nkurunziza.'

My fingers hovered over the keyboard to write the first word, and a butterfly flew in through the library window.

Psyche is the Greek word for soul and the Greek word for butterfly. The butterfly flew over the quill pen and settled on the top right-hand corner of my screen, its wings trembling.

I looked at it, and I wondered if it remembered being a caterpillar. Dying in the chrysalis. And coming to life again.

My fingers wrote the first word.

There.

I sat back.

Were.

What were there?

> *There were butterflies.*
> *They flew in a huge red swarm over Lake Tanganyika.*
> *Three hundred thousand butterflies, the souls of the dead.*

I got up.

I tried to imagine three hundred thousand dead bodies.

But I couldn't.

I wondered how many you could fit on the floor of the library, and what it would be like to see them all here at my feet. I looked down. Then I looked up. On the noticeboard on the wall, there was an advert for a new library assistant – experience not essential.

I spoke to the woman called Jean who'd been there for years, the one who pulled her hair out, and she gave me the job. On the spot.

Olly wrote me letters on thick cream writing paper with his farm address printed in gold, and he put in dragonfly facts he'd found on the internet:

The dragonfly symbolises transformation.

Can move direction very suddenly.

Is capable of flying across oceans.

I didn't spend much time thinking about Olly.

I thought how much I'd like to fly across an ocean.

* * *

Before Easter, Julia and I went online and bought a dolphin stunt kite for Diego and an octopus one for Olly because I liked alliteration.

On Easter Monday, the day our break was officially over, we flew them at the top of Old John Brown's, the four of us, the four kites, diving into each other in the sky, wrapping around each other and collapsing in huge whooshes on top of us like tents.

For Olly and me, it was *deciding day.*

But, despite the Easter mood of resurrection, I knew I'd already decided, and I was pretty sure he had.

Our relationship was dead, and the stone would not be rolled away.

I had no interest in his farm in Cirencester, and he had no interest in my farm in Bujumbura, where roses grew.

I'd never read him *The Pedlar's Caravan.*

I never could have done.

That said all there was to say.

This was the last day that Olly and I would ever spend together, after all those happy hours of thinking we were in love, or of being in love – if there's a difference. This finitude gave the day a strange clarity. Our words had more resonance, and sounded louder. The wind blew against our faces with more force. I noticed the layered petals of every daisy on our way up, the gold plumpness of their centres, the green-ness of the grass, the blue-ness of the sky.

Daffodils grew on the hillside, but their yellow trumpet coronas were drying up, and they had nothing new or extraordinary to announce.

The boys, perhaps knowing that there would be no lifetime of obligation, chatted fluently, at ease with each other.

My dragonfly came down, belly up.

Olly's octopus crashed down on top of it, astride it with its multiple legs.

We both stared at them.

'Happy memories!' said Olly.

I laughed, but my laughter sounded awkward, as if the two of us were watching ourselves having sex.

It seemed odd that we ever had, looking at him all buttoned up inside his clothes.

Olly and I walked down Old John Brown's, crossing the stile at the bottom, where the mud was gluey thick, walking along the stream where mallards swam in twos, and we were still a pair, for the last time, as we made our way towards the level crossing.

'The novel's coming together,' I said.

Olly said to me, 'Time to fly, Dragonfly.'

I thought this was the most generous-hearted thing I'd ever heard. Until he started going out with Cressida only three weeks later – Cressida from Cirencester, from the Polo Club. They were engaged within the year. She wore a green tweed shooting jacket on their honeymoon.

When Julia's engagement was announced, my father pulled out half of his shrubs and flowering plants, and he started growing white rose bushes round and round the garden – like the one he'd planted for Princess Diana – tending them with a care bordering on the neurotic, covering them in manure, staring at the buds as they opened, preparing for his next loss.

He trod carefully through the world these days as if he sensed that the sinkhole which had opened at the door of Stanley Hope Uniforms when the bell went ding for the last time would only get bigger now.

'I have the title,' I said to Julia. 'It's going to be called *The Rose Farmer of Bujumbura.*'

In the evenings, my father was back in his study with his squared paper and his stubby pencil, calculating the expenses of the wedding.

'We could always do Bring and Share,' said my mother, standing on the metal divide between the carpets.

My father wrote and rubbed, wrote and rubbed, ripped the page.

'What do you take me for?' he said.

'Or a stand-up buffet?' said my mother.

'We will all sit down – every last one of us.'

My father grabbed his ruler and started ruling columns.

'Don't press so hard,' said my mother.

'I'll press as hard as I damn well like.'

'We could have salad.'

'No daughter of mine will marry on salad,' said my father.

For Julia's wedding breakfast, at the church hall in Higgots Close, we would eat poached salmon with lemon mayonnaise followed by summer berry meringues.

For her wedding bouquet, Julia would have a circular mass of roses, pressed together, a mix of buds and open flowers, white on white, sepia-edged and resting in gypsophila, like a nest of sprayed lace.

As Julia dressed on the morning of her wedding, I was transfixed by her, and losing her in a way that only a twin would probably understand. She was radiant in ivory silk; I wore a bridesmaid dress the same colour as my arms.

Julia looked in the mirror only once, when I'd fastened her wedding dress with forty-five tiny silk buttons up her curved back.

'Fine,' she said.

She looked into Diego's dark eyes and saw their children running up Old John Brown's with kites in their hands.

We threw confetti over the two of them, and that's the photo I took to La Higuera, Julia's head inclined upwards, and the rose petals falling around her face.

It was June, and the sun shone.

They walked from the echoey church hall to their maisonette on Higgots Close, where Diego had secretly installed a dovecote the day before in the coral bark Japanese maple, so that they arrived home to doves flying around their heads.

I went back to number 1 Willow Crescent, to the room I'd shared with Julia my whole life. Her bed was made. She'd left her soft toys at the bottom: the white dove, the white rabbit and the threadbare polar bear. I opened the wardrobe door and I looked at myself in the mirror. My dress had mud around the hem, and there were petals of rose confetti in my hair.

It was very still.

I sat on my bed.

Then I took out *The Rose Farmer of Bujumbura*. I started to write. I wrote most of the night, and all the next day.

'I think it would do you good to get out,' said my mother.

But I was out, walking with women balancing baskets on their heads, and bundles of firewood and five-gallon plastic containers full of water.

'We've got the photos back from the wedding!' called my mother.

'I'll be down in a minute!'

I was out amongst the ambling policemen, smooth-skinned and lazy with heat and power, their AK 47s slung across their shoulders, chewing gum.

'Lunchtime!' called my mother.

I was out amongst the expat houses whose gardens waved their traveller palms like ladies' fans to keep out the smell of one hundred human bodies killed every day. I was out in thatched communities where the graves were fuller than the houses. Where no foreign journalists came. Because people in their sitting rooms in the West had had their fill of Rwanda. And didn't have the stomach for any more.

'Grandma's here!' called my mother, and of course she was, she was here for her wedding debrief – and no guest would have escaped the force of her judgement.

But I didn't go down because I was far away, with a young man, who went on planting roses for love, row after row, he didn't stop. He would grow roses across the whole country if he had to. The African mourning doves paddled at the edge of the lake, their eyes pink with tears.

I looked at the empty bed, and the white fur dove I gave Julia for her tenth birthday, whose fur had dissolved with loving, which she hadn't taken with her.

Understandably.

Our life together was over, and would never again exist, which is the true pain of it.

It was so quiet.

Julia was working at Rainbow Nursery, walking there in the early mornings, in her special rainbow smock, embroidered with tiny pots of gold.

The children asked her whether there really was a pot of gold at the end of the rainbow, and Julia said yes of course there was. The nursery manager, a thin woman called Eileen, whose husband was dying of cancer, said that nobody ever reached the end of the rainbow.

Julia wanted the children to believe in pots of gold, in the tooth fairy and the Easter Bunny and Father Christmas, but Eileen said they should manage the children's expectations at Rainbow Nursery.

'Life isn't a picnic, you know,' she said.

Parfait

When I drove back to Tarifa with more paintings for the gallery, the owner greeted me like an old friend. All my paintings had sold, he said, people loved them.

'I'm so pleased for you,' said Antonio, as we sat drinking coffee and eating pastries in the Paseo de la Alameda, where we'd first met.

'It's you who rescued me,' I said, feeling the sun on my skin, and feeling good, so good, like I never thought I'd feel again. 'I'll always be grateful. None of this would have happened without you.'

'So,' said Antonio. 'Are you making lemonade?'

He winked.

'What do you mean?' I said.

'Love?' said Antonio. 'Have you fallen in love? You've been gone a while. We assumed it was a woman.'

I shook my head.

'I've been painting.'

'Oh, come on,' said Antonio. 'Life's for living.'

I thought of my sisters, but it never did me any good thinking of them. Then I thought of Pierre, and Wilfred, and Víctor. I wanted all of them to live too – if life was for living.

I felt bad about my easy life.

I went back to the coach and called Pierre, who now had a phone.

'I'll pay for you to come to Spain,' I said. 'Life's so much easier here.'

'I'm not looking for an easy life,' he said.

'What are you looking for?' I said.

'Justice,' said Pierre.

'Not revenge, I hope,' I said.

'It's only language,' said Pierre. 'Call it what you like.'

'Can I change your mind, Pierre?' I said.

'I'll never leave Burundi,' he said.

'I'd like to send you some money,' I said. 'Please will you spend it on something that would make you happy.'

Though who knows what made Pierre happy these days?

I rang Víctor.

'Do you and Wilfred want to come over here? I'll pay for you both.'

'I've got my school and Wilfred's got his farm, Parfait,' said Víctor. 'But thank you – and I'll tell him.'

'I'm going to send you both money,' I said. 'Please will you try to enjoy it?'

I didn't feel better.

I felt churned up, as if I'd tried to buy what shouldn't be bought: peace, or goodness, or something.

I went down to the streets to dance.

'Are you the artist?' said a young girl with a long dark plait, sitting close to me on the sofa, drawing me, tempting me with the smell of her perfume and her glistening red lips, which would be soft to kiss.

'You're the one whose brother drowned, aren't you?' she said.

I jumped.

She stroked my cheek and leant herself against me.

The one whose brother drowned?

I got up and left.

But I was restless.

I didn't sleep well.

In the early morning, I turned on the radio, and I heard on the news that a migrant boat, with 515 people on board, had sunk near Lampedusa, in Italy. The Italian coastguard had rescued 155 of them.

515 - 155 = 360. Nearly the same number of days in the year. A dead person for every day.

I went to get out my easel.

I set it up outside the coach.

Then I stopped.

The one whose brother drowned.

More brothers had drowned.

I knew that painting wasn't enough.

I should do something.

Deeds, deeds, my father used to say.

I thought of Daffodil Wilfred, and I thought of Víctor.

I should drive to Lampedusa and try and help, I thought, but I couldn't face it, I'm ashamed to say, not on my own.

So I sent some money instead.

Augusta

As Julia walked back from the nursery in the evenings, she realised that Eileen was making her sad, and she knew that she didn't want to be sad.

'Wouldn't you be sad if your husband was dying of cancer?' I said to Julia.

'There will always be someone somewhere dying of cancer,' said Julia. 'I want to choose to be happy.'

I'm still thinking this through – whether it's OK.

Julia and Diego asked me to stop telling them about Burundi and about all the other horrible things that were happening in the world. They sat eating dinner in the little conservatory they'd added at the back of their maisonette, watching the doves fly and the leaves of the coral bark Japanese maple turn from rich green to butter yellow.

'We don't watch the news,' Diego said to me. 'It's too depressing – and anyway, we have our own lives to live, our own worries.'

'No honeymoon baby,' said Julia. 'I hope it's all going to be all right.'

Although she could love the babies at her nursery, she said, she couldn't make the light shine in their eyes like their mothers did. Even the mothers who didn't seem nice at all.

But when she did, quickly, get pregnant, her eyes didn't shine at all.

'Everyone is someone's baby,' she said. 'I've never thought of that before.'

I laughed.

'It's not funny,' she said.

'Are you OK?' I said.

'It's just being pregnant,' she said. 'Hoping it all goes OK.'

I pushed the trolley around the library, putting books back on shelves, feeling like a tea-lady. You got a First from Durham University, I said to myself, and here you are – a library assistant in Hedley Green. You need to do something with your life.

My novel was stalling.

'Do you think you can write about a country you haven't visited?' I said to Julia.

'You know more about it than the people who live there,' she said. 'But I guess it's hard to imagine things we haven't been through.'

'There really *is* a guy who's set up a rose farm outside Bujumbura,' I said. 'I read about him on the internet – and he's lost nearly his whole family. All that's left are his roses, and there's only so much you can write about roses.'

'Could you un-kill his family?' said Julia. 'Bring them back to life. I wish we could do that, don't you? In real life.'

'What? Undo time?' I said. 'Who would you un-kill first?'

She half-closed her eyes and shook her head.

'Jules, what *is it*?' I said.

'If I decided to climb a tree, and you were watching and I fell off and died, whose fault would it be?' she said.

'Yours for climbing the tree,' I said. 'Especially if it was a stupid tree to climb.'

'Oh good,' she said. 'Oh good – is that right?'

'Yes, as long as I at least *tried* to help.'

'Don't say that,' she said.

'If I didn't try to help, would I go to hell?' she said.

'What?' I said.

'Grandma's always talking about hell,' said Julia. 'She says it's the whole point.'

'The whole point of what?' I said.

'Can you go to hell for not helping?' said Julia.

'I don't know anything about hell.'

'Perhaps hell is not being able to get away from things we've done wrong.'

'Jules, you've never done anything wrong,' I said.

'You won't leave me, will you?' said Julia.

'Eventually I'll have to,' I said. 'I'll need to get a real job, and that job won't be in Hedley Green, will it, let's be honest.'

'Please stay until I have the baby,' said Julia.

'I'm going to call her Rose Augusta,' said Julia.

I put my arm around her.

'I'm honoured,' I said. 'And you are totally sure about this pink colour for the room, aren't you?'

She nodded, smiling.

'It's definitely a girl, isn't it?' I said, as I dragged the roller through a tray of candy-floss-coloured paint, wincing.

'Surely you of all people would be happy with pink for a boy?' said Julia, eyeing me quizzically, her face so radiant suddenly, happy, I thought, yes, happy.

She started cutting up her old childhood dresses to make a patch-work quilt for the cot, and I pointed at the hexagons of material and said, 'Our fifth birthday. The Christmas we got the trikes. That sunny day in Mousehole. Grandma's birthday at the hotel.'

I kind of wished, for a reason I didn't fully understand, that she wasn't cutting up our duplicate dresses, but that was ridiculous, so I said nothing.

Julia bought a white cot, a fold-out bed (in case of disturbed nights) and a Moses basket with white lace lining on a stand. The ceiling light was a hot-air balloon with a basket underneath. I bought a little plug-in dome which projected gold stars and a crescent moon onto the ceiling.

On the window sill, Julia put a tiny sleeping cat with the smoothest black fur, curled up in a basket. It was so real that it actually breathed – you could see its tiny ribcage expanding and contracting.

It was Friday night, the night Diego went to the gym and my grand-mother came round. My mother was cooking spag bol – does anyone say that any more?

'Just like old times,' said my mother, handing tea through the serving arch as we all gathered in the lounge to watch TV.

'I never knew snakes could move so fast,' said my father.

'Why aren't you watching, Augusta?' said my mother.

'I'm watching *and* reading.'

'What a horrible title,' said my mother. 'What is that book? *Blood Wedding?*'

'I've told you about it before – it's a Spanish play.'

'What's it about?'

'Kind of everything really – and more every time I read it, if you know what I mean, life, death . . .'

'She's stopped moving,' said Julia, running her hands over her stomach.

'Don't worry, darling,' said my mother. 'She'll be having a little sleep.'

'But she normally moves all the time.'

'Can you feel anything?' said my father. 'Do you want me to run you up to the hospital?'

'Oh, there's her little foot,' said Julia, and she took my hand.

'I think that's her heel,' I said.

It was so strange to feel a living heel inside Julia, pushing through her skin, like pastry, four and twenty blackbirds baked in a pie, that was in my W. B. Rands book too, squealing little blackbird beaks. I remembered Julia's chicks, especially the last chick, which crashed into the plastic side of the incubator and died before it had lived outside the shell.

The television snakes came at the young deer from all directions, and they crushed it to death in a scaly ball of knotted squirming muscle.

'You can see why Satan is seen as a snake,' said my grandmother, seeming energised.

'Shall we turn off the snakes?' said my father.

'But it's true,' said my grandmother. 'Satan was the one who made childbirth painful, wasn't he? As a punishment for eating the apple.'

'She only ate an apple!' I said, laughing.

'But the most important thing is that you forget very quickly,' said my mother firmly. 'Giving birth was the best moment of my life.'

'A woman soon forgets her suffering because of her joy that a child is born into the world,' said my grandmother, pushing her glasses down her nose and looking over them.

My mother nodded gratefully.

'And in my case,' said my mother. 'Not one child but two wriggling little bundles. First Julia, pale and calm, like a little china doll . . .'

'Don't tell me,' I said. 'Then me – red and cross with thick black hair like a dog.'

'You were my best-ever gifts,' said my mother.

'I talk to Rose when I can't sleep,' said Julia. 'I feel like I was born to be her mother.'

When Diego arrived from the gym, he was brimming with confidence inside his taut manly body, as if he was about to break out of himself.

'I think it's time for bed,' said Julia.

'I'll drive you home, Mother,' said my father, whose own mother, Rose, had died when he was a boy. His father had told him she'd gone away and would soon be back, and maybe he was still waiting. Maybe that was why his fingers shook.

My grandmother, Nellie, got to her feet, clutching her black patent handbag with her stiff hands.

'If men had to have babies,' she said, 'the human race would die out!'

My mother smiled at her, but my grandmother didn't smile back.

I think my mother has always felt she doesn't measure up, which I understand.

So strange, the way we pass things on, perhaps the things we least want to.

I must remember that.

'Have you heard of a TENS machine?' said my grandmother to Julia. 'Supposed to be very good. That's what Constance said anyway.'

'The hippie woman recommended it,' said Diego.

'She's keen on natural childbirth,' said Julia. 'No drugs. No epidurals. She said women were *made to give birth*.'

'She wouldn't have been accounting for Satan.'

'She's quite right,' said my mother.

'Women can do other things,' I said.

'I'll be right there by your side,' said Diego. 'Down at the south stand!'

'South stand!' said my father, laughing appreciatively, as no doubt had the men in the changing room at the gym.

The TENS machine was useless in the end, Julia told me, like trying to mop up the Atlantic Ocean with a small piece of blotting paper.

Diego didn't want me at the birth.

He didn't want my mother either.

We wouldn't have made any difference, and, anyway, I didn't want to watch.

The contractions started to come quickly and hard, and they rushed to the hospital.

'Gates up,' Diego texted.

'Arrived.'

'Agony.'

'Unbearable to watch.'

'TENS machine no good.'

'Epidural.'

Later, much later, when we arrived in Spain, a year and a half later, he said that he'd believed the hippie woman. He thought women's bodies *were* made for it. He couldn't believe it had to be so difficult.

Yet it is so ordinary to be born, and so ordinary to die.

350,000 births per day, apparently.

And 150,000 deaths.

Approximately.

Around the world.

That's 15,000 births and 6,300 deaths per hour.

250 births each minute and 105 deaths.

Count to one.

Four babies have arrived.

Count to two.

Two of us have left the world.

Right now.

As you click your fingers.

If only we left the earth in pairs.

Like animals leaving the ark.

Two by two hurrah.

Hand in hand.

Or died together like roses on the same bush.

It would be so much less scary.

'I asked her if she wanted me to turn up the TENS machine,' Diego said to me on the beach, once we arrived in La Higuera. 'And she said something. I haven't told anyone else. It was so out of character.'

I waited, a bit nervous.

'She swore,' said Diego.

'All women swear when they give birth,' I said, relieved.

'But not Julia,' he said.

'Even Julia.'

'She said, *Fucking TENS machine!* And that's when I got a bad feeling.'

'It can be a good word, Diego,' I said to him. 'Swearing can really help, I've heard.'

I wonder if it does.

'But not Julia,' he said. 'She wouldn't say that. Did you ever hear her swear?'

'Twice. One bloody and one fuck.'

We both looked out to Africa – there were tiny lights shimmering in the dusk over the grey glass sea.

Julia was impaled on her child, that's what she said to me, that the baby felt like a rugby ball of flesh, completely solid, hard, immovable, jamming up her vagina, forcing it open.

'I didn't want her to suffer so much,' said Diego. 'She was in so much pain, and the baby wouldn't come, and then one midwife ran out of the room, and I knew something was wrong, and there were people everywhere, like a circle around her bed, and I was pushed back. I hated that. Being pushed back.'

The little girl was pulled out of her with the suction-thing, a ventouse, I think it's called, and her tiny left arm was sticking up, apparently.

'She must be exhausted,' Julia said. 'Poor little thing.'

That's what she thought when the baby didn't cry.

'Oh,' said the midwife.

And there was silence.

'Oh.'

'It is a girl, isn't it?' Julia said. 'Because I've painted everything candy-pink!'

But nobody answered.

'Rose Augusta,' she said. 'That's her name.'

She lay back on the pillow.

She remembered someone saying, 'Just a few stitches.'

People everywhere, talking over her.

Not talking to her.

Later they asked if she'd like to hold her baby, her baby who was dead.

'I'm so sorry,' said the midwife. 'This must be very painful for you.'

'I don't know,' she said.

Diego said no.

He walked out.

He walked back in.

Julia was holding her.

She had pale hair, and she was wrapped up in a white sheet with no creases in it.

'Two perfect little heels,' Julia said to me later. 'The way they used to kick. You felt them. Do you remember?'

Julia stared at Rose.

And Diego stared at Julia.

And she asked for some scissors.

And she cut a tuft of her fine blonde hair from her baby's head.

And gave it to Diego.

Who wrapped it in a tissue.

And later gave it to me because he couldn't bear to have it.

'Did she drown inside me?' said Julia.

'We don't know exactly,' said the midwife. 'It's very unusual.'

'Unusual?' said Julia.

She looked down at her little dead baby.

She started singing.

She sang 'Twinkle Twinkle Little Star' at her.

Up above the world so high,
Like a diamond in the sky.
Twinkle twinkle little star.
How I wonder what you are.

She rocked her in her arms.

Then she stopped.

She said, 'This is ridiculous.'

She looked strange and far away, Diego said.

'Where did you come from?' she whispered to the baby.

'Why did you leave me?' she said.

Then she said, 'Where shall I put her?'

'Shall we take her away?' said the midwife.

'No,' said Julia. 'Put her here in this plastic thing next to me.'

'The cot?'

'Is that a cot?' said Julia.

'I don't like looking,' said Diego. 'Do you mind if I don't look?'

'It's like the chick incubator,' said Julia. 'Do you remember?'

He nodded.

'Would you like to take a photo?' said the midwife.

'Yes,' said Julia.

'I don't know if I can,' said Diego.

'You have to,' said Julia. 'From lots of different angles. Every single bit of her. Undo the sheet. Don't miss anything. So we'll never ever forget any part of her.'

Her tiny snub nose, that's what struck me.

And the whorls of her perfect little ears.

Like ammonites.

'I want to dress her,' said Julia.

'Granny made you a cardigan, Rose,' she said to the dead baby.

The midwife helped her put it on, which was difficult, the left arm, the fiddly little fingers, in particular.

The cardigan had a satin ribbon, which she tied in a bow.

'I couldn't get the bow right,' she said to me.

'Her arms were like dolls' arms, but her skin was all flaky,' she said.

'It was seeing her in Mum's cardigan,' she said. 'That's when it hit me.'

She let out the most heart-rending cry, that's what Diego said.

'I'm so sorry,' she said to the baby. 'I'm so sorry. I'm just so so sorry.' Over and over again.

'Everything about her was perfect,' she said to me. 'Except that she was dead.'

I held her in my arms.

'I could taste my tears,' she said. 'They came in big waves, and I couldn't get rid of the taste of salt – whatever I ate. I scrubbed at my tongue with a toothbrush, and I made it bleed. But I could still taste the salt, mixed up with the blood.'

We had been poised.

On the cusp.

Of something.

But we got something else.

The Moses basket lay empty, its blankets tidily folded.

The day after Rose was born dead, my father had a stroke. His face split in two along the hairline crack which I saw coming the night that Mr Green watched his house fall down, and my father lost the left side of his body too.

Julia had also split in two.

They sewed the tear at the opening of her vagina with needle and thread.

But there was no needle and thread for her soul.

They buried Rose in a tiny green rectangular coffin.

Because green is the colour of life.

Julia planted a rose bush so that roses would grow from her dead baby, and butterflies would fly above and settle on the pinky sepia petals – above the thorns.

'Talk to me, Julia,' I said. 'Talk to me.'

'Words are no good,' she said.

My novel had stalled.

Because the rose farmer didn't have any words either.

*   *   *

Julia sat with the patchwork quilt, feeling the textures of the different fabric hexagons with her fingers, rubbing them against her cheek, which was sweating.

Diego said he was going to bed.

I said goodnight to him.

'Don't go,' she said when I got up to leave. 'There's that folding bed in Rose's room. I put it in there in case she was unsettled in the night. I didn't want to disturb Diego if he had work in the morning. But really I think I wanted to sleep next to her. To check she was OK. To keep looking at her – do you know what I mean?'

I didn't.

'I'm sorry, Jules,' I said. 'I don't know what to say to help you.'

'Nothing helps,' she said. 'Because I'd planned my whole life being with her.'

She sat staring at the television.

'My whole life,' she said again.

I'm not sure I understood then how a tiny baby inside you, who you'd never met, could take up the whole of the rest of your life.

We sat watching the news, on repeat.

'Shall we go to bed, Jules?' I said. 'It's late. And Diego will be waiting for you.'

'Not yet,' she said.

Her lips trembled, and she flicked through the channels.

We watched the headlines again.

President Poroshenko declares a unilateral ceasefire in Ukraine.

Again.

Then he declared it again.

'I can't remember what unilateral means . . .' said Julia.

'Affecting one group or one person,' I said.

'Oh,' she said.

'Come on, Jules,' I said.

'Not yet,' she said. 'Please. Not yet. Don't make me.'

We sat saying nothing.

'Can you turn the telly off, Aug?' she said. 'I can't stand that advert.'

It was a family in a kitchen.

I turned it off.

'I can't stand the silence,' she said.

'Shall I turn the telly back on?' I said.

'Not that kitchen,' she said.

'Maybe we should go into the garden,' I said. 'It's so hot.'

We sat on the new swing seat in the dark, and we rocked back and forward, sitting together side by side, with our thighs touching.

Flesh on flesh, slightly sweaty.

'I imagined that I'd be out here all summer, sitting here with her, rocking. So happy.'

I nodded.

'So happy,' she said.

I couldn't breathe.

A car drove into next door's drive.

'He's very late,' I said.

The door slammed.

'He works shifts,' said Julia. 'That's his normal life. Everyone else's lives go on the same.'

We heard his key in the side door.

'That's why I bought it,' said Julia. 'So it would rock. And also so the shade would keep the sun off her head.'

We sat in the dark, rocking back and forward. The night sky was pale with clouds, and between them, the moon peeped out, like a fat face.

'They say babies like rocking because it reminds them of being in the womb,' said Julia.

I nodded.

'She was so beautiful,' she said. 'I wish you'd seen her.'

'I wish I'd seen her,' I said.

And Julia started to cry again.

'I'm too frightened to go to bed,' she said. 'I'm too frightened to close my eyes.'

Diego came stumbling into the back garden.

'You could have told me,' he said. 'I didn't know where the hell you were.'

'Leave me alone,' said Julia. 'Go back to bed.'

'Come to bed with me,' said Diego.

She shook her head.

'She's too frightened,' I said.

'What of?' said Diego.

'Closing my eyes,' said Julia.

'I'll be with you,' said Diego.

'Not when I close my eyes,' she said. 'That's when all of us are on our own.'

Neither Diego or I spoke.

'Rose is all alone now,' she said. 'Without me.'

Diego took her hands and he pulled her up from the swing seat, and he tried to hold her hand, but she wouldn't hold his.

'I'm frightened of my life, Aug,' she said. 'What it's going to be now.'

They disappeared through the back door into the kitchen.

I went to Rose's room.

As I walked, something grazed the top of my head.

I jumped.

The basket of the hot-air balloon.

I turned on the light.

The empty balloon basket was swinging back and forward in the breeze from the fanlight window.

I stood by the window.

The rose curtains were open and I stared into Higgots Close, where every light but one was off. There was a guy upstairs, sitting at a computer in a yellow glowing window. I wondered what he was doing.

The tiny black cat breathed in and out, in and out, on the window sill, as if it were alive.

*　　*　　*

Julia, her breasts swelling with unwanted milk, which made dry streams inside her bra, had taken to playing my father's old records on a vintage turntable that Diego had bought her on eBay.

When I think of that time, I see the black album cover lying on the carpet – Art Garfunkel's shock of blond hair, and Paul Simon's face, half-light and half-shadow. I had the feeling that we were deep in the shadows – 'the valley of the shadow of death,' said my grandmother.

Julia took the needle, and it crackled with dust, and there went the song again, track 4, *Homeward Bound*, she was sitting in the railway station . . .

'Why do you play this one so much?' I said. 'Do you want me to take you somewhere on the train? We could go up beyond Durham and walk across the causeway to Holy Island. Or we could get the Eurostar to France and go back to Quimper – what do you think? Do you want to get away? Is that it, Julia?'

Round and round went the vinyl album. Julia would take the metal arm, replace the scratchy little needle at the outer circumference, and *Homeward Bound* would start again.

I wondered whether home was no longer here, no longer me, no longer any of us.

My mother would watch the doves fly through the garden at number 1.

'Do you want to fly kites, Jules?' I said.

'Or go for a picnic on Tattershall Common?'

'Get drunk on cider?'

'Make a fire behind the shed?'

'Augusta,' she said. 'Can you shut the fuck up?'

I didn't tell anyone she'd said that.

But it kept coming at me. Like the needle was stuck in a groove.

I couldn't sleep for hearing it.

It made me tremble.

I'd lost my confidence that I could make her better.

I'd lost my confidence that I knew her at all.

I couldn't find our warm secret places.

They'd evaporated.

All we had was the cold, quiet, separate present.

I crept in and out of the maisonette in Higgots Close, treading my way through the thick air in the hall, making her cheese-and-ham pancakes, which used to be her best thing, but I feared that everything I did was wrong.

My mother was also split in two.

When she was with my father at the hospital, she felt she should be with Julia. And when she was with Julia, my father kept phoning her and speaking in his new slurry voice so that she couldn't understand what he was saying. But he was always saying, Where are you?

'It's like a tug of war,' she said.

'Stay with him, for God's sake,' said Julia. 'No one can help me.'

'You're very brusque, darling,' said my mother.

'Is she brusque with you, Augusta?' she asked me.

I said no.

Because it hurt me too much to say yes.

I felt now that I would never, could never, leave her.

Yet I couldn't bear to be with her, that's the truth.

My mother made batches and batches of cupcakes, icing them in pastel colours and covering them in small sugared flowers and white rabbits left over from Easter. She rushed to the corner shop and bought several varieties of polish. She polished the furniture, and Diego's shoes.

'Please don't put roses on the cakes,' said Julia.

'You don't need to polish my shoes, Jilly,' said Diego. 'I'm not going anywhere.'

So she polished my father's shoes instead, and left them in a tidy row by the back door, though he only ever wore his brown corduroy slippers, which sat on the little plastic foot-rest of the wheelchair, with his feet inside them.

My mother and I ate cakes in my father's grey ward, where old men cried and burped and asked to go home. Then we ate cakes in Julia's conservatory as the doves crapped above us, and their guano dripped like paint down the slanted glass.

I went on working at the library.

I hovered about the self-help section looking up Stillborn Babies and Loss of Speech after Strokes.

I longed to get away.

I felt full of guilt.

I wished I hadn't gone on about dying.

I wished I hadn't read out bits of *Blood Wedding*.

I wished I hadn't done my dissertation on Symbols of Death in Spanish Literature of the Early Twentieth Century.

I wished I'd never chosen Burundi as my favourite country.

I wished I'd married Olly Macintosh and moved to Cirencester.

Far far away.

And worn green tweed jackets and tended horses.

And had a baby, myself.

And from where, on the phone, I would have said, in a calm and measured voice, 'I can't leave the horses/my husband/the farm/my baby. Do send Julia lots of love.'

My father came home in his wheelchair, and I slid him up the new metal ramp and into the porch.

My mother was given compassionate leave from the pet shop.

Diego was given compassionate leave from the council.

We went on eating my mother's cakes.

We all put on half a stone.

I dreamt of La Higuera.

Julia had counselling and drugs.

More counselling.

More drugs.

We went to Old John Brown's to watch the sun rise because we couldn't sleep, and when we walked home, the level crossing gates came down. We stood waiting in silence.

I tried to think of something to say, which made me nervous, aiming for words which were not too sad, not too happy. Better to mention the baby? Or better not to? Call her *the baby*? Call her *Rose*? Tell her how sad I was that she didn't invite me to the funeral. They didn't invite anyone.

I wanted to put my arm through hers.

But I didn't.

Her hands were in her pockets.

The tension bubbled into possible sentences I might say.

I saw us, through the ages, waiting by the gates, growing taller, changing school uniforms. I imagined us on fast forward, like those sped-up films you see on nature documentaries, about the growth of trees.

Blossoming, flourishing, that's what we expect.

We didn't expect this.

Nobody does round here.

The train sped past, passengers a blur, zooming towards London, as Julia and I stood.

'Do trains remind you of time?' I said to Julia.

She laughed.

The sound of it shocked me.

I hadn't heard her laughter for a while.

'Do you remember when we got drunk before I left for Durham?' I said.

Julia creased her eyes like someone looking for something they can't see.

'You must remember. I read you the Lotos-Eaters poem by Tennyson. *Time driveth onward fast . . .*'

'Oh, Aug,' she said. 'Will you never change?'

The steady beat of the disappearing train faded into silence.

'If trains do remind you of time,' I said, anxious and tripping on my words, 'it's good news, Julia. We move on. It doesn't seem as if we will, but we do. These days I hardly think of Olly Macintosh. You will have more babies. You will be the best mother in the world.'

The train noise was eaten by the air as the gates came up, and we walked through, on our way back to Willow Crescent.

I shouldn't have mentioned Olly Macintosh.

How could I think of comparing poncy Olly Macintosh with his ridiculous floppy hair to her dead baby?

We walked on in silence, and Julia came to a stop on the pavement, outside the party shop and the jeweller's.

She took a big breath, hesitated, then took another breath.

She put her hand on my upper arm.

'I don't want to move on, Aug,' she said. 'That's the point. Don't you get that? I don't want to *hardly think of Rose*. Having more babies isn't the point at all. The point is that *I killed her.*'

I stopped.

I breathed.

I gathered myself together.

And I said, 'What do you mean you killed her?'

'She was alive and swimming about inside me. But there you are. An eye for an eye. A tooth for a tooth. Like Grandma says.'

'What was the first eye then? The first tooth?'

'There was a boy. And I didn't save him. *I didn't save him.*'

'What are you talking about?'

'When we went to Spain. The morning we had breakfast on the beach. Saw the sun rise. And you didn't come. That's the thing I never told you. The thing that happened. Here's the newspaper cutting. The photo. I cut it out. You have it.'

She took it out of her pocket.

'This is the newspaper Dad didn't let us buy. I stole it from the shop,' said Julia, handing it to me.

'I knew something was wrong and I kept asking you. But you wouldn't tell me. Why wouldn't you tell me?'

'I promised Dad I wouldn't.'

There was our special spot, the holey rocks, the pine trees, the white sand, the buried *patera* boat, there were the sunrise fish clouds – and there was a black man, face down on the beach.

'He was probably one of the guys from the building site,' I said. 'Sleeping on the beach. You didn't need to save him.'

'Not him,' she said, and she was white with the fluorescent light of the street lamp. 'No, there was someone out at sea, I'm sure there was. There was just his hand. Like your poem.'

Then Diego arrived.

He clamped his arm around Julia's shoulder and she stopped talking, and, as we walked, his arm slipped down and fell off right off her.

Someone out at sea?

A hand like in my poem?

I couldn't ask.

In case Diego didn't know.

Because husbands are supposed to know everything, and I couldn't risk it, especially with things so strange.

I'd find a way to bring up the conversation when I next saw her.

Which was never, the time I next saw her.

'Chin up,' Diego said to her the following morning as she sat on the bed.

The sun rises.

The new day always comes.

Yet you don't always want it.

Sometimes you know you don't want it, and sometimes you don't.

But it doesn't make any difference.

'Why did I say chin up?' Diego asked me.

Julia's chin, when he looked back on that last moment together, had not been up. It had been down. Her eyes had been down too. Looking at the floor, and not at him.

Again.

He should have asked her to look up, that's what he said, because he might have seen something in her eyes, something which would have told him, which could have stopped it, which would have made him go with her to Amy's.

Or *I* should have warned him, that's what he said later – did I see any signs?

I didn't tell him about the newspaper cutting she'd given me, in case that was a sign, and I'd missed it.

'Aren't twins supposed to feel these things?' he said.

Julia, eyes down, fiddling with the towelling belt of her bathrobe, as Diego remembered it, said, 'I'm going to walk over to Amy's later and give her the pram. I don't want to have the pram in the hall any more. I think it will be a step, don't you? A *step forward.*'

Diego liked the sound of a step forward that morning. Because they'd stepped endlessly backwards.

'I'm being repaid,' said Julia.

'You're not being logical,' Diego said.

'My baby died and you talk to me about logic!' she said.

'I feel like I'm going mad,' said Diego.

'*You're* going mad?' said Julia.

'Well, perhaps we both are.'

'Anyway, I'm going to take the pram to Amy's. She's two weeks away.'

'Is that hard for you?' said Diego.

'What do you think?'

'I'm sorry.'

'And I'm sorry,' said Julia. 'For how horrible I am these days.'

Diego didn't tell her he forgave her.

He wanted her to feel bad.

He wanted her to know how horrible she was these days.

He was late for work, and he hated his job.

Because he hated everything.

So all he said was, 'See you later, darling. Chin up.'

'Chin up,' said Diego. 'Who says "chin up"?'

'You could have said much worse things, Diego,' I said. 'Think of all the things you managed not to say that morning.'

'She was always saying I mustn't try and fix things. She told me not to give her solutions.'

'Don't try and fix it, Diego,' said their counsellor, black-eyed Virginia. 'Show you're listening by repeating back what she says to you. Let's try. Julia. Say something.'

'I keep thinking about a secret I carry,' said Julia.

'Repeat it back,' said Virginia.

'You keep thinking about a secret you carry,' said Diego flatly.

He was weary.

He couldn't stand Virginia, and he couldn't stand reflective listening.

'Actually, why don't you tell Virginia about the secret?' said Diego. 'It might help to get it out, rationalise it somehow . . .'

Virginia shook her head vigorously.

'No no no, Diego,' she said. 'That's not reflective listening.'

'No!'

That's what I shrieked down the phone when I heard.

I didn't let Diego finish.

I was standing in our bedroom.

The little silver jewellery box was on the bed in a bag.

I dropped my phone.

And the wardrobe door was open.

I was watching myself in the mirror.

The way my face stilled, drained, paled, crunched up.

The way my arms hung.

I lifted one up.

To my face.

Like a puppet.

'No, no, no,' I said.

To the pale face.

I felt a strange swelling at the base of my spine, in my coccyx.

I turned around.

It was still light, a golden glow of late afternoon sun.

It was hard to believe that the sun would still be out.

I walked to the window.

My mother had put a vase of late-flowering chrysanthemums on the window sill, bright yellow.

She'd cut them from the garden.

I picked one flower out of the vase and stared at the way its stem had been cut on the diagonal.

It looked alive but actually it was dead.

Julia.

Julia.

The garden was still there.

A drop of water hit my sock.

Through the window, I saw my mother open the back door.

And her hand came out.

She didn't know.

Her hand reached for her wellington boots.

What a joy for her.

To be bringing in her wellington boots.

Her last moment of peace, it came to me.

Of the peaceful ordinary.

Dead leaves blew across the lawn, little flurries of wind lifting them – they rose and they fell.

Because my father couldn't use his rake.

And the pain of that had seemed.

Until now.

So big.

The pain of Rose.

So big.

Until now.

Everything, in an instant, had changed size and shape.

We'd never had all these dead leaves blowing around our garden before.

Because my father liked it tidy.

They both did.

They liked tidy.

And there was no tidy.

Julia.

Julia.

But I didn't cry.

The tears didn't come.

There was only the terrible pain at the base of my spine.

'My mouth still tastes of salt,' Julia said to Diego before he left.

'Kiss me,' said Diego.

'I don't want to,' said Julia. 'Go to work.'

And Julia took that step forward.

Straight into the train.

The train had always been coming.

It was timetabled.

It came down the track from London.

As it did so, I was at the counter of the jewellery shop, picking up the locket with the ringlet of Rose's blonde hair, a white rose petal and the engraved date of her birth: 10 July 2014.

The woman handed me the silver box and she said, with a cheery smile. 'I hope your sister likes it.'

But I didn't know, I didn't know, I was buying her a locket which I was planning to give to her in a silver box later that day, or maybe the next.

'I'm sure she will,' I said.

I walked home.

To Willow Crescent.

A three-minute walk.

Went up to my room.
Put the box on my bed.
Took off my shoes.

Time driveth onward fast,
And in a little while our lips are dumb.
Let us alone. What is it that will last?

She'd been eaten up.
    By the mouth of the train.
    The empty pram was mangled in its jaws.
    It was 5 November, and we were twenty-four years old.
    And Julia would only ever be twenty-four years old from now on.
    And Jules.
    Weren't we going to?
    Weren't we going to?
    So much.
    I'd planned my whole life being with her.
    Isn't that what she said?
    And I hadn't understood.
    I would be twenty-five.
    Twenty-six.
    Fifty-six perhaps.
    Who knows?
    Or seventy-six.
    She would forever be twenty-four.
    And I wasn't a twin any more.
    I was already older than her.
    I didn't sense it.
    I was her twin, and I should have done.
    Everything should have stopped.
    To mark her stopping.
    But nothing stopped.

Except the traffic which queued at the level crossing.

People hooted and got out and shouted at the policemen.

They said they had a fireworks show to go to.

Open the bloody gates.

Diego sat without her kiss, with her voice saying over and over again, I don't want to, I don't want to, I don't want to.

His un-kissed lips felt like ice.

As if they'd died too.

He shivered.

Diego said to my parents that she was getting better, she was taking the pram to Amy's – it's only that she never got there.

'She's always day-dreaming,' said my mother.

We sat staring out of the window, our shaking hands trying to hold cups of tea, our shaking mouths trying to form words and sentences although there were no words in the whole of the dictionary that were suitable for this day.

My parents looked at me, and I looked at them.

What we felt, I think, though this is odd, was embarrassed.

By the way we weren't OK.

We weren't at all OK.

We were supposed to be normal.

We weren't this kind of family.

We had no setting for drama.

Or for feelings.

Feelings like this, which wanted to explode through our skin and shatter us, like a grenade.

We needed to pull ourselves together.

I tried to act normal.

My mother made more tea.

The tea tasted of copper.

'Did she kiss you goodbye?' said my mother.

'Yes,' said Diego, lying.

'It's the anti-depressants,' said my mother. 'They blur your mind.'

Diego didn't answer, and for a second I thought we were talking about anti-depressants, a conversation we'd had before, she's depressed, it's quite normal, it'll pass.

Then it came at me.

My phone lying on the floor.

The stem cut on the diagonal, with its last drop of life.

The bag with the locket in a silver box on the bed.

My mother's hands reaching out of the back door for her wellington boots.

The first people to come and ring on the doorbell at number 1 Willow Crescent were Jim and Barbara Cook.

'We came to say that there are no words.'

That's what they said, not alluding to the fact that there had been no words from my father for the past twelve years.

Other people, though they knew, they knew, all of Willow Crescent knew within minutes, were pulling on their coats and gloves and climbing into their cars to go to the fireworks at Tattershall Common, giving themselves time to go the *long way round*, avoiding the *incident* at the level crossing.

They would keep going.

They would keep putting on their gloves.

'Put your gloves on!' they called to each other in hallways.

If they put their gloves on, they wouldn't be frightened of the kinds of things that could happen in life, their lives too. Like when someone tells you they have cancer, and you want to feel more scared for them than you do for yourself.

Life couldn't stop, they thought, on Fireworks Night, not for a death. Death is what happens to other people – let's go to the fireworks display to show that we're alive. Bang bang bang!

Barbara opened her arms, and my mother clenched her teeth, you could see her jaw under her skin, tightening – and she stared at Barbara.

'Let me give you a hug,' said Barbara.

'I don't know how to,' said my mother.

'Julia,' she said, looking around her.

Barbara didn't know what to say.

'She's always here,' said my mother. 'Isn't she? Round at our place? Even though she's married . . .'

'She . . .' Barbara hesitated – the present tense, the past tense, how could one switch over so quickly?

'She's such a perfect daughter,' said my mother.

'She is,' said Barbara, wincing, at the tense, the wrong tense, the right tense. 'Yes, she is.'

I stared at Barbara as she took my mother's hand.

I noticed the veins standing up on it, and a little brown age spot in the shape of a kidney bean.

Jim bent to the wheelchair.

My father clung to him.

'I told her she'd have more babies,' said my mother.

I'd told her that too.

I'm not sure it helped.

She didn't want her dead baby to be replaced.

My father was crying.

She had perhaps preferred to die and be with Rose.

She'd wanted to be *homeward bound,* ever since she lost her, like the song.

Where are you? I thought, and the fear of it sent me running up the stairs, to our bedroom, where I got into Julia's cold bed, deep deep down, all of me, under the duvet, which was too tight because my mother always tucked the bedspread in under the mattress.

Parfait

Oddly, this little spot at the back of the beach had become home. Despite what happened here, or perhaps because of it. Because sometimes it's the pain of a place that draws us to it.

Every home has known pain, I guess. It's what gives it texture.

When I turned onto the beach road, I could hear the waves and smell the pines, and I felt a tingling in my stomach.

I parked, and I climbed onto the roof of the coach to check Africa was still there. Then I looked the other way – to the cows in the fields. The moon was in the sky, though it wasn't quite dark, and its light shone on the egret tree, where the birds were flying in to roost.

That's when I had the idea.

A Refugee Tree?

Deeds, deeds, that would be a deed.

Not as good as actually going there, but still.

Maybe this Christmas?

Augusta

When I went to see her body, which they had tried to put back together again, I couldn't look.

I didn't look.

I did look.

Between my fingers.

She was under a sheet.

Like her baby.

All except her hand.

All the king's horses and all the king's men
Couldn't put Humpty together again.

We used to say it so fast that the words blurred into each other.

I peered from under my hand, between my fingers, and I stared at her hand, the only part of her undamaged, they said.

'Of course she didn't kill herself,' my mother kept saying to me – she'd passed over to the past tense as you have to, you just have to. 'How ridiculous that anyone would say that. She had everything to live for.'

Her diamond ring.

I will always remember her hand.

So will Diego.

'She kissed Diego goodbye,' said my mother on the phone. 'Everything was quite normal. It's a freak accident.'

I couldn't see the freckle on her left ring finger.

And I didn't want to turn her dead finger to find her dead freckle.

In case it wouldn't move.

I didn't want to touch her.

And find her cold.

I didn't know what dead people felt like.

I didn't want to take my own hands from my face.

I didn't want.

Anything that was here.

I turned around and left.

And still the tears didn't come.

I'd turned to lead.

To osmium, the densest of all elements.

My legs wouldn't move.

My heart was so heavy it sank into my bowel.

They tried to find the chain with the double ring and the A and the J, which had been around her neck, but they said they were sorry, it obviously got damaged. Was it valuable?

'It didn't use to be,' I said.

I didn't want to think about her damaged neck.

Olly Macintosh could snap a bird's neck with his hands.

We gathered around the hole into which Julia's pale birch coffin would go now we had taken off the arrangements of white roses, abundant and pressed together like her wedding bouquet. I tried to calm myself by remembering facts about doves, a word that (rightly) rhymes with loves.

Facts facts facts facts to blot out the fear I felt inside.

Fear, all the time.

I never knew grief felt so much like fear.

Somebody else said that.

I thought grief would feel like sadness.

Where are you, Jules?

I need you right now.

To help me get through this.
Which is.
Obviously.
Absurd.
I closed my eyes.
I must tell Julia.
A pain in my chest, too intense to breathe at first.
About this terrible day.
She'd know what to say.
And she'd hold my hand.
A little shard of glass had lodged in my heart.
I felt it every time I breathed.
I guess this feeling is ordinary.
We smiled on the day of the funeral, greeting our friends, like robots – what did we care who came?
'We wanted to be here,' they said, one after another.
Did you? I thought.
Thinking nothing.
Other than that I didn't.
Other than that I had this piece of glass in my heart, which hurt every time I breathed.
I looked up at the doves, and I saw a tiny aeroplane higher up, tracing a white line in the sky, and I thought that there must be a line from me to her, if only I could see it.
Doves have exceptional eyesight, I thought. They can see things our eyes can't see. Is there some way of seeing her, or feeling her, I wondered. Wherever she is.
'She's looking down on you,' said Hilary Hawkins.
Is she? I thought.
The vicar said he didn't know if she was or she wasn't.
Nobody knows.
This is the one thing nobody knows, although we think we know everything.

We released the dove she loved most, the one with the Z-shaped ruffle of feathers on her head.

We looked up.

Then down.

A tremor started to run up my leg.

It ran around my body, stopping where it couldn't move through, there at that place at the base of my spine, where the fear had gathered in a huge knot.

Everyone was staring at the ground. They couldn't bear to look. They couldn't bear, especially, to look at me. To look at my mother. To look at my father. To look at Diego.

My father was embarrassed by what he'd become.

So was I.

I didn't want to be an object of pity, talked about behind net curtains.

I didn't want these people here watching me.

I didn't want them to see my fear.

Or my shaking legs.

You don't invite people to funerals; they just come.

So, at this most private of moments, as your sister is lowered into a hole in the ground, there are people there you didn't choose and you didn't invite and you didn't want.

Watching you.

People like Robin Fox, with some girl you've never met, in a black dress, and neither of them giving a shit.

Talking about you afterwards.

When you wanted to be invisible.

My mother pushed my father in his wheelchair.

'Let me,' I said.

'He's my husband,' she said.

So I stepped to one side, and I felt unwelcome, and I remembered my mother saying to Barbara Cook, 'She's such a perfect daughter.'

I don't measure up, I thought, like my mother.

My grandmother didn't come – she said she was coming down with something.

And down she went.

Down we all went.

My mother's face had sort of imploded inwards. She'd covered it in white powder and chosen a hat with a black veil, which gave me the horrible feeling that her face was dissolving behind it. She said nothing. She gripped the handles of the wheelchair.

She clenched and she clenched and she gritted and held on. And then, in the silence, she couldn't stop herself, she let out a long low moan, which felt to me as if it would never stop.

A long low moan like a cow in calf.

Cards fell through the letterbox, making the faintest of sounds as they hit the wire bristles of the mat which said WELCOME.

'Thinking of you,' they said.

And sometimes they were.

And sometimes they weren't.

I heard a man enquiring about condolence cards in the newsagent by the station.

'I think we've run out,' said a girl chewing gum.

They would be restocked, she assured him, there'd been a lot of demand for them recently.

New condolence cards would arrive, which would sit waiting for the next name, right next to the birth cards.

Lola Alvárez gave me an old book by Francis of Assisi, sepia-coloured and slightly falling apart.

I leafed through it. All the darkness in the world cannot extinguish the light of a single candle, that's what it said.

But it wasn't true – two candles had already been extinguished.

And before we knew it, another one was.

The third candle was Graham Cook.

I ordered a bus made of red roses, and Jim and Barbara put it on his coffin with their own. I was his only friend. His girlfriend. Though they didn't say that any more. Words are unpredictable. You never know how they'll be received. And that makes me nervous as I write. But, most of all, I rehearsed all the words I'd ever said to Julia. They gathered in a cloud above my head, and rained on me, constantly, so that I was always covered in a damp film of regret.

I shouldn't have said that.

I should have said this.

This particular word, phrase, sentence might have stopped her.

Why, and how, didn't I notice how bad she was feeling?

Why didn't I realise when she handed over the newspaper cutting outside the party shop? When she told me about the hand out at sea?

It felt like the ultimate and most terrible failure, and it followed me like a ghost.

Two funerals in fairly quick succession underneath the doves at the church on Higgots Close. I guess that's what churches are for. The ordinary business of dying.

Not so many people came to Graham's funeral, though most of those who were there had never taken a second's notice of him in his life.

My grandmother rallied herself for this one.

'It's not the same with Graham,' she said.

'They always said he'd die young,' said my mother, nodding.

'It is the same,' my father wrote in biro on the spiral pad.

My mother cried.

I cried.

Because Stanley Hope, in all his hopelessness, made me feel more hopeful these days. We took my mother's scones to the Cooks. Barbara made ginger cake, and my mother reciprocated with coffee and walnut sponge.

Our grieving was an exchange of cakes through the winter because sometimes the only things you can do in response to big things are small things.

There aren't big enough big things.

Diego and I would go for walks and remember Julia, telling each other new stories about her, ones that the other didn't know. Then the stories ran out, and there was no more new.

She was lying in the ground with the worms, her skin was drying to parchment, she would soon be dust.

I listened to voicemails that I hadn't deleted.

And winced at the sound of her undusty voice.

And wondered where her life had gone – the warm livingness of her.

I dreamt she was a butterfly.

I caught her in a net.

She had wings and her own face.

And somehow, by mistake, I let her fly out.

I raced around with the net.

'You'll never catch her,' said my mother.

It was winter.

The wintriest winter.

There were no butterflies.

I read poetry.

Frantically.

They looked for me in cafés, in cemeteries, in churches,
But they didn't find me.
They never found me.
No.
They never found me.

Diego went with his family to La Higuera for the Living Nativity – horses on the beach, camels in the square and a real baby in the manger, so they said.

Parfait

I watched the Advent celebrations in La Higuera from the roof of my coach with Antonio, Paco and Luis, who'd come over from Tarifa. I liked the way it felt – sitting up there, the four of us, together. On my patch. I had a patch. I had friends.

Mary and Joseph left Nazareth and started their journey up the beach, crowds of people following them.

Throughout December, the festivities continued, with real shepherds coming down from the hills with their sheep, robed travellers from the surrounding villages descending on the square in a great brouhaha of eating and drinking for the census, and, by Christmas Eve, Mary was coming into the square on a donkey, and people from all along the coast gathered, cheering in Christmas.

I'd persuaded the priest to put a Refugee Tree outside the church, where the four of us were standing.

'What if no one comes forward?' I said to Antonio, suddenly anxious.

'What if people don't want to pay for the gold stars?'

'What if the whole thing bombs?'

The huge fir tree towered over the Nativity stable – and just before midnight, I took my place at the microphone, nervous as anything, waiting for the crowd to stop talking, not sure what I'd do if they didn't.

But they did.

283

I invited the people who'd gathered in the square to buy a gold star and name it for a lost loved one. I said there was a star for each one of the refugees who'd drowned at sea this year, and that all donations would be going to those who'd made it, but had lost family, home, pretty much everything, in fact.

'I would be so grateful if you could help,' I said into the microphone.

Paco was first in the queue to remember his mother.

Then Antonio, to remember his.

Luis bought two stars, but wouldn't talk about either of them.

Then everyone else seemed to surge forward: old ladies with sticks, old men in caps, small children running.

The donation bowl overflowed.

I flicked the switch.

The tree trembled with light.

A baby cried in the stable.

The new year dawned, and the wise men came on camels.

Augusta

Barbara made us fruit cake and mince pies, and my mother and father and I fled to a wet cottage in Wales with pink acrylic curtains which let in the light, where the three of us did jigsaws together, not talking.

We returned to Willow Crescent, and the exchange of cakes began again between number 1 and number 2.

Spring came, and we went to Diego and Julia's maisonette in Higgots Close and mowed the lawn. The coral bark Japanese maple had pinkish green leaves growing on its branches, and underneath it grew circles of daffodils, with their trumpets for announcing extraordinary things and new beginnings. We picked them and put them around the window sills in little jugs.

Diego moved back in with his parents and resigned from his job. The council said they'd keep it open for him. He told them not to bother.

We put Julia's clothes in suitcases and wheeled them round to number 1, as if we were all going on a jolly holiday.

'We must take these to the charity shop,' I said.

'That would be horrible,' said my mother. 'Seeing the neighbours walking around in her clothes.'

'Janice Brown can put them in her plastic sacks and send them on to Africa,' I said.

'I want to put them back in your wardrobe,' said my mother, and her voice was breaking, and a little hair above her lip was trembling.

'I really don't want them in my wardrobe.'

'Then they will stay in the cases,' said my mother. 'We don't need the cases any more.'

I looked at her.

I would always need cases.

I wish I lived in a caravan.

I could hear my own breathing.

We put the cases on the landing, and Diego moved the dovecote he'd built for Julia into my parents' garden.

I went back to the station and squeezed between the barbed wire. The glade seemed to have shrunk in on itself, all its dimensions had changed and the bluebells were bowed down, staring at the ground.

I looked at the flat branch where we used to sit together.

I closed my eyes and walked away.

I didn't ever want to come here again.

I wanted to move on.

Somehow.

Somewhere.

When I got home, Jim and Barbara Cook were drinking tea with my mother and father, and my father was sitting in his wheelchair staring at the doves through the glass doors he'd once smashed with his chair.

'We need to have some new dreams, all of us,' I said to them. 'Did you have any dreams when you were young?'

My mother looked around her, as if she might be able to find some dreams above the sofa.

'Or maybe this was your dream,' I said. 'The house.'

'The house and the family,' said my mother.

And we found that we couldn't speak.

'I wanted my own steam train when I was a boy,' said Jim Cook into the silence, a resistant kind of silence, which made talking much harder than normal, as if you had to push your words through it. 'Or a barge. I think I got the idea from reading *Wind in the Willows*. How about you, Augusta?'

'Let me tell you my poem,' I said.

My mother looked nervous.

'It's more of a nursery rhyme, Mum,' I said. 'Don't worry.'

'Not like those awful poems of yours?' she said.

'It's called *The Pedlar's Caravan.*'

After I'd stopped saying the poem, they looked awkward.

Except Jim Cook didn't look awkward.

He looked slightly flushed.

The poem was my way of broaching the subject.

That I was going.

That I couldn't stay.

That I wished I lived in a caravan with a horse to drive like the pedlar man.

That I wished I didn't live here.

That I couldn't live here any longer.

Parfait

I sat high up in the hills above Tarifa, and I painted the storks as they arrived in their millions, crossing the Straits of Gibraltar from Africa all through the early spring, petering out as the sun got hotter and the days got longer and people started building *chiringuito* beach bars out of wood and thatch on the sand.

Summer was coming.

Augusta

The daffodils died, and the bluebells died, and I was quietly dying too as summer came and my parents sat staring into the back garden with their cups of tea. I sat staring with them. In the evenings and at weekends. They didn't like to leave the house any more.

Sometimes Diego joined us.

But that didn't help.

'Your parents are not your responsibility,' Barbara Cook said to me when she came to see me in the library. 'You have your life to lead, Augusta, and you always wanted to get away.'

'How can I possibly now?' I said.

'We need to get your mum and dad out of the house,' she said. 'I'm feeling a bit better since I started doing things. And I've got an idea. They're holding a steam fair on Tattershall Common on the fifth of July.'

'That'll be eight months to the day since she died,' I said.

'I'm going to get them there, whatever it takes,' she said.

And she did.

As we got out of the car, you could smell roasted chestnuts and candy floss. There was an old-fashioned merry-go-round, which I couldn't bear to think about, with that same organ music and palomino ponies with leather stirrups. There were steam yachts and swing boats in swirling red-and-yellow patterns. *Look, Julia, look*. We went over to the far side of the fairground which had a sign saying VINTAGE CARAVANS FOR SALE. There were rows of them called Small Southern, Royal Windsor, Proctor, Vosper and Brayshaw. But I had eyes for only one.

'*100 years old, living wagon belonging to fairground people in the age of horse-drawn vehicles.*'

It was old and wooden, its paint peeling off, its wheels bare and flaking. Jim Cook and I climbed inside. There was a little card fixed to the wooden slats, giving the caravan's dimensions – external length 3.9 m, width 2 m, height 3.25 m (excluding mollycroft). Mollycroft – I nearly shrieked with pleasure. A new word! They didn't come along so often nowadays. Jim was staring at the shabby wooden interior.

'Julia said she'd buy me a gypsy caravan if she ever got rich,' I said as we climbed down the steps to meet the others.

Nobody answered.

It was the sound made by her name.

Such an ordinary sound all those years.

But now you had to force yourself to say it.

For a fraction of a second, I saw her, as she was, and the leaves stopped blowing in the trees, the fair music paused, the birds stilled up above.

Her dove was on her hand.

But it all re-started.

Jim Cook re-started. He made a little stamp with his foot, and then his foot kept on tapping, as if his body was filling with energy, as if he was being unleashed.

'I ran out of money,' said the pale man who was selling the caravan. 'It will be beautiful once it's restored. It's sad, but there we are.'

'Tell us about its history,' said Jim, foot tapping away, as if, if we weren't careful, he would start involuntarily dancing a jig, like some kind of Victorian gypsy-man.

'Built in 1914. Made by F. J. Thomas of Chertsey, who also made hooplas and roundabouts. Used by travellers. England, Belgium,

France, possibly Spain,' said the pale man gloomily, pulling the plaited end of his beard.

'Spain?' I said. 'Whereabouts?'

He shook his head.

Gypsies who danced flamenco?

It was possible.

Parked up in the shadows of Seville or Córdoba or Granada. Flagons of wine and fires under the stars. When Lorca was still alive.

'Did people live in this caravan?' I asked.

'Gypsy people,' said the man. 'They raised their kids in it. Six of them.'

'I'll have it,' said Jim Cook.

Everyone gasped.

'You and me, Stan,' Jim said to my father in the wheelchair. 'Restoration job. That'll keep our mind off things.'

The gypsy caravan was delivered on a trailer to the paved drive of number 2, and, after the Cooks' holiday in August, restoration began.

It sat looking hopeful.

My father was commissioned to do the paintwork, from his wheelchair, using his dextrous right hand, and he started studying the intricate patterns in the old photographs which the owner of the caravan had handed over, as well as the watercolour illustration in my W. B. Rands book, peering through a black plastic magnifying glass which was kept on his study desk.

Parfait

I phoned Víctor from the roof of the coach to ask what had happened in the election.

'The opposition boycotted the vote because they said it was illegal,' said Víctor. 'And Nkurunziza has been restored to power.'

I noticed how tired Víctor sounded.

How unlike himself.

'What's the atmosphere like?' I said.

'Chaos,' said Víctor.

He never said chaos.

Even when it was.

'Violent?' I asked.

'The soldiers and the police killed about ninety people between them in Bujumbura at the weekend. One of them was a young boy called James who'd gone out for sugar. I don't know what it is but I can't seem to get that boy out of my mind.'

'Why don't you come home to Spain?' I said. 'Bring Wilfred too.'

'I'm wondering,' said Víctor.

He'd never said that before either.

When the call ended, I painted rose petals the colour of blood falling from the sky over Burundi and floating over the lake so that the whole of its surface was scarlet red.

Augusta

For our next outing, I bought tickets for my mother and father, Diego, Lola and Fermín to go to the Tower of London to see 888,246 ceramic red poppies, which tumbled out of a bastion window, representing every serviceman – British or colonial – who had died in World War 1.

The blood swept lands and seas of red
Where angels dare to tread . . .

The anonymous poem had been found in a soldier's unsigned will.

There was a homeless man outside the station, and when I stopped, my father stopped his wheelchair.

'Can I get you a sandwich?' I said.

'Anything,' said the homeless man, who had sores all over his face.

My father didn't say that we shouldn't get wrapped up in it, he didn't say that it wasn't our business, there were so many of them, half of them were on drugs and the other half were crooks – no, he didn't say any of that.

Julia, he didn't say any of that.

No, you won't believe this, but he came with me to the Co-op and chose tuna and cucumber and added in a bottle of Lucozade and a Mars Bar.

* * *

My father and Jim went on painting. Neighbours came over and climbed aboard the Victorian caravan and chatted. Barbara Cook moved her white plastic garden furniture from the back lawn to the front, so that people could come and sit with her and pass the time of day.

'When I first arrived,' said Lola Alvárez, 'I could never understand why you sat at the back of your houses and locked your neighbours out. In Spain, we sit at the front. The old ladies bring their armchairs onto the pavement.'

'That would look rather a mess,' said my mother.

'Oh, Jilly,' said Lola Alvárez, and tears welled up in her eyes, which always happened when she spoke to my mother.

Barbara bought fake-fur rugs for the plastic chairs, and she made the neighbours hot chocolate as the leaves started to blow across the crescent and we headed towards 5 November, the one-year anniversary.

I must tell Julia.

What?

About the anniversary of her own death?

About the pedlar man's caravan, which was coming to life in front of our eyes, and which would never have been bought if she and Graham hadn't died.

I sat at the white plastic table with Lola Alvárez and Barbara Cook, watching my father and Jim as they worked away, quietly, together.

'Jim and I have moved back into the double bed,' said Barbara, blushing. 'He's started going to AA, and then of course there's the whole business of the restoration, which is part of it.'

'Restoration,' I said. 'That's a very big word.'

'It will take months,' said Barbara. 'Jim's going to build a shelter for the caravan so that they can work in the rain, him and your father. It'll keep them going through the winter, don't you think?'

Parfait

In November, Pope Francis went to Africa: to Kenya, Uganda and the Central African Republic, the first time a pontiff had flown into active armed conflict.

Wilfred took a knife and cut big pieces of cardboard from the boxes in his store, and he put them together in a long line on the hillside, and he wrote across them with black marker pen, PAPA HELP MY COUNTRY BURUNDI.

It made me cry when Víctor told me.

Víctor said to Wilfred that he wasn't sure the Pope was calling in on Burundi. Wilfred shrugged his shoulders and pointed to the sky.

'Maybe he was hoping his aeroplane might divert to read his message,' said Víctor.

'Maybe,' I said.

Yes, maybe the Pope would remember that there was a forgotten country in the world called Burundi — a dark country full of heavy hearts whose name was light as a feather.

It rained on the cardboard and the ink dissolved and the words flowed down the hillside into the lake to be eaten by crocodiles.

The Pope never came by.

Augusta

In Hedley Green, it rained through December.

Cheerful Christmas songs came on in the shops.

Over a year had passed.

Mum and Dad had the caravan, and the caravan community who now gathered on Barbara's plastic chairs, under the party gazebo that Jim Cook had borrowed from the Dunnetts. He'd also bought a *chimenea* from Homebase to keep everyone warm.

I knew I couldn't be here for another Christmas.

I went to number 13.

I told Diego I was leaving.

He asked if he could come too.

He assumed I was going to La Higuera.

I assumed I was too, though the thing in my head was more of an idea than a plan.

Lola Alvárez said we were welcome to have the house. She and Fermín were planning to stay in England for Christmas anyway.

'Have it as long as you like,' she said. 'You can stay six months, as far as I'm concerned. Go and enjoy the sunshine! You really need it.'

I went to pack my case and found it full of Julia's clothes. I put them on Julia's bed.

'Leave them there,' said my mother. 'It makes me feel she's coming back.'

She sat amongst them, feeling them with the palm of her hand, and later she laid Julia's wedding dress over her pillow.

As I packed, she did up the forty-five silk buttons, and undid them again.

My mother and father, and Lola Alvárez, drove us to Gatwick Airport on 5 December. On the radio, a young boy with a haunting voice sang 'Silent Night' but the night felt neither calm nor bright. *'Sleep in heavenly peace,'* he sang, filling the car. *'Sleep in heavenly peace.'*

I half-loved half-hated flying in aeroplanes.

'We're nowhere,' I said to Diego.

He frowned.

'I found a new word for heaven,' I said. 'I've reached *I* again in the dictionary.'

'You're not reading the dictionary *again*, Augusta?'

'It consoles me.'

I dragged the huge dictionary out of my hand luggage.

'Look!' I said. 'I never noticed this word before. Iriy. *In Slavic mythology, storks were thought to carry unborn souls from Iriy to earth. Iriy is a mythical place where birds fly for winter, from where babies emanate and where souls go after death.'*

'It's all bollocks,' said Diego.

He put his jumper over his head and went to sleep. Like Olly Macintosh. Do all men do this, I wondered. But there were several un-jumper-headed men around me.

I flicked idly through J to L, to love, which had the shallowest and most pathetic of definitions. I closed the dictionary.

I picked up the free newspaper and I read about a probe that was circling Saturn, taking photos of Earth.

When Diego woke, we couldn't find anything to say to each other.

We landed.

We caught a taxi.

We hardly spoke.

As we approached La Higuera, through the olive fields, you could see huge kites like bunting in the sky, to the left of the beach. I held my breath as we came into the village, and the taxi turned left along the beach road, and it pierced me, the sight of it all, as we drove past Restaurante Raúl, and past the shop where Julia stole the newspaper.

The taxi stopped.

We got out.

I looked down to the dunes.

There was the artist I'd seen with Olly Macintosh: he was on the beach, painting. I paid the driver and I walked towards him. I looked at his face, his smooth dark skin, his fat bunch of tied black plaits, his muscular arms, his right hand, run with veins, flicking his brush. I wasn't sure what he was painting – he'd just started.

For a moment, I forgot.

I stood and looked at him. I was fascinated by him, like you might be by a work of art, or a sculpture, or the character in a book who you dream about for years after you finish reading.

Diego said, 'What are you looking at?'

And I said, 'Nothing.'

In the square, there was one bar open, the bullfight sending crackly TV applause across the cobbles.

'Let's go and eat something,' said Diego. 'Come on!'

The clock on the church tower chimed eight times.

There was the artist again. He was pulling a huge Christmas tree out of a coach with two other men – one with a hat and a ponytail, one with a vest and tattooed arms.

'That's the artist who was on the beach,' I said to Diego. 'I think he lives in that coach.'

Diego didn't answer.

As the men pulled the tree into position outside the church, with ropes and ladders, we walked over to them.

'This is new,' said Diego, nodding at the huge tree.

I held back, saying nothing.

'We'll have the ceremony on Christmas Eve,' said the artist in Spanish. 'I hope you'll both come.'

He made dimples in his dark cheeks when he smiled.

'It's in aid of the refugees – a tree to remember the dead,' he said.

Oh, not the dead.

We'd come here to forget them.

'We never had a tree before,' said Diego as we went into the bar. 'I wonder who the guy is.'

Precisely, I thought.

Stop it, I thought.

We sat at the bar, and ordered tapas: *tortilla*, spicy *patatas bravas*, prawns in garlic.

There was Raúl who owned the restaurant – his dark eyes twinkling under wild eyebrows, chewing a toothpick – with the old men in grey trousers and grey caps gathered around him, elbows on the tiled counter, half-watching the bull collapsing onto the sand.

'Now don't I recognise you two?' said Raúl, and he slapped Diego on the back and kissed me on each cheek as we re-introduced ourselves.

Once we'd finished eating, he took us out across the square, down a side street, past the cats eating fish skeletons on the plastic bins, tumbling out of cereal packets and old shoes. I crouched down, and the cats fled back into the rubbish, but a tiny black kitten pushed its nose out of a can. She nuzzled my fingers, rubbing her heart-shaped face against my palm.

I felt like crying.

But I didn't know how to.

No tears had come.

Not one.

Since the day she died.

'Come on!' said Diego.

But I didn't want to leave the little cat.

I wanted her to go on nuzzling my hand.

I stood up, and the three of us walked to Raúl's house, climbing the outside steps to his roof terrace, which overlooked his restaurant and the beach beyond. Next door to his restaurant, a *foreigner* had built a concrete cube with glass sides, which he'd turned into an art gallery.

'It doesn't suit the place,' said Raúl. 'Why would we need an art gallery in La Higuera?'

He pulled aside a hanging checked tablecloth on the line to show us his new telescope, and I looked through it at the huge glittering sky. I thought of the probe circling Saturn, showing us that Earth was a tiny star like all the rest, with all of us crowded onto it. Everything – *everything* – is mysterious, I thought.

'Come on, Augusta,' said Diego. 'I'm knackered.'

I wondered if Diego had kept saying *Come on* to Julia all the time.

We walked down the steps and into the kitchen to greet Raúl's wife, Teo, in a haze of frying prawns. She threw her arms around me. Her hair had turned white, and she was quite beautiful.

'Would you like to come riding with us?' said Raúl. 'Now your father's not here to stop you?'

He laughed.

I saw my father standing – *standing* like he used to when his legs worked – with his pink knees, saying '*Sombrero! Sombrero!*' with a horrible English *o*.

'I'd love to come,' I said. 'I don't care about riding hats.'

Back at the house, in my bedroom, I wrapped myself in a blanket, but I was still cold. I remembered lying here, naked in the heat, fanning Julia with one of those little battery-fans. Fanning away, laughing, so un-warned.

In the morning, Diego and I went to the bar in the square for break-fast – tomato and garlic on toasted bread.

'Do you remember when Julia was a shooting star in that dance show?' I said to him. 'She twirled across the stage so fast we all thought she was going to take off?'

'I don't want to talk about her any more,' said Diego. 'It's all we ever talk about.'

'We're keeping her alive,' I said.

'We can't keep her alive,' said Diego. 'We have to let her die.'

The garlic turned to metal on my tongue.

'Do you want to drive to Cádiz to buy a telescope for *our* roof terrace?' I said. 'It could be our Christmas present to each other. Light.'

'I've had enough of feeling depressed,' said Diego. 'This is the end of it. The start of a new life. It's got to be.'

Don't forget her so quickly, I thought, you loved her half her life.

'You can't stop being sad,' I said, 'and it's a big pressure trying. I think Julia tried too hard to be happy.'

'We've got to get over it,' said Diego, knocking back his little glass of coffee and slamming it on the table. 'Draw a line. You might not want to, but I want to be happy. You only live once.'

'Do you think you only love once?' I said.

But he didn't answer.

'I don't expect to get over it,' I said. 'It's inside me, and I expect things to grow from it. Like in flower beds, you put shit on the mud, and plants grow.'

'That's where we're different,' said Diego, raising his hand at the waiter. 'I want to leave the shit behind now. Find another flower bed. For me it's time to move on.'

'That sounds a bit callous, Diego,' I said. 'I don't get what you mean. Another flower bed? It's only been a year. What are you saying? You're going to start dating again?'

'I didn't mean that,' he said. 'But I can't live in the past forever.'

He ordered another coffee.

I stared at him.

'I'd feel a bit weird if you started bringing girls back to the house,' I said.

He didn't answer.

But I had a strange fizzing feeling inside me.

He tipped his coffee down his throat, and we got up to walk home.

Outside the shop behind the beach, there were white doves, which made us both think of her – instantly – but we didn't say.

'They come from Palomar de la Breña,' said Diego. 'Did you ever go and see it?'

'See what?'

'It's like an enormous old dovecote, with its own streets. It used to produce about a hundred thousand birds a year for meat, I think.'

'People don't eat doves.'

'They did in the past,' said Diego. 'It was to feed the crew who were going off to conquer new lands, when we were an empire.'

'What is it with Europeans and conquering?' I said. 'Couldn't we just call by for a visit? Did we have to nick their countries?'

'Why do you make everything such a big deal?' said Diego. 'Can't you accept things?'

'Please let's go to Cádiz and buy a telescope,' I said to Diego because I didn't want to argue. 'I want to learn about the moon and the tides and the names of stars.'

I went into the shop to buy some bottled water, and the woman, still in the light blue housecoat, with her fat upper arms filling the short sleeves, asked after Julia.

'She died a year ago,' I said. 'We needed to get away.'

I paused, and then I said, to my surprise, 'My mother preferred her.'

There, I'd said it.

It was easier to say it in Spanish words – I didn't know why.

'Or was it that *your sister* preferred your mother?' said the woman, her mouth now pinched with bitterness.

I looked at her.

'I have daughters too,' she said, unsmiling.

I'd trusted in her fat arms, but her words hurt me.

'*Es recíproco,*' she said. '*El amor.*'

Is love reciprocal, I wondered.

Is it some kind of Pavlovian reaction?

Someone decides to love you so you just love them back.

Had I loved Olly Macintosh all those years simply because he loved me? And if somebody else had chosen to love me, would I have loved them instead? Was I that biddable? If so, I was a danger to myself.

And isn't it the job of mothers and fathers to love first, and to love equally, and to love better than their children? Or was I supposed to help them love me by being what they wanted me to be?

Whatever that was.

I knew, of course, exactly what that was.

They wanted me to be Julia.

She was exactly what they would have chosen.

We bought the telescope in Cádiz on Christmas Eve, though I don't think Diego especially wanted to, and by the time we arrived for the ceremony in the square, there were baskets of gold cut-out planets and stars, and pots of black felt-tip pens and collection dishes for the migrants and their families.

Diego and I walked forward and gave our donation.

I let him pick a planet, layered with gold oil paint. I wrote Julia on the back. I let him pick a star. I wrote Rose on the back. Then I wrote one for Graham Cook.

Men climbed the step ladders, and small children crawled under branches with their grandparents' names written in smudged black pen, which is what we all become in the end.

A series of letters.

A word.

Which gradually falls out of use.

The artist spoke into the microphone.

'The authorities say that approximately three thousand seven hundred and seventy migrants and refugees lost their lives trying to cross the Mediterranean Sea to reach a place of hope in Europe this year,' he said.

'We can't possibly take them all,' I heard Raúl say to Teo. 'We'll be over-run. It isn't practical.'

'Have you seen the news?' I whispered to Raúl. 'Would *you* like to stay in Aleppo? In Mosul? Someone has to take them in.'

'Before we met tonight,' the artist went on, 'there were 3,770 stars on the tree for the refugees who died. Now you've added the names of those you've loved and lost, we'll turn on the lights.'

I stared at the artist's face.

I made myself look away.

The tree was lit, and the square was grave and quiet.

But still no tears came.

I was dammed up.

In the live Nativity, the baby's cry broke the silence, and the big electric star was turned on above the stable.

A man from the local government with a gold chain around his neck took the artist's arm, and paused for the photographer. Look at me with the migrant, he seemed to be saying. Then the entourage sat down at a table with a white cloth, with the artist and the priest, for dinner.

I couldn't help staring at him.

Diego and I walked down to the beach, looking up at the stars, which were unusually bright, forming clouds of light against the blue-black sky.

'The Romans named the planets after their most important gods,' I said, and I noticed I was gabbling. 'As Venus was the brightest, it was named after the goddess of love. It has two huge continents on it.'

'How do you know all these things?' said Diego.

'It's all on our phones these days,' I said. 'I used to keep it in my brain. It bored Julia, all this stuff. Drove her mad. Does it bore you?'

He shook his head.

'It's weird the way we keep our brains in our pockets now,' I said. 'Do you think our brains will gradually evolve to hold less and less information? And soon we'll be Neanderthals again but with iPhones?'

Diego smiled at me.

'Then our brains will shrink like our appendixes did,' I said. 'But our phones will grow cleverer, and eventually phones will rule the world! They'll keep human beings in their pockets, but we'll all be apps by then.'

There was something strange in Diego's smile.

I wasn't sure what it was.

'You're a one-off, Augusta,' he said.

We spent Christmas Day on the beach.

It was warm and sunny.

We walked right down to our special spot, but the buried boat wasn't showing any more. We barbecued sardines, which were very bony, on a little foil tray.

'Happy Christmas,' we said to each other, unhappily.

The new year appeared.

The Refugee Tree disappeared.

So did the artist.

I kept an eye out for his coach, but it never came back.

The big old tree lay, bare-branched, by the bins on the main road, on its side like the skeleton of some great dinosaur, and gold cardboard stars flew about on the wind. I wondered if Julia or Rose would ever fly by. But they didn't.

Raúl, Teo and I rode the horses down the beach in the early morning, or sometimes at dusk, or in the dark. A strange tingling feeling would come over me, like a cloak, as the mottled moon glowed silver, as the egrets flew against the dark sky and the horses' hooves thudded on the wet sand, spraying sea in our faces.

Inside this cloak, I had the momentary sense that *all was well*, that there was a reality beyond reality, something else, which compensated, consoled, completed me.

We'd untack the horses, and I would feel peaceful, alive, numinous somehow – and soothed – though it didn't last.

'When did the artist first arrive here?' I asked Raúl as we sat at the bar drinking coffee, after riding, 'You know, the Refugee Tree guy?'

I tried to sound as casual as I could.

'I think he came over in a boat,' said Raúl. 'He started out as a labourer at the great complex that never happened. Before someone in Tarifa spotted his talent.'

'Where does he come from?' I asked again, casually.

'Nobody knows,' said Raúl. 'But over there.'

'And what about the coach?'

'He lives in it, travels about the place. I haven't seen him since the tree came down.'

I wish I lived in a caravan,
With a horse to drive, like the pedlar man!
Where he comes from nobody knows,
Or where he goes to, but on he goes!

At Easter, there was still no sign of the artist.

I'd started working in Raúl's restaurant for the summer season, and this made me feel a bit more like a normal person with a normal kind of life. I quite liked the feeling, which scared me. Wasn't that what I'd prided myself on hating? The days trotted by, one after another, with days off and payday, and April becoming May.

When I rang my parents, they seemed strangely enlivened by the prospect of chucking out the foreigners and reclaiming Britain for the British.

On the day of the Brexit vote, in June, I was walking past the roundabout, at the back of the beach, when I saw the artist's coach turning in. I looked determinedly out to sea as he drove past.

When I went down to the square, he was there, chatting to people by the market stalls. I sat at the corner table in the bar, and I watched him: his wide smile, the way he held his hands out, moving them up and down when he spoke.

Later, I saw him on the beach, doing football tricks with some children.

The next day, my mother phoned.

'We did it,' she said.

Diego mouthed, 'Be nice!'

So I said, 'Well done. Congratulations!'

'It's your country too,' she said.

But I wasn't sure it was.

'We're going to turn back the clocks,' said my mother.

'Great,' I said, thinking that clocks don't turn back, even if we want them to.

'I'd love to speak to Dad,' I said.

'He's trying to sweep out the garages for the Brexit party,' she said. 'Though it's not very easy for him these days. Even with the shorter broom.'

My chest ached at the thought of him struggling round the garage in his wheelchair trying to keep it *spick and span*, as he likes to say, as nobody says.

'Well, enjoy your party,' I said to my mother, and I walked out along the beach road, carrying my rubbish bags to the plastic bins where I'd first seen the kitten. But she wasn't there. There were just some boys, who ran off, throwing fire-crackers.

The rubbish lorry arrived, stinking, and the cats dived off into an old pipe.

Down on the beach road, I saw some movement inside the art gallery, and I walked through the open glass doors.

The artist came in a minute later.

He wore his jeans low.

You could see the waistband of his boxer shorts and where his hip bones jutted out.

You shouldn't have been looking, that's what Julia would have said.

I was looking.

Let's be honest.

He propped his paintings up against the wall, went out, brought more paintings, in and out, in and out. I tried not to stare at him.

'Sorry!' I said, I don't know why.

Which was awkward.

My voice echoed in the empty cube.

What was I doing here?

Why was I *sorry*?

And how could I get out?

I couldn't concentrate on anything. He made me feel funny. I blushed at nothing.

'Do you want to give this painting a title?' he said.

I liked the way his voice sounded on the air.

I liked the way his eyes glinted.

I had a strange feeling that my voice wasn't going to come out when I opened my mouth.

I looked at his painting – a huge rubbish dump, with prowling storks the size of the smallest children.

He nodded at the painting.

'How about Gehenna? As a title?' I said, colouring slightly.

'I know that word,' he said.

'It's the rubbish dump outside Jerusalem,' I said.

'And it's used to mean hell, isn't it?' he said.

He wrote *Gehenna* in perfect italics on the white card.

I held my breath, as if I had hiccups.

'In my country, people walk barefoot through the rubbish every day,' he said, sticking the white card, *Gehenna*, to the wall, 'looking for scrap metal and plastic for selling. Or for making things. In the rain, the rubbish mixes with the sewage.'

I nodded.

I was still holding my breath.

'Would you not leave if you could?' he said.

I let my breath out – it made a strange gasp.

'Apparently,' I said, 'people have started using plastic as firewood, and it's killing them. The fumes are getting into their food.'

I looked at the dark backs of his hands, at the black inky shapes of the letters of Gehenna. Then I walked off, facing away from him, looking at the view of the sea through the square window, and I felt as if tears were bubbling in my chest.

'How about another title?' he said to me.

I came back.

'You look sad,' he said, and his eyes were so kind. 'Were you crying?'

'No, I can't cry,' I said, though the more I looked at his eyes, the more I thought maybe I could.

He started writing – a letter M and then a y.

The warm cloak came over me, like dawn on the beach – the moon, the spray, the egrets. I remembered I used to feel the same watching Julia write italics, hearing the tiny scrape of the pen nib on the paper, watching the flow of ink, the way the card drank it, porously. It comforted me.

My.

He smiled, and his kind eyes were bright against his dark skin.

Friend's.

He looked at me and I wondered if I could be his friend.

My Friend's Tears. My Tears.

That's what he wrote.

I tingled.

'Five hundred people have drowned off the coast of Greece,' said the artist. 'It's so tragic. They paid around two thousand dollars – all they had – to drown.'

'Did you know they use doves to spot people drowning at sea?' I said. 'Their eyes are better than people's.'

'Some people's eyes are better than others',' said the artist, and he smiled at me again.

'They're really brave too, doves,' I said.

'So are people,' he said. 'I've known some extraordinary people. I bet you have too.'

I nodded, thinking, I don't know if I have.

In Willow Crescent.

At Durham University.

I remembered telling Julia that I wanted to be extraordinary, and I knew I wasn't.

Not yet anyway.

I couldn't think what to say.

So I walked out without saying goodbye.

I thought: Why the hell did I talk about doves?

Five hundred people dead – and I said that *doves were brave.*

I blushed.

I meant pigeons anyway – not doves. The ones they used in wars.

I would never ever be able to talk to him again.

I had embarrassed myself beyond belief.

When I walked past the gallery each day, I turned my head away so we didn't catch each other's eye.

And, every time I thought of going in, my legs went off in a different direction.

On Julia's birthday, I was up on the roof terrace and there were birds flying above me, on the wind. They were either late, drifting north, or very early, getting ready to head south.

Every morning, Diego headed off to work in Conil, and Raúl and I got up to exercise the horses, swimming in the sea before the crowds descended on the beach. I was working in Raúl's restaurant, with hardly a day off, since Teo fell off her horse. She was now home from hospital, with a broken leg, her neck in a collar – fingers crossed, said Raúl, her head looked fine in the scan.

I didn't speak to the artist again.

Not about pigeons.

Not about anything.

The exhibition was over – every painting had sold, so people said in the bar in the square.

I saw his coach turn right at the roundabout on the beach road, and he was off again.

Oh no, not today.

Surely he wouldn't be gone another six months.

How ridiculous that I hadn't spoken to him again.

Course you feel sad, I said to myself, it's Julia's birthday.

But it wasn't only that.

My mother phoned me.

When I answered, neither of us could speak.

'The worst day,' said my mother.

'But then again, are there better days?' I said. 'Or just more days without her?'

Then we didn't say anything.

I felt I should offer her something hopeful, but I couldn't think what that something might be.

'Shall I catch you up on the crescent?' said my mother.

I sat not listening to my mother's updates, watching the birds, which were now magnetic filings against the sky fading into specks, into pinpoints, into nothing.

'So what's your news?' said my mother.

'The same really,' I said. 'Working at the restaurant, swimming in the sea, riding Raúl's horses . . .'

'I hope you wear a riding hat,' said my mother.

'Yes,' I lied.

'That lady in the newspaper was paralysed from the neck down,' said my mother.

'Don't worry,' I said.

'And your flamenco dancing?'

'The lessons stopped for summer,' I said.

'Do you think you'll ever get married, Augusta?' said my mother. 'You'll be twenty-six tomorrow.'

I said I didn't know, I would need to find someone to marry first, ha ha – it wouldn't work so well without the bridegroom's speech.

'It's a lovely thing, marriage,' my mother said. 'You stick together through thick and thin. Because you promised. Without the promise, it would be much harder, I imagine.'

'It *is* a lovely thing, Mum,' I said. 'You and Dad are so good at it. You're real pros at marriage, you two. You've shown me how it's done. How to really keep your promises.'

'You stick at it,' said my mother.

There was a long pause.

Then she said, 'Thank you, Augusta.'

'It's a pleasure,' I said.

'I think that's the nicest thing you've ever said to me,' she said.

It made me feel nice, and it made me want to put down the phone and savour it. Because it wouldn't last.

'And what are you going to do for your birthday tomorrow?' said my mother.

'Watch the birds,' I said. 'Ride the horses.'

'I don't know why you want to live there,' she said. 'When you haven't got any friends to celebrate your birthday with. If you were here, half the crescent would come out.'

'Mum,' I said. 'I've been meaning to tell you this for a long time. The thing is. I hate Willow Crescent.'

There was a long silence.

I wished I hadn't said hate.

I wished I'd said don't like.

'But that doesn't mean I hate *you*,' I said. 'I love *you*.'

I should have emphasised the *love* more than the *you*. I'd half hoped she might say I love *you* back. But it would probably have been embarrassing in real life, the way it isn't in your mind, where you can both be different people from the ones you are.

'I think it's better to be honest,' I said. 'So that you can adjust your expectations.'

'So, when do you think you'll be coming back?' said my mother. 'To Hedley Green?'

'Mum,' I said. 'I'm not coming back to Hedley Green. I'm staying here.'

Then she didn't have anything left to say, and I felt horrible and guilty because Julia said the whole point of families was to stick together.

The next morning, when I got back from riding, my mother phoned again.

Diego had tied balloons to the door before he left for work, and there were fresh *ensaimada* pastries in a box on the table, tied with a bow.

'Happy birthday,' said my mother flatly on the phone.

'Thank you,' I said, flatly, back.

'Her doves still fly over every evening,' said my mother.

'I couldn't watch,' I said.

'It comforts me,' said my mother.

'I'm glad,' I said.

'Speak to your father,' said my mother.

He made some noises at me, and I thought of Graham Cook, and how much my father had hated the noises he'd made, noises that told him that bad things happened to good people. Now he was making those noises, himself, because bad things had happened. No matter how many times he'd said *Nothing to worry about*, there were, in the end, things to worry about, and he couldn't stop them.

My mother came back on the phone.

'Diego will have told you Pally's having a baby,' she said. 'Lola came round to tell me last night. To bring good news on a bad day, she said. She can't wait to be a granny. She says I can be an honorary granny too.'

'That's lovely,' I said.

'Might you think of having a baby?' said my mother.

'Yes, I might, Mum, I might think of that some time,' I said, though I wasn't thinking of it at all.

'It was the best time of my life,' she said.

'Yes,' I said. 'I know.'

'It seems such a long time ago now.'

'It does.'

'I loved making your clothes – little matching dresses.'

'I know you did.'

'I kept them all – for, you know.'

'I know,' I said. 'Although Julia cut some of them up for the patchwork quilt. Which was . . .'

'I hope you'll have some grandchildren for us. I wondered if perhaps. I mean, we have spoken about it, your father and I . . .'

'I don't have a boyfriend, Mum, like I said yesterday.'

I could hear my father making noises at her.

'Well, have a lovely day anyway,' she said.

At that moment, the sky inflated with clouds, stacking one above another, and the wind blew up, and it was raining, when it never rains in August in La Higuera. I let the wind blow at me and felt the warm blobs of rain fall on my cheeks, slowly at first, then faster.

Inside the wind, there we were, Julia and I, sitting out on the porch as the dove landed on the top of the magnolia tree; up at the pond, under the willow, feeding the seven goldfish; making a fire behind the shed; flying kites at Old John Brown's; fishing for minnows on Tattershall Common; sitting on the flat-branched tree at the bluebell glade; killing ourselves laughing at Dad's Y-fronts on our beds; waxing our legs with strips that didn't work; and there she was walking down the aisle, forty-five buttons down her back, and so beautiful; and pregnant with Rose, and so sad.

How could I have been so blind?

How didn't I notice?

How didn't I stop her?

The irretrievable past.

I felt contractions of nostalgia inside me.

The *algos* – ache – of *nostos* – home.

And home was a person.

Who wasn't here.

'It's just started to rain,' I said to my mother.

'It's lovely here,' she said.

'It never rains in August,' I said.

'I won't keep you,' she said.

The smell of hot earth was pungent in the puddles, and the doves were landing on the wet mud.

I went and got my Lorca books and brought them up to the roof terrace, where the damp coated their pages.

Whilst I read the familiar poems, I drank a bottle of wine.

Alone on the roof terrace without Julia.

I went down for my dictionary and let it fall open.

It opened at H.

Hobby horse.

Oh no, please not hobby horse.

Keep reading.

Find a new word.

'*Hodegetria*', said the dictionary.

I always, always love a new word.

Whatever I'm feeling.

'An iconographic depiction of the Virgin Mary holding Jesus at her side.'

That's what the dictionary said.

I opened another bottle of wine.

Perhaps there's a Hodegetria in the church in La Higuera, I thought, they're extremely keen on the Virgin Mary round here.

Perhaps I could find it.

I had to do something.

Such a treat, have a day off for your birthday.

There were no birds in the sky today.

I started walking along the back of the beach, my head swimming a little and my legs heavy with wine. I walked past the shop and up the narrow road where the cats were on the bins, licking tuna brine from cans.

There was the little black cat. I crouched down, and she stretched out her neck and lay her heart-shaped face in my hand. But there was Raúl, and she ran off.

'We've run out of tomatoes,' he said. 'The restaurant's jam-packed because of the rain.'

I nodded.

'Are you OK?' he said.

'It's a hard day,' I said.

'Light a candle in the church,' he said. 'It'll make you feel better.'

'I'm on my way as it happens,' I said.

'Don't forget it's the start of the *feria* tonight,' he said.

He put up his thumb.

'Teo's collar's off,' he said, 'and all the scans are clear. So it's just the leg. We can cope with the leg!'

'I'm so pleased,' I said – and I was.

My wet feet slipped off my flip-flops into the puddles.

People huddled in bars, looking at the grey August sky, checking the weather on their phones. In the market, they picked up Buddhas and tried on Indian skirts.

I walked into the church.

There was a dark painting of the Virgin Mary and the baby, a Hodegetria perhaps, I wasn't sure, and there was a row of lit candles, like a birthday cake.

I sat on a pew in front of the candles, and I found that I was whispering the Lord's Prayer, which we used to say every morning at school.

Forgive us our trespasses as we forgive those who trespass against us.

I was wet and cold when Diego arrived.

'You're shivering,' he said.

I realised I was.

He'd bought me red roses for my birthday, and champagne.

Julia liked roses.

I preferred daffodils.

When we went outside, the *feria* had started. The coloured lights made patterns on our faces as the men played guitars and the girls danced flamenco and the children rode the dodgems and jumped on trampolines, making star shapes with their bodies.

Diego put a red rose in my hair, we finished the champagne and drank paper cups of *fino*, returning home drunk, arm in arm, telling each other stories of Julia which we already knew, and we lay out on the Moroccan bed on the wet cushions, and this was a bad idea, to allow this to happen, to warm to each other's arms, to look inside each other to see if we could find her, to allow ourselves to dig like frenzied dogs after the smell of her.

There was no comfort there, inside each other, but still we let ourselves in, we trespassed on each other – and on her.

We heard only the low moan of our pain, disguised, for a brief moment, as pleasure – *la petite mort*, the little death, the brief lost consciousness – it joined my mother's voice behind the veil at the funeral, and it sank into the muddy pools beneath the fig trees, moaning into the earth, downwards.

We untangled our bodies and lay back, separate.

I felt anguish in my veins and the damp recall of him between my legs, dripping down my thigh. Like the guano on their glass roof.

Diego said nothing.

There was nothing I wanted to hear from him.

Nothing I wanted to say to him.

I wanted more than anything, nothing.

I wanted the sky to be black.

So that I couldn't see myself.

I wanted the air to be thick.

So that I couldn't hear the crickets.

Crickets, frogs and the lurking night . . .

There were frogs among the rocks in the natural pool.

Next door's dog strained on its chain, barking. The dog at the back raised his howl to the moon. The farm dogs behind joined in, in great yelping moans and shrieks. The dog howls spread across the dry earth. Back, back, to the scattered farmsteads inland, where the hills began.

As summer ran out, the beach began to empty, and Diego and I sat inside the open doors at the back of the house, away from the clouds of dust and the insects swarming down from the mountains in the wind.

'I've been thinking,' said Diego.

He looked strange.

And he paused.

And something was happening to his face.

He started to speak.

Then he stopped.

His face turned red.

He couldn't make his lips work.

'We could get married, Augusta, you and me.'

I stared at him.

He held out his hand, which was small like my father's.

And I said, 'No, Diego, never.'

Never – '*at no time, not under any circumstances, on no account*' – that's what the dictionary says.

Diego's cheeks coloured.

'But we've been living here eight months together,' he said, 'and we've, you know.'

He stopped and reached for my hand again. 'After the *feria*.'

I didn't take his hand.

I turned away.

'That was such an unbelievable night,' said Diego. 'I haven't been able to stop thinking about it. But I didn't know what to say to you. So I guess I said nothing. I wondered if you maybe felt the same.'

Breathe, breathe, breathe.

It wasn't an *unbelievable* night.

Or perhaps it was.

It was something that I couldn't, or wouldn't, believe I had done.

'Diego,' I said, 'This feels really hard to say – but the truth is, I don't feel the same.'

'I'm in love with you, Augusta, so why don't we . . .'

'Did you hear me, Diego? Love is reciprocal. Two people have to feel it. And I'm so sorry but I don't.'

'But what about that night?' he said, and now his dark face had reddened.

'It was a mistake,' I said. 'It was the *feria*, and we were both drunk. And I was sad and cold and lonely. And it was Julia's birthday. And then mine. And it was all too awful. Erase it from your mind – it was one big mistake.'

'But I didn't force myself on you, Augusta,' said Diego.

'No, it's not that. You did nothing wrong. Or, if you did, we both did.'

He reached for my hand again.

'I don't think it was wrong,' he said. 'We don't need to resist it. It doesn't matter what people say.'

Again, I didn't take his hand.

'Did you think I could be your new flower bed?' I said.

'What?'

'You wanted to leave the shit behind and find a new flower bed.'

'You twist things,' said Diego. 'This was supposed to be a nice conversation.'

'I'm sorry,' I said. 'I don't mean to.'

'We could have a baby,' he said. 'Your mother . . .'

'No, Diego,' I said. 'You loved *her*, not me.'

'Well, why can't I love both of you?'

'It's so wrong,' I said.

'Then we can't stay here together in the house,' said Diego.

'You know how much I love this house,' I said quietly.

'So that was it, was it?' said Diego. 'That was all it was.'

I got up and I went to my bedroom, and I lay on my bed, on the coral bedcover, and I looked at the stone walls, the driftwood shapes on the window sill and my long red dress on the back of the door, and I thought that yes, that was all it was.

I couldn't bear not to live here.

If I didn't live in this house, where would I live?

What would I do?

No thoughts came.

What if I couldn't even come here?

Couldn't ever again see the baby frogs swimming up and down in the natural pool, see the familiar twists of fig bark, the swirling threads of sea sewn into the fabric wall hangings.

I didn't turn on the light.

It was hot in the room, despite the wind outside, and the air was thick around my face, and a fly was stuck between the mosquito screen and the wooden shutter, and I slept and I woke, and it buzzed, and in the morning, Diego and I met each other in the dark stone passage.

He opened his mouth.

I opened mine.

Neither of us moved, backwards or forwards.

'Should we go for a walk?' he said. 'Talk some more?'

'I think we should try and end well,' I said. 'For everyone's sake.'

'Don't talk about endings,' he said. 'I've had enough of endings.'

I went out of the back door into the light, with my eyes blinking.

'I want us to go to the end of the beach,' he said.

'I thought you didn't like endings,' I said.

'I'm not sure it's the moment for jokes.'

'It was a crap one anyway.'

We walked out to the dunes.

There was the artist, painting.

Row after row after row of roses in straight lines.

He was back again – and so soon.

'Why are you painting roses?' I said to him.

I said to him.

I spoke to him.

'Can you talk about this another time?' said Diego.

We went down to the sea.

I took off my espadrilles and walked at the edge of the water. Diego walked on the dry sand, a few feet away from me.

We kept going without speaking, our heads down – and Julia walked between us.

'What are you thinking?' I said.

'I still feel like she'd be happy for us,' he said.

We walked.

'What are *you* thinking?' Diego asked.

I was thinking that the flocks of birds were flying wrong in the sky, that the pebbles were sitting wrong on the beach, that the artist was painting red roses in rows, that I wished I could go back and ask him what they meant.

I said nothing.

I shrugged.

'I'm in two minds,' said Diego.

'About what?'

'About telling you something.'

'You'll have to tell me now,' I said.

'But I don't know if it's right to,' he said.

'Nothing we've done is right,' I said.

The waves kept up their rhythm, breaking in little spumes of spray, which shimmered over my legs. Diego stayed on the dry sand.

'Thing is, she told me not to tell you,' he said.

We were drunk on cider on Tattershall Common, but now I think of it, perhaps it was only me who promised not to have secrets.

He sat down.

I sat down, to the right of him.

I picked up a pebble and threw it, then another, and another, into the sea.

The wind had calmed, and there was a thin layer of cloud over the sun. Cirrostratus cloud, I remembered from somewhere.

'There was one thing she never told you,' said Diego.

'Something that happened right here?'

He nodded.

'She told me,' I said. 'The day before she died.'

'The day before she died?' said Diego. 'And you didn't think to tell me?'

'I thought it would be hurtful to find she'd kept a secret from you. I didn't know you knew.'

'You didn't wonder why she was telling you on that particular day, after all those years?' he said, and he stood up, agitated. 'Wasn't it obvious, Augusta? Why the hell didn't you tell me? Then I might have guessed what she was about to do.'

'That's cruel,' I said. 'I'm sure we both wish we'd picked up the signs, but we have to forgive ourselves.'

'You knew how fragile she was.'

I sat staring at the sea.

He stood staring at the sea.

Did I know how fragile she was?

Was it obvious?

Was it?

'She didn't finish the story, Diego. We were outside the party shop, the day before, do you remember? You came and she stopped talking.'

'Oh, so you're blaming me?' he said, looking down at me.

'You were blaming me,' I said. 'I said we both had to forgive ourselves.'

I looked up at him, and it was odd seeing his face from this unfamiliar angle – his Adam's apple looked enormous, and he was breathing deeply, in, out, in, out.

'Then she was dead,' I said, 'and I couldn't ask her. So will you please tell me the full story? I want to know.'

The three of them headed down here for their picnic, that's what Diego said. That morning, the morning when the clouds were puffer fish.

'Your dad was all worked up and freaked out. He hadn't slept, and he kept saying it wasn't wise being out so early, when no one was about. Except a guy on a horse who disappeared.'

'Probably Raúl,' I said.

'Julia saw a black man lying on the beach – and your father told her to come away.'

Diego was pacing about as he spoke, almost as if he was acting out the story, here where it happened.

'So she came away. But then she turned back towards the sea. She thought she'd seen someone out there and she wanted to check.'

Diego looked out to sea, before turning to look at me.

'But your father was yelling at her, really yelling at her. Like he'd totally lost it,' he said. 'You know how he gets.'

'How he *used to* get,' I said.

Julia asked if she could please just look.

But my father said she was seeing things.

And my mother said it was someone swimming, someone waving at them. For fun. Probably.

By now my father was going hysterical – about crooks on the beach. Or something. And Julia wouldn't move. Which wasn't like her. She'd never disobeyed him before.

So he slapped her.

In the face.

'Do as you're told,' he said, and he yanked her away. 'We're not getting wrapped up in this.'

The red cheek.

My mother slathering aftersun.

And everyone ashamed.

'She always had a thing about hands, didn't you notice?' said Diego. 'She had nightmares about that hand. Out at sea.'

'Not waving but drowning,' I said to Diego. 'The poem.'

'That fucking poem,' he said, shaking his head at me.

I watched a wave that was sheeting up the beach.

'When Rose was born, her hand was sticking up,' said Diego. 'It sent her crazy. She said the baby drowned inside her . . .'

The waves came in and out.

Julia, I thought, why didn't you tell me?

I should have gone with them for breakfast on the beach that day, and everything would have been different. Lives would have been saved. If I hadn't been so lazy. So selfish. So desperate to be on my own.

I should have noticed how bad she was after Rose died.

Should have.

Could have.

Would have.

The worst tense of all.

If I had, if I hadn't – all too late.

'Do your parents really think that she didn't see the train?' said Diego, and his eyes looked cold. 'How would you not see a train? It's laughable.'

He laughed.

He actually laughed – in the same breath as he said train.

'Let them think whatever helps them,' I said.

'Let's make it up,' said Diego, coming closer. 'For her sake. Make a home with me, Augusta, up at the house. You know how much you love that house. You can write your book. We could have children here. They could grow up on the beach.'

'You tell me I could have stopped it, you laugh at my parents and in the next breath you want to have my children.'

'I don't want you in my house any longer, Augusta,' said Diego, his voice flat and cold, and he started to walk up the beach, turning around to say, 'And don't tell me you don't laugh at your parents!'

I went to my room and I packed my suitcase.

'You can have the telescope!' I called through Diego's bedroom door.

'I never wanted the bloody telescope in the first place,' he called back.

'Which tells me everything I need to know about you!' I shouted.

'Can you only like people who like telescopes? That sounds typical of you!' he shouted back.

I walked out of the gate, and my fingers were shaking.

Like my father's.

I wanted to phone him and tell him that he didn't only kill the boy. He killed Julia too – by not letting her save him. He ruined her life with the guilt of it. Except I couldn't hate him when I thought about his wheelchair and his corduroy slippers and his shaking fingers and his face with the crack down the middle.

I dragged my case across the road and down the boardwalk over the dunes, and I left it there because its wheels wouldn't roll over the sand.

Then I saw the artist.

'Can you keep an eye on my case?' I said to him, not looking at him. I always found I couldn't look at him, not straight, eye to eye, though I so wanted to. I so wanted to talk to him again.

'I need to go down to the end of the beach,' I said, still not looking at him. 'To think something through.'

I looked up.

He nodded.

I headed back to *our special place.*

I drew a huge X in the sand with my heel.

X marks the spot.

I sat next to the X.

I don't know how long for.

Trying to find a path through my thoughts.

Throwing stones.

My teeth were chattering though it was warm and humid, a sea mist forming across the beach.

The artist came down.

I didn't look at him.

He stood next to me.

I still didn't look at him.

I tried to stop my teeth chattering.

'I'm leaving the beach now,' he said. 'I can't concentrate. Come for the case when you want it. I'll hold it in my coach.'

He pointed, and I nodded.

'Are you staying down here?' he said.

I nodded again.

'So what's the X?' he said.

'Nothing,' I said. 'Or maybe everything. Like in Maths.'

I turned around.

He was staring at the X, and at the rocks, and the pine trees, and out to the hazy sea, now almost flat.

'Would you like to stay in the coach tonight?' he said.

'How did you know?'

'I knew. There's a space at the back, with a bed. It's totally separate from me.'

'Thank you,' I said.

He looked at the X again, and he untied his sweater from his waist and put it around my shoulders. But it didn't stop my teeth chattering.

He sat down next to me, about a foot away, but I felt him.

We both looked forwards – the way you might sit in a gypsy caravan, going from town to town. Except there was no road – only sea. In a gypsy caravan, you'd be closer together.

Which would be.

What would it be?

Unbearable.

'So,' he said. 'Why the X? And why here? Tell me . . . '

'I don't want to,' I said. 'You tell me something.'

Still looking forwards, taking up the reins of our imaginary horse, on our imaginary road.

'OK,' he said. 'What kind of thing should I tell you?'

'It has to be something to do with X,' I said because it was the first thing that came into my head.

He laughed.

We still looked forward.

'People drew Xs on the face of our president – on posters,' said the artist. 'And the president killed them for it. For drawing two simple lines. How weird is that?'

I know this, I thought, I read it, I researched it.

I didn't move.

Or, to put it another way, I couldn't move.

'Pretty good, don't you think?' he said. 'Right on theme. And with so little warning.'

I tried to smile at the same time as I tried to breathe, at the same time as I tried to form words. Four words I was trying to form, four simple words – quite normal words in normal circumstances.

'Where are you from?' I said.

I could feel I was hunching my shoulders, frowning, waiting to hear.

I turned to look at him.

He turned to look at me.

He smiled, and his mouth made dimples on his cheeks.

'Burundi,' he said.

The world had to keep turning.

But, even if it was turning, I was stuck.

Held.

Not breathing.

It came over me – the feeling. Was it a feeling? Or was it some change in the atmosphere like before a storm? Whatever it was, it was heavy and warm – and it seeped out of the letters of Burundi, dripping over me from the capital B and the u and the r and the u and the n and the d and the i, it came pouring out of the word I chose when I was seven years old, when I turned the globe in Hedley Green library, but I'd never heard it before like this, I'd never heard it before in his gravelly voice, I'd never heard it said right.

I was covered from head to toe in Burundi.

Burundi, Burundi, Burundi.

Say something.

I heard my mother's voice – *I can't imagine what you're going to do with all those books of notes.*

And I *could* imagine what I was going to do with them.

'Your President Nkurunziza, who seemed so hopeful, has robbed you of hope again,' I said to him, looking straight at him. 'How much more can your poor country suffer?'

Now he looked straight at me too.

Our eyes locked.

'How do you know all this?' he said. 'Nobody knows anything about Burundi. They never put it on the news in Europe.'

'On the twenty-fourth of August 2015,' I said, and I was gabbling now, of course I was gabbling, the words tumbled out, as if they'd piled up at the bottom of my throat, 'the commission concluded that the president could run for as many terms as he likes. So that means a fourth term, I suppose. And that means more bloodshed in your country. And still no happy ending.'

'Tell me how you know, Augusta.'

Augusta.

I melted at the sound of my name.

'You know my name?'

'I've heard you on the beach, riding, early, with the other two,' he said. 'But tell me how you know all this stuff about Burundi.'

He turned around on the sand, and so did I, and we sat cross-legged, opposite each other, and his face had opened up.

'I picked Burundi when I was seven years old.'

'What do you mean you *picked* it?'

'As my favourite country. I liked the sound of the word. I didn't know what was hiding inside its letters then. I didn't know about Lake Tanganyika or massacres or three hundred thousand people dead. I found that out later.'

'I picked Spain. Like you, I didn't know.'

I stared at him, as he looked away, and I was seven years old in front of the big rotating globe, with all the land masses separated by the same blue sea.

Or was I?

No.

Definitely not.

I was twenty-six years old and riding a gypsy caravan.

Somewhere.

Somewhere.

Anywhere.

With him.

'So,' I said. 'Tell me how you came from Burundi to La Higuera.'

He came a bit closer.

I let him.

We were both still cross-legged, like at school.

Except – everything.

His knees, sticking out of the rips in his baggy jeans.

A bit closer.

His skin.

The feel of it.

Knee to knee.

Say something.

'I came on a boat,' he said, and I looked at him, though I could hardly bear it, the looking. 'Like the others. The Senegalese selling stuff on the beach. But you don't meet many here from Burundi. No one else is mad enough to walk.'

He laughed.

'You really walked?'

'I walked.'

I saw the map in my head.

'I arrived with nothing,' he said. 'And I worked over there.'

He gestured to the road behind the village.

'You know, the holiday complex that never happened.'

'I saw it years ago,' I said, 'when I was fourteen, when it was being built. In 2004.'

'In 2004?' he said, turning his head. 'Fourteen?'

Puffer fish clouds.

Sunrise.

Dolphins in Tarifa.

Julia.

'Then, later, I escaped. Like you.'

'That's going in the wrong direction,' he said. 'Nobody wants to escape from England.'

'I did.'

'Why an X and why here?'

'Can you tell me some more stories about the X because I don't want to tell you mine?'

'I'll do my best.'

'To tell me your story?'

'No, not my story,' he said. 'I don't want to say much more about that.'

'I understand,' I said.

We looked at each other, and though we didn't yet know, we knew.

'Go on then,' I said. 'More about the X.'

'You know the flag of Burundi has an X with a circle in the centre?' he said.

I nodded.

'I do know that,' I said.

We smiled at each other.

Keep it light.

Keep it surface.

The waves left a layer of foam on the sand.

Keep it foam.

Don't go underneath.

Don't go into the water yet.

You might drown.

'You may not know,' I said, 'that, in my country, the X is also a warning sign for the point where a railway line intersects a road at a level crossing.'

'Oh really?' he said.

Keep it foam.

Don't go underneath.

Don't go into the water yet.

You might drown.

He could think of nothing he wanted to say about railway lines intersecting roads.

And who could blame him?

This was entirely understandable.

'I *hate* level crossings,' I said.

'Do you?' he said.

I couldn't breathe.

'Your turn,' I said.

He was silent for a while, looking out at sea.

Then he turned.

'The top and bottom triangles of the X are red to show that my country has been bleeding for so many years.'

Bleeding.

Your country?

Or you?

I think maybe you.

'The level crossing sign is white outlined in red,' I said. 'They used to call my sister Snow White and me Rose Red. Tell me something white or red.'

'My brother Wilfred grows red roses.'

I couldn't breathe.

What are you going to do with all these pages of notes?

'He's the Rose Farmer of Bujumbura then?'

He laughed aloud.

'How do you know? How do you know he's in Bujumbura?'

'I've read about him. He's actually your brother? Tell me about him,' I said.

'You've read about *my brother*?'

Now, total incomprehension in his face, as he narrowed his eyes at me.

'Yes. A journalist went to interview him. But he wouldn't speak. Tell me why he doesn't speak.'

'This is amazing!' he said, and he got to his feet.

'Amazing,' he kept saying. 'Amazing.'

I got to my feet too.

He turned around as if he was going to hug me, and we moved towards each other.

But then we just stood there, saying again and again, 'Amazing.'

'You didn't tell me why he doesn't speak,' I said.

'He has nothing left to say.'

'So tell me another colour – something white.'

'I can't think of anything white,' he said. 'This is quite stressful.'

We both laughed.

'You must be able to think of something white,' I said.

'Oh shit,' he said.

Another burst of laughter.

'That's not white,' I said.

We both laughed.

We both stopped.

'Come on!' I said. 'It's easy. Doves, sea spray, fingernails – or maybe yours aren't.'

'Look,' he said. 'We don't have black fingernails!'

Now we were both really laughing – what was it about this man? Course I knew nobody had black fingernails. What was the matter with me?

He was holding out his hands, his definitely white fingernails.

And we couldn't stop laughing.

And I couldn't stop blushing.

'Sorry,' I said. 'I don't know what I was thinking.'

Then we were quiet again, but the laughter was still hovering underneath.

'Choose another colour,' I said.

'The two sides of the X are green for hope. *Esperanza*,' he said. 'If I have a daughter, I'll call her *Esperanza*.'

'My surname is Hope.'

'Your *name* is Hope?'

I nodded.

'Tell me something else,' he said.

'I bought a telescope to look at the stars, but I left it behind in the house and now I wish I hadn't. Your turn. Tell me something about stars.'

I was speaking so fast.

And so was he.

We couldn't stop.

It all poured out.

'There are three stars at the centre of our flag,' he said. 'For Hutu, Tutsi and Twa. For *Unité, Travail et Progrès.*'

'Unity, Work and Progress?'

'You speak French?'

'And Spanish. And English. And Latin,' I said.

'But not Kirundi?' he said, smiling so wide, with a wicked look in his eye, teasing me. 'So disappointing!'

Another burst of laughter.

Then silence again.

As we both stared at the X.

'X is a confluence – where people come together,' I said.

People come together, I thought, people do come together – and my heart was racing – and not just apart.

Could we come together?

'X is where the apostle Andrew was crucified,' he said.

People are crucified, they really are, not only the apostle Andrew, but normal people, like me – sometimes life crucifies the rest of us too.

'The *crux decussata*,' I said.

'I don't know any Latin,' he said. 'But you could teach me.'

'You could teach me Kirundi,' I said.

And possibly, we could also resurrect.

He said, 'Let me introduce myself. I'm Parfait.'

'Parfait?'

'That's right.'

'*Perfect, parfait, perfecto, perfectus* all come from the same root, did you know? It's the Latin *per* – meaning completely – joined to *facere* – meaning do. Done completely. So you're the finished article. Entire and complete and perfect.'

'You're too kind,' he said, and I laughed.

He pulled up his plaits into a bunch and tied them with a grey cotton band.

'Shall we go?' he said.

We?

Shall *we*?

Anything.

Anything.

With you.

We started walking up the beach towards the coach, and, as we went in the door, I saw a cross made of driftwood hanging on a hook.

Then I saw a painting on the wall.

A girl dancing.

The skirt of her dress was made of satin ribbons, and as she turned, the ribbons became paint, splashing the white walls around her.

I thought, *I want to be that girl.*

'You will be quite safe here with me,' he said, and he showed me my little room behind the plastic partition.

I thought, I don't want to be safe with you.

I want to be unsafe with you.

Parfait would disappear for hours to paint – or I supposed he was painting. And when he came back, we were both a bit nervous around each other.

We'd start talking at the same time.

Then we'd both stop.

I'd feel myself blushing.

And I'd busy myself.

Or he would.

It was quite ridiculous.

I'd never known myself like it.

Anyway, there was something else on my mind, and this eventually took me to the chemist, and it was on the way back from the chemist that I saw the stall selling flamenco dresses.

'Do you have one in orange?' I asked.

The woman went to the back of her van and pulled out a dress. She held a blanket to shield me as I tried it on. I stared at my flat stomach, muscular, same as always – it would all be fine.

The woman held up a cracked mirror.

There I was: cracked, in an orange flamenco dress.

My mother's mirror broke and Julia turned it into a mosaic, which is what you can do with broken things. You can turn them into something else.

The dress was goldfish orange, with tiny white dots on the frills – *volantes*, from the Spanish word *volar*, to fly.

I wouldn't fly away from here.

I would find a way.

The woman wrapped the dress in tissue and put it in a white plastic bag.

'I don't use plastic bags,' I said to her. 'The bags are killing the dolphins out in the Straits of Gibraltar. And the whales. And the fish. And ultimately us, you see. Because we eat the fish.'

The woman creased her brow.

I took the dress out of the plastic bag and gave it back to her, and I headed for Restaurante Raúl, passing the art gallery.

I went into the tiled hall of the restaurant and swung open the door to the Ladies. I locked myself in, unwrapped the package and read the instructions.

I tried to make myself pee.

Count to one.

And two.

And three.

And four.

And five.

Then have a look at the line.

The line was turning blue.

Is that blue? I thought, looking at the blue line.

That can't be blue, I thought, looking at the blue line.

That *is* blue, I thought, looking at the blue line.

I put the plastic stick in my pocket, and I couldn't think where I could hide.

So I went into the church.

Because it was dark in there.

The blue line is – *there was a painting I hadn't noticed before* – my child.

The holy child embraced his mother, pushing himself up against her with great energy, cheek to cheek. Mary, in the painting, in her blue dress, looked almost embarrassed by the child's physicality.

I knew I was embarrassed by my own – it had always been a shock to me. But, of course, I would now be revealed.

The blue line is my child.

I put my hand on my belly, and then I went and knelt, I'd no idea why. It's something people do in churches. But I wasn't kneeling before God. I was kneeling before Julia.

I was pregnant, by her husband, and she was dead, and her husband blamed me for it, and the candles were flickering.

Now Parfait definitely won't love me.

Not now.

I'm so sorry, Jules, I'm so sorry.

For my words – if they hurt you. For telling you things you didn't want to hear about the world. For making your life not simple.

I got to my feet to light a candle, which is another thing people do in churches.

I looked around me – nobody was in here.

Julia, I whispered, I'm sorry if you had to watch us, Diego and me, I hope you didn't, I don't know how it works. And I know it was wrong. Very wrong. And also, I'm sorry if I could have helped you and I didn't. If I could have stopped you, and I didn't.

Forgive us our trespasses.

If you wanted to be stopped.

That stopped me, that thought.

I looked at Mary, at her son's cheek pressed up against hers. Like Rose's cheek was never warm against Julia's. And for a fraction of a second, I understood.

Julia wanted to be with her, to feel her warm cheek, like Mary had.

Mary knew what it was to be pregnant at the wrong time, although, obviously, she'd done nothing wrong, and was just a vehicle, I supposed, for the story.

I wondered if she minded being a vehicle.

I wondered if I minded being a vehicle.

She couldn't have known what her journey would be.

None of us does.

I looked at Mary's baggy blue dress. I would wear baggy dresses, like she did. I like baggy dresses anyway.

This orange one I'd bought was tight, like flamenco dresses always are, but I'd bought it before I peed on the line. To have faith in not being pregnant, I bought a tight dress.

I only slept with Diego once, and by mistake. Such a mistake. And because I was sad.

Shit shit shit, I thought.

The whole thing's probably over.

The thing I most want.

I walked out of the church, holding the dress.

They were moving the silver Virgin into position for the procession.

I went to Restaurante Raúl, to the Ladies again, and I changed into the dress. I glanced in the mirror. I wondered if I might – perhaps – be beautiful tonight. With my sunned face, and my black hair pulled up with a mantilla comb, and my orange flamenco dress, like the dancers wore on Mr Sánchez's film.

All the things you've ever done, that's what Mr Sánchez asked – would it be heaven or hell?

Now I knew.

I arrived at the *feria* after the Virgin had passed by. Parfait came down the hill towards me, and we walked back, side by side, to the striped canvas *caseta* where everyone was sitting on hay bales, drinking sherry from Jerez, a town just up the motorway, where they train horses to dance.

The women were wearing coloured dresses like mine, and we looked like the songbirds which they still sadly keep on their balconies in cages in La Higuera.

'One day I'll dance the streets releasing them,' I told Parfait. I liked the picture it made in my head. It felt hopeful. Like the painting of the girl with satin ribbons for a skirt which was hanging in the coach.

Augusta *Hope.*

Maybe.

Parfait put a white rose in my dark hair.

The music began.

You remember what Mr Sánchez said.

He said that *duende* came only sometimes.

That the conditions had to be right.

Just right.

It was dark that night.

The guitar moaned and wept, and a lone female voice, dusty and low, was carried on the warm air. The guitar and the voice melted into the clapping of the crowd, and Parfait started to dance, slowly, and an intoxicating energy bubbled under the surface of his smooth conker skin, like boiling water.

He knew how to do this.

He must have been taking lessons too.

I started to dance.

Parfait reached for me and withdrew.

Reached and withdrew.

I leaned right back, and I let my body say the things I hadn't been able to say to him.

He did too.

As my body stretched, I could feel my extremities fizzing, the tips of my toes, my nipples, my fingers – and my scraped-back hair pulling the skin of my scalp.

We shaped ourselves to each other's bodies, outlines of each other, but we couldn't touch, that's the dance, you mustn't touch.

We raised our hands, grazing each other, nearly.

But not.

Duende.

Here it was, curling up the street, like a genie.

We were not touching.

But we were so close.

We were echoes of each other, reaching for each other, like a surgeon, on the cusp.

Of opening up a body.

Of plunging in his hand.

The purpose being healing.

The strings of the guitar wept.

And we were three parallel lines of fire.

Parfait, *duende* and I.

Withholding ourselves.

Exposing our pain.

Going underneath.

I don't know how long we danced.

But I noticed that the guitar had stopped playing, that all the people had gone home. That we were a man and a woman on a street. Alone. That the polished Virgin had been long returned to her dark box in the dark church.

There were thrown roses on the street, cut down, like my mother and father used to scythe the blue flowers which they thought were weeds.

Your weeds are my flowers, that was what Lola Alvárez said, do you remember?

It was soon dawn, I was still wearing the flamenco dress and we were on the beach, but I still didn't tell Parfait what was happening inside my body – why he wouldn't want me.

Parfait sliced an orange into four.

I put a quarter-orange in my mouth.

And Julia collapsed with Diego behind Mr Dunnett's shed.

I want to collapse too.

With this man.

'Tell me the rest of your story will you, Parfait?' I said, feeling him like heat beside me.

Which is something you can do, tell your stories.

Instead of collapsing.

I suppose.

He breathed deeply, the way he always does, as if he's sampling the air for the first time, and a bright orange dragonfly, the same colour as my dress, hovered above the damp sand, like a spark of fire.

'They come over from Africa,' I said. 'Orange-winged Dropwings.'

Parfait smiled.

'I assume it's easier for them,' he said. 'The journey!'

It landed on my hand.

Parfait stared at the dragonfly as it darted from my hand to my dress.

'It makes me think of my father,' he said. 'He loved beauty.'

He told me more about his father, and his mother, about Víctor who'd come with hope and would perhaps be beaten by Burundi, like Parfait was. He told me about the hillside and the stream and the rainbow Fischer's lovebird, and about a day they all went swimming together in the lake and the sun shone and they were happy.

'You've left lots of things out, haven't you?' I said.

He nodded.

'But I think you get it anyway,' he said.

I nodded.

He moved a little closer to me, and I could hear him breathing.

'You feel somehow like home,' he said.

Now I could hear myself breathing.

'You do too, Parfait,' I said, and I wanted to reach out to him, to touch him, but I didn't, I went on talking, as a substitute. 'It's called *nostos* in Latin. That's how we get the word nostalgia. It means aching for home.'

'I always had some kind of ache inside me,' said Parfait.

'Me too,' I said. 'I didn't know anyone else had that ache.'

'I always assumed everybody had it,' he said.

We were talking fast now, our words crashing against each other.

'I thought I'd been born into the wrong life,' I said.

'Everyone I knew was born into the wrong life,' said Parfait. 'So I came looking for the right one.'

'Me too,' I said.

A pause.

'Maybe I was looking for you, waiting for you, before I even met you? Is that possible?' he said. 'Because it's kind of cool.'

'That's like time travel. I like that. Chronology is so suffocating, isn't it?' I said, smiling.

'If only we could rewind,' he said. 'Do you ever think that?'

'Shall we go in the water?' I said, and I started to get up, and maybe he'd follow.

If only we could rewind.

'I don't like to,' he said. 'Not any more. I used to love swimming in the lake.'

'With the cichlid fish?' I said, smiling. 'Two hundred and fifty species of them!'

I walked down to the edge of the water because I couldn't sit so close to him any longer, without exploding.

He stayed sitting.

'If you could rewind your life,' he said, 'but you could only change one thing, what would it be?'

Sleeping with Diego, I thought.

Then I felt sick.

Julia dying.

Obviously.

What was I thinking?

I turned around.

'My sister once asked me if people could be un-killed,' I said.

'When will you tell me about your sister, Augusta?'

'Not today,' I said.

If you could change one thing.

Only one thing.

We said nothing.

The sun came up behind us, pink flames from the mountains.

On 5 November, I worked.

Didn't think.

Couldn't bear to think.

It had been two whole years since I'd heard her voice.

Parfait was painting, all the time.

Dragonflies, butterflies, chrysalises, wombs.

I didn't want to think about wombs.

He seemed consumed, so I tried to seem consumed too – which is quite hard to fake. I don't know if you've tried it.

At night, I wrote bad poems.

There was a volcano rising up. Or there was in me, anyway, and possibly in him. He was harder to read.

He never once made any attempt to cross the plastic partition at night, though I lay awake, shamefully wishing that he would.

'Parfait, I've been wanting to ask,' I said to him, finally, sitting outside the coach, finding it easier to talk in the dark. 'Is there anything I should know about you? A girlfriend? Or . . . ?'

'No,' he said.

'Have you ever been in love?' I said.

'No,' he said.

'Are you serious?'

He nodded.

'Are you scared?'

He looked up.

'Maybe,' he said.

I went into the coach for my scarf – to hide my belly, which wouldn't, ultimately, hide.

'Why haven't you been in love?'

'I've been waiting for the right person,' he said. 'And also.'

'Also what?'

'Never mind.'

My scarf was made of coral silk flecked with blue dragonflies.

Olly Macintosh gave it to me.

I wasn't properly in love with Olly Macintosh, I knew that now. He was more of a trial run.

'Didn't you want to have a trial run?' I said.

'No,' he said. 'I watched the soldiers rape my sisters, you see. Again and again and again. And there was nothing I could do.'

'I'm so sorry.'

'It made me feel ashamed to be a man. I felt, somehow, stained by what had happened to them. And I chose a different way. With my body. To make it up to my sisters. And to please my father, I guess. He waited for my mother, you see, and . . .'

'I admire you for that,' I said. 'For choosing.'

'And maybe for myself too,' he said. 'And maybe also for . . .'

'So you mean you've never slept with a woman?' I said, creasing my brow.

He nodded.

'Don't look so worried,' he said, smiling.

'But you'd like to?' I said. 'One day?'

He smiled.

I felt embarrassed.

I fiddled with my scarf.

I wished I was a dragonfly.

Then I could be free.

I wished he was a dragonfly.

Then he could be free too.

I wondered why it was so complicated being a person.

'Can we go dancing again tonight?' he said, drumming his fingers on the wooden table. 'Will you put on your orange dress again? You looked so . . .'

'I can't wear my orange dress tonight,' I said.

'Why not?'

More drumming.

'Can we go for a walk?' I said. 'I feel antsy.'

'Which means?'

'Restless. About to explode.'

'Perhaps you should explode.'

'I don't want to. Perhaps *you* should. You keep drumming your fingers on the table.'

'Where shall we go?'

'Anywhere.'

We set out along the beach road.

As we were approaching Raúl's house, where the road turns right into the square, we heard the most terrible sound, like a child squealing in pain.

We increased our pace, heading in the direction of the cry.

It took us up the road where the bins are.

We looked around us.

Down into a pool of light from the street lamp.

And there she was.

Amongst the glass shards and the ants.

Lying twisted.

Terrible to look at.

We stopped dead.

The small black cat with the heart-shaped face.

Caught up in a spiral of barbed wire around her body, cutting into her neck.

It almost looked as if someone had wrapped it round her.

She was bleeding, in spirals, and her fur was shot with little star-shaped holes.

Her little ribcage rose and fell, rose and fell, so fast, with the pain.

Parfait knelt down, and he picked her up.

He stroked the bits he could stroke.

As he held her, she stopped screeching, and he started, very gently, to unpick the wire knots from her skin.

He said nothing.

I tried to stem the wounds with my coral scarf, but there were too many, so all I could do was press it against her miniature body, cutting my fingers on the wire knots.

Parfait went on undoing the wire, with great care, with great concentration, unhooking it from her skin.

Her ribcage fell, rose, fell.

We both stared at her tiny black body, willing it to rise.

Rise again.

It never rose again.

Parfait put his big hand against the kitten's back, and I laid my palm over her tiny head.

We stopped, conscious of some great gravity held in that little dead body.

Parfait's face was set.

Almost immobile.

He dug a hole in the sandy earth with a stick, and he buried the kitten under a fig tree.

'Are you OK?' I said.

But he didn't speak.

All of him was clenched and taut.

Like a dam, holding back a tide.

Then, unexpectedly, the tide came – except it was my tide, not his.

Here, at last, were the tears I'd been waiting for.

For two whole years.

They rose up from inside me.

When I'd stopped crying, I knew the moment had come.

'You know when you arrived here in 2004? I have a photo here of a man lying at the end of the beach,' I said, taking the folded newspaper cutting out of my pocket. 'And, although I really hope it isn't, I think it might be you.'

'How do you have that?' he said, and I could tell he felt exposed. 'It was years ago.'

'What happened?' I said. 'What were the bits you left out of your story?'

'There was a storm,' Parfait said to me.

'Go on.'

'I killed my baby brother, who'd trusted me with his life.'

I didn't want to hear, I couldn't bear it.

'A Spanish priest in Tangier gave us his boat. He was worried by the weather, and he told me not to go. It was the wrong boat and the wrong time, he said. But it looked calm from where I was standing. I knew nothing about the sea. And we'd walked all the way from Burundi and I was impatient to arrive. I tried to hold him. But . . .'

He gestured to the sea.

I remembered the wind on the beach that day, and the way it shook the shutters at night.

'What was your brother called?' I asked, though I wasn't sure I wanted a name.

'He was called Zion, and I'd promised him a better life, right back from when he was a little boy. It was such a terrible journey, but I thought it was worth it. To save him. Save both of us. Our family died you see. One by one.'

'Mine too,' I said. 'Kind of.'

'In England? People don't die in England,' he said.

'People die everywhere,' I said.

'You never forget it when you let someone down that badly,' said Parfait.

'I know,' I said.

'My sisters were so badly damaged, and then they disappeared, and I don't know if I'll ever see them again.'

'Are there any other brothers or sisters you haven't told me about, apart from Wilfred?'

'There's Pierre – he's left Bujumbura for the north. I've got a bad feeling about what he's doing. And then my brother, Claude.'

'Yes?'

'He burnt to death. I think I could have stopped it. But I didn't. I didn't save any of them. Not one.'

I got ready.

My heart was beating.

'My mother and my father were there at the beach, where I drew the X,' I said. 'With my sister. It was the tenth of August 2004, like it says on the newspaper page. We were here on holiday. They were having breakfast, and they didn't help Zion. I am so so sorry, Parfait. Sorry beyond words. That we can't rewind.'

Parfait

'I don't think your family can have been there,' I said to Augusta. 'It was very early.'

'They were there,' she said, and she stared intently at me, and I said nothing. I was trying to take it in.

'I'd understand if you didn't want to know me any more,' she said, and she tried to smile at me. 'But I had to tell you.'

Didn't want to know her any more?

'You weren't there, were you, Augusta?' I asked.

'I didn't go with them,' she said. 'I stayed behind.'

We sat, staring at each other.

'How old was he?' she said.

'Fourteen.'

'Julia was fourteen too,' she said. 'And very obedient. My father told her to walk away. He said he didn't want to get wrapped up in it. He was always saying that. It's how he was. Afraid, I suppose. Or selfish.'

What could I say to her?

What should I think?

I didn't blame her, that's what I thought, it would be ridiculous to blame her for what her family had or hadn't done. Who knows what Pierre was doing these days? And, whatever it was, I couldn't be blamed.

'You once told me that some people's eyes are better than others,' she said.

I still said nothing.

'Julia changed from that day onwards. She was never really peaceful again, never truly happy, and when she lost her baby, she thought she was being punished for not saving your brother.'

That's when I saw it.

She'd unwittingly got wrapped up in my story.

This tragedy wasn't only mine.

'So she killed herself,' said Augusta. 'She was twenty-four.'

'Because of Zion?' I said. 'Because of me?'

'No, not because of you,' she said, and her dark eyes stared at me from underneath her straight fringe.

'Please say something,' she said.

But I couldn't find any right words to say to her.

So we sat in silence, until Augusta said, 'I came here to La Higuera with Julia's husband, with Diego, to try to recover . . .'

Augusta

Parfait said to me, 'If I'd never come to Spain in the priest's boat, Julia wouldn't have died.'

'No,' I said. 'No, don't say that.'

'I can't bear to think that it was me who killed her,' he said.

'No, no,' I said, 'it wasn't you. It was my father who killed your brother.'

'Look at us,' said Parfait, trying to smile, 'arguing about who killed who.'

'Who are we crying for, do you think?' I said to him.

'Let's be crying for each other,' he said. 'Because I'm not sure our own tears can heal our own pain.'

'Like, if you tickle yourself, you can't laugh?' I said.

Parfait laughed.

'I suppose that could be a good definition of love,' I said. 'Crying for another person – like their pain is yours. Because we do need a new definition. The dictionary one is absolutely pathetic – it says *deep affection or fondness* – and that's it. Like the dictionary really doesn't get it at all.'

'Maybe it's time to give up on the dictionary?' said Parfait, smiling at me.

'I've been relying on words my whole life,' I said.

'Perhaps it's time to rely on something else,' he said.

'There's another thing,' I said, 'which may be even harder to tell you because I made a bad mistake.'

'What's that?' he said.

'My mistake?' I said.

'No, look, at the road, Augusta. Look at that! It's so beautiful.'

'I know exactly what that is,' I said, my cheeks burning with the shock of it.

Right down at the end, beyond the coach, there was a car parking, and there was a trailer behind the car, and on the back of the trailer was a gypsy caravan in gleaming red and yellow, with big wooden spoked cream wheels and a tiny chimney pot.

My heart was beating with the strangeness of.

Well.

Everything.

'It's my parents,' I said, 'and my next-door neighbours, Jim and Barbara. Jim always had dreams up his sleeve, from when I was a little girl. You remember I told you about Graham Cook – they're his parents.'

My two worlds were coming together – and it felt impossible.

There was Jim Cook, with his checked shirt open to his smooth balloon-belly, and Barbara Cook, in her wrap-around Indian skirt. My mother got out and unfolded the wheelchair, and they shuffled my father into it.

'You're here!' I said. 'You must have brought this all the way by boat!'

They all nodded, and my father, in his strange voice, said what I could just about work out was, 'We came by ferry.'

'Plymouth to Santander,' said Barbara.

'You came all the way down through Spain?' I said.

I knew the courage that my mother and father would have needed to do that.

'We booked up hotels,' said my mother, licking her finger and stooping to rub a mark from her white sandal. 'We did it from our laptop. Booking dot com.'

'Online!' said my father in his strange slow voice. 'For you.'

At least I think he said *for you.*

And looking back, it could only have been for me that they did it.

'That's amazing,' I said. 'I'm so sorry. I should introduce you. This is my friend, Parfait.'

I wiped my face with my hand and hoped they couldn't see we'd both been crying.

Parfait stepped forward, and his dark hand reached out to shake my father's small white hand.

His good hand, as we called it.

I wondered if it was a *good* hand.

The hand that had stacked shirts and folded socks and put them in drawers.

And slapped Julia in the face.

And dragged her away from saving Zion.

And walked her down the aisle with such pain in his eyes, such love.

My father eyed Parfait's black hand.

'Is that par-fay?' said my mother. 'Like in cooking. The dessert you make with whipped cream and eggs?'

Parfait smiled.

I admired him for smiling at my mother and father.

'He's the pedlar man,' I said.

'That's the poem,' said Jim Cook. 'That's where you got the idea for the caravan. And we restored this for you, Augusta – your father and I did the outside. With that old book of yours open. We've put it on the bookshelf above the bed for you.'

'Barbara and I did the inside,' said my mother.

'It's a gift for you,' said Barbara Cook. 'With our love.'

'It's brought the crescent together,' said Jim Cook. 'We've all got to know each other, even the Hassans joined in. And we've found it . . .'

'Comforting,' said Barbara.

My mother said, '*His caravan has windows too, And a chimney of tin that the smoke comes through*' – that's what the poem says. So that's what Jim told us to follow. We had to have the wood-burner. It made it nice and cosy.'

She hesitated, and took a breath.

'Julia would have loved it too,' she said.

Her name hung on the air.

I smiled at my mother, and she smiled, and the warm cloak fell on me, it actually fell on me for a second, looking at her, then we felt awkward, looking into each other's eyes, and we both looked away.

'This poem's so much nicer than your normal ones,' said my mother.

'You're right,' I said.

'*He has a wife with a baby brown, and they go riding from town to town,*' said my mother.

I blushed because that still sounded racist to me.

Also, I didn't want to think about babies.

I went and sat out at the front of the caravan, and I gestured for Parfait to sit next to me on the painted bench seat, as if we were setting off on a journey.

I wanted to say something to him but I wasn't exactly sure how it was going to come out.

Jim Cook appeared as I started to open my mouth, and Parfait suggested that we wheel the caravan down from its trailer onto the sand, beside his coach.

I climbed the wooden steps and went inside.

Parfait followed me.

'Might you be able to forgive my father?' I said. 'I'd understand if not.'

Parfait's phone rang.

'You're coming home!' he said, walking down the steps of the caravan.

Through the open door, I heard him say, 'Are you bringing Wilfred?'

Then I heard him say, 'I can't stand the thought of him being there all alone.'

There was a wooden bed and slatted cupboards, and tin pans hanging from hooks, and there was a tiny wooden cuckoo clock, ticking loudly, with the little bird inside a carved arch, waiting to mark the hour, waiting to leap.

I sat on the bed, and I thought how perfect everything could be.

If only.

I felt a terrible wave of guilt.

No, I said aloud.

I didn't want to transmit a single negative thought from my brain down through the umbilical cord.

Because it wasn't fair.

On.

The.

I didn't yet dare think the word *baby* – I wasn't ready.

'Will you live in this caravan now?' said Parfait, coming back inside. 'It suits you.'

And what I wanted to say was, 'Will you live here too? And can we go travelling from town to town?'

I moved my things out of Parfait's coach into the caravan. I lay on my bed, staring at the *mollycroft* ceiling, not sleeping, rehearsing ways to tell Parfait without saying *pregnant* or *baby* or *Diego* – which was problematic.

I got out of bed and went down the steps, wondering if perhaps he was outside.

He wasn't.

I shone the light of my phone into the windows of his coach, accidentally on purpose (as Julia and I used to say). Maybe he'd come out when he saw the light.

As I moved my phone around, the light caught the side of the gypsy caravan, and I saw that my father had painted the exact markings of the tiny butterflies' wings.

And a tear rolled down my cheek because my father loved me enough to paint the Adonis Blue, the ragged orange-black Comma, the luminous Green Hairstreak and the purple-eyed Peacock. He'd got them just right.

I'd been wrong to think that beautiful things couldn't come out of Willow Crescent.

Do you hear me, Julia?

And do you forgive me my judgement?

I went back inside and lay on the bed.

I felt the awful awe-ful awesome curve of my stomach.

I was terrified about Parfait's reaction.

Especially now.

He said that my father didn't know what he was doing.

But did I know what I was doing?

When Diego and I lay down on the Moroccan bed?

Parfait let himself out of his coach at around three in the morning, and we sat in the dark between the coach and the gypsy caravan.

It wouldn't be long until sunrise, and it was cold. I wanted him to come closer. But he didn't.

'Why wouldn't you wear the orange dress last night, Augusta?' he said.

'There's no easy way of saying this,' I said. 'I've been practising – and whichever words I use, it doesn't sound any better.'

He nodded.

'It's because I'm pregnant, Parfait. And I can't do up the zip.'

He took my hand.

'I hope I'm crying for you,' I said. 'Because I should be. Like we said. But I don't think I am.'

'Who do you think you're crying for?' said Parfait.

'Myself,' I said. 'In case you can't forgive me.'

'Say something,' I said.

'Say anything,' I said.

'What do you feel about it all now, Augusta?' he said, very quietly.

'I don't know,' I said.

Parfait closed his eyes.

'Say something,' I said again.

'Can you give me a bit of time?' he said.

'Time to do what?'

'To think,' he said. 'To take it all in.'

'Please tell me what you're feeling,' I said.

'I'm not quite sure,' said Parfait. 'But are you OK, Augusta?'

I nodded.

'At least your parents are here,' he said.

'I won't tell them,' I said. 'It's strange but they don't comfort me. They never have.'

'Perhaps you could put the caravan in Raúl's field,' he said. 'To be close to Raúl and Teo.'

I nodded.

'What can I do for you?' he said.

'I don't know,' I said. 'What can *I* do for you?'

'I'll be fine,' he said.

'So will I,' I said. 'I don't need looking after.'

Our hands fell apart.

I wished we hadn't let our hands fall apart.

He nodded towards my stomach.

'Is this the one thing you would undo?' he said. 'If you could.'

I shook my head.

'Not this, it couldn't possibly be this. That wouldn't be . . .'

'It isn't?' he said. 'Oh, I'd thought that perhaps . . .'

'I'd never undo . . .'

'Don't worry,' he said. 'You don't have to explain. I mean, it's nothing to do with me.'

Nothing to do with you? Is that true?

'I'll see you in a little bit then, Augusta,' he said. 'I need to get my

357

thoughts straight. I'm sure you do too. If that's OK. If there's nothing else I can do. Also, Víctor's coming back to Spain. And that means Wilfred will be totally alone. And everything feels . . .'

He stopped.

He couldn't find a word for what everything felt.

And who could blame him?

He took my hand, and I think he was about to let it go, but he changed his mind and he kissed the back of it, and he looked inside my eyes, and his eyes weren't sparkling, like they always were – they were full of pain.

'I think you've put on a bit of weight,' my mother said, standing back and looking me up and down, when she arrived after breakfast.

'It must be all the paella!' I laughed, pulling my scarf over me.

'And where's your friend, Parfait?'

'Oh, he's like the pedlar man. He's always on the move,' I said in the most cheerful voice I could manage. 'Thank you so much, all of you. I'm not sure I thanked you enough yesterday. The caravan is beautiful – and I'm so touched.'

'Our pleasure,' said Barbara Cook. 'I'll never forget how kind you were to Graham.'

'Me neither,' said Jim Cook.

'I loved Graham,' I said.

Then we all stared at each other, and nobody spoke.

'I really did,' I said. 'He was the purest person I've ever met because he couldn't make himself lovable to make us love him.'

Nobody spoke.

'The beds were rather hard,' said my mother. 'At the hotel.'

'But the view was lovely,' said Barbara.

'I told Barbara he wasn't your boyfriend. I said you'd never have a coloured boyfriend.'

'Black, Mum. We say black.'

'I thought that was rude.'

358

'No, it's factual.'

'Well, not really black, he's more brown, to be honest.'

'Yes, and you're more pink, Mum, but we call you white.'

'Anyway, I'm pleased he's not your boyfriend,' said my mother. 'Though he did seem very nice.'

'He's from Burundi,' I said.

'Oh, that's that country you were always going on about.'

Jim and Barbara took me out to lunch with my parents at Restaurante Raúl.

My father sat in his wheelchair at the head of the table.

Jim sat the other end.

There were four chairs left.

Barbara, my mother and I sat down, leaving one empty.

Raúl came and took the chair away.

We all pretended not to notice.

'Why don't you try the *chanquete* fish?' I said to my father.

And he popped one in his mouth, tail and eyes, the whole thing.

He winked at me.

'Baby squid?' I said.

'Oh go on!' he said.

And down it went, tentacles and all.

My eyes filled with tears, but I don't think they showed.

Raúl wouldn't let them pay.

It was time for my parents and the Cooks to start the long drive back to Santander.

My mother rushed forward and kissed my cheek.

My father held out his good hand and I squeezed it.

Jim and Barbara hugged me.

And their car with the empty trailer turned up towards the main road.

Raúl and Teo's donkey pulled my caravan to the back of their field, needing quite a lot of encouragement.

When I went for a walk, I could see Parfait's coach, still parked behind the dunes, but I didn't feel I should call by.

He'd said he wanted to think.

So I should let him think.

How long would this type of thinking need, I wondered.

I found it quite unbearable being without him.

And that made me feel weak.

And feeling weak made me feel furious.

I kept walking down the beach road, hoping to bump into him, staring up at the coach, longing for him to come and find me. I sat at the edge of the sea, hurling pebbles at the rocks, and when I walked back, his coach was gone.

Had he gone for a drive, or had he gone?

My body seemed to freeze at the thought of him not being here, and, as I walked back, I couldn't unfreeze it.

Raúl suggested we went riding.

'You know, Augusta, I'm pleased you're living here,' he said. 'I didn't like you being in the coach with the artist.'

'Didn't you?' I said, not looking at him.

'They have different ways over there,' he said, waving at Africa. 'And last time they came, they took over the place.'

'Last time who came?'

'The Moors.'

'That was in the Middle Ages, Raúl,' I said, crossly.

'We only got rid of them in 1492,' said Raúl. 'Kicked them out of Granada. And somehow they're creeping back again.'

'Don't take any notice of him,' said Teo.

When we rode along the beach, I rode ahead.

Teo caught up with me.

'Are you sure you should be riding?' she said.

'Yes,' I said.

'You're really not yourself, Augusta. Is there anything I can do?' she said.

But there was nothing anyone could do.

Except him.

It might sound pathetic.

Or needy.

But that's how it is sometimes.

'Are you in love with him?' said Teo nervously.

'No, why?' I said.

'Let's take it easy today,' said Raúl. 'No galloping.'

His coach still wasn't there.

We untacked the horses in silence.

Teo appeared in my caravan. She said she was taking me on a surprise trip.

I had this terrible feeling that Parfait might take his own trip back to Burundi. To be with Wilfred. To get away from, well, me. The dilemma I was proving to be.

If I left La Higuera, I felt, oddly, that he was more likely to leave too.

But I didn't know how to say no to Teo.

So we both got in the car, and she drove me up the motorway to Jerez, trying to make me tell her I was pregnant, which eventually, unwillingly, I did. We went to the School of Equestrian Art to watch white horses dancing for tourists in an indoor arena, and tasted sherry in the famous *bodegas* and stayed the night with her sister.

And although it should have been lovely, it wasn't.

Parfait

I drove along the coast to Tarifa after lunch to see if the boys were around. I felt it would help to talk to them.

'*I know there is no straight road,*' Paco read to me, back in the lorry park in Tarifa, pulling at his ponytail.

'No straight road in this world
Only a giant labyrinth of intersecting crossroads.'

'You're a man who likes a straight road,' said Luis, who never normally spoke much, nodding at me. 'But none of us gets one in this life, Parfait, that's the truth.'

A giant labyrinth of intersecting crossroads, that's what struck me. The line repeated itself over and over in my mind.

'Do you hear what we're saying to you?' said Paco.

'But she said she didn't want to undo it,' I said. 'So what does that mean? What do you think she feels about the other guy?'

'Go back and ask her,' said Antonio. 'You shouldn't be away from her right now. It's no good sitting around reading poems at a time like this.'

'And the baby needs a father,' said Paco.

'Hasn't the baby got a father?' I said. 'A father who isn't me?'

'Has she even told him?'

'I don't know.'

'Well, why the hell didn't you ask?'

'I'm not sure.'

'Is it difficult to be a father to another man's child?' I said.

'Perhaps you should ask Víctor that,' said Paco.

I thought of the way Víctor loved Wilfred, and I thought of his deaf and blind children, wearing pink cotton uniforms, dancing in the dust.

'Get back to her,' said Antonio.

I thought of her radiant, questioning, wild face framed with jet-black hair.

Her orange dress with the frills.

Dancing with a white rose in her hair.

Diving off the rocks to swim.

Galloping down the beach.

I pictured her reading that great huge dictionary outside the coach wrapped up in her scarves, with a crease above the bridge of her nose, trying to find a definition of love.

A definition of love?

I saw her sitting on the painted bench of the gypsy caravan in her denim dungarees, as if she was ready to set off on some new road.

Some new road?

'Yes,' I said to myself. 'Yes.'

But when I got back, I couldn't find her.

Augusta

Teo and I were back in time for the tree ceremony, and Joseph led Mary into the stable on Raúl's donkey.

Parfait had the microphone.

I couldn't take my eyes off him.

'It's four thousand six hundred and sixty-three people who died trying to cross to Europe this year,' he said.

I went forward to queue.

He took a pen and he started to write, leaning on the table in front of me.

He wrote Julia on a gold planet, and then he wrote Rose.

And then he wrote Graham Cook.

'Will you forgive me?' he said.

'What for?'

'Leaving you alone.'

It was one of those moments.

I took a breath.

I took a star.

I took a pen.

I wrote Melchior.

Another star.

I wrote Claude.

Another star.

I wrote Zion.

Another star.

I wrote Aurore.

It was hard to concentrate with him watching, and my fingers not working right – they'd tensed up, with my heart, which had contracted and was ticking violently like one of those old-fashioned alarm clocks.

Parfait was called away to light the electric star above the stable, and there was the mayor getting his photo with the migrant, and there was dinner laid out on white tablecloths for them all.

I watched him.

The holy baby cried.

And the cry woke something up in me.

I was carrying a baby too.

A baby who was real.

As I walked away I felt a movement inside me.

As if the baby was turning.

The baby.

My baby.

I threw off my scarf and walked on the sand, digging in my toes. Then, checking there was nobody around because I wasn't in the mood for naturism these days, probably never had been, I took off my red dress and my underwear, down on the dark beach, alone, and I dived into the waves, and I imagined the baby hearing the slap slap slap of water, inside and out. More than that, I imagined my baby. Being mine. Being here. Being he or she. Being happy to see my face. Lighting up at the sight of me. That's what Julia said. That's what she wanted more than anything.

I thought of the womb that Parfait was painting which was called *The Baby Doesn't Believe there is a Mother.*

'Do you believe there's a mother?' I whispered to my baby, the first time I'd dared to speak to him, to her.

I hoped my baby wasn't lonely in there, all alone, and I thought of all that was coming in the other life, outside the womb, all that the baby couldn't yet possibly imagine.

I wondered if there was another life beyond this one, one we couldn't possibly imagine, full of people we'd loved, we still loved, you can't stop loving them even when you can't see them any more.

Again I felt the baby turning, this baby I couldn't yet see.

I wondered what it would feel like to give birth.

How much it hurt.

I thought of Julia swearing.

I wondered if it had helped.

I don't suppose Mary swore, I thought, it might have worried the angels.

I smiled as I swam.

Jesus passed through the birth canal, as my mother loved to call it, the vagina, as she didn't love to call it. This was the route God chose into the world.

I suddenly saw the dignity that had been given to my body by it.

I dived under a wave.

Zambullirse, they say in Spanish, to dive, to submerge oneself, and it can also mean to dedicate oneself utterly. That's what I thought as I dived. I thought, I'm diving into this. Motherhood. Headfirst.

'The sea is beautiful, you wait and see,' I whispered to my child, my body buoyant on the water, my spirits suddenly buoyant too.

I felt that this was the beginning of something.

The beginning of loving.

The real way.

The crying-for-someone-else way.

Which I saw, in a flash, was the kind of love that parenthood would be.

I got out and put my dress on and wrapped my scarf around me, shivering, and I remembered Parfait asking me if this was the thing I'd undo.

I remembered his face.

His worried face.

When I said no, I said no for the baby.

Because I would, of course, do anything to undo the fact that, on the night of my twenty-sixth birthday, I lay down on the Moroccan bed with my sister's husband.

But I never explained that to Parfait, did I?

He said it was nothing to do with him and he backed away.

I thought at the time – if you love me, it's everything to do with you. Because I'm to do with you. So perhaps you don't love me.

But now I saw.

He didn't want to look as if he was judging me for not waiting for him.

He'd waited for a woman who he'd hoped had been waiting for him.

And, actually, I had been waiting for him all along.

I was still waiting for him.

Even now.

But maybe he was somewhere else waiting for me.

Or maybe he wasn't.

I ran back to the square – to the smart dinner in the corner by the church.

The mayor.

Local officials.

President of the Neighbours' Association.

The priest.

But not Parfait.

Had he left?

Was he already on his way to the airport?

To go and see Wilfred in Bujumbura?

I ran along the beach road, heading towards *our special spot*.

If I wasn't wrong, there was a fire down there.

And people.

As I came closer, I could make out the shape of chairs.

*　　*　　*

The flames flared up.

Blowing in the wind.

A person.

Maybe more than one.

But I could only really make out one.

When Parfait saw me, he held out his arms.

I wanted so much to fall into them.

Which I hadn't done before.

He'd never touched a woman.

And this felt such a beautiful thing.

All of a sudden.

That he hadn't had a trial run.

Even if I had.

'Will you forgive me?' he said.

'You don't need forgiving,' I said. 'I need forgiving.'

He wrapped his arms around me.

'You look cold,' he said. 'And you're wet.'

He took a blanket, and he wrapped me in it. I sat down. He got a towel and he started to dry my hair. I closed my eyes, and felt his hands against my head, his fingers drying my hair, working through each strand to the end. It didn't feel anything like Barbara Cook in the swimming pool changing rooms in Hedley Green. I never knew I had so many nerve endings on my scalp. I never knew that this was a feeling that could come through my head.

He let my hair fall, put a log on the fire, sat down on the other chair and drew it close to me.

'So, Augusta, I assume that the baby is Diego's,' said Parfait.

I nodded.

'You see, we both loved her so much, and perhaps we thought we'd find her in each other. If that makes any sense. Or maybe I'm making excuses. Trying out nice-sounding words to make myself look better.'

He held my hand.

'We were very sad. And very drunk. And we did it once. And never again.'

'What do you feel about it now?'

'It was the wrong thing to do. For both of us. But the baby is here, and deserves to be thought of as right. That's why I said I didn't want to rewind. To undo. I don't want to undo my baby.'

'I like it that you don't,' said Parfait. 'I think I misunderstood you at the time. And I'm sorry it took me so long to think. Maybe I'm a very slow thinker.'

I smiled.

He smiled back.

'It's only that the baby . . .'

'Isn't yours?' I said.

'Isn't mine,' he said.

'And so?' I said, though I hardly dared ask.

'I felt jealous. I wanted you to be all mine, and if there was going to be a baby, I guess I wanted that to be mine too. Is that a bad thing? Wanting to have you all to myself?'

'I think that might be not so much a bad thing. As a . . .'

'Good thing?' said Parfait. 'Could it be?'

'Yes.'

'I'm sorry I left you alone when you most needed me to be with you,' he said. 'It's just I wanted . . .'

'It doesn't matter now,' I said.

'There's this poem by Federico . . .'

'García Lorca?' I said.

'It talks about a giant labyrinth . . .'

'Of intersecting crossroads,' I said.

'If I hadn't left for Europe, Zion wouldn't have died. And, if Zion hadn't died, maybe Julia wouldn't have died. And then this baby wouldn't have been conceived. If you think about it.'

'I guess I still had a choice,' I said.

He stood up.

'Diego is very dark-skinned,' I said. 'If that helps at all. It won't be quite so obvious.'

Parfait laughed.

He actually laughed.

Which made me laugh.

'I think you're being a little optimistic,' he said.

'I feel like being optimistic,' I said.

'Does Diego know?' he said.

I shook my head.

'Did you ever love him, Augusta? So that I know.'

'Possibly for a week or two when I was nine years old and I was impressed that he could carry four cardboard boxes at a time.'

'I'm sure I can carry five,' said Parfait, and his smile stretched from one ear to the other. 'Or fifty-five.'

I smiled.

'And the baby you're carrying, I'll carry with you,' said Parfait. 'As if he – or she – was mine. That's a promise.'

'I always thought promises were problematic,' I said, and I couldn't stop smiling either. 'But, you know, I think they might be growing on me.'

'They might?'

'I need a word for this,' I said, looking around me. 'This moment. This feeling. This. Everything.'

The clock chimed in the square.

And the cloak fell on me.

The fleeting feeling.

Of beyond.

It was midnight.

Weirdly, Christmas.

It didn't feel anything like Christmas.

At exactly the same moment, there were fireworks outside Restaurante Raúl.

The cuckoo would be jumping out of the clock in my caravan.

'I've got the word!' I said. 'Chimingness. You and me.'

'How do you translate that?' said Parfait.

'It's untranslatable,' I said. 'I always hoped I was untranslatable too. Might I be, do you think?'

Parfait nodded, smiling.

'Chimingness is a bit of an ugly word,' I said, 'on second thoughts.'

'So let's forget about words,' said Parfait.

'Come and swim with me – it's so beautiful in the water,' I said.

'I haven't swum since Zion died.'

'If *I've* started crying, *you* can start swimming,' I said.

We went down to the water, and I felt coy.

I didn't know what he might expect.

In terms of the taking off of clothes.

But he was on the sand taking off his jeans and his T-shirt.

He ran, somersaulting, into the sea in his shorts, and when he stood up, under the moon, there was a kind of lustre to his wet skin.

'Come on, Augusta!' he called.

I ran towards the sea, still wearing my dress.

Under the moon, he picked me up in his arms.

He whirled me around.

I was the girl in the painting with the ribbon-skirt.

And all the secret bits of me were going to come flying out.

Any minute.

Epilogue

I'm crouched over, digging holes, and in each hole, I plant a daffodil bulb. Hundreds and hundreds of them. All around our little patch of land, out beyond the fields, behind La Higuera.

There's mud clustered around the ring on my left hand, the ring finger, so it's hard to read the words.

Ecc 3:4-5 – Parfait had it engraved.

I looked it up.

A time to weep and a time to laugh.

Julia's locket hangs down from my neck over the earth as I dig.

A time to mourn and a time to dance.

Esperanza, six months old, dark-haired and caramel-skinned, is in the big old pram, giggling, under the palm tree, beside the gypsy caravan, where we're sleeping until the house is ready. Raúl's donkey is getting the hang of her new role.

The coach is parked at the back. We're going away, the three of us, to Calabria for a month to help the refugees – we'll be teaching English and writing and art. Raúl and Teo think we're mad. Parfait says he has amends to make. I guess we both do.

Then we'll come back here, where we're making our home – so perhaps I've sold out.

Julia, are you laughing at me?

Are you saying, it's different when it's a person?

By the time we're back, the daffodils will be out, all around our little white house – where I suppose, though it seems unthinkable now, there will be both pain and joy, there probably always is.

We'll go off again, perhaps to Lesvos next, and when Esperanza is old enough, we'll go to Bujumbura, to the rose farm, to see Wilfred.

The cattle egrets are pecking ticks off the cows' ears.

I go on planting bulbs.

Teo's frying prawns over the fire.

Raúl is building a stone wall.

A time to scatter stones and a time to gather them in.

I can smell saffron and paint on the warm wind.

Parfait comes outside, and he walks over to where I'm digging.

I stand up.

Julia's silver locket falls, hot, against my chest.

He kisses me.

He tastes of the earth, this earth, our earth, home, *nostos.*

Acknowledgements

I come from a family of irrepressible storytellers, so perhaps the journey started around the kitchen table all those years ago. Mum (no longer with us, but utterly with us), Dad and Richard – I'm so grateful for your daily stories.

My beloved headmistress, who was (honestly) called Miss Leader, said that books were sacred – and this felt true to me. Books have marked my way, like milestones.

As soon as I could write, I wrote stories. My childhood friends let me read my stories to them on rowing boats, in woodland dens, under willow trees. A few grown-up friends have done the same, over the years, in slightly less interesting places. Some are the same people. Every friend, every pupil, every colleague, in fact, every person who's cheered me on – you are all living milestones, and you've marked my path in the loveliest of ways.

To the endlessly wonderful and endlessly freeing Mark, Charlie and Nina – special thanks for loving me and letting me be.

Thank you to the writer, Niall Williams, the Kiltumper class of November '16 and other writerly friends, for your part in the crafting, the dreaming and the believing.

To my school Spanish teacher, Miss (now Dr) Rawlings, whose Hispanic passion ran quiet and deep – and to the hot earth of Andalusia, which never fails to touch my soul.

To my agent, the (somehow) effortlessly extraordinary Sue Armstrong, who spotted Augusta in a crowd – thank you for everything. Heartfelt thanks to the most delightful and insightful of editors, Carla Josephson, and to my publicist, the fabulous and dynamic Ann Bissell. And to the multi-talented Borough Press and HarperCollins teams: Fleur and Katy, brimming with marketing magic, and Holly, designer of the gorgeous gold dragonflies. You're all brilliant professionals and you're lovely people too.